Dear Reader,

With a plethora of fast cars, luxurious destinations and drop-dead-hunky men, you'd think my addiction to watching FORMULA 1 races was by design, right? Sadly not. It was born out of being forced, yes, forced to watch motor sports on lazy Sunday afternoons by my brothers.

When I noticed the distinct lack of female race drivers, I had to redress that balance. Cue the idea for *The Price of Success.* Sasha's the epitome of my perfect female driver—snarky, supertalented yet vulnerable—and the ideal match for frozen-hearted team boss Marco, whose only interest was protecting his brother, Rafael, my hero in *His Ultimate Prize.*

I was thrilled to revisit the world of motor racing in *His Ultimate Prize,* and enjoyed watching sparks fly between legendary race driver and irreverent playboy Rafael and sexy physiotherapist Raven.

I hope you enjoy reading about the de Cervantes brothers and the women who win their hearts.

Maya x

Maya Blake

—

His Ultimate Prize

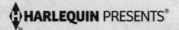

HARLEQUIN PRESENTS®

Recycling programs
for this product may
not exist in your area.

ISBN-13: 978-0-373-13205-8

First North American Publication 2013

HIS ULTIMATE PRIZE
Copyright © 2013 by Maya Blake

THE PRICE OF SUCCESS
Copyright © 2012 by Maya Blake

Printed in U.S.A.

CONTENTS

To Lucy Gilmour, for making my dream come true,
and also because I know she loves bad boys!

His Ultimate Prize

CHAPTER ONE

'PUT YOUR ARMS around me and hold on tight.'

The rich, deep chuckle that greeted her request sent a hot shiver down Raven Blass's spine. The same deep chuckle she continually prayed she would grow immune to. So far, her prayers had gone stubbornly unanswered.

'Trust me, *bonita*, I don't need guidance on how to hold a woman in my arms. I give instructions; I don't take them.' Rafael de Cervantes's drawled response was accompanied by a lazy drift of his finger down her bare arm and a latent heat in ice-blue eyes that constantly unnerved her with their sharp, unwavering focus.

With gritted teeth, she forced herself not to react to his touch. It was a test, another in a long line of tests he'd tried to unsettle her with in the five weeks since he'd finally called her and offered her this job.

Maintaining a neutral expression, she stood her ground. 'Well, you can do what I say, or you can stay in the car and miss your nephew's christening altogether. After agreeing to be his godfather, I'm sure you not turning up in church will go down well with your brother and Sasha.'

As she'd known it would, the mention of Sasha de Cervantes's name caused the atmosphere to shift from toying-with-danger sexual banter to watch-it iciness. Rafael's hand dropped from her arm to grip the titanium-tipped walking stick tucked between his legs, his square jaw tightening as his gaze cooled.

Deep inside, in the other place where she refused to let anyone in, something clenched hard. Ignoring it, she patted herself on the back for the hollow victory. Rafael not touching her in any way but professionally was a *good* thing.

Recite. Repeat. Recite. Repeat—

'I didn't agree…exactly.'

Her snort slipped out before she could stop it. 'Yeah, right. The likelihood of you agreeing to something you're not one hundred per cent content with is virtually nil. Unless…'

His eyes narrowed. 'Unless what?'

Unless Sasha had done the asking. 'Nothing. Shall we try again? Put your arms—'

'Unless you want me to kiss that mouth shut, I suggest you can the instructions and move closer. For a start, you're too far away for this to work. If I move the wrong way and land on top of you, I'll crush you, you being *such* a tiny thing and all.'

'I'm not *tiny.*' She moved a step closer to the open doorway of the sleek black SUV, stubbornly refusing to breathe in too much of his disconcertingly heady masculine scent. 'I'm five foot nine of solid muscle and bone and I can drop kick you in two moves. Think about that before you try anything remotely iffy on me.'

The lethal grin returned. '*Dios,* I love it when you talk dirty to me. Although my moves have never been described as *iffy* before. What does that even mean?'

'It means concentrate or this will never work.'

Rafael, damn him, gave a low laugh, unsnapped his seat belt and slid one arm around her shoulders. 'Fine. Do with me what you will, Raven. I'm putty in your hands.'

With every atom in her body she wished she could halt the stupid blush creeping up her face, but that was one reaction she'd never been able to control. In the distant past she tried every day to forget, it had been another source of callous mirth to her father and his vile friends. To one friend in particular, it had provoked an even stronger, terrifying reaction. Pushing away the unwelcome memory, she concentrated on the task at hand, *her job.*

Adjusting her position, she lowered her centre of gravity, slid an arm around Rafael's back and braced herself to hold his weight. Despite the injuries he'd sustained, he was six foot three of packed, lean muscle, his body honed to perfection from years of carefully regimented exercise. She needed every single ounce of her physiotherapist training to ensure he didn't accidentally flatten her as promised.

She felt him wince as he straightened but, when she glanced at him, his face showed no hint of the pain she knew he must feel.

The head trauma and resulting weeks-long coma he'd lain in after he'd crashed his Premier X1 racing car and ended his world championship reign eight months ago had only formed part of his injuries. He'd also sustained several pelvic fractures and a broken leg that had gone mostly untreated while he'd been unconscious, which meant his recovery had been a slow, frustrating process.

A process made worse by both his stubborn refusal to heed simple instructions and his need to test physical boundaries. Especially hers.

'Are you okay?' she asked. Because it was her job to make sure he was okay. Nothing else.

He drew himself up to his full height and tugged his bespoke hand-stitched suit into place. He slid slim fingers through longer-than-conventional hair until the sleek jet-black tresses were raked back from his high forehead. With the same insufferable indolence with which he approached everything in life, he scrutinised her face, lingered for an obscenely long moment on her mouth before stabbing her gaze with his.

'Are you asking as my physiotherapist or as the woman who continues to scorn my attentions?'

Her mouth tightened. 'As your physio, of course. I have no interest in the…in being—'

'Becoming my lover would make so many of our problems go away, Raven, don't you think? Certainly, this sexual tension you're almost choking on would be so much easier to bear if you would just let me f—'

'Are you okay *to walk*, Rafael?' she interjected forcefully, hating the way her blood heated and her heart raced at his words.

'Of course, *querida*. Thanks to your stalwart efforts this past month, I'm no longer wheelchair-bound and I have the very essence of life running through my veins. But feel free to let your fingers keep caressing my backside the way they're doing now. It's been such a long time since I felt this surge of *essence* to a particular part of my anatomy, I was beginning to fear it'd died.'

With a muted curse and even redder cheeks, she dropped her hand. The professional in her made her stay put until Rafael was fully upright and able to support himself. The female part that hated herself for this insane fever of attraction wanted to run a mile. She compromised by moving a couple of feet away, her face turned from his.

For the second time in as many minutes, his laugh mocked her. 'Spoilsport.'

She fought the need to clench her hands into agitated fists and faced him when she had herself under sufficient control. 'How long are you going to keep this up? Surely you can find something else to amuse yourself with besides this need to push my buttons?'

Just like that, his dazzling smile dropped, his eyes gleaming with a hard, cynical edge that made her shiver. 'Maybe that's what keeps me going, *guapa*. Maybe I intend to push your buttons for as long as it amuses me to do so.'

She swallowed hard and considered staring him down. But she knew how good he was at that game. Heck, Rafael was a maestro at most games. He would only welcome the challenge.

Reaching behind him to slam the car door, she started to move with him towards the entrance of the church where baby Jack's ceremony was being held. 'If you're trying to get me to resign by being intolerable, I won't,' she stated in as firm a tone as possible, hoping he'd get the hint. Aside from the need to make amends, she needed this job. Her severance package from Team Espíritu when Marco de Cervantes had

sold the racing team had been more than generous, but it was
fast running out in light of her mother's huge treatment bills.
It would take a lot more than Rafael's sexual taunts to make
her walk away.

He shrugged and fell into step beside her. 'Good. As long as
you're here tormenting yourself with your guilt, I feel better.'

Acute discomfort lodged in her chest. 'I thought we weren't
going to speak about that?'

'You should know by now, rules mean nothing to me. Unspoken rules mean even less. How's the guilt today, by the
way?'

'Receding by the second, thanks to your insufferable
tongue.'

'I must be slacking.' He took a step forward, gave a visible wince, and Raven's heart stopped, along with her feet.
He raised a brow at her, the hard smile back on his face. 'Ah,
there it is. Good to know I haven't lost my touch after all.'

Ice danced down her spine at his chilled tone. Before she
could answer, the large bell pealed nearby. Pigeons flew out
of the turrets of the tiny whitewashed church that had been
on the de Cervantes's Northern Spanish estate for several
hundred years.

Raven glanced around them, past the church poised at the
summit of the small hill that overlooked miles of prime de
Cervantes vineyards, to the graveyard beyond where Rafael's
ancestors lay interred.

'Are we going to stand here all day admiring the landscape
or do we actually need to go *inside* the church for this gig?' A
quick glance at him showed his face studiously averted from
the prominent headstones, his jaw set in steel.

She drew in a deep breath and moved towards the arched
entrance to the church. 'It's not a *gig;* it's your nephew's christening. In a church. With other guests. So act accordingly.'

Another dark chuckle. 'Or what, you'll put me over your
knee? Or will you just pray that I be struck down by lightning if I blaspheme?'

'I'm not rising to your baits, Rafael.' Mostly because she had an inkling of how hard this morning would be for him. According to Rafael's housekeeper, it was the first time he'd interacted with his family since his return to León from his private hospital in Barcelona. 'You can try to rile me all you want. I'm not going anywhere.'

'A martyr to the last?'

'A physiotherapist who knows how grumpy patients can be when they don't get their way.'

'What makes you think I'm not getting exactly what I want?' he rasped lazily.

'I overheard your phone call to Marco this morning… twice…to try and get out of your godfather duties. Since you're here now, I'm guessing he refused to let you?'

A tic in his jaw and a raised brow was her only answer.

'Like I said, I know a grumpy patient when I see one.' She hurried forward and opened the large heavy door.

To her relief, he didn't answer back. She hoped it was because they were within the hallowed walls of his family's chapel because she was close enough to feel his tension increase the closer they got to the altar.

De Cervantes family members and the few close friends who'd managed to gain an invitation to the christening of Sasha and Marco de Cervantes's firstborn turned to watch their slow progress up the aisle.

'Shame you're not wearing a white gown,' Rafael quipped from the side of his mouth, taking her elbow even as he smiled and winked at a well-known Spanish supermodel. But, this close, Raven could see the stress lines that faintly bracketed his mouth and the pulse throbbing at his temple. Rafael *really* did not want to be here.

'White gown?'

'Think how frenzied their imagination would be running right about now. It would almost warrant a two-page spread in *X1 Magazine*.'

'Even if I were dressed in bridal white with a crown on my

head and stars in my eyes, no one would believe you would actually go through with anything as anathema to you as a wedding, Rafael. These poor people would probably drop dead at the very thought of linking you with the word *commitment*.'

His grip tightened for a minuscule moment before that lazy smile returned. 'For once, you're right. Weddings bore me rigid and the word *marriage* should have a picture of a noose next to it in the dictionary.'

They were a few steps away from the front pew, where his brother and sister-in-law sat gazing down adoringly at their infant son. The sight of their utter devotion and contentment made her insides tighten another notch.

'I don't think that's how your brother and his wife see it.'

Rafael's jaw tightened before he shrugged. 'I'm prepared to accede that for some the Halley's Comet effect does happen. But we'll wait and see if it's a mirage or the real thing, shall we?'

Her breath caught at the wealth of cynicism in his tone. She couldn't respond because an usher was signalling the priest that it was time to start.

The ceremony was conducted in Spanish with English translations printed out on embossed gold-edged paper.

As the minutes ticked by, she noted Rafael's profile growing even tenser. Glancing down at the sheet, she realised the moment was approaching for him to take his godson for the anointing. Despite her caution to remain unmoved, her heart softened at his obvious discomfort.

'Relax. Babies are more resilient than we give them credit for. Trust me, it takes a complete idiot to drop a baby.'

She was unprepared for the icy blue eyes that sliced into her. 'Your flattery is touching but the last thing I'm thinking of is dropping my nephew.'

'You don't need to hide it, Rafael. Your tension is so thick it's suffocating.'

His eyes grew colder. 'Remember when I said weddings bore me?'

She nodded warily.

'Christenings bore me even more. Besides, I've never been good in churches. All that *piety*.' He gave a mock shudder. 'My *abuela* used to smack my hand because I could never sit still.'

'Well, I'm not your grandmother so you're spared the smacking. Besides, you're a grown man now so act like one and suck it up.'

Too late, she remembered certain words were like a naked invitation to Rafael. She was completely stunned when he didn't make the obvious remark. Or maybe it was a testament to just how deeply the whole ceremony was affecting him.

'I just want this to be over and done with so I can resume more interesting subjects.' Without due warning, his gaze dropped to the cleavage of her simple, sleeveless orange knee-length chiffon dress. The bold, heated caress resonated through her body, leaving a trail of fire that singed in delicate places. 'Like how delicious you look in that dress. Or how you'll look *out* of it.'

Heat suffused her face. It was no use pointing out how inappropriate this conversation was. Rafael knew very well what he was doing. And the unrepentant gleam in his eyes told her so.

'Rafa...' Marco de Cervantes's deep voice interrupted them.

Raven glanced up and her eyes collided with steel-grey ones which softened a touch when they lit on his brother.

Like most people who'd worked the X1 Premier circuit, she knew all about the de Cervantes brothers. Gorgeous beyond words and successful in their individual rights, they'd made scores of female hearts flutter, both on and off of the racing circuit.

Marco had been the dynamic ex-racer team boss and race car designer. And Rafael, also insanely gifted behind the wheel, had at the age of twenty-eight founded and established himself as CEO of X1 Premier Management, the multi-billion euro conglomerate that nurtured, trained and looked after racing drivers. Between them they'd won more medals and championships than any other team in the history of the sport.

The last year had changed everything for them, though. Marco had sold the team and married Sasha Fleming, the racing driver who'd won him his last Constructors' Championship and stolen his heart in the process; and Rafael had spectacularly crashed his car, nearly lost his life and stalled his racing career.

The icy jet of guilt that shot through Raven every time she thought of his accident, and her part in it, threatened to overwhelm her. Her breath caught as she desperately tried to put the incident out of her head. This was neither the time nor the place.

But then, when had timing been her strong suit?

Over and over, she'd proven that when it came to being in the wrong place at the wrong time, she took first prize every single time. At sixteen, it was what had earned her the unwanted attention that had scarred what remained of her already battered childhood.

As a grown woman of twenty-three, foolishly believing she'd put the past behind her, she'd been proved brutally wrong again when she'd met Rafael de Cervantes.

Rafael's mouth very close to her ear ripped her from her painful thoughts. 'Right, I'm up, I believe. Which means, so are you.'

Her heart leapt into her throat. 'Excuse me?'

'I can barely stand up straight, *pequeña*. It's time to do your duty and *support* me just in case it all gets too much and I keel over.'

'But you're perfectly capable—'

'Rafa...' Marco's voice held a touch of impatience.

Rafael's brow cocked and he held out his arm. With no choice but to comply or risk causing a scene, Raven stood and helped him up. As before, his arm came around her in an all-encompassing hold. And again, she felt the bounds of professionalism slip as she struggled not to feel the effortless, decidedly *erotic* sensations Rafael commanded so very easily in her. Sensations she'd tried her damnedest to stem and, failing that, ignore since the first moment she'd clapped eyes on the legendary racing driver last year.

What had she said to him—*suck it up*? She took a breath and fought to take her own advice.

They made their way to the font and Raven managed to summon a smile in answer to Sasha's open and friendly one. But all through the remainder of the ceremony, Raven was drenched with the feeling that maybe, just maybe, in her haste to assuage her guilt and make amends, she'd made a mistake. Had she, by pushing Rafael to take her on as his personal physiotherapist, jumped from the frying fan into the proverbial fire?

Rafael repeated the words that bound the small person sleeping peacefully in the elegant but frilly Moses basket to him. He firmed lips that wanted to curl in self-derision.

Who was he to become *godfather* to another human being?

Everything he touched turned to dust eventually. Sooner or later he ruined everything good in his life. He'd tried to tell his brother over and over since he'd dropped the bombshell on him a month ago. Hell, as late as this morning he'd tried to get Marco to see sense and change his mind about making him godfather.

But Marco, snug in his newfound love-cocoon, had blithely ignored his request to appoint someone else his son's godfather. Apparently, reality hath no blind spots like a man in love.

Was that a saying? If not, it needed to be.

He was no one's hero. He was the last person any father should entrust with his child.

He gazed down into his nephew's sweet, innocent face. How long before Jack de Cervantes recognised him for what he was? An empty shell. A heartless bastard who'd only succeeded at two things—driving fast cars and seducing fast women.

He shifted on his feet. Pain ricocheted through his hip and pelvis. Ignoring it, he gave a mental shrug, limped forward and took the ladle the priest passed him. Scooping water out of the large bowl, he poised it over his nephew's head.

At the priest's nod, he tipped the ladle.

The scream of protest sent a tiny wave of satisfaction through him. Hopefully his innocent nephew would take a look at him and run screaming every time he saw him. Because Rafael knew that if he had anything at all to do with his brother's child, the poor boy's life too would be ruined.

As well-wishers gathered around to soothe the wailing child, he dropped the ladle back into the bowl, stepped back and forced his gaze away from his nephew's adorable curls and plump cheeks.

Beside him, he heard Raven's long indrawn breath and, grabbing the very welcome distraction, he let his gaze drift to her.

Magnet-like, her hazel eyes sought and found his. Her throat moved in a visible swallow that made his fingers itch to slide over that smooth column of flesh. Follow it down to that delectable, infinitely tempting valley between her plump breasts.

Not here, not now, he thought regrettably. What was between the two of them would not be played out here in this place where dark memories—both living and dead—lingered everywhere he looked, ready to pounce on him should he even begin to let them…

He tensed at the whirr of an electronic wheelchair, kept his gaze fixed on Raven even as his spine stiffened almost painfully. Thankfully the wheelchair stopped several feet behind him and he heard the familiar voice exchange greetings with other family members. With every pulse of icy blood through his veins, Rafael wished himself elsewhere…anywhere but here, where the thick candles and fragrant flowers above the nave reminded him of other candles and flowers placed in a shrine not very far away from where he stood—a constant reminder of what he'd done. A reminder that because of him, because of callous destruction, this was his mother's final resting place.

His beloved Mamá…

His breath caught as Sasha, his sister-in-law, came towards him, her now quietened son in her arm.

Sasha…something else he'd ruined.

Dios…

'He's got a set of lungs on him, hasn't he?' she laughed, her face radiant in the light slanting through the church windows. 'He almost raised the roof with all that wailing.'

He took in the perfect picture mother and child made and something caught in his chest. He'd denied his mother this—the chance to meet her grandchild.

'Rafael?'

He focused and summoned a half-smile. '*Sí*, my poor eardrums are still bleeding.'

She laughed again as her eyes rolled. 'Oh, come on, my little champ's not that bad. Besides, Marco tells me he takes after you, and I don't find that hard to believe at all.' She sobered, her gaze running over him before piercing blue eyes captured his in frank, no nonsense assessment. 'So…how are you? And don't give me a glib answer.'

'Thoroughly bored of everyone asking me how I am.' He raised his walking stick and gestured to his frame. 'See for yourself, *piqueña*. My clever physiotherapist tells me I'm between phases two and three on the recovery scale. *Dios* knows what that means. All I know is that I'm still a broken, broken man.' In more ways than he cared to count.

She gently rubbed her son's back. 'You're far from broken. And we ask because we care about you.'

'*Sí*, I get that. But I prefer all this caring to be from afar. The up-close-and-personal kind gives me the…what do you English call it…the *willies*?'

Her eyes dimmed but her smile remained in place. 'Too bad. We're not going to stop because you bristle every time we come near.' Her determined gaze shifted to Raven, who was chatting to another guest. 'And I hope you're not giving her a hard time. From what I hear, she's the best physio there is.'

Despite telling himself it wasn't the time or place, he couldn't stop his gaze from tracing the perfect lines of Raven Blass's body. And it *was* a perfect body, honed by hours and hours of gruelling physical exercise. She hadn't been lying when she said she was solid muscle and bone. But Rafael knew, from being up close and personal, that there was soft femininity where there needed to be. Which, all in all, presented a more-than-pleasing package that had snagged his attention with shocking intensity the first time he'd laid eyes on her in his racing paddock almost eighteen months ago.

Of course, he'd been left in no uncertain terms that, despite all indications of a *very* mutual attraction, Raven had no intention of letting herself explore that attraction. Her reaction to it had been viscerally blunt.

She'd gone out of her way to hammer her rejection home… right at the time when he'd been in no state to be rejected…

His jaw tightened. 'How I choose to treat my physiotherapist is really none of your business, Sasha.'

A hint of sadness flitted through her eyes before she looked down at her son. 'Despite what you might think, I'm still your friend, so stop trying to push me away because, in case you need reminding, I push back.' She glanced back at him with a look of steely determination.

He sighed. 'I'd forgotten how stubborn you are.'

'It's okay. I'm happy to remind you when you need reminding. Your equally demanding godson demands your presence at the villa, so we'll see you both there in half an hour. No excuses.'

'If we must,' Rafael responded in a bored drawl.

Sasha's lips firmed. 'You must. Or I'll have to leave my guests and come and fetch you personally. And Marco wouldn't like that at all.'

'I stopped being terrified of my big brother long before I lost my baby teeth, *piqueña*.'

'Yes, but I know you wouldn't want to disappoint him. Also, don't forget about Raven.'

He glanced over his shoulder at the woman in question, who now stood with her head bent as she spoke to one of the altar boys. Her namesake hair fell forward as she nodded in response to something the boy said. From the close contact necessitated by her profession, Rafael knew exactly how silky and luxuriant her hair felt against his skin. He'd long stopped resenting the kick in his groin when he looked at her. In fact he welcomed it. He'd lost a lot after his accident, not just a percentage of his physical mobility. With each groin kick, he ferociously celebrated the return of his libido.

'What about Raven?' he asked.

'I've seen her in action during her training sessions. She's been known to reduce grown men to tears. I bet I can convince her to hog-tie you to the SUV and deliver you to the villa if you carry on being difficult.'

Rafael loosened his grip on his walking stick and gave a grim smile. '*Dios*, did someone hack into my temporary Internet files and discover I have a thing for dominatrixes? Because you two seem bent on pushing that hot, sweet button.'

Sasha's smile widened. 'I see you haven't lost your dirty sense of humour. That's something to celebrate, at least. See you at the villa.'

Without waiting for an answer, she marched off towards Marco, who was shaking hands with the priest. His brother's arm enfolded her immediately. Rafael gritted his teeth against the disconcerting pang and accompanying guilt that niggled him.

He'd robbed his family of so much...

'So, which is it to be—compliance without question or physical restraints?' Raven strolled towards him, her gaze cool and collected.

The mental picture that flashed into his mind made his

heart beat just that little bit faster. Nerves which his doctors had advised him might never heal again stirred, as they'd been stirring for several days now. The very male satisfaction the sensation brought sent a shaft of fire through his veins. 'You heard?'

'It was difficult not to. You don't revere your surroundings enough to keep your voice down when you air your… peccadilloes.'

The laughter that ripped from his throat felt surprisingly great. He'd had nothing to laugh about for far longer than he cared to remember. Several heads turned to watch him but he didn't care. He was more intrigued by the blush that spread over Raven's face. He leaned in close. 'Do you think the angels are about to strike me down? Will you save me if they do?' he asked sotto voce.

'No, Rafael. I think, based on your debauched past and irreverent present, all the saints will agree by now you're beyond redemption. No one can save you.'

Despite his bitter self-condemnation moments ago, hearing the words repeated so starkly caused Rafael's chest to tighten. All traces of mirth were stripped from his soul as he recalled similar words, uttered by the same voice, this same woman eight months ago. And then, as now, he felt the black chasm of despair yawn before him, growing ever-wider, sucking at his empty soul until only darkness remained. Because knowingly or unknowingly, she'd struck a very large, very raw nerve.

'Then tell me, Raven, if I'm beyond redemption, what the hell are you doing here?'

CHAPTER TWO

I'M NOT HERE to save you, if that's what you think.

The words hovered like heat striations in Raven's brain an hour later as she stood on the large sun-baked terrace of Marco and Sasha's home. This time the rich surroundings of the architecturally stunning Casa León failed to awe her as they usually did.

I'm not here to save you...

She snorted. What a load of bull. That was *exactly* why she'd begged Marco to let her visit Rafael in hospital once he'd woken from his coma all those months ago. It was why she'd flown to León from London five weeks ago, after months of trying to contact Rafael and being stonily ignored by him; and why she'd begged him to let her treat him when she found out what an appalling job his carers were doing—not because they were incompetent, but because Rafael didn't seem inclined in any way to want to get better, and they'd been too intimidated to go against his wishes. It was most definitely why she continued to suffer his inappropriate, irreverent taunts.

She wanted to make things right...wanted to take back every single word she'd said to him eight months ago, right before he'd climbed into the cockpit of his car and crashed it into a solid concrete wall minutes later.

Because it wasn't Rafael's fault that she hadn't been able to curb her stupid, crazy delusional feelings until it was almost too late. It wasn't his fault that, despite all signs that he was nothing but a carbon copy of her heartless playboy father, she hadn't been able to stop herself from lusting after him—

No, scratch that. Not a carbon copy. Rafael was no one's copy. He was a breed in his own right. With a smile that could slice a woman's heart wide open, make a woman swoon with bliss even as she knew her heart was being slowly crushed. He possessed more charm in his little finger than most wannabe playboys, including her father, held in their entire bodies.

But she'd seen first-hand the devastation that charm could cause. Swarthy Spanish Lothario or a middle-aged English playboy, she knew the effect would be the same.

Her mother was broken, continued to suffer because of the very lethal thrall Raven's father held over her.

And although she knew after five weeks in his company that Rafael's attitude would never manifest in sexual malice, he was in no way less dangerous to her peace of mind. Truth be told, the more she suffered his blatant sexual taunts, the more certain she was that she wanted to see beneath his outwardly glossy façade.

With every atom of her being, Raven wished she'd known this on his unfortunate race day. But, tormented by her mother's suffering, her control when it came to Rafael had slipped badly. Instead of walking away with dignified indifference, she'd lashed out. Unforgivably—

'So deep in thought. Dare I think those thoughts are about me?' Warm air from warmer lips washed over her right lobe.

'Why would you think that?' she asked, sucking in a deep, sustaining breath before she faced the man who seemed to have set up residence in her thoughts.

'Because I've studied you enough to recognise your frowns. Two lines mean you're unhappy because I'm not listening to you drone on about how many squats or abdominal crunches you expect me to perform. Three lines mean your thoughts are of a personal nature, mostly likely you're in turmoil about our last conversation before my accident.' He held out a glass of champagne, his blue eyes thankfully no longer charged with the frosty fury they'd held at the chapel. 'You're wearing a three-line frown now.'

She took the proffered drink and glanced away, unable quite to meet his gaze. 'You think I'm that easy to read?'

'The fact that you're not denying what I say tells me everything I need to know. Your guilt is eating you alive. Admit it,' he said conversationally, before taking a sip of his drink. 'And it kills you even more that I can't remember the accident itself but can remember every single word you said to me only minutes before it happened, doesn't it?'

Her insides twisted with regret. 'I...Rafael...I'm sorry...'

'As I told you in Barcelona, *I'm sorry* won't quite cut it. I need a lot more from you than mere words, *mi corazon.*'

Her heart flipped and dived into her stomach. 'And I told you, I won't debase myself like a cheap paddock bunny just to prove how sorry I am for what I said.'

'Even though you meant every single word?'

'Look, I know I shouldn't have—'

'You meant them then, and you still believe them now. So we shall continue as we are. I push, you push back; we both drown in sexual tension. We'll see who breaks first.'

Her fingers tightened around the cold glass. 'Is this all really a game to you?' The man in turmoil she'd glimpsed at the chapel seemed very distant now. But she'd seen him, knew there was something else going on beneath all the sexual gloss.

'Of course it is. How else do you expect me to pass the time?'

'Your racing career may be stalled for the moment but, for a man of your wealth and power, there are a thousand ways you can find fulfilment.'

A dull look entered his eyes but disappeared a split second later. '*Fulfilment*...how New Age. Next you'll be recommending I practise Transcendental Meditation to get in touch with my chakra.'

'Meditation isn't such a bad thing. I could teach you...'

His mocking laugh stopped her in her tracks. 'Will we braid each other's hair too? Maybe share a joint or two while we're at it?'

She tried to hide her irritation and cocked her head. 'You know something? I have no idea what all those girls see in you. You're cocky, arrogant and dismissive of things you know nothing about.'

'I don't waste my time learning things that hold no interest for me. Women hold my interest so I make it a point to study them. And I know plenty about women like you.'

She stiffened. 'What do you mean, women like me?'

'You take pleasure in hiding behind affront, you take everything so personally and pretend to get all twisted up by the slightest hint of a challenge. It's obvious you've had a… traumatic experience in the past—'

'That's like a psychic predicting someone's been hurt in the past. By virtue of sheer coincidence and indisputable reality, half of relationships end badly, so it stands to reason that most people have had *traumatic experiences*. If you're thinking of taking up clairvoyance, you'll need to do better than that.'

His bared teeth held the predatory smile of one who knew he had his prey cornered. '*Claro*, let's do it this way. I'll make a *psychic* prediction. If I'm wrong, feel free to throw that glass of vintage champagne in my face.'

'I'd never make a scene like that, especially not at your nephew's christening.'

The reminder of where they were made him stiffen slightly but it didn't stop him moving closer until his broad shoulders and streamlined body blocked out the rest of the party. Breath catching, Raven could see nothing but him, smell nothing but the heady, spicy scent that clung to his skin and seemed to weave around her every time she came within touching distance.

As if he knew his effect on her, his smile widened. 'No one will see my humiliation *if* I get it wrong.'

Afraid of what he'd uncover, she started to shake her head, but Rafael was already speaking.

'You've been hurt by a man, someone you really wanted to depend on, someone you wanted to *be there* for you.' He waited, his eyes moving to the fingers clenched around her glass. When she didn't move he leaned in closer. 'Since that relationship ended, you've decided to take the tired *all men are bastards* route. You'd like nothing more than to find yourself a nice, safe man, someone who *understands* you.' His gaze moved to her face, his incisive stare probing so deep Raven wanted to take a step back. With sheer strength of will, she stood her ground. 'You hate yourself for being attracted to me but, deep inside, you enjoy our little skirmishes because the challenge of sparring with me makes your heart beat just that little bit faster.' His gaze traced her hopefully impassive face down to her throat.

For a blind moment, Raven wished she'd worn her hair down because even she could feel the wild tattoo of her pulse surging underneath the skin at her throat.

She tried to speak but the accuracy of his prediction had frozen her tongue.

'Since my face is still dry, I'll take it Psychic Rafa is accurate on all accounts?'

His arrogance finally loosened her tongue. 'Don't flatter yourself. I told you when you started playing these games that I wouldn't participate. I know you're challenged by any woman who doesn't fall for your charms, but not everyone subscribes to the OMG-Rafael de Cervantes-makes-my-knickers-wet Fan Club.'

Rafael's smile was blinding, but it held a speculation that made her hackles rise. '*Piqueña*, since there's only one way to *test* that you're not a member, I now have something to look forward to. And just like that, my days suddenly seem brighter.'

Heat punched its way through her pelvis but, before Raven could answer, a deep throat cleared behind them.

Marco de Cervantes was as tall as his brother and just as visually stunning to look at but he wore his good looks with a smouldering grace where Rafael wholeheartedly embraced his irreverent playboy status.

Marco nodded to Raven, and glanced at his brother.

'I need to talk to you. You don't mind if I borrow him for five minutes, do you, Raven?'

Relief spiked, headier than the champagne she'd barely drunk. 'Not at all. We weren't discussing anything important.'

Rafael's eyes narrowed at the thin insult, his icy blue eyes promising retribution just before they cleared into their usual deceptively indolent look.

Lifting her glass in a mocking salute, she walked away, piercingly aware that he tracked her every step. Out of his intoxicating, domineering sphere, she heaved in a breath of pure relief and pasted a smile on her face as Sasha beckoned her.

Rafael turned to his brother, mild irritation prickling his skin. 'What's on your mind?' He discarded his champagne and wished he had something stronger.

'You need another hobby besides trying to rile your physiotherapist.'

His irritation grew as Raven disappeared from sight, pulled towards a group of guests by Sasha. 'What's it to you? And why the hell does everyone feel the need to poke their nose into my business?'

Marco shrugged away the question. 'Consider the matter dropped. The old man's been asking for you.' Grey eyes bored sharply into his. 'I think it's time.'

Every bone in his body turned excruciatingly rigid. 'That's for me to decide, surely?' And if he didn't feel he was ready to ask for forgiveness, who was anybody to decide otherwise?

'There's been enough hurt all around, Rafa. It's time to move things forward.'

He spiked tense fingers through his hair. 'You wouldn't be trying to save me again by any chance, would you, brother?'

An impatient look passed through Marco's eyes. 'From the look of things, you don't need saving. Besides, I cut the apron strings when I realised you were driving me so nuts that I was in danger of strangling you with them.'

Rafael beckoned the waiter over and exchanged his untouched champagne for a crystal tumbler of Patrón. 'In that case, we're copacetic. Was there anything else?'

Marco's gaze stayed on him for several seconds before he nodded. 'You sent for the papers for the X1 All-Star event coming up?'

Rafael downed the drink, welcoming the warmth that coursed through his chest. 'Unless I'm mistaken, I'm still the CEO of X1 Premier Management. The events start in three weeks. You delegated some of the event's organisation but it's time for me to take the reins again.'

His brother's gaze probed, worry lurking within. 'Are you sure you don't want to sit this one out—?'

'I'm sure. Don't second-guess me, *mi hermano*. I understand that my racing career may be in question—' He stopped as a chill surged through his veins, obliterating the warmth of moments before. Although he didn't remember his accident, he'd seen pictures of the wreckage in vivid detail. He was very much aware that *lucky to be alive* didn't begin to describe his condition. 'The racing side of my career may be up for debate,' he repeated, beating back the wave of desolation that swelled up inside his chest, 'but my brain still functions perfectly. As for my body...' He looked over as a flash of orange caught his eye. The resulting kick gave him a surge of satisfaction. 'My body will be in top condition before very long.'

Marco nodded. 'I'm happy to hear it. According to Raven, you're on the road to complete recovery.'

'Really?' Rafael made a mental note to have a short, precise conversation with his physio about sharing confidential information.

'...*Dios*, are you listening to me? Never mind, I think it'll be safer for me not to know which part of your anatomy you're thinking with right at this moment. *Bueno*, I'll be in touch later in the week to discuss other business.'

'No need to wait till next week. I can tell you now that I'm back. I own fifty per cent of our business, after all. No reason why you should continue to shoulder my responsibilities.

Come to think of it, you should take a vacation with your family, let me handle things for a while.' He glanced over to where Sasha stood chatting to Raven. As if sensing their attention, both women turned towards them. Marco's face dissolved in a look so cheesy, Rafael barely stopped himself from making retching noises.

'Are you sure?' Marco asked without taking his eyes off his wife. 'Sasha's been on my back about taking some time off. It would be great to take the yacht to the island for a bit.' They joint owned a three-mile island paradise in the Bahamas, a place neither of them had visited in a very long time.

'Great. Do it. I'll handle things here,' Rafael responded.

His brother looked sceptical.

'This is a one-time offer, set to expire in ten seconds,' he pressed as his sister-in-law and his physiotherapist started walking towards them. For the first time he noticed Raven's open-toed high heels and saw the way they made her long legs go on for ever. Sasha said something to her. Her responding smile made his throat dry.

Hell, he had it bad if he was behaving like a hormonal teenager around a woman who clearly had *man issues*.

He barely felt it when Marco slapped his shoulder. 'I'll set things in motion first thing in the morning. I owe you one, brother.'

Rafael nodded, relieved that the disturbing subject of his father had been dropped.

'What are you looking so pleased about?' Sasha asked her husband as they drew level with them.

'I have news that's guaranteed to make you adore me even more than you already do.' He kissed her soundly on the lips before leading her away.

Rafael saw Raven looking after them. 'I do believe if they had a *like* button attached to their backs you would be pressing it right about now?'

Her outraged gasp made him curb a smile. He loved to rile her. Rafael didn't hide from the fact that while he was busy riling Raven Blass, he was busy not thinking about what this place did to him, and that gained him a reprieve from the torment of his memories.

She faced him, bristling with irritation and censure. 'Whereas if you had a *like* button I'd personally start a world-wide petition to have it obliterated and replaced with one that said *loathe*.'

He took her elbow and, despite her resistance, he led her to an exquisitely laid out buffet table. 'We'll discuss my various buttons later. Right now you need to eat something before you wither away. I noticed you didn't eat any breakfast this morning.'

She glared at him. 'I had my usual bowl of muesli and fresh fruit.'

'Was that before or after you spent two hours on my beach contorting yourself in unthinkable shapes in the name of exercise?'

'It's called Krav Maga. It works the mind as well as the body.'

He let his gaze rake her from top to toe. 'I don't dispute the effects on the body. But I don't think it's quite working on the mind.'

He stopped another outraged gasp by stuffing a piece of chicken into her mouth. Her only option, other than spitting it out, was to chew, but that didn't stop her glaring fiercely at him.

Rafael was so busy enjoying the way he got under her skin that he didn't hear the low hum of the electric wheelchair until it was too late.

'*Buenos tardes, mi hijo.* I've been looking for you.' The greeting was low and deep. It didn't hold any censure or hatred or flaying judgement. In fact it sounded just exactly as it would were a loving father greeting his beloved son.

But every nerve of Rafael's being screeched with white-hot pain. His fist clenched around his walking stick until the metal dug excruciatingly into his palm. For the life of him, he couldn't let go. He sucked in a breath as his vision blurred. Before the red haze completely dulled his vision, he saw Raven's concerned look as her eyes darted between him and the wheelchair-bound figure.

'Rafael?'

He couldn't find the words to respond to the greeting. Nor could he find the words to stem Raven's escalating concern.

Dios mío, he couldn't even find the courage to turn around. Because how the hell could he explain to Raven that he and he alone was responsible for making his father a quadriplegic?

CHAPTER THREE

'Do you want to talk about it?'

'The *therapy* in your job title pertains only to my body, not my mind. You'll do well to remember that.'

Raven should've heeded the icy warning, should've just kept her hands on the wheel of the luxury SUV and kept driving towards the stunning glass and steel structure that was Rafael's home on the other side of the de Cervantes estate from his brother's villa.

But her senses jumped at the aura of acute pain that had engulfed Rafael the moment he'd turned around to face the old man in the electric wheelchair. The same pain that surrounded him now. Grey lips were pinched into a thin line, his jaw carved from stone and fingers clamped around his walking stick in a white-knuckled grip. Even his breathing had changed. His broad chest rose and fell in an uncharacteristically shallow rhythm that screamed his agitation.

She pulled over next to a tall acacia tree, one of several hundred that lined the long winding driveway and extended into the exquisitely designed landscape beyond. Behind them, the iron gates, manned by twenty-four-hour security, swung shut.

Narrowed eyes focused with laser-like intensity on her. 'What the hell do you think you're doing?'

'I've stopped because we need to talk about what just happened. Your mental health affects your body's recovery just as much as your physiotherapy regime.'

'Healthy mind, healthy body? That's a piss-poor way of trying to extract the hot gossip, Raven *mia*. You'll need to do much better than that. Why don't you just come out and ask for the juicy details?'

She blew a breath, refusing to rise to the bait. 'Would you tell me if I asked you that?'

'No.'

'Rafael—'

Arctic-chilled eyes narrowed even further. 'In case you didn't already guess, that was my father. Our relationship comes under the subject line of *kryptonite—keep the hell out* to any and all parties.'

'So you can dissect my personal life all you want but yours is off limits?'

His smile was just as icy. 'Certain aspects of my personal life are wide open to you. All you have to do is say the word and I'll be happy to educate you in how we can fully explore it.'

'That is not what I meant.'

'You've taken pains to establish boundaries between us since the moment we met. This is one of *my* boundaries. Attempt to breach it at your peril.'

She frowned. 'Or what? You'll fall back on your default setting of sexual innuendo and taunts? Rafael, I'm only trying to help you.'

His hand slashed through the air in a movement so far removed from his normal laid-back indolence her mouth dropped open. 'I do not need your help unless it's the help I've hired you to provide. Right now I want you to shut up and *drive*.' He clipped out the final word in a hard bite that sent a chill down her spine.

After waiting a minute to steady her own shot nerves, she set the SUV back onto the road, aware of his continued shallow breathing and gritted-jaw iciness. Her fingers clenched over the titanium steering wheel and she practised some nerve-calming breaths of her own.

From the very first, Rafael had known which buttons to push. He'd instinctively known that the subject of sex was anathema to her and had therefore honed in on it with the precision of a laser-guided missile.

Seeing his intense reaction to his father—and she'd known immediately the nearly all-grey-haired man in the wheelchair was his father—had hammered home what she'd been surprised to learn this morning at the chapel, and had somewhat confirmed at Marco's villa: that Rafael, as much as he pretended to be shallow and sex pest-y, had a depth he rarely showed to the world.

Was that why she was so driven to pay penance for the way she'd treated him several months ago—because deep down she thought he was worth saving?

Raven shied away from the probing thought and brought the car to a stop at the end of the driveway.

The wide solid glass door that led into the house swung open and Diego, one of the many staff Rafael employed to run his luxurious home, came down the steps to open her door. In silence, she handed him the car keys and turned to find Rafael rounding the bonnet. The sun glinting off the silver paint cast his face into sharp relief. Her breath snagged in her chest at the masculine, tortured beauty of him. She didn't offer to assist him as he climbed the shallow steps into the house.

In the marble-floored hallway, he shrugged off his suit jacket, handed it to Diego and pulled his shirt tails impatiently from his trousers. At the glimpse of tanned golden flesh a pulse of heat shot through her belly. Sucking in a breath, she looked away, focusing on an abstract painting that took up one entire rectangular pillar in the hallway for an infinitesimal second before she glanced his away again, to find him shoving an agitated hand through his hair.

'Do you need—?' she started.

'Unless I'm growing senile, today's Sunday. Did we not agree we'd give the Florence Nightingale routine a rest on Sundays?'

Annoyance rose to mingle with her concern. 'No, *you* came up with that decree. I never agreed to it.'

Handing his walking stick to a still-hovering Diego, he

started to unbutton his shirt. 'It's a great thing I'm the boss then, isn't it?'

Her mouth dried as several inches of stunning flesh assaulted her senses. When her brain started to short-circuit, she pulled her gaze away. 'Undressing in the hallway, Rafael, really?' She tried to inject as much indifference into her tone as possible but was aware her voice had become unhealthily screechy. 'What do you think—that I'm going to run away in virginal outrage?'

His shameless grin didn't hide the strain and tension beneath. 'At twenty-four, I seriously doubt there's anything virginal about you. No, *mi dulzura,* I'm hoping you'll stay and cheer me on through my striptease.'

The sound that emerged from her throat made his grin widen. 'Don't you want to heal completely? That limp will not go away until you work hard to strengthen your core muscles and realign the bones that were damaged during the accident. If you'd just focus on that we can be rid of each other sooner rather than later.'

Although she thought she saw his shoulders stiffen as he turned to give his shirt to Diego, his grin was still in place when he faced her. 'You're under the impression that I want to be shot of you but you couldn't be further from the truth. I want you right here with me every day.'

'So I can be your whipping girl?'

'I've never been a fan of whips, myself. Handcuffs, blindfolds, the odd paddle, certainly…but whips?' He gave a mock shudder. 'No, not my thing.'

His hand went to the top of his trousers. Deft fingers freed his button, followed by the loud, distinct sound of his zip lowering. She froze. Diego didn't bat an eyelid. 'For goodness' sake, what *are* you doing, Rafael?'

He toed off his shoes and socks. 'I thought it was obvious. I'm going for a swim. Care to join me?'

'I…no, thank you.' The way her temperature had shot up, she'd need a cold shower, not the sultry warmth of Rafael's azure infinity pool. 'But we'll need to talk when you're done. I'll come and find you—' She nearly choked when he dropped his trousers and stepped out of them. The way his designer cotton boxer shorts cupped his impressive man package made all oxygen flee from her lungs. Utterly captivated by the man whose sculpted body, even after the accident that had laid him flat for months, was still the best-looking she'd even seen or worked with, Raven could no more stop herself from staring than she could fly to the moon.

His thighs and legs bore scars from his accident, his calves solid powerful muscle that made the physio in her thrilled to be working with such a manly specimen. Dear Lord, even his feet were sexy, and she'd never been one to pay attention to feet unless they were directly related to her profession.

Helplessly, her gaze travelled back up, past his golden, sculpted chest and wide, athletic shoulders to collide with icy blue eyes.

'My, my, if I didn't enjoy it so much I'd be offended to be treated like a piece of meat.'

She snapped back to her senses to see Diego disappearing up the granite banister-less staircase leading to Rafael's vast first floor suite. The click of his walking stick drew attention back to the man in question. One brow was raised in silent query.

'What do you expect if you insist on making an exhibition of yourself?'

One step brought him within touching distance. 'That's the beauty of free will, *querida*. The ability to walk away when a situation displeases you.'

'If I did that every time you attempted to rile me, I'd never get any work done and you'd still be in the pathetic shape I found you in five weeks ago.'

Another step. Raven breathed in and clenched her fists against the warm, wicked scent that assailed her senses.

'You know what drew me to you when you first joined Team Espíritu?' he breathed.

'I'm sure you're going to enlighten me.'

'Your eyes flash with the deepest hypnotic fire when you're all riled up but your body screams *stay away*. Even the most seductive woman can't pull that off as easily as you can. I'm infinitely fascinated to know what happened to make you this way.'

'Personal subjects are off the table. Besides, I thought you had me all worked out?'

His gaze dropped to her lips. She pressed them together to stop their insane tingling. 'I know the general parameters of your inner angst. But I can't help but feel there's another layer, a deeper reason why you want me with every cell in your body but would chop off your hand before you would even bring yourself to touch me in any but a professional way.'

The ice that encased her soul came from so deep, so dark a place that she'd stopped trying to fathom the depths of it. 'Enjoy your swim, Rafael. I'll come by later to discuss the next steps of your regime.'

'Of course, Mistress Raven. I look forward to the many and varied ways you intend to *whip* me into shape.' With a step sideways that still managed to encroach on her body space and bring even more of his pulsing body heat slapping against her, he adjusted the walking stick and sauntered away in a slow, languid walk.

Hell, even a limping Rafael de Cervantes managed to move with a swagger that made her heart race. Tearing her traitorous gaze away from his tight butt, she hurried up the floating staircase to her room. Gritting her teeth against the firestorm of emotions that threatened to batter her to pieces, she changed into her workout gear. The simple act of donning the familiar attire calmed her jangling nerves.

But she couldn't forget that, once again, Rafael had cut through the outer layer of her defences and almost struck bone, almost peeled back layers she didn't want uncovered.

She pushed the niggling sensation away and shoved her feet into comfortable trainers. After a minute's debate, she decided on the gym instead of her preferred outdoor regime. Even though the day was edging towards evening, the Spanish sun blazed far too hot for the gruelling exercise she needed to restore balance to her equilibrium.

She took the specially installed lift that divided her suite from Rafael's to the sub-basement level where the state-of-the-art gym was located. It was the only room in the whole house that didn't have an exhibitionist's view to the outside.

Rafael's house held no concrete walls, only thick glass interspersed with steel and chrome pillars. At first the feeling of exposure had preyed on her nerves, but now the beauty of the architecturally stunning design had won her over. Nevertheless, right this minute she was grateful for the enclosed space of the gym. Here she didn't need to compose herself, didn't need to hold back her punches as she slammed her gloved fist into the punching bag. Pain repeatedly shot up her arms, and gradually cleared her mind.

She was here to do her job. Which started and ended with helping Rafael heal properly and regain the utmost mobility. Once she achieved her aim and made peace with her part in his accident, she could walk away from the crazy, bone-deep, completely insane attraction she felt for the man who was in every shape and form the epitome of the man who'd fathered her.

The man whose playboy lifestyle had mattered to him on so deep a level he'd turned his back on his parental responsibilities until they'd been forced on him by the authorities. The same man who'd stood by and barely blinked while his friends had tried to put their hands on her.

Punch!

Her hand slipped. The bag continued its lethal trajectory towards her. Only her ingrained training made her sidestep the heavy-moving bag before it knocked her off her feet. Chest heaving, she tugged off the gloves and went to the climbing frame and chalked her hands.

Clamping her lids shut, she regulated her breathing and forced herself to focus.

Rafael would not derail her. She'd made a colossal mistake and vocalised her roiling disgust for his lifestyle at the most inappropriate moment. Whatever the papers had said, Raven knew deep down she was partly, if not wholly, responsible for putting Rafael in the dangerous frame of mind that had caused his accident. She also knew things could've turned out a million times worse than they had. This was her penance. She would help him get back on his feet. Then she would leave and get on with the rest of her life.

Reaching high, she grabbed the first handhold.

By the time she reached the top seven minutes later, her new course of action was clearly formulated.

'I've laid out the itinerary for the next three months. If you cooperate, I'm confident I can get you back to full health and one hundred per cent mobility with little or no after-effects,' she started crisply as she opened the door and entered Rafael's study. She approached his desk, only to stop when she noticed his attention was caught on the papers strewn on his glass-topped desk.

'I'm talking to you, Rafael.'

'I heard you,' he muttered, and held out his hand for the sheet without looking up. After a cursory glance, he started to shake his head. 'This isn't going to work.' He slapped it down and picked up his own papers.

Raven waited a beat. When he didn't look up, she fought a sharp retort. 'May I ask why not?'

'I have several events to host and meetings to attend between now and when the X1 season starts. Your itinerary requires that I stand still.'

She frowned. 'No, it doesn't.'

'It might as well. You've upped the regime from two to three times a day with sports massages thrown in there that would require me to be stationary. And was that *acupuncture*

I saw in there?' His derisive tone made her hackles rise higher. 'I'll be travelling a lot in the next three months. You're sorely mistaken if you think I intend to take time off to sit around being pricked and prodded.'

She watched the light glint off his damp hair. 'What do you mean, you'll be travelling a lot? You're supposed to be recuperating.'

Steely blue eyes met hers and instantly Raven was reminded of the unwavering determination that had seen him win several racing championships since he'd turned professional at nineteen.

'I have a multi-billion-dollar company to run, or have you forgotten?'

'No, I haven't. But wasn't…isn't Marco in charge for the time being? He told me he had everything in hand when we discussed my helping you—'

His eyes narrowed. 'What else did you discuss with my brother?'

Mouth dry, she withstood his stare. 'What do you mean?'

'I expected an element of confidentiality when I hired you…'

'What *exactly* are you accusing me of?'

'You will not discuss details of my health with anyone else but me, is that clear?'

'I didn't—'

'You're glowing.' His gaze raked her face down to her neck and back up again.

'Excuse me?'

'You look…flushed. If I weren't painfully aware of the unlikelihood of it, I'd have said you had just tumbled from a horizontal marathon in a lover's bed. Not quite tumbled to within an inch of your life, more like—'

'Can we get back to this, please?' She waved the sheet in his face then slammed it back in front of him.

He shrugged and sat back in his plush leather chair, the cool, calm businessman back in place. 'Marco has his own company to run…and a new family to attend to. Besides, he's taking a well-earned break, so I'm managing his company as well.'

A wave of shock nearly rendered her speechless. 'And you didn't think to speak to me before you decided all this?'

'I wasn't aware I needed your permission to live my life or run my business.' His voice, a stiletto-thin blade, skimmed close to her skin.

She took a breath and searched for calm, a state which she'd concluded long ago was near on impossible when in Rafael's presence. 'It's part of the contract we agreed. If you're going to take on any substantial amount of work I'll need to know so I can formulate your therapy accordingly. For goodness' sake, you can't go from zero to full-time work in the space of an afternoon. And I really don't know what you were thinking, telling your brother you'd take on this amount of work for the next goodness knows how long!'

Rafael's gaze dropped to her annoyed almost-pout and fought not to continue downward to the agitated heaving of her breasts. Peachy…the smooth skin of her throat glowed a faint golden-pink. He'd long been fascinated by how a woman with jet-black hair such as hers could have skin so pale it was almost translucent. He knew she took care to stay out of the sun and practised her exercises before daybreak.

An image of her, streamlined, sleek and poised upside down in a martial arts pose, slammed into his brain. The groin-hardening effect made him grip his pen harder. His gaze fell once more on her lips and it was all he could do not to round his desk, clasp her face in his hands and taste her. Or maybe coax her round to him, pull down that prim little skirt she'd donned and discover the delights underneath.

Dios, focus!

'Luckily, I don't answer to you, *mi dulzura*.' He certainly had no intention of enlightening her on what he'd been working steadily on for over a month; what he hadn't stopped thinking of since he'd woken from his coma.

Because finding a way to occupy his mind was the only sure way of keeping his many and varied demons at bay.

'…I hope to hell you're not thinking of adding racing to this insane schedule.' She paled a little as she said it and the usual kick of satisfaction surged.

'And what if I am?' He moderated his voice despite the cold fist of pain that lodged in his gut. Unless a miracle happened, his racing career was over. A part of him had accepted that. Deep inside his soul, however, it was another matter.

'I'm hoping it won't come to that. Because you know as well as I do, you're in no shape to get into a racing cockpit.'

He raised an interested brow. 'And how exactly do you intend to stop me?'

Her delectable lips parted but no words emerged, and her eyes took on a haunted look that made him grit his teeth. 'I can't, I suppose. But I think you'll agree you're not in the best shape.'

'Physically or mentally?'

'Only you can judge your mental state but, as your physiotherapist, I'd say you're not ready.'

He finally got his body under enough control to stand. He caught her sharp inhalation when he rounded the desk and perched on the edge next to where she stood. Hazel eyes, wide and spirited, glared at him.

Taking the sheet from her hand, he dropped it on the table, reached across—slowly, so she wouldn't bolt—and traced his forefinger along her jaw. 'Your eyes are so huge right now. You're almost shaking with worry for me. Yet you try and make me think you detest the very ground I walk on.'

Her hand rose to intercept his finger but, instead of pushing it away, she kept a hold of it, imploring eyes boring into his. 'I don't detest you, Rafael. If I did, I wouldn't be here. I'll admit we're…different but—' her shoulders rose and fell under the thin layer of her cotton top '—I'm willing to put aside our differences to help you recuperate properly. And racing before you're ready…come on, you know that's crazy.

Besides, think of your family, of Sasha. Do you think you're being fair to them, putting them through this?'

He froze. 'I've never responded well to emotional blackmail. And leave Sasha out of this. I'll tell you what, if you don't want me to race, you'll have to find other ways to keep me entertained.'

She dropped his hand as if it burned, just like he'd known she would. 'Why does everything always circle back to sex with you?'

'I didn't actually mean that sexually, but what the hell, let's go with it.'

'Stop doing that!'

'Doing what, *mi encantador*?'

'Pretending you're a male bimbo whore.'

'Are you saying I'm not?' He pretended astonishment, the fizz of getting under her skin headier than the most potent wine.

She nodded at the papers on his desk. 'You just reminded me that you run a multi-billion-dollar corporation. I don't care how great you claim to be in bed; you couldn't have made it without using some upstairs skills.'

He leaned back on the table when a twinge of pain shot through his left hip. 'How do you know?'

'You shouldn't sit like that. You're putting too much pressure on your hip.'

Annoyance replaced his buzz. He didn't deny that Raven had made much progress where his previous physios had failed. After all, it was the reason Team Espíritu had hired her as his personal therapist last year. She was the best around and got impressive results with her rigorous regime. But she'd always been able to brush him off as if he were a pesky fly.

He remained in his exact position, raising a daring brow when her gaze collided with his. His blood thickened when she took the dare and stepped closer.

Without warning, her hand shot out and grabbed his hip. Her thumb dug into his hipbone where the pain radiated from.

A few rotations of pressure-based massage and he wanted to moan with relief.

'Why do you fight me when you know I'm the best person to help you get better?' she breathed.

'Because my *mamá* told me I never took the easy way out. You will never get me to ask how high when you say jump.'

She paused for a second, then continued to massage his hip. 'You never talk about your mother,' she murmured.

Tension rippled through him. 'I never talk about anyone in my family. The prying all comes from you, *bonita*. You've made it a mission to upturn every single rock in my life.'

'And yet I don't feel in any way enlightened about your life.'

'Maybe because I'm an empty vessel.' He tried damn hard not to let the acid-like guilt bleed through his voice.

'No, you're not. You just like to pretend you are. Have you considered that by pretending to be something you're not, all you're doing is attracting attention to the very thing you wish to avoid?'

'That's deep. And I presume that thought challenges you endlessly?'

Her hand had moved dangerously close to his fly. If she looked down or moved her actions a few inches west, she'd realise that, despite their verbal sparring skimming the murkier waters of his personal life, he was no less excited by her touch.

In fact, he wasn't ashamed to admit that he found the return of his libido exhilarating. For a few weeks after he'd emerged from his coma it'd been touch and go. His doctors had cautioned him that he might not resume complete sexual function. Raven Blass's appearance in his hospital room five weeks ago had blown that misdiagnosis straight out of the water.

'No,' she responded. 'I know better than to issue challenges to you.'

'You're such a buzzkill,' he said, but he felt relieved that she'd decided to leave the matter of his mother alone.

He saw the faintest trace of a smile on her face before it disappeared. Her fingers moved away, rounded his hip and settled into his back. The movement brought her closer still, her chest mere inches from his. Firm, relief-bringing fingers dug into his muscle. Again he suppressed a moan of relief.

'I know. But think how smug I'd feel if you got back into racing before you were ready and reversed your progress. You'd never hear the end of it if you proved me right.'

The sultry movement of her mouth was a siren call he didn't try very hard to resist. His forefinger was gliding over her mouth before he could stop himself. Her fingers stilled before digging painfully into his back. The rush of her breath over his finger sent his pulse thundering.

'Or I could die. And this relentless song and dance could be over between us. Once and for all.'

CHAPTER FOUR

THE CALM DELIVERY of his words, spoken with barely a flicker of those lush jet eyelashes, froze her to the core.

'Is that what you want? To die?' Her words were no more than a whisper, coated with the shock that held her immobile.

'We all have to die some time.'

'But why, Rafael? Why do you wish to hurry the process when every rational human being fights to stay alive?'

'*Mi tesoro*, rational isn't exactly what most people think when they look at me.'

'That's not an answer.' She realised she was hanging on to him with a death claw but, for the life of her, Raven couldn't let go. She feared her legs would fail her if she did. And hell, she wasn't even sure *why* Rafael's explanation was so important to her. For all she knew, it was another statement meant to titillate and shock. But, looking closer, her blood grew colder. Something in his expression wasn't quite right. Or, rather, it was too right, as if he held his statement with some conviction. 'What is it, Rafael? Please tell me why you said that.'

'Quid pro quo, sweetheart. If I bare my soul, will you bear yours?'

'Would that give you something to live for?'

Raven could've sworn she heard the snap of his jaw as he went rigid in her arms. Grasping her by the elbows, he set her away from him and straightened to his impressive six foot three inches. His lids shuttered his expression and he returned to the seat behind his desk.

'The amateur head-shrinking session is over, *chiquita*. Modify your regime to accommodate travel and liaise with Diego if you'll need special equipment for where we'll be travelling. We leave on Wednesday.' He reeled off their intended destinations before picking up a glossy photo of the latest Cervantes sports car.

Knowing she wouldn't make any more headway with him, she turned to leave.

'Oh, and Raven?'

'Yes?'

'We'll be attending several high profile events, so make sure you pack something other than kick-boxing shorts, trainers and tank tops. As delectable as they are, they won't suit.'

Raven fought the need to smash her fist into the nearest priceless vase as she left Rafael's study. Not because he would see her, although the glass walls meant he would, but because *not* losing control was paramount if she wished to maintain her equilibrium.

She'd fought long and hard to channel her tumultuous emotions into useful energy when, at sixteen, she'd realised how very little her father cared for her. For far too long, she'd been so angry with the world for taking her mother away and replacing her with a useless, despicable parent, she'd let her temper get the better of her.

Rafael could do his worst. She would not let him needle her further.

Taking the sheet into the vast living room, she spent the next hour revising Rafael's regime and speaking to Diego about organising the equipment she would need. Again she felt unease and a healthy amount of frustrated anger at Rafael's decision to return to X1 racing. She didn't shy away from the blunt truth that she herself wanted to avoid the inevitable return.

Even though she'd been paid handsomely by Team Espíritu and treated well by the team, she'd always felt ill at ease in that world. She didn't have to dig deep to recognise the reason.

Sexual promiscuity had almost a given in the paddock. Hell, some even considered it a challenge to sleep with as many bodies as possible during one race season.

She'd received more than her fair share of unwanted male attention and, by the end of her first season, she'd known she was in danger of earning a *frigid* badge. Ironically, it was Sasha Fleming's catapult into the limelight as the team's lead racer that had lessened male interest in her. For the first time, female paddock professionals were seen as more than just the next notch on a bedpost.

'A two-line frown. I don't know whether to be pleased or disappointed.'

She looked up to find Rafael standing a few feet away, two drinks in his hand and his walking stick dangling from his arm. He held one out to her and she accepted and thanked him for the cold lime based cocktail she'd grown to love since coming to Leon.

'I was thinking about how it would be to return to the X1 circuit.'

'Shouldn't that warrant a three-line frown since I feature in there somewhere?'

'Wow, are you really that self-centred? A psychologist would have a field day with you, you know that?'

With a very confident, very careless shrug, he sank into the seat next to her. 'They'd have to fight off hordes of adoring fans first. Not to mention you.'

'Me? Why would I mind?'

'You're very possessive about me. If you had your way, I'd stay right here, doing your every bidding and following you around like a besotted puppy.'

Eternally thankful she'd swallowed her first sip, Raven stared open-mouthed. Several seconds passed before she could close her mouth. 'I'm stunned speechless.'

'Enough for me to sneak a kiss on you?'

Blood rushed to her head and much lower, between her legs, a throbbing started that should've shamed her. Instead, she exhaled and decided to give herself a break. A girl could only withstand so many shocks in one day.

'Earth to Raven. I don't know how to interpret a wish for a kiss when you go into a trance at the thought of one.'

'I…what?'

'I said kiss me.'

'No. I don't think that's a good idea.'

'It's a great idea. Look at me; I can barely walk. *You'd* be taking advantage of *me*.' His smile held a harsh edge that made the Rafael de Cervantes charm even more lethal.

'Whatever. It's not going to happen. Now, is there anything else I can help you with?'

His sigh was heavy and exaggerated. 'Bianca is almost ready to serve dinner. I figure we have twenty minutes to burn. Shall we be very English and talk about the weather before then?'

'The weather is fantastic. Now, let's talk about your return to X1. I don't wish to get personal…'

His low laugh made heat rush into her face.

'What I mean is…you'll have to be careful when it comes to being…um…'

'Just spit it out, Raven.'

'Fine. Sex. You can't have sex.'

He clutched his chest, then tapped carefully on his sculpted muscle. '*Dios,* I think my heart just stopped. You can't *say* things like that.'

'I mean it. The last thing you need to be doing is chasing after paddock bunnies. You could reverse any progress we've made in the last few weeks. Your pelvis needs time to heal properly. You do want to get better, don't you?'

'Yes, but at what cost? My libido could just shrivel away and die,' he returned without the barest hint of shame while she…she'd grown so hot she had to take a hasty sip of her drink.

'It won't.' She set her glass down on the table. 'Not unless you put too much stress on your body by taking on too much. Look, I'm not asking for much. I'm saying keep your…keep it in your pants for just a little bit longer, until you're more fully recovered.'

He opened his mouth but she raised her hand before he could speak. 'And please don't say you need sex to recover. Despite what you want everyone to think, you're not a sex addict. In fact you were one of the most disciplined men I knew when it came to dedication to racing. All I'm saying is apply that same discipline to your…needs, at least for the time being.'

Sensual masculine lips tilted at the corners. 'I think there was a compliment in there somewhere. Fine, I'll take your lecture under advisement.'

'You need to do more than that, Rafael. Your injuries are too serious to take recovery lightly.'

He shoved a hand through his hair. '*Dios*, did I call you a buzzkill earlier?'

'I believe you did.'

'Congratulations, you've just been upgraded to manhood-killer. Ah, here comes Bianca. Let's hope she's got something to revive me after that complete emasculation.'

'Yeah, my heart bleeds.'

Rafael tried to follow what the financial newsreader was saying on the large high definition screen on his plane. He failed.

Opposite him, ensconced in the club chair, Raven twirled a pen between her lips as she read and made notes on a piece of paper. On any other woman he'd have ridiculed such a blatant sexual ploy. But he knew the woman opposite him was unaware of what she was doing. And its totally groin-hardening effect on him.

Giving up on finding out how the Dow-Jones was doing, he turned off the TV and settled back in his seat.

She raised her head and looked at him with those stunning hazel eyes. 'What?'

'How did you get into physiotherapy?'

She regarded him for several seconds before she depressed the top of her pen. 'The random kindness of strangers.'

He raised an eyebrow.

She shrugged. 'A chance meeting with an ex-PE teacher in my local park when I was seventeen changed my life.'

'Was he hot?'

She rolled her eyes. '*She* realised I loved to exercise but I had no interest in being an athlete. We met and talked a few times. About a month later she took me to the local sports centre where professional athletes trained and introduced me to their head coach. By the end of the day I knew what I wanted to be.'

'And she did this all out of the goodness of her heart?'

'She realised I had…anger issues and worked to give me focus. She didn't have to, so yes, I guess she did.'

He held back the need to enlighten her that nothing in life came free; that every deed held a steep price. 'What were you angry about?' he asked instead.

'Life. My lot. What do most teenagers get angry about at that age?'

'I don't know. I was on the brink of realising my dream and getting ready to step into my very first X1 racing car when I seventeen. I was pretty happy with life at that age.' Blissfully ignorant of the consequences fate had in store for him.

'Of course you were. Well, some of us weren't that lucky.'

'Not all luck is good. Some comes from the devil himself, *bonita*. So, you achieved your light bulb moment, then what?'

Her gaze slid from his. He forced himself to remain quiet.

'Although my teacher helped direct my vision, I couldn't really do anything about it. Not at seventeen. I spent most of that year counting the days until my eighteenth birthday.'

'Why?'

He saw her reticence. Wondered why he was probing when he never intended to get as personal himself.

After a minute, she answered. 'Because turning eighteen meant I could make my own decisions, get myself away from…situations I didn't like.'

Rafael knew she wouldn't elaborate more than that. He respected that but it didn't stop him from speculating. And the directions his thoughts led him made his fist tighten on his armchair.

Raven's attitude towards sex and to him in particular had always puzzled him, not because of the women who had fallen over their feet to get to him since he'd shot up and grown broader shoulders at sixteen.

No, what had always intrigued him was the naked attraction he saw in her eyes, coupled with the fortress she put in place to ensure that attraction never got acted upon.

It didn't take a genius to know something had happened to make her that way. Her little morsel of information pointed to something in her childhood. He tensed, suddenly deciding to hell with respecting her boundaries.

'What happened to you? Were you abused?' he rasped, his fingernails digging into the armrest.

She froze. Darkened eyes shot to his before she glanced out of the porthole. When she returned her gaze to his, the haunted look had receded but not altogether disappeared. 'Have you ever heard of the term—the gift of the gab?'

He nodded.

'Well, my father could make the world's most famous orators look like amateurs. His silver tongue could charm an atom into splitting, so the term *abuse* never could stick, especially if the social worker who dealt with any allegation happened to be a woman. So technically, no, I wasn't abused.'

His teeth gritted so hard his jaw ached. Inhaling deeply, he forced himself to relax. 'What the hell did he do to you?'

She blinked, looked around as if realising where they were, or rather *who* she was with. Her features closed into neutral and she snapped the pen back out. Lowering her gaze, she snatched up her papers from her lap and tapped them into a neat sheaf. 'It doesn't matter. I'm no longer in that situation.'

Rafael almost laughed. Almost told her being out of the situation didn't mean she was out of its control. The past had tentacles that stretched to infinity. He was in the prime place to know.

His father...his mother. Not a day went by that the memories didn't burn behind his retinas—a permanent reminder only death would wipe away. They plagued him in his wakeful hours and followed him into his nightmares. He could never get away from what he'd done to them. No matter how far he went, how much he drank or how many women he let use his body.

'I've revised the regime.' Raven interrupted his thoughts, her tone crisp, businesslike. Her lightly glossed lips were set in a firm line and her whole demeanour shrieked step back in a way that made him want to reach across and *ruffle* her.

Grateful for something else to focus on rather than his dark past, he settled deeper into his seat and just watched her.

She flicked a glance at him and returned her gaze to the papers. 'I've ensured that we'll have a clear hour every morning for a thorough physio session. You already know that if you sit or stand for extended periods of time your body will seize up so I'll recommend some simple exercises for when you're in meetings, although the ideal situation would be for you not to *be* in meetings for extended periods.'

'I'll see about scheduling video conferences for some of the meetings.'

Her head snapped up, surprise reflected in her gaze. 'You will?'

'Don't sound so surprised. My boundless vanity draws the line at cutting my nose off to spite my face. You should know that by now.'

'If you can video conference, then why do you need to be there in the first place?'

'Like any other organisation, there's always a hotshot usurper waiting in the wings, ready to push you off into the great abyss at the slightest hint of weakness. I've grown attached to my pedestal.'

'You speak as if you're decrepit.'

'I haven't had sex in months. I *feel* decrepit. And with your decree of no sex, I feel as if my life has no purpose.'

'You mean you miss your fans and just want to resume basking in their admiration?'

'I'm a simple man, Raven. I love feeling wanted.'

Her lips compressed again, although he saw the shadows had faded from beneath her eyes and her colour had returned to her cheeks. He barely stopped himself from feeling inordinately pleased by the achievement.

She stared down again at the sheet in her hand. 'Why Monaco?'

'Why not? It's the glamour capital of motor racing. Most of the current and ex-drivers live there. It affords the best platform for the launch of the All-Star event.'

'Will there be any actual racing?' she asked.

He caught the wariness in her tone and suppressed another smile. Like it or not, Raven Blass was worried about him.

Just like Marco. Just like Sasha... Just like his father. He had no right to that level of concern from them. From anyone.

The tiny fizz of pleasure disappeared.

'There won't be any actual racing until we get to Monza in two weeks' time.' His brisk tone made her eyes widen. Rafael didn't bother to hide his annoyance. 'Racing is my life, Raven. I haven't decided whether or not I'll ever get behind another steering wheel but that decision will be mine to make and mine alone. So stop the mental hand-wringing and concentrate on making me fit again, *sì*?'

The large, luxurious private jet banked left and Raven felt her heart lurch with it. Below them, the dazzling vista of the Côte d'Azure glittered in the late winter sunshine. With little over a month before the racing season started, the drivers would be in various stages of pre-season tests in Barcelona.

Which was where Rafael would've been had he not had his accident.

At nearly thirty-one, he'd been in his prime as a racing driver and had commanded respect and admiration all over the world. He still did if the million plus followers he commanded on social media and adoring fans from the racing paddock were anything to go by. But Raven hadn't considered how he must be feeling to be out of the racing circuit for the coming year. And what it would do to him if he could never race again.

'I'm sorry. I didn't mean to make this any harder for you than it already is,' she murmured.

She braced herself for his usual innuendo-laden comeback.

'*Gracias*,' was all he came out with instead. 'I appreciate that.'

Before she could respond, a stewardess emerged from behind a curtain to announce they would be landing in minutes.

'Time for the crazy circus to begin. You ready?' He raised a brow at her.

'Sure. After living with you for five weeks, Rafael, I think I'm ready for anything.'

His deep laugh tugged at a place inside her she'd carefully hidden but he seemed to lay bare with very little effort.

'Let's hope you don't end up eating those words, *querida*.'

'I probably will, but…promise me one thing?'

He stilled and his eyes gleamed dangerously at her from across the marble-topped table between them. Finally he nodded.

'Promise me you'll let me know if it all gets too much. No glib or gloss. I can't do my job properly if you don't tell me what's going on.'

His eyes narrowed. 'This job, it's that important to you?'

'Yes, it is. I…I'm here to make amends. I can't ever take back what I said to you, and you don't remember if what I said played a part in your accident. Your recovery is important to me, yes.'

'Hasn't anyone told you being in a hurry to fall on your sword is an invitation to a shameless opportunist like me?'

'Rafael—'

He made a dismissive gesture. 'You won't need me to report my well-being to you, *querida*. You'll be with me twenty-four seven.'

The plane, lending perfect punctuation to his words, chose that moment to touch down. Rafael was up and heading towards the doors before the jet was fully stationary.

Jumping up, she hurried after him.

And realised—once a thousand flashlights exploded in her face on exit—that he hadn't been joking when he'd referred to the circus.

Monaco in late winter was just as glorious as it was during the summer race weekend but with an added bonus of considerably fewer people. But for the paparazzi dogging their every move, Raven could've convinced herself she was on holiday.

After a series of introductions and short but numerous meetings, they were finally driven higher and higher into the mountains above Monte Carlo. Glancing out at the spectacular view spread beneath them, her senses came alive at the beauty around her. It was different to the rugged gorgeousness of Rafael's estate in León, but breathtaking nonetheless.

'Don't you usually stay at the Hôtel de France?' She referred to the exquisite five-star hotel where all his meetings had taken place with the upper echelons of his X1 Premier Management team.

'I prefer to stay there during the race season. But not this time.'

She wondered at the cryptic remark until they arrived at their destination. Wrought iron gates swung wide to reveal a jaw-droppingly stunning art deco villa. The design wasn't unique to the French Riviera but several marked add-ons— large windows and a hint of steel and chrome here and there— made it stand out from the usual.

'Who lives here?' she asked.

'For the next few days, you and me and the usual number of complementary staff. It used to belong to an Austrian countess. I'm toying with the idea of buying it, making this my permanent base.'

She faced him in surprise. 'You're considering leaving León?'

He shrugged, seeming carefree, but his expression was shuttered. 'I haven't really lived full time in León for a very long time. It won't be a big deal.'

'Have you discussed it with Marco and Sasha? Won't they mind?'

'They'd be relieved not to have an invalid cluttering up the place, I expect.'

She suspected his brother and wife thought nothing of the sort but chose not to express that opinion. 'But…it's your home. Won't you miss it?'

'It's only bricks and mortar, *bonita*.'

Realising he meant it, she frowned. '*Is* there a place you actually call home?'

Raven was unprepared for the darkness that swept over his features. In a blink of an eye it was gone, his face restored to its rugged, breathtaking handsomeness that set so many female hearts aflutter whenever the spectacular Rafael de Cervantes made an appearance.

'Rafael?' she probed when he remained silent.

'A long time ago, I did. But, like everything else in my life, I trashed it completely and utterly. Now—' he pushed the door of the limo open, stepped out and held out a hand for her '—come in and tell me what you think. I read somewhere that a woman's opinion is priceless when choosing a house, especially a woman you're not sleeping with. Personally, I disagree with that assertion but I've been known to be wrong once or twice.'

She managed to hold her tongue until the trio of staff who greeted them at the door had taken up their luggage. The min-

ute they were alone, she faced Rafael in the large open style
living room, which had an exquisitely moulded ceiling that
extended over two floors. Once again—and she was beginning to notice a pattern—the room consisted mostly of windows, although this villa had a few solid walls.

'What did you mean when you said you've trashed everything in your life?' she asked.

He flung his walking stick into the nearest chair and made
his way slowly towards her. Stopping a mere foot away, he
glanced down at her.

'I was hoping you'd forgotten that.'

'I haven't, and I don't really think you meant me to.'

His smile was fleeting, poignant, and barely touched his
eyes. 'I guess my probing on the plane makes you feel you're
entitled to a certain…reciprocity?'

'No, I don't. I shared a little of my past with you because I
wanted to. You don't have to feel obliged to return the favour
but I'd like to know all the same.'

'Tell me what you think of the villa first.'

Her gaze took in the various OTT abstract art and cutting
edge sculptures and high-spec lighting and shrugged. Every
item in the room shrieked opulence a little too loudly. 'I like
it but I don't love it. I think it's trying too hard to be something it's not. I don't think it suits you.'

He glanced around at the plush leather chairs and carefully placed art and sculptures, the high-tech gadgets and
priceless rugs.

'Hmm, you could be right. Although that single armchair
looks perfect for…de-stressing.'

'Answer my question, Rafael. Why don't you have a home
any more?'

His smile dimmed slowly until only raw, untrammelled
pain reflected in his eyes. He held his breath for a long, inter-
minable moment, then he slowly exhaled. 'Because, *querida*,
everything that meant a damn to me went up in a ball of
flames eight years ago.'

CHAPTER FIVE

THE GLITTERING BALLROOM of the Hôtel de France had been re-designed to look like a car showroom, albeit a very expensive car showroom, complete with elaborately elegant priceless chandeliers.

A vintage Bentley MkVI Donington Special from Rafael's own car collection gleamed beneath a spotlight in the centre of the room.

Raven stood to one side as guests continued to stream in from the Automobile Club de Monaco where the X1 All-Star event had kicked off with an opening by the resident head of the Monégasque royal family.

Glancing at the door, she caught sight of Rafael as he chatted to the head of one of the largest car manufacturers in the world. Dressed in a black tuxedo with the customary studded shirt and bow tie, it was the most formal she'd seen him. The sheer stomach-clenching magnetism he exuded made her clutch her champagne flute harder to stem the fierce reaction that threatened to rock her off her feet.

As she watched he laughed in response to a joke. Looking at him, it was hard to believe he was the same man who, for a minuscule moment in time, had bared a part of his soul to her at the villa three days ago. The moment had been fleeting—as most of those moments were with Rafael. Hell, he hadn't even bothered to elaborate after that one cryptic statement about the ball of flames. But his pain had been unmistakable, visceral in a way that had cut through her defences.

Far from recoiling from the man he'd revealed, she'd wanted to draw closer, ease his pain.

I'm going loopy.

He glanced over suddenly and held up three fingers. Her

fingers flew up her face to touch her forehead before she could stop herself. Feeling a wave of heat creep up at his knowing smile, she flung a vaguely rude sign his way and turned her back on him.

He found her minutes later. 'Are you avoiding me?'

'Nope. You seem to be in your element. How's your hip?'

'Not well enough to attempt a paso doble but I'm holding my own.'

'You never told me what all of this is in aid of.'

'Have you never been to an All-Star event?' he asked.

She shook her head. 'I don't tend to involve myself in out of season activities. I've heard of it, but only in vague terms.'

'So what *do* you do when the season ends?' He latched onto the revelation.

Raven bit the inside of her lip, then decided she had nothing to lose by revealing just a little bit more about her personal life. 'I work with injured soldiers, mostly from Afghanistan and Iraq.'

His eyes narrowed slightly, a solemn look descending over his face. 'This must seem so very pointless and horribly ostentatious to you in comparison.'

'Since I don't know exactly what *this* is, I'm prepared to reserve judgement.'

'*This* is nothing but a huge elaborate scheme to get rich people to preen and back-slap while reaching into their pockets to fund a few charities.'

'Good heavens, in that case I condemn you all to Hades,' she said around the smile she couldn't seem to stop.

'Some of us would feel at home there,' he murmured. The bleakness in his voice made her glance up at him but his features gave nothing away.

Deciding to let it go, she glanced around the glittering ballroom. 'It must be nice to click your fingers and have everything fall into place for you like this.'

'Not quite…everything.' His gaze dropped to her lips before returning to capture hers.

Her pulse kicked hard. She fought to pull her gaze away from his but it only went as far as his mouth. 'Well...consider yourself fortunate, gluttony being a sin and all that.' She attempted another smile. When Rafael's own mouth curved into a smile, her heart did a hugely silly dance then proceeded to bash itself against her ribcage.

He beckoned a waiter, took Raven's champagne and exchanged it for a fresher-looking glass. He stopped her with a restraining hand on her arm when she went to sip it.

'Take it easy. It may look like champagne but it's not.'

She eyed the drink warily. 'What is it?'

'It's called Delirium. Don't worry, it's not as sinister or as sleazy as it sounds. Sip it slowly, tell me what you think.'

She did and nearly choked on the tart, potent taste. Almost immediately, the tartness disappeared to leave her tongue tingling with a thousand sensations that made her eyes widen. 'Oh my goodness, it's incredible. What's in it?'

'Edible gold dust and the tiniest drop of adrenaline.'

'You're kidding!'

'About the adrenaline, *si*, but not the gold dust. Although, in my opinion, it's wasted in the drink. I can think of much better uses for it.' Again his words held a note quite different from his usual innuendo-laden tone.

The ground didn't quite shift but Raven felt a distinct rumble and decided to proceed with caution. 'You were about to tell me about the All-Star event.'

'It's an event I hold every year to get all the racing drivers across various racing formulas together before the season starts. Here we can be just friends, instead of championship competitors, while raising money. It's also an opportunity for retired motor racers to still feel part of the sport for as long as they want to.'

'How many events are there in total?'

'Six races in six countries.' He waved to a grey-haired man who stood with a towering brunette with the hugest diamond ring Raven had ever seen adorning her finger. When the couple beckoned them over, Rafael sighed and took her elbow.

Raven's irritation at having to share Rafael was absurd considering he was the host. But, short of being rude, she had no choice but to let herself be led to the couple.

'Rafael!' the brunette's husky voice gushed a second before she threw herself into Rafael's arms. Dropping Raven's arm, he deftly caught the woman before she could unbalance him and laughed off her throaty murmurs of apology.

They conversed in fluent French as Raven stood to the side.

'Let me introduce you—Sergey Ivanov and his wife, Chantilly. Sergey owns the Black Rock team.'

'And I own his heart,' Chantilly gushed. But even while she planted an open-mouthed kiss on her husband, her eyes were gobbling up Rafael.

Raven tried not to retch as she murmured what she hoped were appropriate conversational responses. After ten unbearable minutes, she was about to make her excuses and escape to the ladies' room when she saw Chantilly reach into her bag. With her husband deep in conversation with Rafael, neither man noticed as she withdrew an expensive lipstick and pulled closer to Rafael.

Raven barely held back her horrified gasp as she saw what Chantilly was doing.

'Did she write her number on your walking stick?' she asked the moment the couple walked away.

He lifted the stick and peered at it. 'Hmm, I believe she did. Interesting…'

Irrational anger bubbled up through her. 'Excuse me.' She barely spat out the words before marching off to the ladies' room. She forced calming breaths into her lungs, calling on every control-restoring technique she knew to help her regain her equanimity.

But when she couldn't even summon up the will to make conversation on the ride back to the villa, she knew she'd failed.

At the door, she bit out a terse goodnight, nearly tripping over the hem of the black sequined gown she'd hastily shopped for in Monaco that morning. She was unused to such elaborate, expensive outfits, as was her credit card, but as she went up to her room, the slide of the seductive material over her heated skin was unmistakable.

Or was it Rafael's gaze on her bare back that caused sensations to skitter all over her body?

She didn't care. All she cared about was getting away from the man who, in more ways than she was willing to admit, was cut from the same cloth as her father.

'I can feel the volcanic waves rising off your body,' Rafael drawled as they finished the last of his exercises next to the large, sparkling infinity pool the next morning. 'I hope your outrage didn't keep you up all night?' His blatant amusement set her teeth on edge.

She stepped back from the bench she'd set up outside, and especially from the man whose potent sweat-mingled scent made her head swim. Taking a deep breath, she fought the feeling.

'Are you seriously so without a moral compass that you don't see anything wrong with a married woman slipping you her phone number right in front of her husband?' she asked, her insides twisting with raw acid.

'Your claws are showing again, *piqueña*.'

'I don't have claws, certainly not where you're concerned. I'm merely disgusted.'

From his position lying flat on the bench, he rose smoothly into a sitting position. 'But you could be so much more if you'd just say the word.'

Flinging a towel onto a nearby chair, she whirled to face him. She tried to tell herself her heart pumped with outrage but underlying that was another emotion she flatly refused to examine. 'For the thousandth time, I'm here to make sure you heal properly, not be your sex pet!'

He rubbed his chin thoughtfully in the morning light, a smile teasing his lips. 'Sex pet. *Dios*, the sound of that makes my pulse race, especially seeing as you're just the right size and shape for a pet.' He shut his eyes, one long arm lifting to trace the air. 'I can just see my hand gliding over that glorious raven hair, sliding down the side of your elegant neck. Of course, you'd gasp in outrage. That's when I'd slide my finger over your full, sexily kissable mouth. And if you were to nip it with just the right amount of pressure—'

She gulped. 'Dammit, Rafael—'

'Shh! Don't spoil my fantasy. The sweat trickling down your chest now just makes me want to undo those no-nonsense buttons and follow it with my tongue.'

Raven glanced down and, sure enough, a bead of sweat was making its way between her breasts. Heat slammed inside her, setting off trails of fire everywhere it touched as if seeking an outlet. This wasn't good. Fires like this eventually escaped, sought the oxygen they needed to burn. Oxygen that looked temptingly, deliciously like the half-naked man in front of her. She could never let it escape, never let it burn because she had a feeling this particular conflagration would be nearly impossible to put out.

She'd more than learned her lesson. She'd been burned badly. Never again.

'Rafael, unless you want to spend the rest of the morning sitting here burning to a crisp, I suggest you zip it and help me get you indoors.'

With a put-upon sigh, he opened his eyes. His low laugh bounced on the morning air before ricocheting through parts of her she didn't want to think about or even acknowledge. 'All right, sex pet. I'll keep my lustful thoughts to myself. But if at any time you want a demonstration, don't hesitate to ask.'

'I won't.'

His smile grew even more wicked, more dangerous than she felt able to cope with. 'You won't hesitate?'

'I won't ask,' she stated firmly, dragging her eyes from the sweat-sheened torso that gleamed mere feet from her.

For several seconds he held her gaze, challenging her with the unabashed heat in his eyes, as if daring her to refuse him.

Raven stood before him, bracing herself and silently praying he would give up or move. Or something!

Finally, he dropped his gaze and reached for his walking stick. With the other hand he pulled her closer and braced his arm over her waist.

'So, you're concerned about my moral compass?' he asked in a droll voice.

'Don't let it go to your head. Sergey seems like a decent man. Are you not concerned about how he'll feel when he finds out you're intending to call his wife for a tryst?'

His laugh was deep and long.

'A *tryst*? That sounds so…decadent.'

She leaned forward, hoping her hair would hide the renewed flush of her cheeks. 'Don't mock me, Rafael. I can still ensure you never walk again.'

'Spoilsport.' He gave a dramatic sigh. 'Before you unleash your many weapons on me, I have no intention of calling or *trysting* with Chantilly. It's a little dance we do. She slips notes and numbers in my pocket. Sergey and I pretend we don't notice.'

She stopped dead. 'You mean he knows?'

His expression was world-weary and full of cynicism. 'He's old enough to be her grandfather, *bonita*. He knows she's not with him for his virility and good looks. Sorry if that bursts your happy little moral bubble.'

The rest of the slow journey to his study was conducted in silence. Raven concentrated hard on ignoring the relief fizzing through her.

She succeeded only because with every step his body bumped against her, his warm, tensile body making her so hyper-aware of her own increased heartbeat. His scent washed over her. She swallowed, the knowledge that it was wrong to

feel this way about her patient doing nothing to stop the arrows of lust shooting into her abdomen.

By the time the reached the long sofa that faced the large
floor-to-ceiling window in his study, Raven wasn't sure which
one of them was breathing heavier.

Rafael slumped into the seat and rested his head on the
back of the sofa. Lines of strain bracketed his mouth. Her
heart lurched for him.

'Are you okay?'

'Nothing a new hip won't sort out.'

'I can get you some painkillers to ease the pain?'

His jaw clenched. 'No.' From day one, Rafael had refused
pain relief, opting for physical therapy to heal his body.

'You have three meetings tomorrow before we leave. I think
you should cancel them. Your pelvis isn't as fluid as it could
be…and please, no *double entendre*. I mean it. I…I advise
you to rethink and let Marco to take over.'

Every last trace of mirth left his face and eyes. His jaw
clenched tight and he speared her with suddenly cold eyes.
'I'm not cancelling anything. And my brother and Sasha will
be staying exactly where they are.'

The sudden descent into iciness made her shiver. 'Is it true
you tried to break them up?' she blurted before she could
stop herself.

His gaze grew colder. 'You're straying into none-of-your-
business territory, *chiquita*.'

'I thought we were past that? After all, you seem to feel
free to stray into my life whenever you feel like it. I'm merely
returning the gesture.'

He locked gazes with her for endless seconds. Then he
shrugged. 'Okay. Yes, I tried to break them up.'

'Why?'

'Because it seemed like a great idea at the time. Obviously,
it didn't work.'

'It wasn't because you loved her?'

Why was she doing this? Asking questions she was fairly certain she didn't want answers to.

'Love? Yes, love. I did it out of love. Twisted, isn't it? If you had a lover too, I'd probably try to separate you from him.'

She frowned. 'Why would you do that?'

He laughed, a half bitter, half amused sound that chilled her nerves. 'Haven't you noticed yet, Raven? I like chaos. I like to cause as much damage as possible wherever I go. Haven't you learned this of me by now? I'm trouble with a capital T.'

She tried for a shrug. 'Some women go for that sort of thing, I hear.'

'But not you, *si*? You remind me of one of the girls I went to Sunday school with.'

Shock held her rigid. 'You went to Sunday school?'

He nodded, the unholy gleam in his eyes lightening the blue depths. 'Religiously. My mother was very keen I got into heaven.'

She laughed at the very idea. She knew no one more devilish in temperament and looks than Rafael de Cervantes.

His grin widened. 'The idea of me in heaven is laughable?'

'In the extreme. You'd corrupt all the other angels within seconds.'

'And they'd love every minute of it.'

'I bet.'

Laughter faded, slowly replaced by an incisive look that should've been her first warning. 'You hide your pain underneath a veneer of blistering efficiency.'

'While you hide yours under the cover of irreverent, sometimes callous charm.'

He reached out a hand for her, and Raven found herself moving towards him, his aura drawing her in like a moth to a flame.

When he patted the seat next to him, she sat down. 'What a pair we are,' he muttered.

She shrugged. 'I guess we must do what we need to do to protect ourselves.'

'From the outside world, yes. But we know what the other is. So there's no need for pretence with us.'

His smile slowly faded to leave a serious, probing look that made her whole body tingle. Slowly he reached out and clasped his hand around her nape. Effortlessly, he drew her forward. She wet her lips before she could stop herself. His groan echoed the deep, dark one inside her.

'What do you want from me, Rafael?' she muttered, her tongue feeling thick in her mouth.

'Nothing you aren't prepared to give me.'

'Don't pretend you won't take more than your fair share.'

His head dropped an inch closer. 'What can I say, I'm a greedy, greedy bastard.'

'What the hell am I doing?'

'Letting go. Living a little. Just because you were hurt before doesn't mean you have to stop living. Pleasure, in the right circumstances, with the right person, can be the most exhilarating experience in life.'

'But you're the exact opposite of the right person, I can't even see how you can say that with a straight face.'

'*Sí*, I'm the devil. You would never be satisfied with a Normal Norman. You'd be bored rigid in three seconds flat.'

He kissed her before she could countermand his assertion. As first kisses with the devil went, it was soul-stealing and Raven was eternally grateful she was sitting down.

Because Rafael devoured her as if she were his favourite fruit. No millimetre of her mouth went unkissed. When he was done ravaging her lips, he delved between to boldly slide his tongue into her mouth. The toe-curling sensation made her fingers bite hard into his bicep. She needed something solid to hold on to. Unfortunately, Rafael—unyielding, warm— no, hot—heady, sexily irreverent Rafael—was the last anchor she should've been seeking. And yet she couldn't pull away, couldn't summon even the smallest protest as she let him devour her lips.

'*Dios*, you taste even better than I imagined.' He only gave her a chance to snatch a quick breath before he pounced again.

One hand caught her waist, his fingers digging into her flesh to hold her still as he angled his head to go even deeper. Her moan felt ripped from her very soul.

He started to lean her back on the sofa, then he stilled suddenly. Between their lips, the sound of his pained hiss was smothered but Raven recognised it all the same.

Reality came crashing down on her, her dulled brain clamouring to make sense of what she'd let happen. Slowly, painfully, he straightened until he was upright again.

Raven wanted to reach across and help but she was too weak with thwarted lust, too stunned from the realisation that she was still as hopelessly attracted to Rafael as she'd been the first time she was introduced to him as his physiotherapist.

'Shut up,' he ground out hoarsely.

'I didn't say anything.'

'No, but I can hear you thinking. Loudly, noisily. I've never had to compete with a woman mentally working out the Fibonacci Sequence while I was trying to get her naked. And you know what? It's not sexy. It's quite deafeningly unsexy, actually.'

She slid agitated hands into her hair. 'You're being offensive.'

'And you're ruining this electric buzz with all that overthinking. I would much prefer it if you'd shut up and strip for me.'

Her mouth dropped open. Actually dropped opened in a gob-smacked, un-pretty mess that she couldn't stop. 'I really don't know how you managed to snag girlfriend after girlfriend with that insufferable attitude.'

'It's the same way I've snagged you, *piqueña*. It's why you're leaning towards me right now, unable to look away from me as you imagine what it would be like to have me inside you, buried deep, riding us both to ecstasy.'

She jumped back, and her breath whooshed out of her lungs.

'And now you're going to blush.'

As if on cue, heat rose and engulfed her face. 'Crap.'

He laughed, actually laughed at her. Raven had never felt so humiliated. Or so...so hot as he grasped the bottom of his T-shirt.

'Here, I'll go first, shall I? One item of clothing each until we're in flagrante. Deal?'

She wanted to walk out, wanted to tell him what to do with his tight, muscle-packed body and sheer masculine perfection. She wanted to have enough willpower to turn her back on all the things his glinting blue eyes promised. This wasn't her. She wasn't the type of girl who fell casually into sex as if she were choosing the latest hair accessory from a supermarket shelf. So why couldn't she move? Why did every single instinct she had scream at her to move closer to Rafael, to touch, experience the seductive pleasure he promised, instead of running as far as her marathon-trained legs could carry her?

A long-suffering sigh filled with extreme impatience shattered her thoughts. Her gaze sharpened in time to see his hands drop.

'Fine, I get the message. You're about to fall on your puritanical sword, deny yourself pleasure just so you can crawl back into your cold bed and pat yourself on the back. Aren't you?'

'I wasn't...' But she *had* been thinking that, hadn't she? 'Maybe,' she admitted. 'Besides being totally unprofessional, I can't very well advocate no sex for you and then be the one who...who makes you suffer a setback.'

He shook his head, a genuine baffled look on his face. Reaching over carefully, he took her face in his hand. '*Sí*, I get it. More restraint. More suffering for both of us. You're twenty-four so I'm sure you're not a virgin, but are you sure you weren't an inquisitor in a past life?'

Since there was no way she wanted to confirm her virginity, she focused on the second part of his statement. 'I know you don't believe it, but I'm only looking out for you.'

'By torturing me to death? Or is there something else at play here?'

'By making sure you heal as quickly and efficiently as possible.'

He dropped his hand. 'Where's the fun in that?'

Raven kicked herself for immediately missing his touch. 'God, you're unbearable! And what do you mean, "there's something else at play"?'

'Ah. Finally, some fire. Do you have any idea how incredibly hot you look when you're riled?'

Desire dragged low through her abdomen at his heated, husky words. 'You're getting off topic. And that compliment is so clichéd, even a three-year-old wouldn't believe you.'

'Cliché doesn't make it any less true. But yes, I'll get to the point. You like to hide behind a prickly exterior, holding the world at bay because you're afraid.'

'I'm not prickly and I'm most definitely not afraid.'

'You over-think every single move you make.'

'It's called being sensible,' she retorted.

'You're living half a life. Every bone in your body wants to be on the bed with me, yet you're afraid to let yourself just be.'

'Just because I don't put myself about like you doesn't mean I'm not living.'

His lips twisted. 'I wouldn't be this frustrated if I'd been putting it about like you suggest. And don't forget, I was in a coma for several weeks. Have mercy on my poor, withered c—'

'If you finish that sentence I'm walking out of here right now!'

'The C-word offends you?'

'No, your blatant lies do. There's nothing withered or poor about you.'

'*Gracias*…I think.' He tilted his head. 'Now you're about to deflate my ego thoroughly, aren't you?'

'Your ego is Teflon-coated and self-inflating. It doesn't need any help from me.'

He let out an impatient sigh. '*Dios*, Raven, are you going to talk me into another coma or are we going to have a conversation about what's really going on here?'

She shoved her hands onto her hips. 'There's nothing going on. You want to get on with making up for lost time and I happen to be the willing body you've chosen.'

His hands dropped. 'Would it make you feel better if I said yes? It would help you get through the morning-after handwringing if you feel righteous anger for being used?'

She gasped. 'I didn't say that.'

He moved further away. 'You didn't have to. *Santa Maria!* We haven't been to bed yet, and already you're seeking excuses to ease your guilt. How long are you going to let your father win?'

Her gasp was a hoarse sound that scraped her throat raw. 'That's low, Rafael.'

'No lower than the way you treat yourself. Have a little pride. You're a beautiful woman, with a powerfully sexual nature you choose to suppress underneath a staid exterior. But, underneath all that togetherness, your true nature is dying to leap out. To be set free.'

'And you're the man to do it? How convenient for you.'

His face remained sober. 'For both of us. I'm willing to rise to the task. I'm very good at it, too. Trust me.'

'Trust you. The self-proclaimed damaged man who is trouble with a capital T?'

'Think of all the experience I'd bring to the task. You couldn't find a better candidate to bed you if you tried.'

She shut her eyes. Despair wove through her because, deep down, she knew he was right. Her body hadn't reacted to anyone this strongly since…heavens, since never! But that was no excuse to throw well-served caution to the wind. 'No. It's not going to happen.'

He was silent for so long her nerves were stretched to the max by the time he spoke. 'What did your father do to you?'

'What makes you think this is about my father, not about an ex?'

'The first cut is the deepest, no?'

She looked around the too posh living room, at the priceless pieces of furniture that most people would give their eye teeth to own.

She didn't belong here. Her presence in Rafael's life was temporary, transient. Baring her soul to a man who didn't possess one was out of the question. Regardless of what she'd told herself she'd seen in his eyes last night, they were nothing more than ships passing in the night.

In a few weeks she would be gone and Rafael would return, healed, to his regular life. 'Yes, the first cut is the deepest, and yes, my father hurt me. Badly. But my scars don't dictate who I am. I am free to choose who to be with, who I have sex with. And I don't want to have it with you.'

CHAPTER SIX

RAFAEL TOOK HER rejection with more grace than she'd given him credit for, especially considering his reaction to her rejection the day of his last X1 race.

Later that day, after shrugging off her terse pronouncement, they strolled into an exclusive rooftop restaurant overlooking Casino Square. Although a whisper of tension flowed between them, Rafael was as charming as ever.

'So, what are your plans after you're done fixing me?' he asked after the first course had been served.

A strange twinge attacked her insides. Pushing it away, she speared her fork through a plump shrimp. 'I'll either get the agency that allocated me the X1 contract to find me another driver to work with, or I'll find one on my own. I could also try the army facility to see if they need a full-time physiotherapist. I have a few possibilities and I figure after you, every other patient would be a breeze to work with.'

Blue eyes gleamed at her across the table. '*Gracias, bonita.*'

She eyed him suspiciously. 'What are you thanking me for, exactly?'

'I've obviously become a yardstick by which you measure your future clients. I consider it an honour.'

She rolled her eyes and found herself grinning when he laughed. Shaking her head, she took another mouthful of her delicious shrimp pasta. 'I knew you were trouble from day one.'

His laughter slowly disappeared. '*Sí,*' he murmured. 'What did you call me? A useless waste of space who was taking up valuable oxygen more worthy human beings were entitled to?'

Her fork clattered onto her plate. 'You remember? Every single word?' she whispered.

His smile was sharp and deadly, the easy camaraderie from moments before completely annihilated as the tension that had lurked solidified into a palpable wall. 'What can I say, *querida*, you cut me to the bone.'

'Was that…was that why…?' She couldn't quite frame the words.

'Why I attempted to turn myself and my car into a Rubik's Cube the next day? Ask me again when I remember anything from the accident.'

She shut her eyes for a brief second, a shudder of guilt and regret raking over her. 'Please believe me, I don't usually lay into anyone quite like that. That day…' She paused, unwilling to bare her whole life to him. But then she realised she owed him an explanation of some sort. 'It was a *very* difficult day.'

'In what way was it difficult?' he probed immediately.

'My mother called me the evening before the race, just before the team dinner where you—'

'When I *dared* to ask you out?' he asked.

Her gaze dropped as she felt a prickle behind her eyelids. 'Her relationship with my father has always been…tempestuous.' That was putting it mildly but she couldn't elaborate any further. 'When she called, she was very upset… She has…moments like that. She wanted to see him. Nothing I said would calm her down. So I called my father—the father I haven't spoken to in years.'

Rafael's brow hitched up a fraction but he didn't interrupt her.

'He wouldn't lift a finger to help. He was too busy, he said. But I could hear the sound of a party in the background. I swallowed my pride and begged him. He refused. When I called my mother to try to explain, her mood…escalated. I was trying to get her some help when you found me and asked me to dinner.'

'So you attempted to slice the skin off my bones because of bad timing?' His words were light but the chilling ice in his eyes told her he hadn't forgiven her. 'What about the dozen times before then?'

She blew out a breath. 'I've just told you the effect my father has on me and on my mother. Do you honestly think I'd ever want to associate myself personally with a man who reminds me of every despicable trait I witnessed growing up?'

'Watch it, *piqueña*,' he murmured softly. 'You didn't think I was despicable when we kissed this morning.'

A wave of heat crept up her face. 'That was a mistake.'

'Also, you may have claws, but I have teeth. Sharp ones and I'm heartless enough to use them.'

She didn't doubt it. For him to have succeeded in securing several championships over the past decade, he had to have a ruthless streak somewhere beneath the indolent playboy demeanour. Certainly, she'd seen his dedication and absolute focus during the racing season.

'I'm sorry, Rafael. But I didn't really understand why you wanted to go out with me. There were dozens more willing girls who would've jumped at the chance to be with you.' If she were being honest, she still didn't understand why he continued to try and goad her into bed. The only thing she could think of was…no, it didn't make sense. 'I'm hardly your Mount Everest.'

'You're not. Been there, done that.'

Her eyes fell to the jagged scar on his forearm. It might have been ugly at one time but now it just blended into the frustratingly captivating masterpiece that was Rafael de Cervantes. 'You've been to a lot of places, done a lot of things.'

'You've been listening to gossip.'

'Before I came to work for you last year, the agency sent me a dossier on you. Is it true that scar on your arm was from a bull goring you?' She pounced on the change of subject all the more because here was her chance to learn more about Rafael.

'*Sí*, and I thanked the bull for the unique, exhilarating experience.'

She suppressed a shudder. 'What is it exactly that you crave? The thrill of the chase? The rush of adrenaline?'

'It's conquering the fear of the unknown.'

His words were so stark, so raw, her breath caught in her lungs.

'What do you mean?'

'I don't like mysteries, *querida*. Take you, for instance. From the moment we met, you held me at arm's length. No woman's ever done that, not effectively anyway, and definitely not for as long as you have, and this isn't arrogance talking. It's just never happened. You were an enigma to me. I wanted to smash aside all your barriers. Instead you built them up higher. You intrigued me to the point I couldn't see anything beyond having you.'

She had never been able to explain the phenomenon of ice and heat that filled her whenever she was in Rafael's presence. She couldn't explain it now the sensation had increased a thousandfold. 'I don't know that I want to be described that way. You make me sound like I'd become your worst nightmare.'

'You had. I wanted to confront it. Turn it into a dream I liked.'

'God, Rafael. Do you hear how twisted that sounds?'

His laugh was nowhere near a normal sound. 'I'm sorry I don't fit your ideal of the right guy.'

'I'm not looking for a right guy. I'm not looking for a guy, period. I just want to do my job.'

'It's not just that though, is it?' He beckoned the waiter and ordered an espresso for himself and a white coffee for her. 'You're here because you want to do penance.'

'And you've been fighting me and trying to drive me away ever since I arrived.'

'If I'd wanted to be rid of you, I would've succeeded.'

'So you want me to stay?'

He shrugged. 'One of the many discoveries I made while stuck in a hospital bed was this—I like being alone. But I don't like being alone in León.'

She sensed the revelation behind the statement. 'Another of your nightmare scenarios?'

He didn't deny it. He just shrugged. 'Tell me more about your mother.'

'Tell me about yours.'

'She's dead.'

In what felt like mere seconds between one and the other, another forceful blow punched through her middle at the stark announcement. 'How—?'

The word stuck in her throat when he shook his head and picked up his newly delivered espresso. 'You're one of a handful of people outside of my family circle I've disclosed that to. It's not a state secret, but it's not a subject I wish to discuss either, so don't ask any more questions. And yes, I know it's hypocritical of me to demand everything from you and give nothing in return, but we both know I do what I like. Your mother?'

She moistened her lips and tried to arrange her thoughts. 'For what it's worth, I'm sorry about your mother.' She sucked in a deep breath and slowly exhaled. All of a sudden, it wasn't so bad to reveal just that little bit more. Because Rafael had shared *something*.

'Mine is alive but barely conscious half the time. You know why? Because she's completely and utterly hung up on a man who can go for months, sometimes years without giving her a single thought. And yet he only has to crook his finger to have her falling into his lap. At least you know your mother loved you. Do you know how devastating it is to find out your own mother would gladly give you away for free if she could have her one true obsession?'

'Is that why you lived with your father?'

'No. Aside from her obsession with my father, she was also diagnosed with severe bipolar disorder when I was seven. For a few years she took the prescribed medication, but as I got older, she would miss a few days here and there. Then days would turn into weeks, then she would stop altogether.'

His frown was thunderous. 'Did you not have any relatives that could step in?'

'None that wanted to add the burden of a pre-teen on top of the responsibilities they already had. And, frankly, I felt I was better off on my own. By ten I could take care of myself. Unfortunately, my mother couldn't. One day she had an episode in a shop. The police were called. Social services got involved. Eventually they tracked down my father and threatened to report him to the authorities when he wouldn't step up.' Bitterness made her throat raw. 'They *made* him take me. And you know what? Every day until I turned eighteen I wished they hadn't.'

'Did he hurt you?' he rasped.

'Not at first. When I initially arrived at his doorstep, he didn't even care enough to resent me for my sudden appearance in his life.' She laughed. 'And he was rich enough that I had my every material need catered for.'

'But?' he demanded.

Ice drenched her skin as the dark memory surged, its oily tentacles reaching for her.

A tinkle of laughter from a table nearby slammed her back into the present. Chilled and exposed, she rubbed her hands over her arms. 'I don't want to relive it, Rafael.'

His jaw tightened. 'It was that bad?'

'Worse.'

His fingers curled around the small, fragile cup in his white knuckled grip before he carefully set it back in its saucer. '*Dios mio.* When did it—?'

'Rafael…please…'

He sucked in a sharp breath, his gaze still fiercely probing as he sat back in his seat. After several seconds, he nodded and pushed back his chair.

Silently he held out his hand. Before the start of the evening she'd have hesitated. But after what she'd shared with him, after seeing his reaction to how she'd grown up, a tiny voice urged her to trust him a little.

She placed her hand in his and let him help her up. 'I should be helping you, not the other way round.'

'Let's forget we're patient and specialist, just for a few hours, *si*?' The low, rough demand made her breath snag in her throat.

When she glanced up at him, he watched her with hooded eyes that held no hint of their usual teasing. Swallowing, she nodded.

They walked in the unseasonably warm evening along the dock that held some of the world's most extravagant and elegant yachts. Or they tried to walk. Rafael was stopped several times along the way by wealthy Monégasques and visiting celebrities. Again and again, Raven tried not to be enthralled by the sight of his breathtaking smile and easy charm. Even when a paparazzo's camera lens flashed nearby he didn't seem to care. But then she caught the clenched fist around his walking stick. She wasn't surprised when he signalled his driver a few moments later.

When she glanced at him, he merely shrugged. 'We have an early flight in the morning. Don't want you to accuse me of depriving you of your beauty sleep.'

She waited until they were in the car, leaving the bright lights of Monte Carlo behind. 'You strive to put a brave face on it all, don't you?'

'A brave face?'

'I saw how the paparazzi affected you just now. And even though you stopped to speak to people, you didn't really want to be there.'

He tilted his head. 'Your powers of deduction are astounding.'

'Don't dismiss me like that, Rafael,' she murmured. 'You've changed.'

Although his expression didn't alter, she saw his shoulders stiffen beneath his expensive cotton shirt.

'Of course I have, *querida*. My hip no longer works and I carry a walking stick.'

'I don't mean physically. You turned away from the cameras at the airport too. You answer their questions but you no longer bask in the limelight. Oh, the playboy is very much a part of your DNA, probably always will be, but…something's changed.'

'*Sí*, I've turned into a decrepit recluse who's been banned from having a bed partner.'

She ignored the quip. 'I bet you're not going to buy that villa, are you?'

The corner of his mouth lifted in a mirthless smile. 'You assume correctly,' he replied, his gaze steady on her face. 'You were right, it's a little too…stalker-ish for me. I think the owner studied what I liked and tried to replicate it without taking the location into consideration. It's slightly creepy, actually. Besides that, Monaco is great for a visit but not somewhere I prefer to live. But then neither is León.'

'Why?'

'Too many bad memories,' he stated.

Somewhere inside, Raven reeled at the easy access he seemed to be giving her. A strong need to know the man made her probe further. 'Your father?'

He paled a little beneath his tan, but he nodded after several seconds. '*Sí*. Amongst other things. He moved to Barcelona after…for a while, but he's back in León now. Seeing him there reminds me of what a disappointment I've been to my family.'

She gasped. 'A disappointment? How…why? You've won eight world championships and ten Constructors' Championships for Team Espíritu. How in the world can that be termed a failure?'

'Those are just trophies, *querida*.'

'Trophies coveted by the some of the world's most disciplined athletes.'

'Why, Raven, I almost think you're trying to make me feel better about myself.'

'You've achieved a lot in your life. Self-deprecation is one thing. Dismissing your achievements out of hand is an insult to the team that has always supported you. Now, if you're talking about your private life…'

'What if I said I was?'

'I've met your father, albeit very briefly. I saw no trace of disappointment when he tried to talk to you. And, as far as I can see, Marco and Sasha worship the ground you walk on, despite you saying you tried to break them up.'

He lifted a hand, his knuckles brushing her cheeks before she knew what he was doing. 'That may have been an over-exaggeration. Was I annoyed when I woke up from my coma to find my best friend had fallen for my brother? *Sí*. But I'm a big boy, I'll learn to adapt. As for worshipping the ground I walk on—appearances can be deceptive. I've done things—things I'm not proud of; things that haunt me in the middle of the night, or in the middle of the day when I smile and shake hands with people who think I'm their golden boy. They don't know what I've done.'

'What have you done, Rafael? Tell me.'

He shook his head, a bleak expression stamped on his face that sent a bolt of apprehension through her.

'Did you notice the condition my father is in?'

She frowned. 'You mean his wheelchair? Of course I did.'

'What if I told you I put him in that wheelchair?'

Rafael looked into her face, trying to read her reaction while at the same time trying to decipher exactly why he was spilling his guts when he never, ever talked about what he'd done eight years ago.

The car passed under a streetlamp and illuminated for a moment her pale, shocked face. 'H…How did you put him in the wheelchair?'

A deep tremor went through him, signalling the rise of the blistering pain that seemed to live just below his skin. 'Take a wild guess.'

'A car accident?'

He nodded, his peculiar fascination with her escalating

when she made a move as if to touch him. At the last moment, she dropped her hand.

'Where did it happen?'

'On the racing track in León. Eight years ago. I walked away unscathed. My father has never walked since.'

This time when she lifted her hand he caught it before she could lower it and twined his around her slender fingers. The surge of pain diminished a little when her fingers tightened.

'I'm so sorry,' she murmured.

His smile felt broken. 'You don't want to know whose fault it was?'

'I'm not going to force you to relive the emotional pain, Rafael. Like you said, I'm not that type of therapist. But one thing I do know is that, contrary to what you might think, your family…your father, from what I saw, is more forgiving than you realise.'

His father might be forgiving of Rafael's role in making him wheelchair-bound, but the other, darker reason would be more unthinkable to forgive. Hell, he hadn't even dreamed of seeking forgiveness. He deserved every baptism of hellfire he lived through every morning when he opened his eyes. 'That's the problem with family. Forgiveness may be readily provided but the crime is never forgotten.'

'Unfortunately, I wouldn't know. Dysfunctional doesn't even apply to me because I had two people who were connected to me by genetics but who were never family.'

The car was drawing up to the villa when he lifted their entwined fingers to his lips. A soft gasp escaped her when he kissed her knuckles. 'Then count yourself lucky.'

Two hours later, Rafael stretched and held in a grimace of pain when he tried to rise from his chair. He eyed the walking stick leaning against his desk and with an impatient hand he reached for it.

Pelvis, fractured in three places…broken leg…multiple cracked ribs…severe brain swelling…lucky to be alive.

The doctor's recital of his injuries when he'd woken from his coma should've shocked him. It hadn't. He'd known for as long as he could remember that he had the luck of the devil. He'd exploited that trait mercilessly when he was younger, and then honed it into becoming the best racing driver around when he was older. No matter how many hairy situations he put himself in, he seemed to come out, if not completely whole, then alive.

Recalling his conversation earlier with Raven, he paused in the hallway. *I'm not going to force you to relive the emotional pain.*

Little did she know that he relived it every waking moment and most nights in his vivid nightmares. He might have cheated death countless times, but his penance was to relive the devastation he'd brought to his family over and over again.

His phone pinged and before he glanced at it he knew who it was.

His father...

He deleted the message, unread. *Dios*, even if they wanted to grant it, who was he to accept their forgiveness—?

The sound in the library next to his study attracted his attention.

Raven's lusciously heady perfume drew him to the room before he could stop himself. 'It's almost midnight. What are you doing up?'

'I was looking for something to read. The only reading material I have upstairs is boring clinical stuff, and my tablet is charging, so...'

He glanced down at the papers in his hand. He had no idea what he was doing, no idea where this project would take him but... He debated for a few seconds and made up his mind. Closing the distance between them, he stopped in front of her.

'Here.' He tossed a bound sheaf of papers at her, which she managed to catch before they spilled everywhere.

'What is this?'

One corner of his mouth lifted in a dangerous little half-smile that always made her forget to breathe. 'Two articles for *X1 Magazine*…and something new I'm working on.'

'Something new? I didn't know you wrote outside of your monthly *CEO's Snippets*.'

He shrugged. 'Three months ago—while I was trussed up like a turkey in a hospital bed—I was approached by a couple of publishing houses to write my memoirs.' He laughed. 'I guess they figured a has-been like me would jump at the chance to lay it all out there before the moths set in.'

She glanced down at the thick inch of paper between her fingers. 'And you agreed?' she asked as she started to leaf through the pages.

'I said I'd think about it. I had time on my hands after all.'

She read, then read some more. On the third page, she looked up. 'This isn't your memoirs, unless you were a girl who grew up in Valencia in the late forties.'

'*Bonita*, you're getting ahead of yourself. *Por favor*, contain yourself and let me finish.'

She stared up at him. Rafael gave himself a mental slap against the need to keep staring into those mesmerising eyes. 'I started writing and realised fiction suited me much better than non-fiction. I told them no to the memoir.'

'And?' she prompted when he lapsed into silence. 'You told them about this?'

'No. I've told no one about this. Except you.'

Surprise registered in her eyes before she glanced back down at the papers. 'Are you sure you want me to read it?'

'It's pure fiction. No deep, dark secrets in there for you to hold over my head.'

Wide hazel eyes, alluring and daring at the same time, rose to lock on his. 'Are you sure?'

'If you're thinking of flipping through the pages for X-rated material, I'm afraid you'll be disappointed.'

Her blush was a slow wave of heat that he wanted to trace with his fingers. For a woman so fierce in her dedication to her craft and so determined to succeed despite her past, she blushed with an innocence that made him painfully erect. Despite his intense discomfort, he wanted to continue to bait her so she blushed for him again.

Unable to help himself, he lowered his gaze to the shallow rise and fall of her chest.

When she cleared her throat delicately, he forced his gaze upwards. 'So what are you looking for—an honest critique? I'm sure I can read whatever it is you've written and give an honest view, if that's what you want?'

He smiled at her prim tone and forced himself to step back before he gave in to the need to kiss her. Their kiss had only opened up a craving to experience the heady sensation again. But, aside from the insane physical attraction, he was feeling a peculiar pull to Raven Blass he wasn't completely comfortable with.

Keeping his distance from her was impossible considering her role in his life, but he wasn't a hormonal teenager any longer and he refused to make any move towards her that reminded her of her sleazebag father.

If anything was going to happen between them, Raven had to make the first move…or indicate in clear and precise terms that she wanted him to.

'*Gracias*, it is. I await your thoughts on my efforts with bated breath.'

CHAPTER SEVEN

THEIR EARLY MORNING departure to Italy, accompanied by Rafael's executive assistant and a trio of ex-racers, meant that Raven had no chance to discuss Rafael's manuscript with him at any point. A fact for which she was more than thankful.

The story of the young girl was both uplifting and heartbreaking. Rafael's language was lyrical and poignant, clever and funny in a way that had made her feel each and every word, every expression.

Reading his work, she'd felt just that little bit closer to him. Raven wasn't sure if she was more frightened or insane for feeling like that. It was that floundering feeling that had made her take a seat as far away from Rafael as possible.

But even though she made the right noises with the guy next to her—whose name she couldn't immediately remember—she couldn't get Rafael's story out of her head.

Nor could she deny his talent. She'd learned very early on, after reading an unauthorised biography on him before accepting the job as his physiotherapist last year, that Rafael had a magic touch in most endeavours he undertook in his life. That he'd dedicated his life to racing had only meant that the sport had benefited endlessly.

His regular contribution to X1 Premier Management's monthly magazine already garnered a subscription said to be in the millions. If he chose to dedicate his life to writing fiction his fan base would become insane.

And you would probably be his adoring number one fan.

Without warning, Rafael's gaze swung towards her. The sizzling *knowledge* in that look sent sharp arrows of need racing to her pelvis. Her pulse hammered at her throat, her skin tingling with the chemistry of what she felt for Rafael.

'...you ever been to Monza?' The German ex-racer seated next to her—Axel Jung, she remembered his name now—stared at her with blatant interest.

She shook her head but couldn't tear her gaze away from the formidable, intensely charismatic man whose gaze held her prisoner from across the aisle. 'Um, no, I was Rafael's physio last year but Monza wasn't on the race calendar so I missed it.'

'You're in for a treat. It's one of the best racetracks in the world.'

She swallowed and tried to dismiss the intensity of Rafael's stare. 'Yes, so I've been told. The old track was even more spectacular, from the pictures I've seen of it.'

Axel's chuckle helped her break eye contact with Rafael but not before she saw his gaze swing to Axel and back to her.

'If you liked danger with your spectacular view, that was the track to race on,' Axel said.

She made an effort to turn her attention to him and almost regretted it when she glimpsed his deepening interest. 'I suspect that's why it's a thrill for most drivers?' she ventured.

He nodded eagerly. 'I don't know a driver who hasn't dreamt of driving at Monza, either on the old or the new track. The tickets for Monza's All-Star event sold out within minutes of going online.'

Raven had a feeling it had something to do with Rafael's presence, this being one of his first public appearances since his accident. 'That's great for the charity, then?'

'Yes, it is. I'd be honoured if you'll permit me to show you around Monza.' He drew closer. His smile widened, lending his blond-haired, blue-eyed features a boyish charm.

'I'm there to work, I'm afraid. And you'll be driving I expect?'

Axel, a two-time world champion twenty-five years ago, nodded. 'Rafael and I have a friendly rivalry that seems to draw the crowd.' He laughed. The fondness in his voice was clear. 'He's a special one, that one. The playboy thing is just a front. Don't let it fool you. Deep down, there beats the heart of a genius forged in steel. A fierce leader who would fight to the death for what he believes in.'

Having her instincts confirmed that there was more to Rafael than met the eye made her slow to respond. A quick glance at him showed him in deep conversation with a member of his All-Star team. 'I...'

'He single-handedly brought the board members to his way of thinking two years ago when they tried to put off new safety measures for drivers,' Axel said.

'*Safety?*' Raven asked in surprise. 'But I thought...'

'You think because we love speed and hurtle around race-tracks at two hundred and fifty miles per hour we think less of safety? Ask any driver. The opposite is true. We manage to take the risks we do *because* of people like Rafael and the work they do to ensure drivers' safety.'

Feeling wave after wave of astonishment roll through her, she glanced again at Rafael, only to find his attention fixed on her, his blue eyes narrowed to speculative slits. He glanced away again and resumed his conversation.

The floundering feeling escalated. 'Excuse me,' she murmured to Axel when the stewardess entered to take drinks orders. Standing, she made her way towards the large bedroom and the en suite bathroom.

After splashing water on her wrists, she re-knotted her hair in a secure bun and left the bathroom, only to stumble to a halt.

Rafael stood, back braced solidly against the bedroom door. His presence in the enclosed space, larger than life and equally as imposing, dried her mouth.

Heart hammering, she stayed where she was, away from the danger radiating from him. 'I...is there something you need?'

He folded his arms and angled his head. '*Need?* No.' He remained in front of the door.

Raven licked her lips and immediately regretted it. 'Can we return to the cabin, then?'

'Not just yet,' he rasped, then just stood there, watching her with a predatory gleam that made her nape tighten.

Silence stretched for several minutes as he stayed put, seemingly in no hurry to go anywhere, or speak, for that matter.

She searched her mind for what he could possibly want, and felt her heart lurch with disappointment. 'You're not in here because you want to make sure your playboy status is intact, are you?'

'What was Axel saying to you?'

She waved him away. 'Nothing for you to worry about.' He remained in place, that infuriatingly well-defined eyebrow arched. 'Okay, if you must know, he told me that beneath all that lady-killer persona, you're really a Boy Scout. Oh, and he also offered to show me Monza.'

He glanced away but she saw his jaw tighten. 'I hope you told him no?'

'Maybe.' She started to move towards him in the hope that he'd get the hint and move. He remained, rock-still and immovable.

'Stay away from him,' he said, his voice low but no less forcefully lethal.

Her pulse spiked higher. 'Sexually, socially or just for the hell of it?'

With a swiftness she wouldn't have attributed to him considering his injuries, he reached forward, grabbed her arms, whirled her round and reversed their position. Her lungs expended their oxygen supply as she found herself trapped between the hard, polished wood and Rafael's equally hard, warm body.

One hand gripped her nape while the other settled firmly on her waist. Heat ratcheted several notches. Inhaling only made matters worse because Rafael's scent, potent and delicious, attacked her senses with rabid fervour.

'He was looking at you as if he wanted to serve you up on his sauerkraut.'

'And what, you're jealous?'

'Not if you tell me you're not thinking of falling into the clutches of an ex-racer more than twice your age.'

'Axel's only in his mid-forties. And I'm touched you're looking out for me.'

Blue eyes deepened by his blue long-sleeved shirt and navy jeans narrowed even further. 'And he also likes to think he's slick with the ladies.'

'Scared of the competition?'

'Scared I'm going to have to toss his ass out of the plane without a parachute if you don't tell me you'll stay away from him.' Without warning, one thigh wedged between hers. The heat emanating from him made her whole body feel as if it were on fire. Second by inexorable second, he pressed closer against her. His hard chest brushed against hers, stinging sensitive nipples to life. Raven fought a moan and tried to decide whether defiance or acquiescence was her best path.

'Is this what it means to be caught between a rock and a hard place?' she asked, unable to resist baiting him just a little.

His laugh sent a skitter of pleasure through her. 'You're making jokes, *querida*?'

'You're laughing, aren't you?'

'*Sí*,' he agreed. The hand on her waist moved a fraction higher, dug deeper in an almost possessive hold on her ribcage. 'But I'm still waiting for an answer.'

A small voice cautioned her against throwing more fuel onto the flames.

'I spoke to him for fifteen minutes, but I barely remember what he looks like,' she whispered against seriously tempting lips a hair's breadth from hers. 'But why do you care? Really?'

'You were the first person I told about my father outside my family. You haven't condemned me...yet. In my own small way, I'm trying to return the favour by saving you from a potentially unfortunate situation.'

'By trapping me here and threatening to toss a man out of the plane?'

'It's my Latin blood, *pequeña*. It takes me from zero to

growly in less than five seconds.' He closed the gap between their lips and their bodies.

A fervid moan rose from her chest as sensation crashed over her head. Her knees turned liquid and she would've lost her balance had she not been trapped so powerfully against a towering pile of formidable maleness. As they were, with his thigh wedged so firmly between hers, she felt the heat from his leg caress her intimately. Friction, urgent and undeniable, made her pulse race faster. Even more when his tongue delved between her lips. Like the first time they'd kissed, Rafael seemed bent on devouring her. Although she'd been kissed, she'd never been kissed quite like this, with a dedication so intense she felt as if she were being consumed.

When he finally let her up for air, it was to allow her a single breath before he pounced again. Her hands, which had miraculously risen to glide over his shoulders, finally found the wherewithal to push him away.

'Rafael…'

'No, not yet.' His lips swooped, but she managed to turn her head just in time. He settled for nibbling the corner of her mouth, a caress so erotic she throbbed low down with the sensation.

'We need to stop. Everyone out there will think we're in here…doing…having…'

'*Sex*…saying it doesn't make you a dirty, dirty girl, Raven.' His thigh moved, inserting itself even more firmly between hers. Again friction caused sensation to explode in her belly.

She flushed. 'I know that.'

'Then say it,' he commanded, pulling back to stare into her eyes.

Defiance surged back on a wave of desperation. 'Sex. Sex, sex, *sex*—'

He kissed her silent, and damn, but did she enjoy it. When he finally raised his head she was thoroughly and dangerously breathless. 'It's okay, you've made your point. Although I can't say that'll dissuade our fellow travellers from thinking we've joined the Mile High Club.'

A growl of frustration rumbled out before she could stop it. 'Why couldn't you leave this alone until we landed?'

'The same reason you're still caressing my shoulders even though you're protesting my presence here with you.'

She dropped her hands and swore she could feel her skin tingling in protest.

'I...this is crazy,' she muttered under her breath.

'*Si*, but we can't help ourselves where the other is concerned. Are you ready to go back?'

A shaky nod was all she could manage before he withdrew his thigh from between hers. The loss of his support and heat made her want to cry out in protest. She stopped herself in time and checked to see if her buttons had come undone.

With a sigh of relief, she stepped away from the door.

Rafael was very close behind her when they exited the bedroom. 'You didn't tell me what you thought of the story.'

She looked over her shoulder. 'I thought it was incredible.'

He stilled, an arrested look on his face. 'You enjoyed it?'

'Very much. The girl has an amazing spirit. I can't wait to find out more about her journey.' She glanced at him. 'That is if you intend to continue with it?'

A look passed over his face, gone too quickly before she could decipher it. 'With such a rousing endorsement, how could I not? As it happens, I have a few more chapters.'

Pleasure fizzed through her. 'Will you let me read it?'

He smiled. 'You mean you want to read more, despite the lack of X-rated material?'

She huffed in irritation. 'Why did I think a lovely conversation with you would last more than five seconds?'

His low laugh curled around her senses. She was so lost in it, she didn't realise he had led her away from Axel until he pushed her into the seat next to his.

The Monza circuit, perched on the outskirts of the small namesake town, was situated north of Milan. The view from above as Rafael's helicopter pilot flew over the racetrack was spectacular.

A riot of colour from the different sponsor logos and team colours defied the late winter greyness. She felt the palpable excitement from small teams readying the race cars before they landed.

Casting a glance at Rafael, she couldn't immediately see his reaction due to wraparound shades and noise-cancelling headphones, but his shoulders, the same ones she'd caressed barely ninety minutes ago, tensed the closer they got to the landing pad. If they'd been alone she would've placed her hand on his—an incredible development considering this time last week the thought of touching him set her teeth on edge—but she didn't want to attract undue attention. The paddock would supply enough gossip to fuel this event and the rest of the X1 season as it was.

Cameras flashed as soon as the helicopter touched down and demanding questions were lobbed towards them the moment the doors opened.

Are you returning to racing, Rafael?

Will you be officially announcing your retirement today or is this the start of your comeback?

Is it true you're suffering from post-traumatic stress disorder?

His jaw was set in concrete even though his lips were curved in a smile as he stepped out of the helicopter and waved a lazy hand at the cameras.

A luxurious four-by-four was parked a few feet away. He held the door open for Raven and slid in after her.

'I don't know how you can stand them without wanting to punch someone in the face,' Raven found herself murmuring as she watched a particularly ambitious paparazzo hop onto the back of a scooter and race after them.

'They help raise the profile of the sport. They're a necessary evil.'

'Even when they're intrusive to the point of personal violation?'

'When I engage them, I engage them on my terms. It's a skill I learned early.'

With a surprise, she realised that everything the press knew about Rafael was something he'd chosen to share with them, not some sleazy gossip they'd dug up. To the common spectator, Rafael lived his life in the public eye but in the past few weeks she'd discovered he had secrets…secrets he shared with no one, not even his family.

'You give them just enough to keep them interested and to keep them from prying deeper.'

Stunning blue eyes returned her stare with amusement and a hint of respect. 'That is just so, my clever Raven.'

'So, what pierces that armour, Rafael?'

His smile dimmed. 'I could tell you but I'd have to sleep with you.'

Raven's heart lurched and then sped up when, for a single second, she found herself contemplating if that was a barter worth considering. *Sleeping with Rafael…*

A tiny electric shock that zapped her system left her speechless.

'Since you're not slapping my face in outrage, dare I hope the suggestion isn't as repulsive as you found it previously?'

'I…I never thought you were repulsive,' she replied. 'You may have been a little too intense with your interest, that's all.'

'You dislike my intensity?'

She opened her mouth to say *yes,* and found herself pausing. 'I wasn't used to it. And I didn't like that you had everyone falling over themselves for you and yet you weren't satisfied.'

'But now we've spent some time together you think you *understand* me?' His tone held a hint of derision that chilled her a little.

'I don't claim to understand you but I think I know you a little better, yes.'

The warmth slowly left his eyes to be replaced by a look so neutral he seemed like a total stranger.

Their vehicle pulled up in front of the expansive, stunning motor home that had been set up to accommodate the Italian All-Star event. Several dignitaries from the sports world waited to greet Rafael. He reached for the door handle and turned to her before alighting.

'Don't let that knowledge go to your head, *querida*. I'd hate for you to be disappointed once you realise I won't hesitate to take advantage of that little chink in your armour. Underneath all this, there is only a core of nothingness that will stun you to your soul.'

He got out before she could respond. Before she drew another breath, he'd transformed into Rafael de Cervantes, world champion and charm aficionado. She watched women and *men* fall over themselves to be in his company. Basking in the adoration, he disappeared into the motor home without a backward glance.

Rafael waved away yet another offer of vintage champagne and cast his gaze around for Raven.

He'd been too harsh, he knew. Had he—finally—scared her away for good? The thought didn't please him as it should have.

But she'd strayed far too close, encroaching on a deep dark place he liked to keep to himself. He hadn't been joking when he'd warned her about the core of nothingness. How could he? What would be the point in revealing that grotesque, unthinkable secret?

She would hate you, and you don't want that.

His gut tightened but he pushed the thought away.

No one could hate him more than he hated himself. It was better that he ensured Raven harboured no illusions. Although she'd probably claim not to be, she was the type to see the good in everyone. If she didn't she wouldn't have asked for help from a deplorable father who had subjected her to *dios* knew what to save her mother. He suspected that, deep down, she'd hoped her father would reveal himself to be something other than he was.

Rafael wasn't and would never be a knight in shining armour. Not to her and not to any other woman. He took what he wanted and he didn't give a damn.

Above the heads of the two men he was talking to, he saw Chantilly enter the room on her husband's arm. She zeroed in on him with an openly predatory look, her heavily made-up eyes promising filthy decadence.

Rafael felt nothing. Or rather he felt…different. On further examining his reaction, he realised the sensation he was feeling wasn't the cheap thrill of playing games with Sergey's wife. It was self-loathing for having played it in the first place.

He looked away without acknowledging her look and cast his gaze around the room one more time. Realising he still searched for Raven—where the hell was she?—he made a sound of impatience under his breath.

'Is everything all right?' the chairman of the All-Star event asked him.

'The old racetrack has been carefully inspected as I requested?'

The white-haired man nodded. 'Of course. Every single inch of it. You still haven't told us whether you'll be participating.'

Tightness seized his chest. He forced himself to take a breath and smile. 'The event is only beginning, Adriano. I'll let you old folks have some fun first.'

'Less of the old, if you please.'

The laughter smoothed over his non-answer but the tightness didn't decrease. Nor did his temper when he looked up a third time and found Raven standing at the far end of the room with Axel.

She'd changed from jeans into yet another pair of trousers, made of a faintly shimmery material, and a black clingy top that threw her gym-fit body into relief when she moved.

The sound of a nearby engine revving provided the perfect excuse for Axel to lean in closer to whisper into her ear. Whatever the German was saying to her had her smiling and nodding. Obviously encouraged, her companion moved even closer, one hand brushing her shoulder as he spoke.

Rafael moved without recognising an intention to do so, a feat in itself considering his hip was growing stiffer from standing for too long. 'Raven, there you are.'

She turned to him. 'Did you want me?' she asked, then flushed slightly.

'Of course I want you,' he replied. 'Why else are you here, if not to come when I want you?'

A spurt of anger entered her eyes. 'What can I do for you?'

'I need your physio services. What else?'

She frowned. 'According to your itinerary, you're working until ten o'clock tonight. Which is why I scheduled a swim therapy for you afterwards and a proper physio session in the morning.'

His eyes stayed on hers. 'My schedule is fluid and right now I need you.'

'Ah, actually, I'm glad you're here, Rafael,' Axel said.

'Really? And why's that, Jung?'

The other man cleared his throat. 'I was hoping to convince you to let my team borrow Raven's services for a few hours. Our regular physiotherapist came down with a stomach bug and had to stay at the hotel.'

'Out of the question,' Rafael replied without a single glance in his direction.

'Rafael!'

'Need I remind you what your contract states?' he asked her.

'I don't need reminding, but surely—'

He shifted sideways deliberately in a move to get her attention. And succeeded immediately. 'What happened?' she demanded, her keen eyes trailing down his body, making a visual inspection.

'You were right. This whole thing has simply worn me out. I think I'll have an early night.' He turned towards the door. 'Are you coming?'

'I…yes, of course.' Concern was etched into her face. Rafael wanted to reassure her that his hip wasn't painful enough to warrant that level of worry.

But he didn't because he couldn't guarantee that she wouldn't wish to stay, return to Axel. The disconcerting feeling unsettled him further.

'I was away for just over an hour. Please tell me you didn't try and do anything foolish to your body in that time.'

'Where were you, exactly?'

'Excuse me?'

'Were you with Jung all that time?' he asked, an unfamiliar feeling in his chest.

'Are we seriously doing this again?'

'How else would he have got it into his mind to poach you?'

'He wasn't…isn't trying to poach me. He was telling the truth. His team's physio was sent back to his hotel because he fell ill. But they think it's just a twenty-four hour virus. I didn't see the harm in agreeing to give my professional opinion.'

'You should've spoken to me first.'

'In the mood you were in? You bit my head off because I got too close again. I won't be your personal punchbag for whenever you feel the need to strike out.'

He sucked in a weary breath and Raven forced herself to look at him properly for the first time. Not that it was a hardship.

It was clear he was in pain. His skin was slightly clammy and stress lines flared from his eyes. 'What the hell did you do to yourself?' she asked softly.

'You should've stuck around if you were concerned.'

She didn't get the opportunity to answer as they'd arrived at the helipad. The blades were already whirring when she took her seat beside Rafael for the short trip to their hotel in Milan.

As they exited the lift towards their exclusive penthouse suite, she turned to him. 'Lean on me.'

When he didn't argue or make a suggestive comment, she knew he was suffering. Raven was thankful she'd had the forethought to ring ahead to make sure the equipment she needed had been set up.

Back in their hotel, after Rafael stripped to his boxers, she started with a firm sports massage to relax his limbs before she went to work on the strained hip muscles.

By the time she was done, a fine sheen of sweat had broken over his face. Pouring a glass of water, she handed it to him.

He drank and handed the glass back to her.

'I don't like seeing you with other men. It drives me slightly nuts,' he said abruptly.

She stilled in the act of putting away a weighted leg brace. 'You can't have all the toys in the playground, Rafael.'

'I just want one toy. The one sitting on top of the tree that everyone says I can't have.'

'What you can't do is to keep shaking the tree in the hope that the toy will fall into your lap. That's cheating.'

'It's not cheating; it's taking the initiative. Anyway, you can't be with Axel.'

She stopped, head tilted to the side, before she tucked a strand of hair behind one ear. 'Okay, I'll play. Why can't I be with him?'

He gave a pained grimace. 'He has a ridiculous name, for a start. Think how ridiculous your future kids would find you. Raven and Axel Jung. Doesn't rhyme.'

'And I have to have a man whose name rhymes with mine, why?'

'Synergy in all things. Take you and me.'

'You and me?' she parroted.

'Sí. Rafa and Raven rolls right off the tongue. It was meant to be.'

She passed him a towel. 'I'd suspect you were on some sort

of high, but you didn't touch a drop of alcohol at the mixer and you've refused any pain medication.'

'I'm completely rational. And completely right.'

'It must be hunger making you delirious then.' She handed him the walking stick and walked beside him to the living room. 'Room service?'

With a sigh, he sank into the nearest wide velvet sofa, nodded and put his head back on the chair.

'What would you like?' she asked.

'You choose.'

'Would you like me to spoon-feed you when it arrives, too?'

His grin was a study in mind-melting hotness and unashamed sexual arrogance. 'You're not the first to offer, *querida*. But I may just make you the first to succeed in that task.'

Rolling her eyes, she ordered two steaks with a green salad for them. Then, on impulse, she ordered a Côte du Rhone.

The wine wouldn't exactly lay him flat but it might let him relax enough to get a good night's sleep, especially since he refused to take any medication.

After she'd placed the order, she set the phone down and approached the seating area.

Rafael patted the space beside him.

Very deliberately, and sensibly, she thought, she chose the seat furthest from him and ignored his low mocking laugh.

'So, care to tell me what happened today?'

He stilled, then his eyes grew hooded. 'First day back on the job. Everyone was clamouring for the boss.'

Raven got the feeling it was a little bit more than that but she wisely kept it to herself. 'What are the races in aid of this year?' she asked, changing the subject.

He tensed further, wrong-footing her assumption that this was a safe subject.

For the longest time, she thought he wouldn't answer. 'XPM started a foundation five years ago for the victims of road accidents and their families. But we soon realised that giving away money doesn't really help. Educating about safety was a better route to go. So we've extended the programme to testing road and vehicle safety, with special concentration on young drivers.'

'Was…was it because of what happened with your father?'

His eyes darkened. 'Surprisingly, no. It was because a boy racer wiped out a family of six because he wasn't aware of how powerful the machine underneath him really was. I knew exactly how powerful the car I drove was so my transgression didn't come from ignorance.'

'Where did it come from?'

'Arrogance. Pride. I owned the world and could do as I pleased, including ignoring signs of danger.' His face remained impassive, this slightly self-loathing playboy who wore his faults freely on his chest and dared the world to judge him. His phone rang just then. He checked the screen, tensed and pressed the off button. 'Speak of the devil and he appears,' he murmured. His voice was low and pensive with an unmistakable thread of pain.

Raven frowned. 'That was your father?'

'*Sí*,' he replied simply.

'And you didn't answer.'

The eyes he raised to her were dark and stormy. 'I didn't want to interrupt our stimulating conversation. You were saying…?'

She searched her memory banks and tried to pull together the threads of what they'd been talking about. 'You used the past tense when you said you owned the world? You no longer think that?'

'World domination is overrated. Mo' power mo' problems.' Although he smiled, the tortured pain remained.

'Is that why you won't forgive yourself? Because you think you should've known better.'

'My, my, is it Psychology 101?'

She pressed her lips together. 'It is, isn't it?'

'If I said yes, would you make it all better?'

'If you said yes you would feel better all on your own.' The doorbell rang and she looked towards the door. 'Think about that while I serve our feast.'

The emotions raging within him didn't disappear from his eyes as she went to the door to let the waiter in.

By unspoken agreement they stuck to safer subjects as they ate—once again, Rafael taking her refusal to feed him with equanimity.

When she refused a second glass of wine, he set the bottle down and twirled his glass, his gaze focused on the contents.

'So where is this island of yours that Marco and Sasha have gone to?'

'There are a string of islands near Great Exuma. We own one of them.'

'Wow, what does it feel like to own your own island?'

'Much like it feels to own a car, or a handbag, or a pen. They're all just possessions.'

'Possessions most people spend their lives dreaming about.'

'Are you one of those people? Do you dream of finding a man to take you from your everyday drudgery to a life filled with luxury?'

'First of all, I don't consider what I do drudgery. Secondly, while I think dreams are worth having, I set more store by the hard work that *propels* the achievement of that dream.'

'So I can't sway you with the promise of a private island of your very own?'

'Nah, I have a thing about private islands.'

His brow rose. 'A *thing*?'

She nodded. 'I saw a TV show once where a group of people crashed onto one and spent a hellishly long time trying to get off the damned rock.' Her mock shudder made him grin. 'A concrete jungle and the promise of a mocha latte every morning suits me just fine.'

He raised his glass. 'To concrete jungles and the euphoria of wall-to-wall coffee shops.'

'Indeed.' She clinked glasses with him. Then it dawned

on her how easy the atmosphere had become between them; how much more she wanted to stay where she was, getting to know this compelling man who spelled trouble for her. The thought forced her to push her chair back. 'I think I'll head to bed now. Goodnight, Rafael.'

If he noticed the sudden chill in her voice, he didn't react to it. 'Before you go, I have something for you,' he said, pointing to the elegant console table that stood outside the suite's study.

Seeing the neat stack of papers, Raven felt a leap of pleasure. Going to the table, she picked up the papers and, sure enough, it was the continuation of Ana's story.

'Did you write all of this last night?' she asked him.

He shrugged. 'The muse struck when I was awake. No big deal.' But she could tell it was. His gaze was hooded and his smile a little tight. It was almost...almost as if he was nervous about her reading it.

'Thanks for trusting me with this, Rafael.'

He looked startled for a moment, then he nodded. '*De nada. Buenas noches, bonita*,' he replied simply.

The distinct lack of *naughty* left her floundering for a moment. Then she forced herself to walk towards her suite.

'Raven?' His voice stopped her beside the wide, elegant double doors leading into the hallway. When she turned, his gaze had dropped to assess the contents of his wine glass.

'Yes?'

'Don't flirt with Jung.'

Her pulse raced. Later, when she was safely in her cool bed, she tried to convince herself it was the effects of the wine that made her say, 'Quid pro quo, my friend. If I'm not allowed to flirt, then no more numbers on your walking stick. Agreed?'

Blue eyes lifted, regarded her steadily, their brilliance and intensity as unnerving as they'd been the very first time she'd looked into them. After a full minute, he nodded. 'Agreed.'

CHAPTER EIGHT

SHE FOUND HIM in the penthouse pool the next morning. She stood, awestruck, as Rafael cleaved the water in rapid, powerful strokes, his sleek muscles moving in perfect symmetry. He turned his head just before he dived under and executed a turn and, for a split second, Raven became the focus of piercing blue eyes.

One length, two lengths…three.

After completing the fourth, he stopped at the far end, flipped onto this back and swam lazily towards her. 'Are you going to stand there all day or are you going to join in? We leave for the racetrack in half an hour.'

'I'm not coming in, thank you. We were supposed to have a full physio session this morning.'

'I was up and raring to go, *bonita*. You were not.'

It was the first time ever that Raven had overslept or been late for an appointment. She couldn't stem the heat that crawled up into her face as she recalled the reason why. When she'd found herself unable to sleep, she'd opened up Rafael's manuscript and delved back between the pages. If anything, the story had been even better the second time round, renewed fascination with Ana, the heroine, keeping her awake.

'I was only ten minutes late.'

He stopped on the step just beneath where she stood and sluiced a hand through his hair. 'Ten throwaway minutes to you is a lifetime to me.' He hauled himself out of the pool. Raven couldn't stop herself from ogling extremely well-toned biceps and a tight, streamlined body. Even the scars he'd sustained on his legs and especially his hip were filled with character that made her want to trace her fingers over it, test his skin's texture for herself.

She forced herself to look away before the fierce flames rising could totally engulf her. He grabbed the towel she tossed to him and rubbed it lazily over his body.

'Well, since you had the full therapy session last night, I don't see the harm in reversing the regime.'

He glanced over and winked. 'My thoughts exactly.'

Suspicion skittered along her spine. 'You're surprisingly chipper this morning.' Looking closer, she saw that his face had lost its strained edge, and when he turned to toss the towel aside, his movement had lost last night's stiffness.

'It's amazing what a good night's sleep can do. I feel as if I have a new lease of life.' He picked up his walking stick and came towards her, a sexy, melt-your-panties-off grin firmly in place. 'Come, we'll have breakfast and I can tell you how to make your tardiness up to me.'

'Anything less than a pound of flesh and I'll probably die of shock,' she muttered.

He laughed. The sound floated along her skin then sank in with pleasure-giving intensity. 'You wound me. I was thinking more along the lines of your thoughts on the manuscript.'

She didn't answer immediately. She was too caught up in watching the ripple of muscle as he sauntered out of the pool area—and through his bedroom, where discarded clothes and twisted sheets made her temperature rise higher—towards the sun-dappled balcony where their breakfast had been laid out.

Goodness knew how she managed not to stare like some hormonal schoolgirl.

'Wow, should I take your silence to mean it was sheer dross?'

Focus! She sat down at the table, snapped out her napkin and laid it over her lap, wishing she could throw a blanket over her erotic thoughts just as easily.

He poured her coffee—mocha latte—and added a dash of cinnamon, just the way she liked it. Raven decided she was *not* going to read anything into Rafael's intimate knowledge of how she took her caffeine. But inside she felt a long held-in tightness spring free, accompanied by the faintest spark of fear.

'It wasn't dross. I'm sure you know that. I love Ana's transition from girl into woman. And that first meeting with Carlos was what every girl dreams of. I'm happy she's putting her dark past behind her...'

'But?' He scythed through her ambivalence.

'But I think Carlos is coming on too strong, too fast. He risks overwhelming Ana just a little bit.'

He picked up his own coffee and eyed her over the rim. 'But I think she has a backbone of steel. Do you not think she has what it takes to stay?'

Raven nodded. 'I think she does. She sees him as a challenge...welcomes it to some extent, but I'm still a little scared for her.'

'You're invested in her. Which is what a writer wants, isn't it? Maybe she needs to be pushed out of her comfort zone to see what she really wants.'

'I notice she likes racing, just like Carlos.'

He stilled. '*Sí*. It is a racing thriller, after all.'

Raven carefully set her cup down and picked up a slice of toast. 'She wouldn't, by chance, be modelled on your sister-in-law, would she?' she asked, keeping her voice level.

He shrugged. 'Sasha is one of the best female drivers I've known. What's your point?'

She didn't know how to articulate what it made her feel. Hell, she couldn't grasp the roiling feelings herself. All she knew was that she didn't want Rafael to be thinking of a specific woman when he wrote the story.

'I just think you would appeal to a wider audience if the character wasn't so...specific.'

'You mean, it would appeal to you?'

The toast fell from her hand. 'I don't know what you mean.'

'Are you going to play this game? Really?'

The words, so similar to those she'd thrown at him, made heat crawl up her face. 'Fine. Touché.' She hardened her spine and forced out the next words. 'But you know what I'm trying to say.'

'Are we still talking about my manuscript?' he asked, a trace of a smile on his lips.

'We've taken a slight detour.'

'A detour that touches on our…friendship and the adjustments I need to make in order for it to advance?'

Her hands shook at how quickly they'd strayed into dangerous territory. She couldn't look into his probing gaze so she studiously buttered her toast. 'Y…yes.'

He stayed silent for so long she was forced to glance up. Blue eyes pinned her to her chair. 'Don't expect me to turn into something I'm not, *querida*.'

'Take a first step. You might surprise yourself.'

'And you, *pIqueña*, how are you surprising yourself?'

The question, unexpected and lightning-quick, sent a bolt of shock through her. She floundered, unsure of what to say. 'I…I'm not sure…'

'Well, make sure. If I'm to bend over backwards to accommodate you, you have to give something back, *si*?'

That pulse of fear intensified. Opening up to Rafael in Monaco, telling him things she'd never told another human soul, had left her feeling raw and exposed.

Now, by daring her in his oh-so-sexy way to open up even more, he threatened to take it a whole lot further, luring her with a promise she knew deep down he wouldn't keep. That was the essence of playboys. They exuded charisma, invited confidences until they had you in their grasp.

And yet the rare glimpses she'd caught of Rafael threatened that long-held belief. He was alluding to the fact that playboys could have hearts of gold. Raven wasn't sure she was ready to handle that nugget of information.

For years, her mother had believed it—believed it still—and look where it'd got her. If she let Rafael in and he did a number on her, she wasn't sure who she would hate more—Rafael…or herself.

'You don't have to turn into something else. All I ask is to see a little bit more, make my choice with a clear, if not total, view of the facts. Because I can't have sex with you for the sake of it. I would hate myself and I would hate you.'

'Ah, but we're already having sex, *mi amor*. All that's left is for our bodies to catch up.'

Of course, she could *really* have done without that thought in her head. Because, suddenly, it was all she could think about.

She walked beside Rafael along the long paddock an hour later, watching as he stopped at every single All-Star garage to greet and exchange info with the crew. From her stint as his physio last year, Raven knew just how meticulous a driver he was. He understood the minutiae of racing to the last detail and could probably recite the inner workings of a turbo engine in his sleep.

Which was why his accident, judged to be the result of human error—his—had stunned everyone. Some had speculated that it had been the effects of partying hard that had finally done him in. But, in the last few weeks, she'd caught occasional glimpses of the man underneath and knew Rafael de Cervantes wasn't all gloss. He rarely drank more than a glass of champagne at any event and she knew he'd banned smoking in the paddock a few years back.

What she didn't know was how deep the Rafael de Cervantes well ran, or how monstrous the demons were that chased him. It was clear he was haunted by something in his past. At first she'd thought it was his father. But even though that particular revelation had been painful to him, it had been when she'd mentioned his mother that the real pain had surfaced, just for a moment.

She glanced at him, a little overwhelmed by the many facets she had previously been too riled up to see. Rafael had traits she abhorred, traits that reminded her of the man whose DNA ran through her veins.

But he was also so much more.

'I can hear you thinking again.'

'Unfortunately, my active brain cells refuse to subside into bimbo mode just because I'm in your presence.' She cast a telling glance at a groupie who'd just obtained an autograph and was squealing in delight as she ran to her friends.

'You can wow me with your superior intelligence later,' he said as they approached the last garage in the paddock.

The first thing she noticed was the age group of this particular crew. Aside from two older supervisors, everyone else ranged from early to late teens. The other thing that struck her was their synchronicity and clear pride in what they were doing.

When Rafael greeted them, they responded as if he were their supreme deity come to life. She wasn't surprised by their reaction. What surprised her was Rafael's almost bashful response as they gathered around him. Then it all disappeared as he started to speak. Started to teach.

They hung on his every word, and took turns asking him challenging questions, which he threw right back to them. Respect shone from their eyes and the depth of understanding he'd managed to impart in the space of the hour before the race started left Raven reeling.

'Close your mouth, *piqueña*. You'll catch flies,' he quipped as he led her away from the garage towards the VIP Paddock Club.

Her mouth snapped shut. 'That was incredible, the way you got them to listen, got them to apply knowledge they'd forgotten they had.'

'They're a talented bunch. And they love racing. All there is to learn is a respect for speed.' He shrugged. 'It wasn't hard.'

'No. You're a natural teacher.'

'I learned from the best.'

'Marco?'

He shook his head and held the door open to let her into the lift that whisked them up to the top floor VIP lounge. From there they had a panoramic view over the entire race circuit.

Rafael bypassed several A-listers who'd paid thousands of euros to attend this exclusive event and led her into a private roped-off area. He held out a chair for her then sat down opposite her. 'My father. He gave me my first go-kart when I was five. There's nothing about engines that he doesn't know. By the time I was nine, I could dismantle and reassemble a carburetor without assistance.'

'I didn't know your father raced.'

'He didn't. My grandfather had a small hotel business and wanted my father to study business so he could help him run it. But he never lost his love of racing. The moment his business grew successful enough, he enrolled Marco, then me in learning the sport. And he took us to all the European races, much to my mother's distress.'

The pang of envy for what she'd never had made her feel small so she pushed it away. Especially given what she knew of the strain between father and son now.

'That sounds just like what happened to Carlos in your story.'

He glanced at her with a tense smile. 'Does it?'

'Yes.' When he just shrugged, she decided not to pursue the subject of his story. 'So your father took you to all the races? Sounds like an idyllic childhood.'

'Sure, if you're prepared to forgive the fact that back then I was so intent on winning I didn't feel any compunction in crashing into every single car in front of me just to put them out of business. I was disqualified more times than I actually won races.'

'But I'm guessing your father persevered. He saw the raw talent and did everything he could to nurture it.' Something her own father hadn't even come close to attempting with her.

'*Sí*, he showed me the difference between winning at all costs and winning with integrity. And I repaid that by making sure he would never be able to drive a car again.' His face was taut with pain, his eyes bleak with a haunting expression that cracked across her heart.

'I saw how things were between you two at Jack's christening, but have you spoken to him at all since the accident?'

He tensed, waited for the waiter who'd brought their drinks to leave before he answered. 'Of course I have.'

'I mean about what happened.'

'What would be the point?'

'To find out how he feels about it?'

'How he *feels*? Trust me, I have a fair idea.'

Recalling the look on his father's face, she shook her head. 'Maybe you don't. Perhaps you should talk to him again. Or maybe let *him* talk to you. He could have something to say to you instead of you thinking it only works the other way round.'

He frowned suddenly. 'You're head shrinking me again. And how the hell did we get onto this subject anyway? It's boring me.'

'Don't,' she said softly.

A glaze of ice sharpened his blue eyes. 'Don't what?'

'Don't trivialise it. You'll have to tackle it sooner or later.'

'Like you have tackled your father?'

Her breath shut off in her chest. 'This is different.'

'How?' He had to raise his voice to be heard over the sound of engines leaving the garages to line up on the racetrack. Rafael barely glanced at them, his attention riveted on her face.

'Despite everything that's happened, your father loves you enough to want to connect with you. My father doesn't care if I'm alive or dead. He never has, and he never will.'

Rafael saw the depth of pain that slashed across her features before she turned to watch the action unfolding on the racetrack. He wanted to say something, but found he had no words of wisdom or of comfort to give her.

Because he didn't agree with the redeeming quality she seemed to want to find in him. He had no doubt that if she knew the extent of his sins, she wouldn't be so quick to offer her comfort.

An icy vice threatened to crush his chest, just as it did every time he thought of his mother. He'd awoken this morning with her screams ringing in his ears, the image of her lifeless eyes imprinted on his retinas.

No, he had no words of comfort. He'd trashed everything good in his life, and had come close to dismantling his relationship with his brother last year. The last thing he wanted to do was admit to Raven that part of his refusal to speak to his father was because he didn't want to discover whether he was irredeemably trashed in his father's eyes too.

His gaze flicked to the cars lining up on the track. Unlike the normal grand prix races when the cars lined up according to their qualifying time, the six All-Star cars were lined up side by side.

Team El Camino's red and black racer, driven by the young driver he'd been working with, was the first off the mark. Rafael felt a spurt of pride, which he immediately doused.

He had no right to feel pride. All he'd done was take what his father had taught him and passed it on. His father deserved the credit here, not him.

'Don't be so hard on yourself.'

Irrational anger sprang up within him. The fact that she seemed so determined to make him feel better when she was content to wallow in her own *daddy issues* filled him with anger. The fact that he was sexually frustrated—heck, he was going on eight months without having had sex—was setting his teeth on edge. The fact that he was up here, cooling his heels when he wanted more than anything to be down there... behind the wheel of a racing car—

Ice chilled his veins as he acknowledged the full extent of what he was feeling.

'Rafael?'

He didn't respond or turn towards her. Instead he watched the screen as Axel Jung threatened to take the lead from the young driver.

'Rafael, are you okay?'

'Do me a favour, *querida*, and stop talking. You're hold-ing a mirror up to my numerous flaws. There's only so much I can take before I have to revert to type. And since you don't want that, I suggest you let me absorb a few of them and con-centrate on enjoying this race, *si*?'

Far from doing what he expected of her, which was to retreat into sullen silence or—from experience with other women—flounce off in feminine affront, she merely picked up the remote that operated the giant screen in their section and turned it on. Then she picked up the menu, asked him what he wanted for lunch, then ordered it for them, her face set in smooth, neutral lines.

He waited several minutes, despising the emotion that ate away his insides like acid on metal. Guilt. An emotion he didn't like to acknowledge.

Guilt for upsetting her. 'I'm sorry,' he said.

A shapely eyebrow lifted in his direction, then she nodded. 'It's okay. I don't like dredging up my past either. I guess I should learn to respect yours.'

'But I seem to invite you to dig, which is very unlike me.' He frowned.

A tiny, perfect smile played around lips he remembered tasting. A craving such as he'd never known punched through him. Right in that moment, all he wanted to do was taste her again. Keep on tasting her until there were no clothes between them. Then he would taste her in the most elemental way pos-sible. Right between her legs.

He would so enjoy watching her come. Again and again. And again.

Normally, he would have been thrilled by the natural path of his thoughts, but Rafael admitted his need held a previously unknown edge to it…an almost desperate craving he'd never experienced before. He wanted Raven. And yet a part of him was terrified by the depth of his need.

Forcing himself not to analyse it too closely, he returned

his attention to the track and felt a further spurt of discontentment when he saw Axel Jung had taken the lead.

Lunch was delivered and they ate in truce-like silence.

When Axel Jung took the race by a half second, Rafael tried to force back his black mood. As the CEO of the company organising the event, he had to step up to the podium and say a few words.

'If your jaw tightens any further, you'll do yourself an injury,' Raven murmured next to him.

'I'm smiling, *querida*, like the great racer slash CEO that I am,' he muttered back, turning towards her.

This close, her perfume filled his nostrils and invaded his senses. She gave a laugh and raised a sceptical brow. 'We both know you want to throw your toys out of the pram because the team you silently support came second. You're supposed to be unbiased, remember?'

He moved closer to her, felt the brush of her arm against his side and the depth of need intensified. 'I am unbiased. I just wanted my young driver to win, that's all,' he said, unrepentant.

Her teasing laugh and the way she bumped his shoulder in playful admonition unravelled him further. He glanced down into her face and his breath strangled at her breathtaking beauty.

A shout made him turn. Axel had stepped off the podium and was making his way towards them. Or Raven in particular, if the interest in his eyes was anything to go by.

Before conscious thought formed, Rafael moved, deliberately blocking the German from accessing the woman beside him. *His woman.*

'Congratulations, Jung. I think the press want their interview now.' He deftly turned the German towards the waiting paparazzi. As moves went, Rafael thought it was supremely smooth, but Raven's gasp told him the grace had been lost on her.

'Did you just do what I think you did?'

'That depends. Did you want him to come over here and slobber all over you?'

She shuddered. 'No, but I'm not sure I wanted a blatant territory-marking from you either.'

He wanted to tell her that he wished the whole paddock knew to keep away from her. But he knew it wouldn't go down well. It would also point out just how much he detested the idea of Raven with any other man. 'Point taken.'

Her eyes widened. 'Wow, I'm not sure whether to feel suspicious or special that you've conceded a point to me.'

'You should feel special.' His gaze trapped and held hers. 'Very special.'

Raven returned his stare, trying to summon a tiny bit of ire beneath all the high octane, breath-stealing emotions coursing through her. But the excitement licking along her nerve endings put the effort to shame.

Something of her feelings must have shown on her face because his eyes darkened dramatically. His gaze dropped to her lips, the heated pulse beating a wild rhythm in her neck, then back to her face.

Calmly, he breathed out and gave her a slow, electrifying smile. Eyes still locked on hers, he pulled out his phone and spoke in clear tones. Unfortunately, Spanish wasn't her forte so she had no clue what he was saying. But she made out the word *avión,* which made her even more curious.

'What was that about?' she asked when he hung up.

'I've arranged for our things to be packed. I thought we might head to Mexico a couple of days earlier than the rest of the racers.'

'Won't you be needed?'

'Possibly, but for the next two days I'm taking your advice and delegating. Does this make you happy?'

There was a deeper question beneath the stated one, a hungry gleam in his eyes that boldly proclaimed his intention should she agree to what he was proposing.

In a single heartbeat, Raven accepted it. 'Yes.'

It was almost a relief to let go of the angst and the rigid control. At least for a while. She knew without a shadow of a doubt that it would return a hundredfold soon enough.

CHAPTER NINE

SHE WAS GOING to take a lover. She was going to lose her virginity to the very man she'd run a mile from last year. The man who would most likely break her heart into a tiny million pieces long before this thing between them was over.

Nerves threatened to eat her up as their tiny seaplane banked and headed towards the private beachfront of the stunning villa Rafael owned in Los Cabos, Mexico. By now she knew all about the eighteen-bedroom villa, the lower level sauna and steam room, the two swimming pools and the names of every member of the construction crew who'd built the villa to Rafael's exact specification three years ago.

Because she'd needed to babble, to fill her head with white noise to distract her from the urge to spill the fact that she hadn't done this before. The closer they drew to their destination, the higher panic had flared beneath the surface of her outward calm.

Rafael's experience with women was world-renowned. What if she made a spectacular fool of herself? What if he was so put off by her inexperience he recoiled from her? To silence the voices, she babbled some more, found out that he had a staff of five who managed the villa and that he practised his handicap on the legendary golf course nearby when the occasion suited him.

In direct contrast to her nervous chirping, Rafael had been circumspect, his watchful silence unlike anything she'd ever known. Although he'd answered her questions with inexhaustible patience, his eyes had remained riveted on her the whole time, occasionally dropping to her lips as if he couldn't wait to taste, to devour.

They touched down on the water and powered to a stop next

to a large wooden jetty. After alighting, they headed towards an open-topped jeep for the short drive to the villa.

Even though she felt as if she knew the property inside and out, Raven wasn't prepared for the sheer, jaw-dropping beauty of the adobe white-washed walls, the highly polished exposed beams and almost ever-present sea views from the windows of the mission-style villa. Spanish-influenced paintings adorned the walls, lending a rich tapestry to the luxurious interior.

In her bedroom, rich fabrics in earthy colours formed the backdrop to a mostly white theme set against warm terracotta floors. But one item drew her attention.

'What's this for?' She touched the black high-powered telescope that stood before one large window.

He came and stood behind her, bringing that warm, evocative scent that she'd come to associate with him and only him. It took an insane amount of willpower not to lean back into his hard-packed body.

'The waters around here are well-known grounds for sperm whales. They tend to come closer to shore first thing in the morning. If you're lucky you'll spot a few while we're here.'

Again the sombre, almost guarded response caught her off-guard. She glanced at him over her shoulder. He returned her stare with an intensity that made her breath catch. After a full minute, he lifted his hand and drifted warm fingers down her cheek in a soothing, belly-melting gesture.

'You're nervous, *bonita*. Don't be. I promise it will be good.'

Her laugh was aimed at herself as much as at him. 'That's easy for you to say.'

His finger touched and stayed on the pulse jumping in her throat. 'It isn't. I haven't done this for a long time, too. Hell, I don't know if the equipment works.'

He gave a wry smile when her brows shot up. 'You don't?'

'You will be the first since a while before the accident.'

'But I felt…I know you…'

'Can get a hard-on? *Sí*, but I'm yet to test the practical integrity of the machinery.'

'Oh, so I'm to be your guinea pig?' she teased, a little appeased that she wasn't the only one climbing walls about the prospect of them together.

'Guinea pigs don't have mouths like yours, or eyes the colour of a desert oasis. Or breasts that cry out to be suckled. Or the most perfect heart-shaped ass that makes me want to put you face down and straddle—'

'Okay, I get it. I'm hotter than a Greek furnace.' Her eyes strayed to the perfectly made up bed, her imagination running wild. She swallowed. 'I…I'd like a tour of the outside now, if you don't mind.'

His finger drifted up to the corner of her mouth, pressed gently before he put his finger to his own lips and groaned.

'If that's what you want.'

She nodded.

He didn't heed her request right away. He leaned down, placed his lips at the juncture between her neck and shoulder and ran his tongue over her thundering pulse. He answered her groan with one of his own, then he reluctantly stepped back. Raven was glad when he offered his arm because her legs had grown decidedly shaky.

The heeled leather boots she'd worn with her jeans and black-edged white shirt clicked alongside his heavier tread as they went outside.

On one side, an extensive stretch of grass led to a large thatched poolside bar surrounded by potted palm trees.

Beside it, an area clearly designated for relaxing featured a hot tub under long bales of white linen that had been intertwined to form a stunning canopy that offered shade. After the chill of Europe, it was a balm to feel the sun on her face.

'Come, there's something I want to show you.' There was heated anticipation in the low rumble that fluttered over her skin, feeding her own sizzling emotions.

Rafael led her across the grass and down shallow steps to

the private, secluded beach. All through the tour, his hand had been drifting up and down her back, stealing her thoughts and playing havoc with her pulse.

Which meant that she was totally unprepared for the sight that confronted her when he led her round a rock-sheltered cove.

The thick timber four-poster canopy had been erected right on the shore, with a massive day bed suspended by thick intertwined ropes. The sight was so vividly breathtaking, and so unexpectedly raw and pagan, she stopped in her tracks.

There was only one reason for the bed.

Sex. Outdoor sex.

Heat engulfed her whole body as Rafael's gaze met and trapped hers.

'The high rocks shield even the most determined lenses. And see those?' He indicated three discreetly placed floodlights pointing out towards the water. 'They come on at night and send a glare out to sea so any cunning paparazzi out there get nothing but glare when they try and get pictures of the villa.'

She swallowed hard. 'Even so, I can't imagine doing…it so blatantly.'

He caught her hand in his and kissed her palm. 'Never say never. Now, I believe we have a therapy session to work through?'

The fact that she'd forgotten her main reason for being there made her uncomfortable.

She hastened to cover it up. 'Yes, and don't hate me, but we'll need to step things up a bit.'

'Do with me what you will, *querida*. I'm but putty in your hands.'

He led the way back into the villa and into his bedroom. The setting sun threw orange shades across the king-size wooden-framed bed that seemed to dominate the room. When he threw his walking stick on the exquisitely designed recliner facing the double doors leading to a large balcony, she was reminded again why she was here with Rafael in the first place.

She'd cautioned him against sex only a handful of days ago, and yet here she was, unable to think beyond the raging need to strip every piece of clothing from his body.

Guilt ate away inside her.

'I can hear you thinking again. And I don't feel warm and fuzzy about the direction of your thoughts.' He started to unbutton his shirt.

She tried and failed not to let her eyes linger over his muscular chest and down over his washboard stomach, following the faint line of hair that disappeared beneath his jeans.

'Is this where we hold hands and pray about whether we should have sex or not?'

He was back. The irreverent, sexy, endlessly charismatic man who had women the world over falling at his feet.

Or was he?

A careful look into his eyes showed not the gleam of irreverence but a quietly speculative look beneath his words. 'Are you afraid you'll hate sex with me? Or afraid you'll love it so much you'll beg to become a groupie?'

She shook her head. 'As much as I want it to be easy, I've never taken a decision lightly. And I don't think you should either. It's not just me I'm thinking about here, Rafael. What if all this turns around on you? What if we do this and you get even more damaged?'

'Then I'll learn to live with it. Come here,' he said, holding out his hand. Although his mouth was smiling, his eyes held a very firm command.

She had to dig her toes in to stay put. 'You'll live with it because you think you deserve all the bad things that happen to you?'

His smile slowly eroded until only a trace remained. 'Raven, it's time to stop being my therapist and just be my lover.'

'Rafael...'

'Come. Here.'

He held still, hands outstretched. Almost against her will, she found herself moving forward. He waited until she was within touching distance. Then he lunged for her, sliding his fingers between hers to entrap her.

With his other hand he pulled her close, his fingers spreading over her bottom. Moving forward, he backed her against the wall, enclosing her thighs between his. 'I've got you now. No escape. Now, are you going to undress or do you need help?'

She gnawed on her lower lip, rioting emotions tearing her apart. 'I was so sure I wanted this, Rafael, but I'll never forgive myself if I make things worse for you—'

He growled, 'Damn it, just get naked, will you?'

When she remained still, he took the task into his own hands. For a man who hadn't slept with a woman for almost a year, he didn't seem to lack the skill needed to undress her.

She was down to her bra and knickers within seconds. One deft flick of his fingers disposed of her bra. Slowly he took one step back, then another.

'*Dios*, I knew you would be worth it,' he rasped, his fiercely intent gaze making her skin heat up and pucker in all the right places. Grabbing her by the waist, he reversed their positions and walked her back towards the bed. At the back of her mind she knew she needed to tell him about her lack of experience. But words were in short supply when confronted with the perfection that was Rafael's muscled torso.

With one firm push, she lay sprawled on the bed. He placed one knee on the bed, pushed forward, then winced as he positioned himself over her.

Her concerned gasp drowned beneath his kiss. The kiss that rocked her to her very soul. His tongue pushed inside, warm, insistent and pulse-melting as he showed her the extent of his mastery. Unable to bear the torrent of sensation, she jerked, her hands flailing as she tried to find purchase. He moved over her, pinned her more firmly to the bed with his hips flush against her. When he winced again, she wrenched her mouth from his.

'Before you say it, I'm fine. Dampen the mood with another virtuous monologue and I will spank you. Hard.'

She flushed deep and fierce, but it didn't keep her silent. 'I can't...I can't stop caring about your well-being just because it's inconvenient for you. Just tell me if you're okay.'

'I'm okay. But if I had to, I'd cut off my arm just to be inside you, to feel you close around me like you'd never let me go.'

'Bloody hell, do you practice those lines or do they really just fall off your lips?'

'If I plan to relaunch myself as a multimillion euro best-selling writer, *bonita*, then a way with words is a must.' He sobered. 'But that doesn't mean I don't mean them. I mean every single word I say to you.'

Her heart stuttered, then thundered wildly. 'Rafael...' Her eyes drifted shut.

'I'm lethal. I know.' He settled himself more firmly until she felt his rigid size against the fabric of her knickers. He rocked forward and the relentless pressure on her clitoris made a few dozen stars explode behind her closed eyelids.

'You're beyond lethal,' she breathed shakily. 'You're everything I should be running away from.'

His mouth drifted down her cheek to her jaw and back again. He pressed another kiss to the corner of her mouth, then she felt him move away. 'Hey, open your eyes.'

Reluctantly, she obeyed, already missing his mouth on her.

His gaze was solemn. 'Don't run, Raven. I'm broken and cannot chase after you. Not just yet.'

Her breath caught. 'Would you really? Chase after me?'

'Most definitely. Because I get extremely grumpy when I'm cheated out of an orgasm.'

The slap she aimed at his arm was half-hearted because his mouth was descending to wreak havoc on hers once more. When he finally allowed her to breathe, she was mindless with pleasure.

'I've wanted you for so long, I can't remember when I didn't want you.'

'But…why? Because I was the only paddock bunny who wouldn't fall into your bed?'

She expected a clever quip about his irresistibility. Instead, his gaze turned serious. 'Because within that tainted, false existence, you managed to remain pure. Nothing touched you. I craved that purity. I wanted to touch it, to see what it felt like. But you wouldn't even give me the time of day.'

'Because you had enough groupies hanging around you. I…I also thought you were with Sasha.'

He groaned. 'I guess I played the playboy game a little too well.'

'You mean you weren't?'

'I grew jaded a long time ago but some cloaks are more difficult to cast off than others.'

At her half-snort, he laughed. 'Do you know this is the longest I've been in a bedroom with a woman without one of us halfway to an orgasm?'

She knew that he meant the woman, not him. 'How trying for you.'

He pushed against her once more, his erection a fierce, rigid presence. '*Sí*. It's very trying. You should do something about it before my poor body gives out.' He trailed his mouth over hers before planting a row of kisses along her jaw.

'You really are incorrigible,' she gasped.

'Yes, I am,' he murmured, slowly licking his way down her neck to her pulse. 'I am incorrigible. And I deserve to be punished. Mercilessly.' He slid a hand to caress her belly, then lower to boldly cup her. 'Show me who's boss, my stern, sensible Raven. Give me the punishment I deserve.'

Her breath snagged in her chest. The same chest where her heart hammered like a piston about to burst its casing.

His fingers pressed harder, rhythmic, unrelenting. This time the explosion of heat stemmed from her very core and radiated throughout her body. Her legs parted wider, inviting him to embed himself even deeper. Her restless fingers traced the line of his jeans and found firm skin. Her fingers slipped an inch beneath and he moaned. The sound vibrated along her nerves as heat oozed between her legs.

Her hips undulated in sync with the movement of his fingers, and in that moment, Raven felt as if she were melting from the inside out. She moaned at the intensity of it.

'That's it, *precioso*, give it up for me,' he murmured in her ear, then bit on her lobe. Her cry echoed in the room, the sound as alien to her as the feelings coursing through her body. When his hot mouth trailed down her neck, over her shoulder blades, she held her breath, at once dreading and anticipating the sensation of his stubble roughness on her breast.

With a hungry lunge, he sucked one nipple into his mouth and drew hard on it. At the same time, one firm finger pressed on her most sensitive spot.

'Oh God!' Pleasure exploded in a fiery sensation that made her hips buck straight off the bed. She felt Rafael move off her and alongside her, but the pressure of his fingers and mouth didn't abate. Her climax dragged out until she feared she would expire from it. When her tremors subsided, he left her breasts to plant a forceful kiss on her lips. She fought to breathe.

Heavens, he was too much.

She opened her eyes to find his gaze on hers, intense and purposeful. 'If you're thinking of concocting a means of escape now you've come, know now I have no intention of letting that happen.'

'Why would I want to escape? Unless I'm mistaken, the best is yet to come. Yes?'

The relieved exhalation made her guess he'd suspected she was feeling overwhelmed. 'You have no idea. Kiss me.'

Raven's fingers curled into his nape, glorying in the luxurious heat of his skin as she complied with the heated request.

No, she didn't want to escape. Touching him felt so good, so incredibly pleasurable, that fleeing was the last thing on her mind. The thought surprised her, almost tripping out of her mouth. She curbed it in time. Rafael's head was already swollen by the thought that he could turn her on. Admitting how totally enthralled she was by him would make him even more insufferable. Although, the way she was feeling right now, she wouldn't be surprised if his sharp intellect worked it out before long—

'You're thinking again.'

She stared into blue eyes filled with raw hunger and masculine affront. Slowly she let her fingers drift through his hair, experiencing a keen sense of feminine satisfaction when he groaned. 'What are you going to do about it?'

His lips parted in a feral smile. 'Don't challenge a man on the knife-edge of need, sweetheart. You might regret it. If you survive the consequences.'

Without giving her time to answer, he pulled her down on top of him, both hands imprisoning her to his body as he fell back on the bed. Unerringly, his mouth found hers.

Raven stopped thinking.

And gave herself over to sensation. Rafael's pelvic bone might have been broken and pieced back together but there was nothing wrong with his arms. He lifted her above him and held her in place while he feasted on her breasts. When he was done, he lifted even higher. 'Take off your panties for me.'

With shaky fingers she drew them off, experienced a momentary stab of self-consciousness, which was promptly washed away when he positioned her legs on either side of him and looked up at her.

'You might want to hold onto something,' he murmured huskily, taking a sharp bite of the tender skin of her inner thigh.

The statement wasn't a casual boast. At the first brush of his tongue on her sex, her whole body arched and shook. She would've catapulted off him had he not been holding her hips in an iron grip.

Pain shot through fingers which had grasped the wooden

headboard at his warning. He licked, sucked and tortured her with a skill that left her reeling and hanging on for dear life.

When she tumbled headlong into another firestorm, he caught her in his arms and caressed her body until she could breathe again. Then he left her for a moment.

The sound of foil ripping drew her hazy gaze to him. The sight of his erection in his fist made her sex swell all over again.

He caught her stare and sent her a lethal smile. 'Next time, you get to do it.'

Raven didn't know what to do with that. Nor did she know how to find the correct words to tell him she'd never done it before. In the end, they just spilled out.

'Rafael, I'm a virgin.'

He stilled, shock darkening his eyes. A look flitted through his eyes a second before he shut them. The hand he raked through his hair was decidedly shaky.

He sucked in a long harsh breath, then opened his eyes. The raw hunger hadn't abated but the fisted, white-knuckled hand on his thigh showed he was making an inhuman effort to contain it. 'Do you want to stop?' he rasped, jaw clenched as he fought for control.

The thought of stopping made her insides scream in rejection. 'No. I don't. But I wanted you to know before…before it happened.'

He exhaled slowly. His hand unclenched, then clenched again as his gaze slid hungrily over her. 'I can guess your reasons for remaining celibate. What happened to you would make anyone swear off sex. I know the chemistry between us is insane, but you need to be sure you want to do this now, with me.'

'Would you rather I do it with someone else?' she quipped lightly, although the very thought of anyone but Rafael touching her made her shudder in rejection.

He lunged for her, firm hands grasping her shoulders in a rigid hold before she could take another breath.

'Not unless that *someone else* wishes to get his throat ripped out,' he bit out. He pinned her to the bed and devoured her with an anger-tinged, lethally aroused intensity that made fire roar through her body.

By the time he parted her legs and looked deep into her eyes, she was almost lost.

'I'd planned for you to be on top our first time. But I think this will be easier on you.'

His bent arms caged her as he probed her entrance, his gaze searching hers with every inch he slid inside her. The momentary tightening that made her breath catch stilled his forward momentum.

'Raven?' he croaked, tension screaming through his body as he framed her face in gentle hands.

'I'm okay.'

'That makes one of us.'

Her fingers tried to smooth back his hair but the silky strands refused to stay in place. 'I...can I do anything?'

His laugh was tinged with pain. '*Si*, you could stop being so damned sexy.' He pushed another fraction and her breath hitched again. '*Dios*, I'm sorry,' he murmured, bending to place a reverent kiss on her lips.

Raven didn't know what was in store for her but she knew her body was screaming with the need to find out. With a deep breath—because, hell, no pain no gain—she pushed her hip upward. His cursed groan met her hiss of pain, which quickly disappeared to be replaced by a feeling so phenomenal words failed her.

'Raven!' Rafael's response was half praise, half reproach.

Tentatively, she moved again.

He growled. 'Damn it, woman. *Stay still.*'

'Why?'

'Because this will be over sooner than you'd like if you don't.'

Heart hammering, she inhaled and gasped when the tips

of her breasts brushed his sweat-filmed chest. 'But at least we know the equipment is working, right?'

He pushed the last few inches until he was firmly seated inside her. Sensation as she'd never known flooded her. At her cry of delight, he pulled out slowly and repeated the thrust. Her head slammed back against the pillow, her fingers clenching hard in his hair as she held on for mercy.

Yep, there was nothing faulty in Rafael's equipment.

With another hungry groan, he increased the tempo, murmuring hot, erotic encouragement in her ear as she started to meet his hips with tiny thrusts of her own.

This time when she came the explosion was so forceful, so completely annihilating, she wasn't sure whether she would ever recover.

Rafael plucked her hands from his hair and pinned them on the bed, then proceeded to dominate her senses once more until she was orgasming again and again.

When she heard his final guttural groan of release, she was sure she'd gone insane with pleasure overload.

'*Dios*...' His voice was rough. Mildly shocked. 'This must be what heaven feels like.'

A bolt of pleasure, pure and true, went through her.

Don't get carried away, Raven.

To bring herself down to earth, she searched her mind for something innocuous to say.

'If you break out into *At Last*, I'll personally make sure you never walk again.'

His laugh was deep, full and extremely contagious. She found herself joining in as he collapsed onto his side and pulled her body into his.

They laughed until they were both out of breath. Then he fisted a hand through her hair and tugged her face up to his. After kissing her breathless, he released her.

'I was thinking more along the lines of *Again and Again and Again*. If there's a song like that, I'll need to learn the lyrics. If there isn't I might need to write one.' He cupped her nape and pulled her down for another unending kiss that left her breathless and seriously afraid for her sanity. 'I love kissing you,' he rasped.

A bolt of something strong and unfamiliar went through her, followed swiftly by a threat of apprehension. Steadying a hand on his chest, she pulled herself up.

'Where do you think you're going?' he asked.

She averted her gaze from his and fought to find reason in all this madness. 'I need to get up.'

'No. You need to look after me, and my needs demand that, after what you've just done to me, I stay in this bed. Which means you have to stay too.'

Unable to resist, she glanced down his body and swallowed the hungry need that coursed through her. It was unthinkable that she would want him again, so voraciously, so soon. But she did.

'If you carry on licking your lips and eyeing me like that, I'll have to teach you this lesson all over again.'

She blinked. 'I can't…we can't…it's too soon.'

'As you rightly noted, the equipment works so I most certainly can, *pequeña*.' He moved and she saw his fleeting grimace. 'But maybe you need to go on top this time.' He held out his hand and she swayed towards him.

'This is crazy, Rafael,' she protested feebly, even as she let him arrange her over him.

'But crazy good, no?'

She melted into his arms. 'Crazy good, yes.'

'Tell me what really happened with your father. What did he do to make you yearn for your eighteenth birthday?'

Rafael couldn't believe the words tumbling out of his mouth. But then again, he couldn't believe a lot that had happened in the last twenty-four hours. From the moment he'd placed the phone call to set things in motion to fly them to Mexico, he'd felt control and reason slipping out of his grasp.

Not that he'd had much in the way of control when it came

to the woman drifting in and out of sleep only a heartbeat away. Sure, he used the Los Cabos villa for entertaining. But it was mostly on business, never for pleasure. And he'd never let a woman stay over. Until now.

Her raven-black hair spread over his arm and he couldn't resist putting his nose to the silky strands, inhaling the peach-scented shampoo as he waited for the answer to the question that invited shared confidences he wasn't sure he wanted to reciprocate. But what the hell? She'd pried more information out of him in the last few weeks than he'd ever released in years.

A little reciprocity didn't hurt.

She turned towards him and spoke in a low, quiet voice. 'Remember I told you he barely acknowledged my existence at first?'

He nodded.

'Over time, as I got older, that began to change. I noticed from the way he looked at me. I thought I was imagining it. Then I overheard the housekeeper saying something to my father's driver.'

'What did she say?'

'That my father didn't really believe I was his daughter. I couldn't be because I looked nothing like him—he has ash-blond hair and blue eyes. I inherited my mother's colouring. Between fourteen and fifteen, I shot up in height and grew breasts. I tried not to link that and the fact that he'd started entertaining more and more at his house instead of at his private club.'

Rafael's hand tightened into a fist out of her sight and he fought to maintain a regular breathing pattern as she continued.

'He encouraged me to stay up at the weekend, help him *host* his parties. When I refused, he got angry, but he didn't take his anger out on me. The housekeeper's son, who was the general handyman, got fired when my father saw me talking to him, then the gardener went, then his driver of fifteen years. I got the hint and decided to do as I was told. By the

time I turned sixteen, he was entertaining a few nights during the week and most weekends, and the outfits he wanted
me to wear to those parties got…skimpier.'

Rafael's sucked-in breath made her glance up, her eyes
wary. Swiftly he kissed her and nudged her nose with his to
continue. But the white-hot rage inside him blazed higher.

'I knew I had to do something. I asked for the housekeeper's help, even though I knew I was putting her livelihood in
jeopardy. Luckily, she was willing to help. We forged my father's signature and got a DNA test done. When the results
came I showed them to him. He was angry, of course, but he
couldn't refute the evidence any longer.'

'And did things get better?'

She shrugged but Rafael knew the gesture was anything
but uncaring. 'For a time, he reverted to his old, cold indifference. I was hoping he'd take his partying out of the house
but they continued…'

Her lids descended and he saw her lips tremble. Spearing
his fingers in her hair, he tilted her face until she was forced
to look at him. Haunting memory lurked in the green depths.
'Raven, what happened?'

'His…his male friends began to take notice of me.'

'*Que diablos!*' He could no longer stem the tide of anger.
Right that moment, he wanted nothing more than to track
down her bastard of a father and drive his fist into the man's
face. 'They didn't take it further than just noticing, did they?'

The longer she stayed silent, the harder his breathing got.

Ignoring the pain throbbing in his groin and hip, he hauled
himself against the headboard and dragged her up. Tilting her
jaw, he forced her to look into his eyes. 'Did they?'

Her lower lip trembled. 'One of them did. One day after
a party, I thought everyone had left. He…he came into my
room and tried to force himself on me. I'd started training at
the gym so I knew a few moves. I managed to struggle free
and kicked him where it hurt most.'

He passed his thumb over her lips until they stopped trembling. '*Bueno*. Good girl.'

'I ran out of my room. My father was waiting in the hallway. I thought he was coming to help me because he'd heard me scream. But he wasn't…'

Rafael's blood ran cold. 'What was he doing?'

'He knew exactly why his friend had come to my room. In fact, I don't think his friend could've found my room without help.' She shuddered and goose bumps raced over her arms. He pulled her close and wrapped his arms around her.

'Did you report it to the authorities?' he asked.

She shook her head. 'I'd reported him a few times in the past and been ignored. I knew once again it would be his word against mine. I bought a baseball bat and slept with it under my pillow instead and I moved out on my eighteenth birthday.'

'Where is he now?' He entertained thoughts of tracking down the bastard, wielding his own baseball bat.

'I hadn't spoken to him until I called him last year to help my mother but, the last I heard, he'd lost all his money in some Ponzi scheme and is living with his mistress somewhere in Scotland.'

Rafael filed that piece of information away. When she gave another shudder, he kissed her again, a little deeper this time. He made sure when she shuddered again minutes later it was with a different reaction, one that set his blood singing again.

On impulse, he got out of bed and tugged her upright.

'What are you doing?' she asked.

He went into his dressing room and came out with a dark blue T-shirt. 'Put that on.'

'Why? Where are we going?'

'You'll find out in a minute.' He pulled on his shorts and grabbed her hand.

Five minutes later, she pulled at his grip. 'No, I'm not going on there.' She dug her feet into the sand when he would've tumbled her onto the wide beach bed.

'Of course you are. You've been dying to try it since we

got here.' He set down the vintage champagne and flutes he'd grabbed from the kitchen.

'Rafael, it's the middle of the night,' she protested, although her glance slid to the white-canopied bed that gleamed under the moon and starlit night.

'Where's your sense of adventure?'

'Back upstairs, where it doesn't run the risk of being eaten by sharks.'

He let go of her hand and started uncorking the champagne. 'Unless sharks have developed a way of walking on sand, you'll have to come up with a better excuse.'

'I'm not wearing any knickers. I don't want to catch cold.'

His grin was utterly shameless. 'That's a very good reason.' He popped the cork, poured out a glass of golden liquid and handed it to her. Setting the bottle down, he shucked off his shorts and got onto the bed. Casting her a hot glance, he patted the space beside him. 'I'll be your body blanket. If I fail completely in my task you'll be free to return to the safety of my bed.'

He saw her battle for a response. But his insistent patting finally won through. The mixture of hunger, innocence and vulnerability on her face touched a part of him he'd long thought dead. When she set her glass down and slid into his arms, Rafael swore to make her forget everything about her bastard of a father. If only for a few hours.

Why taking on that task meant so much to him, he refused to consider.

He made love to her with a slow, leisurely tempo even though everything inside him clamoured for quick, fiery satisfaction.

When she came apart in his arms, he let himself be swept away into his own release. Sleep wasn't far behind and, gathering her close, he kissed her temple and pulled the cashmere blanket over them.

CHAPTER TEN

THE INTRUSION OF light behind her eyelids came with firm, warm lips brushing her jaw.

'Wake up, *querida*…'

'Hmm, no…don't want to…'

A soft deep laugh. 'Come on, wake up or you'll miss the sunrise.'

'Sun…no…' She wanted to stay just as she was, suspended between dream and reality, entranced by the sultry air on her face and hard, firm…aroused male curved around her.

'Open your eyes. I promise you, it's spectacular.'

She opened her eyes, simply because she couldn't resist him, and found herself gazing into deep blue eyes. Eyes she'd looked into many times. But still her heart caught as if it'd been tugged by a powerful string.

'*Buenos días*,' Rafael murmured. 'Look.' He nodded beyond the canopy to the east. She followed his gaze and froze at the sheer beauty of the gathering sunrise. Orange, yellow and blue where the light faded, it was nature at its most spectacular and she lay there, enfolded in Rafael's arms, silent and in complete awe as the sun spread its stunning rays across the sky.

'Wow,' she whispered.

'Indeed. Does that win me Brownie points?' he whispered hotly into her ear.

Turning from the sight, she looked again into mesmerising eyes. And once again she felt her heart stutter in awe.

'It depends what you intend to use the points for.'

'To get you to come yachting with me today. My yacht is moored at the Marina. We can take her out for the day.'

More alone time with Rafael. *Too much…too much…*

She should've heeded the screeching voice of caution. But

Raven had a feeling she was already too far gone. 'I'd love to. On one condition.'

He mock frowned. '*Condition*…my second least favourite word.'

'What's your least favourite?'

'*No.*'

She laughed. 'That figures. Well, I need to exercise. Then *you* need to have your session. Then we'll go yachting.'

With a quick, hard kiss, he released her and sat back. 'You can do your exercise right here on the beach.'

She felt heat rise. 'While you watch?'

'I'm a harmless audience. Besides, I want to see if this Krav Maga is worth all the hype.'

She bit her lip and hesitated.

'What?' he demanded.

'I…I'm not wearing any knickers, remember?'

His laugh was shameless and filled with predatory anticipation. 'Kinky Krav Maga…sounds even better.' He lounged back against the plump pillows, folded golden muscled arms and waited.

It was the hottest, most erotic exercise routine Raven had ever performed.

The rest of the day went like a dream. Rafael's yacht was the last word in luxury. With a crew of four, they sailed around the Los Cabos islands, stopped at a seafront restaurant for a lunch of ceviche and sweet potato fries, then sunbathed on the twenty-foot deck until it got too hot. Then he encouraged her to join him in the shower below deck.

She clung to him in the aftermath of another pulse-destroying orgasm.

'Hmm…I have a feeling you won't be needing my services for much longer.'

He raised his head from where he'd been kissing her damp shoulder and stared deep into her eyes. 'What makes you say that?'

'You haven't used your cane all day, and your…um…stamina seems to be endless.'

His frown was immediate, edged with tension that seeped into the atmosphere. 'You're signed on for another three months. Don't make any plans to break the contract just yet.' He moved away and grabbed two towels. He handed her one and wrapped the other around her waist, his movements jerky.

'I wasn't making plans. I was just commenting that your movements are a little more fluid. And you haven't used the cane all day today. I think it's a great sign. You should be pleased.'

'Should I?'

His icy tone made alarm skitter over her. 'What's the matter?'

He smoothed a hand over the steamed up mirror and met her gaze over his shoulder. 'Why should anything be wrong?'

'I've just given you the equivalent of an almost clean bill of health. You're reacting as if I've just told you your puppy has died.'

He whirled to face her. 'This clean bill of health, will it pass the X1 training board and see me reinstated as a race driver?'

Her breath caught. 'You're thinking of going back to racing?'

'You sound surprised.'

She licked her lips. 'Well, I am. I thought since Marco had sold the team, and Sasha had quit—'

'What are you saying, that I should follow the family tradition and quit while I'm ahead?'

'No…but—'

'You don't think I can hack it?'

'Stop putting words in my mouth, Rafael. You're almost done with phase three of the physio regime. I'm just trying to find out what your plans are so I can work with you to achieve them.'

He stalked to where she stood and gripped her nape in a

firm hold. His kiss was hot, ravaging and rage-tinged. 'Right now, my only plan is to be inside you again.'

She barely stopped herself from dissolving into a puddle of need. 'And afterwards? We can't stay here indefinitely, indulging in wall-to-wall shagging.'

His eyes narrowed, his grip tightening. 'Are you trying to set a time limit on what's happening between us? Is that what all this is about?'

The shard of steel that lodged in her chest made her breath catch. 'I don't know what you mean.'

'Don't you? From the start you've tried to manage what was happening between us, tried to define it into something you can deal with. Now you want to set a time limit on it so you can walk away once the time comes, *si*?'

'Are you saying you're not? Am I not just one more challenge to you? Can we please not delude ourselves into thinking this is anything more than sex?'

He sucked in a breath as if he'd been punched. Stepping back, he dropped his hand and left the bathroom.

Raven trailed after him into the large, exquisite gold and cream cabin. He was pulling on a pair of boxers, which he followed with cargo shorts and a white T-shirt.

Feeling exposed, she slipped on her underwear and the lilac flowered slip dress she'd worn to go sailing. 'I'm not sure what's going on here, Rafael. Or why you're annoyed with me. I may not know the rules of this sleeping together thing but even I know there is a time limit when it comes to your affairs—'

'*Affairs*? Is that what we're doing, having an affair?' he asked with a cocked eyebrow. 'How quaint.'

'Will you please stop mocking me and tell me what's really bothering you?'

He slammed the drawer he'd just opened none too gently. 'I don't like time limits. I don't being head-shrunk. And I don't like the woman I'm sleeping with hinting that she'll be leaving me the day after we start sleeping together. There, does that sum things up for you?'

'So you want to be the one to call the shots? To dictate when this aff...*liaison* starts and ends?'

He dragged a hand through his damp hair and glared at her. '*Santo cielo*, why are we even having this argument?' he shouted.

'I have no idea but you started it!' she yelled back.

His eyes widened at her tone, then he sighed. 'Forgive me, I'm used to having things my way, *pequeña*. You have every right to shout at me when I step out of line.'

'Thanks, I will.'

He laughed, and just like that the tension broke. Striding to her, he tugged her into his arms and proceeded to kiss the fight out of both of them. They sailed back to the villa shortly after and, once again, she let him coax her into spending part of the night on the beach bed.

They were halfway through their breakfast when the delivery arrived.

'What is it?'

'I've got something for you.' The gleam in his eyes was pure wickedness. Her heartbeat escalated as she eyed the large gold-ribboned package sitting on the floor beside their breakfast table.

'Don't worry, you'll enjoy it,' he promised with a smile so sexy, and so deliciously decadent, her toes curled.

Even though the subject quickly changed to their plans for the rest of the day, Raven's gaze strayed time and again to the package. But Rafael, as she'd discovered in the past two nights, was skilled in delayed gratification. He was also skilled in being the perfect host. She was stunned when she discovered how many details he'd picked up through their conversation. When he shepherded her towards the SUV mid-morning, she gaped in surprise when she found out he'd organised the hang-gliding trip she'd casually mentioned was on her list of things to do.

She'd barely descended from that high when he whisked her by helicopter to the Mayan encampment she'd been dying to explore.

'You're seriously scaring me now by how utterly close I am to adoring you for this,' she said in hushed tones as they were ushered into the hallowed grounds of the ancient burial site.

His breath hissed out. When she glanced at him, he'd paled a little.

'Rafael? Are you in pain?' He'd left his walking stick back at the villa and nothing from his gait told her he'd suffered a mishap. All the same…

He shook his head. A second later the look had disappeared. 'It's nothing.'

She stopped as the full import of her words struck her. Wide-eyed, she turned to him. 'No, I didn't mean…I was only joking…'

'Were you?' The intensity of his gaze pinned her where she stood.

'Yes! Ignore me, I'm babbling because you've made two dreams come true today.'

'So you don't adore me?'

She opened her mouth to refute the comment and found she couldn't speak. Because she realised she did adore him, and more than a little. The Rafael she'd come to know in the past few weeks had a depth she'd never got the chance to explore last year. She felt a connection to this Rafael, and not just because he'd been her first lover.

The depth of the feeling rampaging through her made her shake her head.

One corner of his mouth lifted in a mirthless smile. Then he nodded to the tour guide looking their way.

'Now that we've established that you *don't* adore me, I think you need to go see your artefacts.'

She felt a stab of disappointment. 'Aren't you coming?'

'Been there, done that.' He pulled the phone from his pocket. 'The drivers and cars arrive this afternoon. I need to return a few calls.' He walked away before she could reply.

Disappointment morphed into something else. Something she couldn't put her finger on but which confused the hell out of her. The more she tried to grasp it, the further away it slithered from her.

He was waiting when she finally emerged. Back in the helicopter, he pulled her close and sealed his lips over hers, his mouth hungry and demanding.

She was breathless when he finally pulled away. 'What was that for?' she asked huskily.

His lids swept down over his eyes. 'Maybe I want you to adore me, just a little.'

Rafael watched her breath catch all over again and wondered just what the hell he was doing. Why he was letting the angst riding underneath his skin get to him.

So she didn't adore him. Big deal. There were thousands of women out there who were more than willing to fall into his bed should he wish them to.

But none like the woman in his arms. None like the woman who refused to mould into a being he understood, could predict. Most women would be halfway to falling in love with him by now; would be secretly or not so secretly making plans on how to prolong their presence in his life.

When he wasn't kissing her breathless—a diversionary tactic he'd grown to enjoy immensely—Raven seemed to be counting the days, hell, the minutes until she could walk away from him.

The notion unsettled him enough to make him want to probe, to find an answer.

Had she glimpsed the darkness in his soul? Had opening up to her in Monaco and again in Monza made him into a man she could sleep with but not a man she wanted in her life for the long-term?

The long-term? Santa María. Had he finally lost all common sense? Certainly, reality had slid back these past two days. Being with her had been like living some sort of dream. A dream where he could look at himself in the mirror without being revolted by what stared back at him.

A dream where he could continue the secret writing project he'd started before his accident without feeling as if he was tainting the very memory he wanted to preserve.

He stared down into her face, a face flushed with pleasure from the activities of the day or, he thought semi-cockily, from kissing him. All at once he wanted to blurt his very innermost secret to her.

He stopped himself just in time.

Permanent wasn't part of his vocabulary. He wasn't about to seek it out now. And, really, he should thank his lucky stars because Raven knew his flaws and had adequately cautioned herself against getting too close.

So why did the thought not please him?

His phone rang and he happily abandoned the questions that threatened to flood him. But he didn't abandon his hold on the soft body of the woman next to him. Delight curled in his chest when she slid closer.

'De Cervantes,' he answered.

The conversation was short and succinct. And it raised every single hair on his nape to full, electrifying attention. Feeling slightly numb, he ended the call.

'What's happened?' she asked.

'One of the drivers has pulled out of the remaining races.'

'Can they do that, pull out without warning?'

He shook his head. 'I've never had a driver pull out before. Normally I have them begging to race.' She didn't miss the frown in his voice. 'But he's just been offered a race seat for the coming season and it's an opportunity of a lifetime. I recognise how important that is to a young driver.'

'So what does that mean for your event?' she asked, pulling back to stare up into his face.

He looked down but didn't really see her. The thoughts tumbling through his head both terrified and excited him at the same time.

'They can find a replacement if they search hard enough...'

Raven pulled away further. He wanted to tug her back but he couldn't seem to summon the strength it took because of the feelings rushing through him.

'Or?'

'Or...the general consensus is that I should step in.'

'No,' she said. Naked fear pulsed through the single word.

He finally focused on her, felt a burn in his stomach from the impact of her searing look. 'No?'

'You're not ready.'

'Shouldn't *I* be the judge of that? And didn't you say yourself I was almost healed?' he asked.

'Yes, *almost!* As your physiotherapist, I strongly do not recommend it. You could reverse everything you've achieved in the last several weeks...'

'If I crash?'

She paled a little, and he felt a tug of guilt for pushing her. 'I won't answer that. What I will say is that you're the head of X1 Premier Management. All you need to do is make a single phone call and any one of dozens of drivers will fly out and take your driver's place. You don't have to do this. *Please don't do it.*'

The naked plea in her eyes struck deep. The unsettling angst of a moment before subsided as he traced his finger down her face.

'Dare I believe that you care about me, just a little bit?' He couldn't stop the question from spilling out. But, once it was out there, he *needed* to know.

'I care, Rafael. More than a little bit, I think.' The naked truth struck them both. Their eyes met, locked.

Breaths held until the banking helicopter jolted them. The sight of the villa sprawled beneath them made Rafael want to swear. Instead he activated his phone again.

'Angelo—' he addressed his second-in-command '—call around the teams, find out if there's any driver who isn't testing and offer them a place on the newly available seat on the All-Star event. You know which guys I rate the most. Tell them they're guaranteed a spread in the next issue of *X1 Magazine* and my personal endorsement of whatever charity they choose. Oh, and I want a driver on his way to the racetrack in Los Cabos by the end of the day.' He ended the call and looked down at her.

'Now what?' he asked softly as the helicopter blades slowed to a halt.

Her smile held such radiance he found it hard to breathe. 'Now, I may let myself adore you a little bit more...see where it takes me.'

He regretted that he wasn't healed enough to swing her into his arms and carry her off to his lair. But he was well enough to drag her from the helicopter to his bedroom. And he made sure he kept her fully occupied until neither of them could move.

'You never told me what was in the package,' Raven murmured, drifting somewhere between *I-can't-move* satiation and a drugging need to experience that mind-bending pleasure all over again.

The wicked grin he sent her way made her heart pound all over again. He left the bed and she could no more help herself from visually devouring him than she could stop breathing.

He picked up the package from the foot of the bed and returned it to her. 'This may just buy me a few more Brownie points.'

That got her attention. She dragged herself up to lean on one elbow. The sight of his naked chest threatened to fry her brain cells. 'What is it?' Her mind whirled with the possibilities, then latched onto what she wanted it to be. Could it be the rest of his manuscript?

Her senses now on a high, she stared down at the box,

feeling like a kid on Christmas morning. 'What's in the box, Rafael?'

He lifted the lid. All she could see were sheaves of wrapping paper. 'See for yourself.'

Carefully, she lifted the sheer paper. The first items made her heart knock in her chest. And not in a good way. Praying she was dreaming, she nudged the material aside with her finger and looked underneath. Each layer held more of the same.

'Naughty underwear? *That's* what you got me?' Raven let the garments drop back into the box, unable to stem the cold wave of hurt that washed over her. She wasn't even sure why it hurt so much. But it felt as if she'd climbed a mountain only to look back and find out that she'd only taken a few steps.

He looked genuinely stunned. 'You don't like it?'

'What's wrong with my own underwear?'

His perplexed look deepened. For the first time, Rafael looked seriously nonplussed. It would have been funny had it not been so far from funny.

'I didn't…I just wanted to…' He stopped, a flush lighting his high cheekbones.

If someone had told her as little as a week ago that she'd be sitting in bed discussing naughty lingerie with Rafael, she'd have laughed herself blind.

Now, she forced herself to glance at the lacy silks and delicate satin bows that didn't seem as if they would stand up to any overt pressure.

'That's not even my size, Rafael. I'm a size twelve, remember?'

His flush deepened. 'I have a feeling you'll punch me when I tell you I don't have a clue what size underwear you wear or what yours look like. By the time I get to your panties, I'm nearly insane with lust. Damn it. I've got it spectacularly wrong, haven't I?'

'Not all wrong. You got my favourite colours right.'

He picked up the package and flung it across the room.

Then he tugged her close. 'Is there any way I can make you forget the last ten minutes?'

Against her will and certainly against her better judgement, she glanced at the lilac silk material caught over a chair back. It seemed so delicate and forlorn.

'I don't need expensive lingerie to feel sexy. If you don't want me as I am—'

He caught her chin between his fingers. 'I do,' he breathed. 'Let me prove it…' His head started to descend.

Raven's gaze swung once more to the basque. Pulling herself from his arms, she walked, naked, to the garment and plucked it off the chair. Carefully, she rubbed the material between her fingers and turned. Rafael's breath caught as she slowly traced the warm silk over her body.

A glance from beneath her lashes showed a definite effect on him.

Pure feminine power washed away her misgivings. With a wanton smile she'd never have believed herself capable of, she sauntered back towards him.

'You need to understand one thing, Rafael.'

He nodded but his eyes were riveted on her breasts. '*Sí*?'

'You promise never to buy me lingerie again as long as we're together. I choose my own underwear.'

He swallowed and nodded.

Raven glanced down at the panties and shook her head. 'I can't believe you thought I was a size eight,' she muttered.

'*Por favor!* Forgive me.' He wet his lips in such a blatantly sexual way, a blush suffused her whole body.

'You're just saying that so I hurry back to bed.'

'*Sí*. And you can forget the lingerie if you wish.'

'And give up the chance to see you sweat. No can do.' She slowly, deliberately swept her hair to one side before sliding the lace-trimmed garment over her head.

She nearly bottled it then, but the scorching intensity in his eyes had the direct effect of firing up her courage. The soft lilac tulle basque hugged her breasts in such a blatant caress, she bit her lower lip to stop a moan of excitement. She turned, then glanced back over her shoulder.

'Are you going to help me with the laces?' she rasped.

'*Dios mío*, what are you trying to do?'

'Teach you a lesson.'

He got off the bed, almost a little too eager for his punishment. 'Turn around,' he instructed.

She did, and heard him hiss out a breath as he pulled the delicate laces and tied it.

'Once again, I have no knickers.'

His moan was a heartfelt balm to her soul.

Turning, she placed her hands on her hips, feminine power fuelling her desire as she saw her effect on him.

When he stumbled back and sank onto the side of the bed, she laughed. 'Hoisted by your own petard, Rafael?'

She took a step towards him and gloried in the slide of the silk on her skin. She would never don anything like this again. Naughty lingerie wasn't really her style but, just for tonight, she would allow herself this experience.

His face was strained like the steely erection that jutted from between his legs. Heat oozed between her thighs, made her movements slow as the magnetic force between them pulled her inexorably into his orbit.

When she reached him, she raked her fingers down his chest. 'You won't see me like this again, Rafael, so look your fill.'

His features altered, a look of regret passing through his eyes that made her stomach hollow out. 'You're breathtaking without it, Raven. How can I make this up to you?'

Her heart thundered at the sincerity in his voice. 'You don't need to. Just see me as I am.'

He inhaled, long and deep, and dropped his head between her breasts. For a long moment, Raven held him close. Then his breathing altered. Hers followed as lust sizzled, rose to the fore once more.

She pushed him back on the bed and climbed on top of him. By the time he donned the condom, they were both nearly insane with need. She'd barely positioned her thighs on either side of him when he thrust hard and deep inside her. Raven lost all coherent thought.

In the sizzling, excruciatingly heady aftermath, she curled into him but found she couldn't breathe, even after his deft fingers pulled the basque from her body and flung it away. She'd always known that Rafael's dominance was larger than life. But she'd trusted herself not to get pulled into his devastating, fast-spinning orbit. Her emotions were fast skittering out of control. How long had she watched her mother experience the same devastation over and over? Now she was running the same risk—

'What is it?' he demanded, his intuitiveness almost scary.

'Nothing…' she started to say, then stopped. 'How many times have you done this?' she blurted.

'I think I definitely need a definition of *this,* otherwise I'll have to plead the fifth.'

'Bought risqué underwear for a woman?'

His lids dropped for a second before rising to spear her with that intense blue. 'Never.'

Her snort was borne of disbelief and a sharp pang she didn't want to touch with a dozen bargepoles. She shook her head and started to move away.

He caught her back easily. A shiver ran through her when his finger slid under her chin and tilted her head up. Almost afraid, she looked into his eyes.

'I've never lied to you, Raven. I'm skilled in evading subjects I don't wish to discuss, but I have never and will never lie to you. Understood?'

She was stunned by how much she wanted to believe him, how much she wanted to be the first at something in his life. 'Why haven't you done this before?'

Surprise flared in his eyes. 'You're asking me why I haven't bought lingerie for a woman before?'

She pursed her lips. 'It seems the kind of thing ruthless playboys specialise in.'

His own lips flattened at the label, then he shrugged and relaxed onto the pillows. 'Not specialise. I have knowledge of it because I'm always the recipient. The assumption has always been that I would prefer the bedroom unveiling to be a knock-my-brains-out surprise, not a joint enterprise. I haven't felt the inclination to alter that assumption.'

A small fizz of pleasure started in her belly. Which was really foolish because she knew this particular experiment had been a means to an end for him.

Unwilling to face up to what all this meant, she buried her face in his neck. 'I'm glad.'

'Enough to forgive my grievous error?'

'That depends.'

'On?'

'On whether you'll give me what I expected to find in the box when I opened it.' She told him.

Another peculiar look crossed his face. 'The story has reached a crossroads.'

'Are you saying I did all of that for nothing?'

He pushed her firmly onto her back and leaned his powerful, endlessly intoxicating body over hers. Unable to resist, she let her hands wander at will over smooth muscle.

'For nothing? No, *bonita*, it was most definitely not for nothing. I think you could be the key to unlocking everything.'

Although she went into his arms at his urging, Raven sensed he wasn't as in control as he made out. She'd heard a different note in his voice—part vulnerability, part bravado. She slid her hand up and down his back in a strong need to comfort him. The persistent voice that had cautioned against getting too deep was receding—almost as if it knew the path she'd chosen. She would live in this fantasy now.

This magic, this overwhelming sense that she was exactly

where she wanted to be, was too great to deny. Reality would encroach soon enough.

So where was the harm in experiencing it for a little while longer?

CHAPTER ELEVEN

IT TURNED OUT a little while was all she would get.

Things started to go wrong the moment the helicopter touched down at the Autódromo Hermanos Rodríguez in Mexico City the next morning. The replacement driver Angelo had lined up didn't turn up. As the day went on with no immediate solution, Raven felt the pressure mount as everyone turned to Rafael for a solution.

Even though this was primarily a charity event, high profile sponsors had channelled millions of euros into it in the hope of gaining maximum exposure, courtesy of the sold-out events. Racing five cars instead of the usual six would make the headlines and throw negative publicity on the event—something X1 Premier Management and Rafael in particular couldn't afford to let happen.

Already the paparazzi, sensing blood in the water, were sniffing around, cameras and microphones poised to capture any salacious gossip.

She recalled how they'd decimated Sasha de Cervantes and her gut churned at the thought of what that type of publicity could do to Rafael.

As if she'd conjured him up, Rafael walked past the window, his pace carrying him from one end of the air-conditioned VIP lounge to the other, his gait remarkably improved despite the physical stress she'd put on his body in the last three days.

Feeling a blush creep up her face, she glanced away before he or any of the other management team hastily assembled for the meeting could guess at her thoughts.

Angelo, Rafael's assistant, approached him, a phone in his

hand. Rafael listened for several seconds, his tension increasing with each breath he took.

'Tell him if he threatens me with a lawsuit one more time, I'll personally see to it that his brand of vodka never leaves the icy wilderness of Siberia…*bueno*, I'm pleased you're finally seeing things my way. We will find a driver, and your logo will be emblazoned on the side pod just as we agreed.'

He hung up, glanced around the room and caught a few nervous gazes. 'They want to play dirty; I'm more than happy to oblige.'

A three-time world champion, now in his early sixties, cleared his throat. 'The race starts in three hours. I don't see that we have much of a choice here. You all but agreed to step in two days ago when we were a driver short. I'm not sure what changed your mind but perhaps you'd revisit the idea of racing?'

Raven half rose out of her seat, the scrape of her chair on the tiled floor drawing attention from the rest of the room.

She collapsed back into her seat when Rafael's fierce gaze settled on her. When the quick shake of her head didn't seem to register, she cleared her throat.

His eyes narrowed. Then he turned, slowly, deliberately away from her.

A block of ice wedged in her chest and her stomach hollowed out. From very far away, she heard him address the race coordinator and chief engineer of the driverless team.

'I have a couple of spare seats around here somewhere. Angelo will arrange to supply you with one to fit into the car. I'll be along in ten minutes to go over race strategy with you.' He looked around the room, the devil's own grin spreading over his face. 'Gentlemen, let's go racing.'

The explosion of excitement that burst through the room drowned out her horrified gasp. Manly slaps of his shoulder and offers of congratulations echoed through her numb senses.

When someone suggested a quick press conference, Raven

finally found the strength to stand and approach him as the room emptied.

'R…Rafael, can I talk to you?'

'Now is not a good time, *bonita*.' His voice was brusque to the point of rudeness.

The endearment she was beginning to adore suddenly grated. But she refused to be dismissed. 'I think this is a bad idea.'

'*Sí*, I knew you would think so. But I can't help what you think. Needs must and I stand to become embroiled in all sorts of legal wrangling if this isn't sorted out.'

She frowned. 'But it was the driver who broke the contract. Isn't he liable?'

'No, he isn't. XPM is staging this event, so I'm responsible. I should've taken more time to ensure contingencies were in place before we arrived. Everyone here knows someone's dropped the ball. Unfortunately, they're looking at me to pick it up and run with it.' He was the hard businessman, the ruthless racer who'd held a finite edge over his competitors for years.

He was certainly nothing like the lover who'd taken her to the heights of ecstasy.

She fought to regain her own professionalism, to put aside the hurt splintering her insides. 'As your physiotherapist, I'll have to recommend that you don't race.'

'Your recommendation is duly noted. Is that all?'

Her fists clenched in futile anger. Anger she wanted to let loose but couldn't. Her days of lashing out were far, far behind her. 'No, that's not all! This is crazy. You're risking your health, not to mention your life, Rafael.'

His smile was tight and tension-filled. 'And *you* are running the risk of overstepping, *querida*. I won't be tacky enough to point out just what your role is in my life considering the lines have been blurred somewhat, but I expect you to recognise the proper time and place for voicing disagreement.'

The blunt words hit her like a slap in the face. Regret momentarily tightened his face, then it smoothed once again into the outward mask of almost bored indifference.

It took every ounce of self-control to contain her composure. 'No, you're right. Pardon me for thinking of your health first.' She indicated the frenzy outside, the racetrack and the baking heat under which the cars gleamed. 'Off you go, then. And good luck.'

He reached forward and grabbed her arm when she'd have turned away.

'Aren't you forgetting something?'

'What?' She made herself look into his eyes, determined not to be cowed by the storm of fear rolling through her gut. He returned her look with one that momentarily confused her. Had her thoughts been clearer, Raven would've sworn Rafael was scared out of his wits.

'As my physio, you need to come with me, attend to my needs until I'm in the cockpit. Have you forgotten your role already?'

She had. Whether intentionally or through mental blockage, she'd tried to put her role eight months ago as Rafael's race physio out of her mind. Because every time she thought of it, she remembered their last row. Her rash, heated words; the stunned look on his face as he'd absorbed her bone-stripping insults before he'd walked out to his car. They'd been in a situation like this, momentarily alone in a place that buzzed with suppressed energy. His race suit had been open and around his neck she'd spied his customary chain with the cross on it. The cross he kissed before each race.

In the months since, she'd remembered vividly that Rafael hadn't kissed his cross that day...

Now, Raven was in favour of forgetting all about it. All she wanted to do right now was find a dark corner, stay there and not come out until the blasted race was over. Watching his crash that day had been one of the most heart-wrenching experiences of her life. She would give anything not to be put in that position again.

But she had a job to do. Sucking a sustaining breath, she nodded. 'Of course, whatever you need.' Pulling herself from his grasp, she walked towards the bar and picked up two bottles of mineral water. She handed him one. 'We're a little late off the mark in trying to hydrate you sufficiently so I'd suggest you get as much liquid in as possible.'

He took the bottle from her but made no move to drink the water.

'You think I'm making the wrong decision.' It wasn't a question.

'What I think is no longer relevant, remember?' Her gaze dropped meaningfully to the bottle.

He uncapped it and drank without taking his gaze off her face. She felt the heavy force of his stare but studiously avoided eye contact. When he finished and tossed the empty bottle aside, she handed him the second bottle.

'Drink this one in about ten minutes.' She started to walk towards the door, eager to get away from the clamouring need to throw herself in his path, to stop him putting himself in any danger.

Too late, she realised the media had camped outside the door, eager to jump on the latest news of Rafael's return.

Is this the start of your comeback?

Are you sure you can take the pressure?

Which team will you be driving for when the X1 season starts next month?

Rafael fielded their questions without breaking a sweat, all the while keeping a firm hold on her elbow. Every time she tried to free herself, he held on tighter.

Raven spotted the keen reporter from the corner of her eye.

Is there a new woman in your life?

Without the barest hint of affront, he smiled. 'If I told you that you'd stop hounding me, then my life would no longer be worth living, would it?'

The paparazzi, normally a vicious thrill-seeking lot, actually laughed. Raven marvelled at the spectacle. Then berated herself for failing to realise the obvious. Sooner or later, everyone, man, woman or child, fell under Rafael's uniquely enthralling spell.

She'd fooled herself into believing she could fall only a little, that she could go only so far before, wisely and safely, she pulled back from the dizzying precipice.

How wrong she'd been. Wasn't she right now experiencing the very depths of hell because she couldn't stand the thought of him being hurt again?

Hadn't she spent half the night awake, her stomach tied in knots as she'd wondered why so beautiful a man suffered tortured dreams because of his choices and his determination to shut everyone out?

She hadn't missed the phone calls from his father that he'd avoided, or the one from Marco yesterday that he'd swiftly ended when she entered the room.

Pain stabbed deep as she acknowledged that she'd come to adore him just a little bit more than she'd planned to. She'd probably started adoring him the moment he'd answered her call and agreed to see her in Barcelona seven weeks ago.

Because by allowing her in just that little bit meant he didn't hate her as much as he should. Or maybe he didn't hate her at all.

Or maybe she was deluding herself.

'A three-line frown. Stop it or I'll have to do something drastic, like confirm to them just who the new woman in my life is. Personally, I don't mind drastic but I have a feeling you wouldn't enjoy being eaten alive by the paparazzi.'

She'd been walking alongside him without conscious thought as to where they were going. The sound of the engine revving made her jump. 'No, I wouldn't.'

'*Bueno*, then behave.'

They'd arrived at the garage of the defected racer. Rafael grabbed the nearest sound-cancelling headphones and passed them to her.

She was about to put them on when she spotted Chantilly,

lounging with a bored look on her face on the other side of the garage. The second she spotted Rafael, she came to vivacious life.

'Damn it, your frown just deepened. What did I say about behaving?'

'What's she doing here? In this garage, I mean?'

Rafael followed her gaze to Chantilly, then glanced back at her. 'Her husband owns this team.'

The single swear word escaped before she could stop it. A slow grin spread over Rafael's face but it didn't pack the same charismatic punch as it usually did. Examining him closer, she noted the lines of strain around his mouth.

'Sheath your claws, *chiquita*. I told you, I have no interest in her. Not after discovering the delights of fresh English roses.' A pulse of heat from his eyes calmed her somewhat but it was gone far too quickly for her to feel its warmth.

The chief engineer called out for Rafael and, with another haunted look down at her, he went over to discuss telemetry reports with the team.

The ninety minutes before the race passed with excruciating slowness. With every second that counted down, Raven's insides knotted harder. The walk across the sun-baked pit lane into the race lane felt like walking the most terrifying gauntlet.

She hitched the emergency bag higher on her shoulder and took her place beside Rafael's car, making sure to keep the umbrella above his head to protect his suit-clad body from overheating. She ignored the sweat trickling down her own back to check for signs of distress on him.

'If you feel your hip tightening, try those pelvic rotations we practised by flexing your spine. I know you don't have much room in the cockpit but give it a try anyway,' she said, trying desperately to hang on to a modicum of professionalism.

He nodded but didn't look up. His attention was fixed on the dials on his steering wheel. When the first red light flashed on, signalling it was time to clear the track, Raven opened her mouth to say something…anything, but her throat had closed up.

She took one step back, and another.

'Rafael…' she whispered.

His head swung towards her, ice-blue eyes capturing hers for a single naked second.

The stark emptiness in his eyes made her heart freeze over.

Rafael fought to regulate his breathing. Shards of memories pierced his mind, drenching his spine and palms in cold sweat.

His fight with Marco the night before the Hungary race…

You're dishonouring Mamá's memory by continuing with this reckless behaviour…

Sasha's voice joined the clamouring…*it's not okay for you to let everyone think you're a bastard.*

And Raven's condemning truth…*you're a useless waste of space…who cares about nothing but himself and his own vacuous pleasures…*

He tried to clear his mind but he knew it wouldn't be that easy. Those words had carried him into that near fatal corner that day in Hungary because he'd known they all spoke the truth. What they hadn't known was that the day had held another meaning for him. It was emblazoned into his memory like a hot iron brand.

That day in Hungary had been exactly eight years to the day he'd charmed his mother into the ride that had ended her life…the day he'd let partying too hard snuff out a life he'd now happily give his own to have returned.

Looking into Raven's eyes just now, he'd known she was recalling her words, too; he'd seen the naked fear and remorse in her eyes. But he hadn't been able to offer reassurance.

How could he, when he knew deep down she was right? Since his mother's death, he'd lived in the special place in hell he'd reserved for himself. That *no trespassing* place where no one and nothing was allowed to touch him.

It was a place he planned on staying…

No matter how horrifyingly lonely…

His gaze darted to the lights as they lit up. Jaw tight, he tried to empty his mind of all thought, but her face kept intruding…her pleading eyes boring into his ravaged soul despite every effort to block her out.

Que diablos!

He stepped on the accelerator a touch later than he'd planned and cursed again as Axel Jung and Matteo, the teenage driver, shot past him on either side. Even in a showcase event like this one, a fraction of a second was all it took to fall behind.

Adrenaline and age-old reflexes kicked in but Rafael knew he was already at a disadvantage. He eyed the gap to the right on the second corner, and calculated that he could slot himself in there if he was quick enough. He pressed his foot down and felt his pulse jump when Axel, in a bid to cut him off, positioned himself in front of him.

In a move he'd perfected long before he'd been tall enough to fit into an X1 cockpit, he flicked his wrist and dashed down the left side of the track. Too late, Axel tried to cover his mistake but Rafael was already a nose ahead of the German. From the corner of his eye, he saw the other driver flick him a dirty gesture.

Where normally he'd have grinned with delight behind his helmet, Rafael merely gestured back and pressed down even harder on the accelerator, desperately trying to outrun his demons the way he had that day in Hungary.

You're not all bad…

Yes, he was. Even his father looked at him with pity and sadness.

His father…the man he'd put in a wheelchair. The man who kept calling and leaving him messages because Rafael was too afraid…too ashamed to talk to him.

The car shot forward faster. Inside his helmet, his race engineer's voice cautioned him on the upcoming bend. The words barely registered before disappearing under the heavy weight of his thoughts. He took the bend without lifting off the throttle or easing back on his speed.

He heard the muted roar of the appreciative crowd but the spark of excitement he'd expected from the recognition that he was still in fine racing form, that his accident hadn't made him lose what was most important to him, didn't manifest.

That was when the panic started.

For as long as he could recall, that excitement had been present. No matter what else was going on in his life, racing was the one thing that had always...*always* given him a thrill, given him a reason to push forward.

Fear clutched his chest as he searched for and found only emptiness. In front of him, Matteo had made a mistake that had cost him a few milliseconds, bringing Rafael into passing distance of him.

He could pass him, using the same move he'd used in Hungary. He had nothing to lose. The grin that spread over his face felt alien yet oddly calming, as did the black haze that started to wash over his eyes.

He had nothing to lose...

'Rafael, your liquid level readings show you haven't taken a drink in the last thirty minutes.'

Her voice...husky, low, and filled with fearful apprehension, shot into his head with the power of a thunderclap. He gasped as he felt himself yanked back from the edge, from the dark abyss he'd been staring into.

For a single second, he hated her for intruding.

'Rafael?'

Sucking in a breath, he glanced up and realised Matteo had regained his speed and was streaking ahead. And still, Rafael felt...nothing.

'Rafael, please respond.' A shaky plea.

He didn't, because he couldn't speak, but he took a drink and kept his foot on the pedal until the race was over.

The shoulder slaps of congratulations for coming in second washed right over him. On the podium, he smiled, congratulated Axel and even felt a little spurt of pride when Matteo took the top step, but all through it he was numb.

The moment he stepped off the podium, he ripped off his race suit. He brushed away the engineer's request for a post race analysis, his every sense shrieking warning of imminent disaster.

He rushed out of the garage, for the first time in his life ignoring the media pen, the paparazzi and news anchors who raced after him for a sound bite.

Relief rushed through him as he entered his motor home and slammed the door shut behind him.

'Rafael?'

Dios mío. Had he lost it so completely he was now hearing her voice in his head? Bile surged through his stomach and leapt into his throat. He barely made it to the bathroom before he retched with a violence that made his eyes water.

For several minutes he hunched over the bowl, feelings coursing through him that he couldn't name. No…he knew what those feelings were, it was just that he'd never allowed them room in his life.

He was a racing driver. Racing was his lifeblood. Therefore he had no room for despair or fear. He was used to success, to adrenaline-fuelled excitement. To pride and satisfaction in what he did. So why the hell was he puking his guts out while fear churned through his veins?

Because, *diablo*, he *had* finally parted ways with reality.

With a stark laugh and a shake of his head, he cleaned up after himself, rinsed his mouth thoroughly…

And turned to find Raven in the doorway, her face deathly pale and her gorgeous eyes wide with panic.

'*Madre de dios.* What the hell are you doing here?'

CHAPTER TWELVE

'ARE YOU ALL right?' Raven asked, making a small movement forward.

Rafael instinctively stepped back from her. If she touched him, she would know. And whatever else he was…*or wasn't*, the last thing he wanted Raven Blass, this infuriatingly bright, mind-bendingly sexy woman, to see was his fear.

He took another step back, feeling more exposed than he'd ever felt in his life.

The water he'd splashed over his face chilled his skin. 'Am I all right? Sure. I puke my guts out after every race. Didn't you know that?'

'No you don't.' She took another step closer and, instantly, another more urgent need surged to the fore. The need to grab her, plaster her warm, giving body against his, use her to stem the tide of icy numbness spreading over him.

Use her…

Bile threatened to rise again and he swallowed hard. He stepped past her, entered the bedroom and started to undress.

'Tell me what's wrong.'

Rafael glanced down at his hands and realised they were shaking. The realisation stunned him so completely, his whole body shuddered before he could control himself. The idea that he was losing control so completely, so unstoppably, made irrational anger whip up inside him.

'Stop it, Raven. Stop trying to save me. You've done your penance.'

'Excuse me?' Her voice was hushed but strong.

'That's what you've wanted since you phoned me up two months ago, isn't it? To hear that I forgive you for what you think you did to cause my accident?'

'What I think…' She sucked in a sharp breath. 'Are you saying you remember why you crashed?'

He firmed his lips. *Brava*, Rafael. 'Perhaps I do. Or perhaps I'm just tired of watching you fall on your sword over and over again. I wouldn't be surprised if that was why you gave me your virginity, considering you didn't like me much before then.'

He felt like the lowest form of life when her colour receded completely. But, *dios*, admiringly she rallied.

'You're trying to push me away by being hateful. But I won't leave until you tell me what happened out there today.'

'What do you mean, what happened? I raced. I came second. Considering I've been out of the game for nearly a year, I think that's a commendable start, don't you?'

He shucked his suit and peeled off the fire-retardant long-sleeved gear. Her eyes darkened but she didn't lose her determination.

'Aside from the fact that you didn't hydrate nearly enough, why did you not pass Matteo the half a dozen times you had the chance?'

'What are you talking about? After he recovered his mistake in Sector 4 there was never a chance to pass Matteo…'

'Of course there was. He damaged his front wing when he went too close to the pit wall on his exit but you stayed behind him when you could've passed. And many times you came close to passing him but you pulled back every time. Your race engineer tried to talk to you but you didn't respond.'

He froze, scrambled around to supply the adequate information to refute her words and came up blank. Panic cloaked his skin, sank its claws deeper into him.

'Are you saying you don't remember?' she almost whispered, her voice thick with emotion.

Rafael couldn't breathe. 'I…no, I don't remember.'

The black haze crowded his mind, encroaching rapidly with each excruciating second. He knew he was in deep trouble when he didn't stop her from touching him, from pulling him down to sit on the king-sized bed.

'Rafael, you're freezing. And you're shaking!'

His laugh was hollow. '*Sí.* In case you haven't guessed yet, *querida*, I'm a hot mess right now.'

'Oh God!' She threw her arms around him, her warm hands pressing into his skin.

Another series of shudders raked through him, setting his teeth chattering. Her fingers speared through his hair, pulling him down into the crook of her neck. He wanted to move, *needed* to move. But he stayed right where he was, selfishly absorbing her warmth, her heady scent, inhaling her very essence as if that would save him. But nothing could save him. He was beyond redemption in more ways than he could count.

Blanking out behind the wheel had cemented the realisation.

And still he found himself leaning into her, his lips finding that soft, sweet spot below her ear lobe where he knew she loved to be kissed. He kissed it, felt her try to shift away, and trapped her in his arms.

'Rafael…'

He trailed his mouth down her neck, to the pulse that jumped when he flicked his tongue against it.

The shaking receded a little, the numbness fading under the pulse of seductive heat that was all Raven. Greedily, he tried to grab onto it, to delay the encroaching darkness beneath the bliss of her touch. With a deep groan, he moved to cup her breasts.

Only to fall into a deeper hell when she pulled away and rushed to her feet.

'Sex isn't going to make this problem go away.'

Darkness prowled closer. 'I know, but a guy can still dream, can't he?'

'No, it's time for reality. We need to discuss what happened. When I saw you throwing up, I thought it was a panic attack. But I think it's more than that,' she said.

Ice snapped through him, freezing him once more to the soul. 'Leave it, Raven.'

'No, you need help, Rafael.'

He couldn't hold her gaze—she saw far too much—so he concentrated on his clenched fists. 'And you think you're the one to offer that help?'

He knew his tone was unduly harsh but he had gone beyond remorse. He was in his special frozen place.

'What happened?' Her voice pleaded for understanding.

Since he was at a loss himself, he contemplated silence. Then he contemplated seduction. When bile threatened, he contemplated pleading for mercy.

Through frozen lips, he found himself speaking. 'I remembered everything about the race in Hungary.'

He looked up to see her hands fly to her lips. He gave a grim smile and stared back down at his hands. Hands that shook uncontrollably.

'You know what I remember most about it?'

She shook her head.

'As I went to the wall, I knew, no matter what happened, no matter how hard I tried, I wasn't going to die.'

'You mean you…*wanted* to die?' Horror coated her words.

He shrugged. 'It doesn't matter what I wanted. I knew it wasn't going to happen. My expertise lies in many other areas. Killing myself isn't one of them.'

'I don't… Explain, please.'

He raised his head, took in her tall, proud figure and felt a moment of regret that he'd messed this up too. She was one thing he'd have fought to hang on to, if it hadn't been too late for him.

'I've been dicing with death since I was old enough to walk. If a situation has an element of danger, I'm there. Being born with racing imprinted into my DNA was just a bonus.'

'Even if it ends up consuming you so thoroughly it kills you?'

The look that came over his face was so gut-wrenchingly

stark she felt pain resonate inside her. 'Sorry, I didn't mean it like that—'

He shook his head. 'I won't die from racing.'

'Are you retiring?'

He dashed the hope in her question. 'No. Regardless of everything that's happened, I still crave it. I've been spared death so far. It seems I'm destined for other things.'

A frown formed. 'What do you mean?'

'Haven't you guessed it yet? My skill lies in killing everything I come into contact with. If you haven't woken to the fact that all I'll bring to your doorstep is utter chaos then you're not as bright as I thought.'

'That sounds like…are you trying to warn me off you?'

He laughed. '*Sí*, I am. Which in itself is strange. Normally, I just take what I want and leave the husk behind.'

Pain darkened her eyes. 'Why are you doing this?'

'Doing what, *querida*?'

'Trying to belittle what we have, and don't use that endearment any more. It's a beautiful word you've made tacky because you don't really mean it. You're trying to paint yourself in a vile light, trying to put me off you so I'll walk away.'

'I'm not *trying*. I'm telling you I'm not a great bet for you. I always escape unscathed but everyone I come into contact with sooner or later suffers for it.'

'You make yourself sound as if you've got a contagious disease. Stop it. And no one suffered today. You still need to address exactly what happened during the race but no one had an accident.'

'That's where you're wrong. At the start, when I realised I was getting squeezed out, I contemplated a move that would've taken Matteo out. For a moment, I forgot that I was supposed to be his teacher. I forgot the reason I'm staging the All-Star event in the first place. In that cockpit, I was just a racer, programmed to win.'

'But isn't that what racers do?'

'He's only nineteen, Raven! And I came within a whisker

of taking him out. Do you know his mother is here today? Can you imagine how devastated she'd have been if I'd crossed that line?'

'But you didn't cross it. You pulled back before you did any damage.'

'Yeah, and you know how I felt? Nothing. No remorse, no victory, no sympathy. I felt nothing.'

'Because there was something else going on. You say you remembered your crash in Hungary but then you blanked out the rest of the race. That could be a form of PTSD.'

He raked a hand through his hair. '*Santo cielo!* Stop trying to make excuses for me. Stop trying to make me the sort of man you'll fall for. There is nothing beneath this shell.'

Raven's heart lurched, then thundered so hard she was surprised it didn't burst out of her chest. Surprised she managed to keep breathing, to keep standing upright despite the knee-weakening realisation that it was too late.

She had fallen hard. So very, very hard for Rafael.

'And if I don't fall in with your plan to drive me away? You know me well enough by now to know I'm no pushover.'

He speared her with a vicious look meant to flay the skin from her flesh, and maybe a few weeks ago she'd have heeded the warning, but she'd found, when it came to Rafael, she was made of sterner stuff than that.

'No, but I'm a complete bastard when I'm pushed to the edge, *chiquita*. Are you prepared for that?' he parried.

'You'll have to do more than throw words at me. I *know* you, Rafael. I see beyond your so-called shell. And I know, despite what you say, you love your family and would do anything for them. I also know that you're pissed off right now because you're terrified of what's happening with you. But I'm not walking away, no matter how much you try to push me. I won't let you.'

Anger hissed through his teeth. Rising from the bed, he stalked, albeit with a barely visible limp, to the drawer that held his clothes and pulled it open. 'A few days ago, you were counting the days until this thing between us ended. Now I'm trying to end it and you've suddenly gone ostrich on me?' He returned with a handful of clothes.

'I'm not burying my head in the sand—far from it. I'm trying to understand. What have you done that's so viciously cruel that you think I'll walk away from you?'

He froze before her, his whole body stiffening into marble stillness. Only his lips moved, but even then no words emerged.

A chord of fear struck her. 'Rafael?'

'What does your mother mean to you?' he rasped.

Although she wondered at the change of subject, her answer was immediate. 'Everything. She's the only family I have. She may think I'm her enemy half the time because she doesn't want to be where she is, and she may blame me some of the time, imagining I'm the reason my father doesn't want her, but the times she's lucid, she's a wonderful human being and I love her unconditionally, regardless of what persona she is on any given day. The thought of her, safe and a phone call away, makes me happy. I'll do anything for her...' Her words drifted to nothing when she saw the look on his face. He'd grown paler with each word she'd uttered, the jeans he'd pulled from the drawer crushed in his vice-like grip. His face, hewn from a mask of pain so visceral, made her step towards him.

He stepped back swiftly, evoking a vivid image of carrying the contagion she'd accused him of seconds ago.

'Well, stay away from me, then, and enjoy that luxury. Because once you have me in your life, you may not have her for long.' His voice came from far away, as if from the shell he'd referred to moments ago.

'What on earth are you talking about?'

'You know I put my father in a wheelchair eight years ago. But, even before that, my life was on a slippery downward slope.'

'You've let yourself suffer enough. You have to learn to forgive yourself, Rafael.'

His head went back as if she'd struck him. 'Forgive myself? For not only crippling my own father but for taking away the one person he treasured the most?'

'What did you do?'

'*I killed my mother*, Raven. I put her in my car, drove too fast into a sharp corner and executed a perfect somersault that snuffed her out within minutes.'

The horror that engulfed her had nothing to do with his emotionless recounting of events. No, the dismay that rocked through her stemmed from knowing just how much more he'd suffered, how he'd buried it all under the perfect front.

His laugh was a harsh, cruel sound. 'Now that's more like it. That look of horror is what I expect. Maybe now you'll listen to me when I suggest you stay away from me.'

He pulled on his jeans, fished out a black polo shirt and shrugged into it.

Reeling as she was from the news he'd delivered, it took her a moment to realise what he was saying into his phone.

'You're leaving Mexico?' she asked when he hung up.

'The race is over. The next one isn't for another four days.'

She started in surprise. 'Where are you going?'

He gave her a grim smile. 'No. The twenty questions is over, *quer*—' He stopped, looked around, then shoved more things into the large bag he'd placed on the bed.

Scrambling wildly, she said, 'What about your physio sessions?'

'I've just endured a two-hour race. I hardly think I'm going to crumble into a million little pieces if I go without a session for a few days.'

Her lips firmed but the questions hammered in her mind. 'No, you won't. As long as you're not attempting to skydive over any volcanoes?'

'Been there, done that.'

His phone rang. He stared at it for several seconds, pain rippling in tides over his face. Finally, sucking in a deep breath, he answered it.

'*Sí*, Papá?' he rasped.

Raven's heart caught. The faint hope that help for Rafael would come from another angle was stymied when the conversation grew heated with bursts of staccato responses.

Rafael grew tenser with each passing moment until his body was as taut as a bow.

The moment he hung up, he reached for his bag. The action held an air of permanence about it that terrified her.

'So, I'll see you at the track in Rio?' she asked, hating herself for the desperation in her voice.

He gave her a smile that didn't reach his eyes. He started to answer but his phone rang again. He stared into her eyes, his expression inscrutable save for the tinge of relief she glimpsed before he masked it.

'No, you won't. *Adios, bonita.*'

He pressed the *answer* button, raised the phone to his ear and walked out of the door.

Rafael told himself to keep moving. To walk away before he brought chaos to her life. Time was running out for him.

He knew he wasn't ready to give up racing. Just as he knew it was his guilt that was causing the feelings rushing through him. For him to hang onto the only thing that kept him sane, he had to try to make amends.

No, racing wasn't the only thing that kept him sane. If he admitted nothing else, he would admit that.

Raven Blass kept him sane, made him laugh, made him feel things he hadn't felt in a long time. But for her sake he had to walk away. Keep walking away. He was toxic in this state.

He couldn't allow himself to be swayed into thinking he was anything else but what she'd first thought him to be.

As for what he planned to do… His father had summoned him.

Since he had nothing to lose, he saw no reason to refuse the summons. Just as he saw no reason to examine why his heart felt as if it would burst out of his chest with every step he took away from her.

Gritting his teeth, he walked out, threw a *'no comment'* to a stunned media before he stepped up in his helicopter and buckled himself in. He had no heart. So he had nothing to worry about.

Raven got the email an hour later. She'd been fired. Rafael de Cervantes no longer needed her services. She would be paid her full contract fee and an insanely hefty bonus for her inconvenience. Et cetera…et cetera…

Thing was, she wasn't surprised. Or even hurt. The man she'd fallen in love with was in full retreat mode because she'd got under his skin, had glimpsed the ravaged soul of the outwardly irreverent but desperately lonely playboy who had been grappling with monstrous demons.

She could've fought to stay, cited contract clauses and notice periods, but she knew first-hand how intransigent Rafael could be. And she knew offering her help when it was unwelcome would only set back the progress she'd made.

So she sent an email response. She would leave on one condition. That he let her recommend a physio who could help.

His curt text message agreeing to the condition made her heart contract painfully. Her next request was flatly refused.

No, Rafael stated, he had no wish to see her. But he wished her good luck with her future endeavours.

Raven watched the remaining All-Star events like most people did around the world—from the comfort of her couch. Except she had an extra reason to watch. She told herself she was making sure Rafael's new physio was doing a good enough job. It only took a glimpse of Rafael walking down the paddock en route to his car at the Montreal race to know that he hadn't suffered any setbacks.

At least not physically.

His haggard features told a different story. That and his studious avoidance of the media.

Her heart clenched as she devoured images of him; called herself ten kinds of fool when she froze his latest image and let her gaze settle on his hauntingly beautiful face.

The icy blue eyes staring into the camera still held the hint of devilish irreverence that was never far away but a raw desperation lurked there too, one that made tears prick her eyes. With a shaky hand, she pressed the release button and sat, numb, as the rest of the race unfolded.

Whatever Rafael had been running from still chased him with vicious relentlessness. The thought made her heart ache so painfully, she was halfway to picking up the phone when she stopped herself.

What would she say to him that she hadn't said before? He'd made it painfully clear he didn't want her interfering in his life. Like all his relationships, she'd been a means to an end, a sexual panacea to make him forget. She had no choice but to accept it was over.

She needed to put the past in the past and move on.

Which was why she nearly binned the invitation that arrived a week later.

The All-Star event's last race was taking place in Monaco. To be followed by an All-Star gala in honour of the drivers who'd given up their time to raise money for the road safety programme.

The only thing that stopped her from throwing the invitation away was the hand-written note from Sasha de Cervantes on behalf of her and her husband.

Sasha had been a good friend to her when she'd first joined the X1 Premier. Raven knew she'd put her friendship with Rafael on the line because of her and it had almost caused an irreparable rift between them. Certainly, she knew that not admitting Raven's role in Rafael's accident was what had caused the initial friction between Sasha and Marco.

So although attending the gala would mean she ran the risk of coming face to face with Rafael, Raven slid the invitation and the accompanying first class aeroplane ticket into her bag, then spent the next three days desperately trying to stop her heart from beating itself into exhaustion every time she thought of returning to Monaco.

Rafael stood before the door leading to the study at Casa León, where his father waited. Contrary to his intentions when he'd left Mexico two weeks ago, he hadn't made the trip to León. The indescribable need that had assailed him as he'd lifted off the racetrack in Mexico had led him down another path. A path which had brought him an infinitesimal amount of comfort. Comfort and the courage to grasp the door before him…and open it.

His father was seated behind his ancient desk in the room that seemed to have fallen into a time warp décor-wise.

'*Buenos tardes,* Papá.'

'*Mi hijo,*' his father replied. My son. 'It's good to see you.'

Guilt and sadness welled in Rafael's chest as he let his gaze rest properly on his father for the first time in eight years. His hair had turned almost completely grey and his limbs, paralysed thanks to Rafael, appeared shrunken. But his eyes, grey and sharp like Marco's, sparked with keen intellect and an expression Rafael thought he'd never see again. Or maybe it was just wishful thinking. 'Is it?' he asked, his throat tight with all the emotions he held within.

'It's always good to see you. I've missed you. I miss you every day.'

Rafael advanced into the room on shaky legs, inhaling an even shakier breath. 'How can you say that after all I've done?'

'What exactly do you think you've done, Rafa?'

He let out a harsh laugh and speared a hand through his hair. '*Por favor*, Papá. Condemn me to hell. It's where I belong, after all.'

'I think you've done a good job all by yourself. Now it's time to end this.'

'End this?'

His father nodded to a file on his desk. 'Sit down and read that.'

The hand he reached across the desk felt as feeble as a newborn's. The file contained a three-page report, one he read with growing disbelief.

'What is this?' he rasped through numb lips.

'It's the truth of what happened to your car that day, Rafael. You're not responsible for your mother's death.'

Shock hollowed his stomach. 'No…it can't be. Please tell me you're not making this up in some attempt to make me feel less guilty.'

'As your father, it's my duty to comfort you when you feel bad. It's also my duty to make you see the truth in front of your own eyes. You've been so bent on punishing yourself you've failed to listen to reason or contemplate the evidence. You told me when you first drove the car that you felt something wasn't right. That's what made your brother decide to investigate further. It turned out your hunch was right.'

'It says here all fifteen models of that car have been recalled for the same error. But it doesn't excuse the fact that I was running on fumes that day, high from partying even though my body was exhausted from being up almost twenty-four hours straight.'

'All things you'd been doing since you hit late puberty. All those things combined, while it gave me nightmares as a father, didn't make me think for a second that you would be dangerous behind a steering wheel or I wouldn't have bought you such a powerful machine, and I certainly wouldn't have allowed my beloved Ana in the car with you.'

The pure truth behind his father's words hit him square in the solar plexus. He stumbled backward and sagged onto the ancient leather armchair.

'I can't…I don't know what to say.' His head dropped into his hands and he felt tears prick his eyes.

'Let it go, Rafa. You've punished yourself enough over this. Your mamá wouldn't want this for you.'

The sob choked him, hot and tight and cathartic. Once it started, he couldn't seem to make it stop. He didn't even have the strength to lift his head when he heard the haunting whine of his father's wheelchair.

'Enough, son…enough.'

He looked up through a mist of tears. 'Forgive me, Papá.'

His father's smile touched him in a way that went beyond the physical. 'There's nothing to forgive. There never was.'

Footsteps sounded and Marco walked in, cradling his son, with Sasha right behind him.

She stopped dead when she saw him, her eyes widening in disbelief. 'Good grief, I never thought I'd live to see the day you'd be reduced to tears, Rafa. Quick, Marco, activate your phone's camera. We'll make a killing on YouTube.'

Marco laughed, their father snorted, even baby Jack chimed in with a hearty gurgle.

'So, we're all good here?' Marco asked several minutes later, his grey eyes probing as they darted between his father and his brother.

Rafael's gaze met his father's and the unconditional love he saw made the tightness in his chest give way just a tiny bit further. 'We're getting there.'

He had a feeling he'd never get there completely. Not while he felt a part of himself still missing.

'Pacing a crater through that carpet won't make the next few hours of your life any easier. You're screwed ten ways to Sunday. Accept that now and you'll be fine.'

Rafael glared at the amusement on his brother's face and clenched his fist. 'Don't you have an adoring wife somewhere who's waiting for you to swoon over her?' He walked over to the balcony overlooking the immense ballroom and scoured the crowd again, his stomach clenching when he didn't spot the figure he sought.

'Sí,' Marco replied smugly. 'But watching you twist your-self into knots is fun, too.'

'Keep it up and I'll be twisting my fist into your face.'

Marco grinned, an expression that had been rare in the years after his own personal tragedy of losing his unborn child. Sasha had brought the smile back to his brother's face. A smile that was now rubbing him a dozen different wrong ways.

As if he knew he was skating close to the edge, Marco sobered. 'If it helps, I messed up with Sasha, too.'

'It doesn't. Sasha is a soft touch. I'm not surprised she was fooled by those puppy-dog eyes of yours.'

Marco laughed. 'You're in more trouble than I thought if you're that deluded.' When his brother tapped him on the shoulder, Rafael was ready with a pithy response. Instead he saw Marco nod over his shoulder.

'Your Armageddon is here. I'd wish you luck but I've always thought you were dealt more than your fair share at birth. So I'll just suggest you don't balls it up…'

Rafael had stopped listening. His attention, his whole being was focused on the figure framed in the double doors of the ballroom.

Her black silky hair was caught up in a high, elaborate bun that made her sleek neck seem longer. And her dress, a simple but classy white gown threaded with gold sequined lines, followed her curves in a loving caress that made his mouth dry.

The vision of her, so stunning, so held together while he was falling apart inside, made his fingers tighten over the banister railing.

He watched Sasha approach and hug her. Her smile made his breath catch and, once again, Rafael felt a bolt of dismay at the thought of what he'd thrown away.

A waiter offered her a glass of champagne. She was about to take a sip when her gaze rose and collided with his.

The force of emotion that shot through him galvanised his frozen feet. He was moving along the balcony and the stairs before he'd taken a full breath.

Sasha saw him approach, gave him a stern *don't-mess-this-up-or-I'll-castrate-you* look and melted away into the crowd. Raven made no move to walk away, and he wasn't sure whether he was relieved or disturbed because her face gave nothing away.

No pleasure. No censure. Just a careful social mask that made his heart twist.

'You're late.' Ah, *brava*, Rafa. *Brava*.

'My flight out of London was delayed due to fog. I explained to Sasha. She's forgiven me.'

The not-so-subtle barb found its mark. *I'm not here for you.*

He wanted to touch, wanted to feel the warmth of her skin so badly, he had to swallow several times before he could speak.

'I need to talk to you.'

Her eyes widened. 'Why? I thought you said all you had to say in Mexico.'

He tried for a careless shrug. 'Perhaps I have a few more things to say.'

She glanced away and gave her still-full glass to a passing waiter. 'I don't want to hear it. We were never friends, not really. And you fired me from being your physio. That leaves us nothing in common.'

'I'm seeing a therapist,' he blurted out.

Shocked eyes returned to his. 'You are?'

His smile felt false and painful. 'Yes, I figured I must be the only high-profile figure without the requisite head-shrinker as an accessory. Now I'm a fully fledged, card-carrying whack-job. But I still want to talk to you.'

She pressed lightly glossed lips together and shook her head. 'I don't think it's a good idea.'

Feeling the ground rock under him, he reached out and captured her wrist. 'You were right.'

Her breath caught. 'About what?' she whispered.

He started to answer but a burst of laughter from nearby guests stopped him. 'Not here.' He pulled her towards the doors and breathed in relief when she didn't resist. The lift ride up to his VIP suite was made in silence. After shutting the door, he threw his key card on a nearby table and shrugged off his tuxedo jacket.

'You were right about everything.'

She turned from the window overlooking the stunning marina. Her gaze slid over him, a hasty assessment which nevertheless made the blood thrum in his veins.

'Even I can't take responsibility for *everything*.'

'According to my shrink, I'm suffering from a combination of survivor's guilt and PTSD. Together, they make for one sexy but volatile cocktail of emotions.'

She licked her lips then curved them into a quick smile. An impersonal smile. She started to move towards the door. 'Well, I'm happy that you're getting some help. If that's all, I'll return downstairs. I don't wish to be rude to Sasha—'

'I also spoke to my father.'

She froze. He took advantage of her hesitation and stalked after her. Catching her around the waist, he pulled her body into his. She gave the tiniest gasp but didn't fight to get away.

Rafael took that as a good sign. 'I finally flew to León and spoke to my father.' He gave her the gist of their family meeting.

'Why are you telling me all this, Rafael?' she whispered.

He pulled her closer until he felt the sweet curve of her bottom against his groin. For a quick second, he lost himself in her scent, breathed her in and let her warm his frozen soul. The past three weeks had shown him there was an even worse hell than the one he'd previously inhabited. Because in that one he'd lost Raven.

Hell without Raven was a whole new reality. One he was desperate to escape.

'You made me face up to my flaws, to seek help before I hurt anyone else.' He couldn't stop himself from brushing his lips against her nape.

Her delicate shudder gave him hope but her next words dashed them completely. 'So you wanted to thank me? I accept your gratitude. Let me go, please.'

He held on tight. 'I'm seeking help, Raven, learning to change. But I need you. Without you, all this will be for nothing.'

She finally turned in his arms. The look on her face threatened to stop his breath. 'You can't do this because of me. You should want to seek help for yourself.'

'*Sí*, even I get that. But nothing I do will have any meaning unless you're part of that change.'

'What exactly are you saying?' she whispered.

Go for broke, Rafa. Hell, there was nothing left to lose. No, scratch that. There was everything to lose. Without her, his life had no meaning. So he took the biggest gamble he'd ever taken.

'*Lo siento*. I got it horribly wrong. I'm sorry.'

'What did you get wrong?'

'Not seeing the treasure I had in you until it was too late.'

She shook her head and grimaced. 'I'm no treasure, Rafael. I am just as damaged as you. I fooled myself into thinking a half-life was better than letting myself feel. You made me see that I'd let my father's treatment of me cloud my judgement so I pushed everyone away.'

His hand tightened on her waist. 'You know what I want to do?'

She shook her head.

'I want to track him down and ram my fist so far down his throat, he'll never speak again.'

'Don't let your shrink hear you say that.'

His smile felt grim and tight. 'I said I was trying to change. I never said I was aiming for saint of the year.' He sobered. 'I'm disgusted that my behaviour brought up what happened to you when you lived with him.'

'That's just it. Deep down I knew you were nothing like him but I'd programmed myself so thoroughly I let myself grasp the excuse when everyone told me you were nothing but a ruthless playboy.'

'And of course I went out of my way to prove them right.'

'If you were, you'd never have agreed to stop flirting with other women. Never have refused Chantilly's blatant invitation.'

Raven saw the flash of self-disgust and pain in his eyes.

'There was a time when I wouldn't have.'

'Past tense. You're a better man now. A better person.'

'Because of you.' His knuckle brushed down her cheek in a gesture so soft and gentle, tears threatened.

Despite the foolish hope that threatened, Raven's heart remained frozen. She couldn't remain here. If she did, she'd end up making a total fool of herself.

'I have to go—'

'I love you,' he rasped in a whisper so fierce it sizzled around the room.

'I...*what?*'

His heartbreakingly beautiful face contorted in a grimace. 'I'm still broken, *querida*, not so much on the outside any more, but I'm a long way from being perfect. And I know it's selfish of me but I want you so very desperately that I have to ask you to consider taking a chance on me, flawed and hideous as I am.' Acute vulnerability shone from his eyes and, when he grasped her arms, Raven felt the tremor in his fingers.

'You love me?'

'I have no right to, and I can't promise that I won't be a complete bastard on occasion, but *sí*, I love you. And I'll do anything to make you agree to hitch a ride with this broken wagon.'

'Rafael...'

He kissed her silent, as if he was afraid of what she'd say. She kissed him back, infusing every single drop of what she felt into the act. Somehow, he got the message.

He pulled back sharply, the question blazing its intensity in his eyes.

'Yes, my gorgeous man. I love you too.'

A frenzied tearing of clothes followed that sweet, soul-shaking confession. They made love right there in the living room, on the plush, expensive rug helpfully supplied by the five-star hotel.

She held her breath as Rafael slid on the sheath and prowled his naked body over hers. Hardly believing that this beautiful man was hers, she caressed her fingers down his firm cheek. He turned his head and kissed her palm, then, being the shameless opportunist he was, he kissed his way down her arm to her shoulder, then over her chest to capture one rigid nipple in his mouth.

At the same time, he parted her thighs with his and entered her in one bold thrust. Their coupling was fast, furious, their need for each other a raging fire that swiftly burned out of control.

When they'd caught their breaths, Rafael moved, picked her up and walked her into the bedroom.

'Should you be doing that?' she asked.

'I'm a renewed man. I can move mountains.' He let go of her and she tumbled onto the bed. Before she got totally lost in the effortlessly skilled seduction she knew he was aiming her way, she placed a hand on his lips.

'We haven't talked about your racing.'

His settled his long frame next to hers, his eyes serious. 'I think I need to concentrate on getting myself mentally in shape before I get behind the wheel. I've turned down a seat for this season.'

Knowing what it must have taken for him to turn down what he loved doing, her heart swelled. 'You take care of the mental aspect. I'll make sure your body is whipped into shape in time for next year's season.'

He grinned and tugged her close. 'I'd expect no less from my take-no-prisoners future wife.'

Her breath stalled. 'Is that a proposal, Rafael?'

'It's whatever you want it to be. If you don't think I'll make a good enough husband, you can take me as your sex slave. Or your boy toy. Or your f—'

She stopped him with a kiss before he finished. His incorrigible laugh promised retribution. And, for the life of her, Raven couldn't think of a better way to be punished.

'Sasha is going to hate me for disappearing from her gala,' she said an hour later.

'No, she's not. I begged her to send you the invitation. We both agreed I owe her big.'

She mock glared at him. 'You're right, you haven't changed one little bit.'

He laughed, a rich sound that made her soul sing. When he stared deep into her eyes her heart turned over. 'I have something to show you.'

Curious, she watched him reach into his drawer and pull out a sheaf of papers.

'You finished it?'

'Yes,' he answered. There was no laughter in his voice, no shameless lust monster lurking behind the stunning blue eyes.

There was only a careful, almost painfully hopeful expectancy.

She took the papers from him. Seeing the one word title, her heart caught—*Mamá*.

'I knew it. I knew Ana and Carlos were your parents.'

Two hours later, she looked up, tears streaming down her face. He'd sat with her back tucked against his front, in watchful silence while she read, all the while knowing he'd been reading his words alongside her.

The sheen of tears in his eyes rocked her soul.

'It's beautiful, Rafael.'

'*Gracias*. I hope, wherever she is, she forgives me for what I did.'

'She's your mother. That's what mothers do. And I promise to remind you of that whenever the nightmares threaten.'

The look in his eyes made hers fill all over again. '*Mi corazon*. I don't deserve you.'

Her smile was watery. 'No, you don't. But I'll let you have me anyway.'

EPILOGUE

'So what do I get for winning the bet?' Raven asked as they stood in another luxurious room, surrounded by well-heeled guests, the very best vintage champagne and excellent food.

'What more could you possibly want, *mi amor*? You have my slavish adoration by day and my hot body by night.'

'Yes, but do you know how draining it's been to reassure you every day for the last three months that your book will be a smashing success? That more than one person will turn up at this launch?'

Rafael mock frowned. 'Have I been that needy?'

'Yes, you have, but don't think I wasn't fooled by what that neediness got you. You owe me big.'

'I seem to owe everyone big. Okay, how about...' He whispered a very hot, very dirty suggestion of payment. She was still blushing several minutes later when they both heard the whine of an electric wheelchair.

Rafael's father stopped beside them. An electronic copy of Rafael's book had been programmed into a tablet on his wheelchair, and the front page showed a picture of Rafael's mother, her face creased in a stunning smile as she laughed into the camera.

Rafael told her he'd taken that picture the year before she died.

'Carlos, please tell your son to stop worrying about his book. He thinks one of us has been bribing the critics to give it rave reviews.'

Carlos smiled and glanced at his son. Then he started to speak to him in Spanish. Slowly, Rafael's smile disappeared until his face was transformed into a look of intense love and gratitude. With a shaky hand, he touched his father's shoulder, then bent forward and kissed both his cheeks.

'*Gracias,* Papá.' His voice was rough as he straightened.

Carlos nodded, his own eyes holding a sheen of tears as he rolled his chair away.

'What did he say?'

'He's proud of me. And my mother would be too if she were here.'

As hard as she blinked, the tears welled. 'Damn it, you de Cervantes men sure know how to ruin a girl's make up.'

He caught her around the waist and pulled her close into his hard body.

'You're now a de Cervantes too. You can't take back your vows.'

She gave a mock grimace. She was still getting used to her new name, just as she was getting used to wearing the exquisite engagement and wedding ring set that had belonged to Rafael's mother. 'Raven de Cervantes is such a mouthful.'

'Hmm…' He nuzzled her neck, instantly melting her insides. 'We could shorten it.'

'You mean like just initials or a symbol like that rock star?'

'Not quite.'

'What have you in mind?' she asked, her fingers toying with buttons she couldn't wait to undo later. The promise of exploring the flesh underneath made her hot.

He worked along her jaw until he reached the side of her mouth. With a whisper-soft kiss, he raised his head and looked directly into her eyes. 'How about just…*amor querida*?'

Her heart, her soul and the rest of her body melted into him. When his thumb brushed her cheek, she blinked back tears. 'That works. That works very well for me.'

* * * * *

The Price of Success

First and foremost, for my dear sister, Barbara, who gave me the book that started this wonderful journey. For my husband, Tony, for his unwavering support and firm belief that this dream would become reality. For my HEART sisters—your incredible support kept me going right from the beginning—thank you! And finally, for my darling MINXES! You are the best cheerleaders a girl can have and I'd be totally lost without you.

CHAPTER ONE

THE MOMENTS BEFORE the crash played out almost in slow motion. Time paused, then stretched lethargically in the Sunday sun. And even though the cars were travelling at over two hundred and twenty kilometers an hour, there seemed an almost hypnotic, ballet-like symmetry in their movement.

Sasha Fleming stared, frozen, her heart suspended midbeat, terrified to complete its task as Rafael's front wing clipped the rear tyre of the slower back marker. Hundreds of thousands of pounds' worth of carbon fibre bent backwards, twisted in on itself. Ripped metal tore through the left tyre, wrenching the car into a ninety-degree turn.

The world-renowned racing car launched itself into the air. For several brief seconds it looked more like a futuristic aircraft than an asphalt-hugging machine.

Inevitably, gravity won out. The explosion was deafening as sound erupted all around her. The screech of contorting metal rang through her head, amplified by the super-sized loudspeakers all around her. In the next instant the white concrete wall just after the Turn One hairpin bend was streaked with the iconic racing green paint of Rafael's car.

'He's crashed! He's crashed! The pole sitter and current world champion, Rafael de Cervantes, has crashed his Espíritu DSII. Only this morning the papers said this car was uncrashable. How wrong were they?'

Sasha ripped off her headphones, unable to stomach the frenzied glee in the commentator's voice or the huge roar that rose around the Hungaroring circuit.

Her heart, now making up for its sluggishness, was beating so hard and so fast it threatened to break through her ribcage. Her eyes remained glued to the bank of screens on the pit wall, and she and two dozen pit crew members watched the horrific events unfold.

'Turn up the sound,' someone yelled.

Curbing a wild need to negate that command, she clamped her lips together, arms folded tight around her middle. Memories of another time, another crash, played alongside the carnage unfolding on the screen. Unable to stem it, she let the memories of the event that had changed her for ever filter through to play alongside this appalling spectacle.

'Sometimes the only way to get through pain is to immerse yourself in it. Let it eat you alive. It'll spit you out eventually.'

How many times had her father told her that? When she'd broken her ankle learning to ride her bike. When she'd fractured her arm falling out of a tree. When she'd lost her mum when she was ten. When she'd suffered the desperate consequences of falling for the wrong guy.

She'd got through them all. Well…almost.

The secret loss she'd buried deep in her heart would always be with her. As would the loss of her father.

The commentator's voice scythed through her thoughts. *'There's no movement from the car. The race has been red-flagged and the safety car is on its way. So is the ambulance. But so far we haven't seen Rafael move. His engineer will be frantically trying to speak to him, no doubt. I must say, though, it's not looking good…'*

Sasha forced in a breath, her fingers moving convulsively to loosen the Velcro securing her constricting race suit. A shudder raked her frame, followed closely by another. She tried to swallow but she couldn't get her throat to work.

Alongside the thoughts zipping through her head, her last conversation with Rafael filtered through.

He'd been so angry with her. And the accusations he'd flung at her when she'd only been trying to help…

Ice clutched her soul. Was this *her* fault? Had *she* played a part in this carnage?

'The ambulance is there now. And there's Rafael's brother,

Marco, the owner of Team Espíritu. He's on his way to the crash site...hopefully we'll get a progress report soon.'

Marco. Another fist of shock punched through her flailing senses. She hadn't even been aware he'd finally arrived in Hungary. In her two years as reserve driver for Team Espíritu, Marco de Cervantes hadn't missed a single race—until this weekend.

The whole paddock had been abuzz with his absence, the celebrities and royalty who jetted in from all over the world specifically to experience the de Cervantes lifestyle, visibly disappointed. From Rafael's terse response when she'd asked of his brother's whereabouts, Sasha had concluded the brothers had fallen out.

Her heart twisted tighter in her chest at the thought that Marco had finally arrived only to witness his brother's crash.

A daring cameraman broke through the flanking bodyguards and caught up with Marco. Tight-jawed, his olive skin showing only the barest hint of paleness, he kept his gaze fixed ahead, his set expression not revealing the slightest hint of his emotional state as he strode towards the courtesy car waiting a few feet away.

Just before he got into the car he turned his head. Deep hazel eyes stared straight into the camera.

Sasha's breath stilled. Icy dread flooded her veins at the banked fury in their depths. His features were pinched, his mouth a taut line, the lines bracketing his mouth deep and austere. Everything about him indicated he was reining in tight emotion. Not surprising, given the circumstances.

But, eerily, Sasha knew his emotion extended beyond the events unfolding now. Whatever emotion Marco was holding in, it went far beyond his reaction to his brother's horrific accident.

Another shiver raked through her. She turned away from the screen, searching blindly for an escape. The back of the garage where the tyres were stacked offered a temporary sanctuary.

She'd taken one single step towards the opening when he heart sank. Tom Brooks, her personal press officer, broke away from the crew and made a beeline for her.

'We need to prep for an interview,' he clipped out, finger flying over his iPad.

Nausea rose to join all the other sensations percolating in side her. 'Already? We don't even know how Rafael is.' Or even if he was still alive.

'Exactly. The eyes of the world will be on this team. Now not the time to bungle our way through another disastrou soundbite,' he said unsympathetically.

Sasha bit her lip. Her heated denial of a relationship wit Rafael only a week ago had fuelled media speculation, an brought unwanted focus on the team.

'Surely it's better to be well informed before the interview than to go on air half-cocked?'

His face darkened. 'Do you want to be a reserve drive for ever?'

Sasha frowned. 'Of course not—'

'Good, because I don't want to play press officer to a re serve driver for the rest of my career. You want to be one o the boys? Here's your chance to prove it.'

A wave of anger rose inside her. 'I don't need to be heart less to prove myself, Tom.'

'Oh, but you do. Do you think any of the other driver would hesitate at the chance that's been presented?'

'What chance? We don't even know how Rafael is doin yet!'

'Well, you can sit on your hands until the moment's snatche from you. The handful of female X1 Premier Racing driv ers who've gone before you barely made an impact. You ca choose to become a meaningless statistic, or you can put your self in the driver's seat—literally—and lay the paddock ru mours to rest.'

She didn't need to ask what he meant. A wave of pain rolle

hrough her. Pushing it back, she straightened her shoulders. I don't care about rumours. I'm a good driver—'

'You're also Jack Fleming's daughter and Derek Mahoney's x. If you want to be taken seriously you need to step out of heir shadows. Do the interview. Stake your claim.'

As his fingers resumed their busy course over his iPad, unase rose inside Sasha. As much as she disliked Tom's acerbic attitude, a part of her knew he was right. The move from eserve to full-time driver for Team Espíritu was a once-in-a-lifetime opportunity she couldn't afford to squander—not f she wanted to achieve her goals.

'I have a reporter ready to meet—'

'No.' Her gaze flicked to the screen and her resolve strengthened. 'I won't give an interview until I hear how Rafael is.'

Two ambulances and three fire engines now surrounded the mangled car. Sparks flew as the fire crew cut away the chassis.

Marco de Cervantes stood scant feet away, ignoring everyone, his impressive physique firmly planted, hands balled into fists, his unwavering gaze fixed on his brother's still form. Sasha's heart squeezed tighter.

Please be alive, Rafael. Don't you dare die on me...

Tom's stern look mellowed slightly as he followed her gaze. 'I'll prepare something while we wait. Find a quiet place. Get yourself together.' He glanced around, made sure he wasn't overheard and leaned in closer. 'This is the chance you've been waiting for, Sasha. *Don't blow it.*'

Marco de Cervantes stepped into the private hospital room in Budapest, sick dread churning through his stomach. He clenched his fists to stop the shaking in his hands and forced himself to walk to his brother's bedside. With each step the accident replayed in his mind's eye, a vivid, gruesome nightmare that wouldn't stop. There'd been so much blood at the crash site...*so much blood...*

His chest tightened as he saw the white sheet pulled ove
his brother's chest.

Absently, he made a note to have the staff replace the sheet:
with another colour—green, perhaps, Rafael's favourite col
our. White hospital sheets looked…smelled…too much lik
death.

Rafael wasn't dead. And if Marco had anything to do with
it this would be his last senseless brush with death. Enough
was enough.

He drew level with the bed and stared down into hi:
brother's pale, still face. At the tube inserted into his mouth
to help him breathe.

Enough was enough.

Marco's throat closed up. He'd chosen to give Rafael time
to come to his senses instead of forcing him to listen to reason
And by doing so he'd allowed his brother to take the whee
behind the world's most powerful car while still reeling from
emotional rejection.

Unlike him, his brother had never been able to compart-
mentalise his life, to suppress superfluous emotions that led
to unnecessarily clouded judgement. Rafael coalesced hap-
piness, sadness, triumph and loss into one hot, sticky mess.
Add the lethal mix of a seven hundred and fifty horsepower
racing car, and once again *he* was left picking up the pieces.

His breath shuddered. Reaching out, he took Rafael's un-
moving hand, leaned down until his lips hovered an inch from
his brother's ear.

'You live—you hear me? I swear on all things holy, if you
die on me I'll track you to hell and kick your ass,' he grated
out, then swallowed the thickness in his throat. 'And I know
you'll be in hell, because you sure as heck won't get into
heaven with *those* looks.'

His voice caught and he forced back his tears.

Rafael's hand remained immobile, barely warm. Marco
held on tighter, desperately infusing his brother with his own

life force, desperately trying to block out the doctor's words... *his brain is swelling...there's internal bleeding...nothing to do but wait...*

With a stifled curse, he whirled away from the bed. The window of the ultra-private, ultra-exclusive, state-of-the-art hospital looked out onto a serene courtyard, with discreet fountains and carefully clipped flowers meant to soothe the troubled patient. Beyond the grounds, forests stretched as far as the eye could see.

Marco found no solace in the picturesque view. He found even less to smile about when his eyes lit on the paparazzi waiting beyond the hospital's boundaries, powerful lenses trained, ready to pounce.

Shoving a hand through his hair, he turned back to the bed.

A flash of green caught the corner of his eye. He focused on the flat-screen TV mounted on the wall and watched Rafael's accident replayed again in slow motion.

Bile rose to his throat. Reaching blindly for the remote, he aimed it at the screen—only to stop when another picture shifted into focus.

Anger escalated through him. Five minutes later he stabbed the 'off' button and calmly replaced the control.

Returning to Rafael's bedside, he sank onto the side of the bed. 'I know you'd probably argue with me, *mi hermano*, but you've had a lucky escape. In more ways than one.'

Jaw clenching, he thanked heaven his brother hadn't heard the interview just played on TV. Marco had first-hand knowledge of what people would sacrifice in their quest for fame and power, and the look of naked ambition in Sasha Fleming's eyes made his chest burn with fury and his skin crawl.

His fist tightened on the bed next to his brother's unmoving body.

If she wanted a taste of power he would give it to her. Let her acquire a taste for it the way she'd given Rafael a taste of herself.

Then, just as she'd callously shoved Rafael aside, Marco would take utter satisfaction in wrenching away everything she'd ever dreamed of.

'Excuse me, can you tell me which room Rafael de Cervantes is in?' Sasha infused her voice with as much authority as possible, despite the glaring knowledge that she wasn't supposed to be here.

The nurse dressed in a crisp white uniform looked up. The crease already forming on her brow caused Sasha's heart to sink.

'Are you a member of the family?'

'No, but I wanted to see how he was. He was…*is* my team mate.' The moment the words left her lips she winced. *Way to go, Sasha.*

True to form, the nurse's frown dissolved as realisation dawned. 'His team mate…? You're Sasha Fleming!'

Sasha summoned her practised camera smile—the one that held the right amount of interest without screaming *look at me*, and lifted the oversized sunglasses. 'Yes,' she murmured.

'My nephew *loves* you!' The nurse gushed. 'He pretends not to, but I know he thinks you rock. Every time he sees you during Friday Practice his face lights up. He'll be thrilled when I tell him I met you.'

The tension clamping Sasha's nape eased a little. 'Thanks. So can I see Rafael?' she asked again. When the frown threatened to make a comeback, Sasha rushed on. 'I'll only be a moment, I promise.'

'I'm sorry, Miss Fleming. You're not on my list of approved visitors.'

Steeling herself against the nerves dragging through her, Sasha cleared her throat. 'Is Marco de Cervantes here? Maybe I can ask him?'

She pushed the mental picture of Marco's cold, unforgiving features to the back of her mind. She was here for

Rafael. Surely, as his team mate, his brother wouldn't bar her from seeing him?

'No, he left half an hour ago.'

Shock slammed into her. 'He *left*?'

The nurse nodded. 'He didn't seem too happy, but considering the circumstances I guess it's to be expected.'

For a moment Sasha debated asking if the nurse would make an exception. Break the rules for her. But she dismissed it. Breaking her own rules, getting friendly with Rafael, was probably the reason he'd ended up in this situation. She refused to exacerbate it.

Plucking her sunglasses off her head, she slid them down to cover her eyes. In her jeans and long-sleeved cotton top, with a multi-coloured cheesecloth satchel slung across her body, she looked like every other summer tourist in the city. Her disguise had helped her evade the paparazzi on her way in. She prayed it would hold up on her way out.

With a heavy heart she turned towards the elevator doors, which stood open as if to usher her away from here as fast as possible.

'Wait.' The nurse beckoned with a quick hand movement and leaned forward as Sasha approached the desk. 'Maybe I can sneak you in for a few minutes,' she whispered.

Relief washed over Sasha. 'Oh, thank you so much!'

'If you don't mind signing an autograph for my nephew?'

A tinge of guilt arrowed through her, but the need to see Rafael overcame the feeling. With a grateful smile, Sasha took the proffered pen.

'What the hell are you doing in here?'

Sasha spun round at the harsh voice, and gasped at the dark figure framed in the doorway. A few minutes, the nurse had said. A quick glance at her watch confirmed her sickening suspicion. She'd been here almost an hour!

'I asked you a question.'

'I came to see Rafael. There was no one here—'

'So you thought you'd just sneak in?'

'Hardly! The nurse—' Sasha gulped back her words, realising she could be putting the nurse's job in jeopardy.

'The nurse what?'

Marco advanced into the room, his formidable presence shrinking the space. She scrambled to her feet, but she still had to tilt her head to see his face.

His cold-as-steel expression dried her mouth further.

She shook her head. 'I just wanted to see how he was.' She stopped speaking as he drew level with her, his hard eyes boring into her.

'How long have you been here?'

She risked another glance at her watch and cringed inwardly. Dared she tell him the truth or blag her way through? 'Does it really matter?'

'How long?' he gritted, his gaze sliding over his brother as if assessing any further damage.

'Why are you checking him over like that? Do you think I've harmed him in some way?' she challenged.

Hazel eyes slammed back to her. His contempt was evident as his gaze raked her face. 'I don't *think*! I *know* you've already harmed my brother.'

His tone was so scathing Sasha was surprised her flesh wasn't falling from her skin.

'Rafael told you about our fight?'

'Yes, he did. I can only conclude that your presence here is another media stunt, not out of concern for my brother?'

'Of course it isn't!'

'Is that why the media presence at the hospital gates has doubled in the last hour?'

Her gaze drifted to the window. The blinds were drawn against the late-afternoon sun, but not closed completely. She'd taken a step to look for herself when steely fingers closed on her wrist. Heat shot up her arm, the reaction so unfamiliar she froze.

'If you think I'm going to let you use my brother to further your own ends, you're sorely mistaken.'

Alarmed, she stared up at him. 'Why would you think I'd do that?'

A mirthless smile bared his teeth, displaying a look so frightening she shivered.

'That press conference you gave? About how much you cared for him? How your thoughts were with him and his family? *About how you're willing to step into his shoes as soon as possible so you don't let the team down?* What were your exact words? *"I've earned the chance at a full-time seat. I've proven that I have what it takes."*'

Sasha swallowed, unable to look away from the chilling but oddly hypnotic pull of his gaze. 'I…I shouldn't have….' The echo of unease she'd felt before and during the interview returned. 'I didn't mean it like that—'

'How *did* you mean it, then? How exactly have *you*, a mere reserve driver, earned your place on the team? Why do *you* deserve Rafael's seat and not one of the other dozen top drivers out there?'

'Because it's my time! I deserve the chance.' She wrenched at her captured arm. His hand tightened, sending another bolt of heat through her body.

Straight black brows clamped together. His arresting features were seriously eroding her thought processes. Even livid to the point where she could imagine heat striations coming off his body he oozed enough sex appeal to make her finally understand why his bodyguards were forever turning away paddock groupies from his luxury hospitality suite. Rumour had it that one particularly eager groupie had scaled the mobile suite and slipped into his bedroom via the skylight.

'*Your time?* Why?' he challenged again, stepping closer, invading her body space and her ability to breathe. 'What's so special about *you*, Sasha Fleming?'

'I didn't say I was special.'

'That's not what I got from the press junket. In fact I deduced something along the lines that the team would be making a huge mistake if you weren't given Rafael's seat. Was there even the veiled threat of a lawsuit thrown in there?'

The thought that this might be her only chance to find a decent seat had resonated in the back of her mind even as she'd felt sickened at the thought of how wrong the timing was.

'Nothing to say?' came the soft taunt.

She finally managed to wrench her wrist from his grasp and stepped back. 'Mr de Cervantes, this is neither the time nor the place to discuss this.'

Her glance slid to Rafael, her throat closing in distress at the tubes and the horrid beeping of the machines keeping him alive.

Marco followed her gaze and froze, as if just realising where he was. When his gaze sliced back to hers she glimpsed a well of anguish within the hazel depths and felt something soften inside her. Marco de Cervantes, despite his chilling words and seriously imposing presence, was hurting. The fear of the unknown, of wondering if the precious life of someone you held dear would pull through was one she was agonisingly familiar with.

Any thought of her job flew out of her head as she watched him wrestle with his pain. The urge to comfort, one human being to another, momentarily overcame her instinct for self-preservation.

'Rafael is strong. He's a fighter. He'll pull through,' she murmured softly.

Slowly he pulled in a breath, and any hint of pain disappeared. His upper lip curled in a mocking sneer. 'Your concern is touching, Miss Fleming. But cut the crap. There are no cameras here. No microphones to lap up your false platitudes. Unless you've got one hidden on your person?' His eyes slid down her body, narrowing as they searched. 'Will I go on the internet tomorrow and see footage of my brother in his sick bed all over it?'

'That's a tasteless and disgusting thing to say!' Spinning away, she rushed to the leather sofa in the suite and picked up her satchel. Clearly it was time to make herself scarce.

Careful not to come within touching distance of Marco de Cervantes, she edged towards the door.

'Any more tasteless than you vying for his seat even before you knew for certain whether he was alive or dead?' came the biting query.

Sasha winced. 'I agree. It wasn't the perfect time to do an interview.'

A hint of surprise lightened his eyes, but his lips firmed a second later. 'But you did it anyway.'

Blaming Tom would have been easy. And the coward's way out. The truth was, she *wanted* to be lead driver.

'I thought I was acting in the best interests of the team. And, yes, I was also putting myself forward as the most viable option. But the timing was wrong. For that, I apologise.'

That grim smile made another appearance. Her body shuddered with alarm. Even before he spoke Sasha had the strongest premonition that she wasn't going to like the words that spilled from his lips.

'You should've taken more time to think, Miss Fleming. Because, as team owner, *I* ultimately decide what's in the best interests of Team Espíritu. Not you.'

He sauntered to his brother's bedside and stood looking down at him.

Sasha glanced between the two men. This close, the resemblance between them was striking. Yet they couldn't have been more different. Where Rafael was wild and gregarious, his brother smouldered and rumbled like the deepest, darkest underbelly of a dormant volcano. The fear that he could erupt at any moment was a very real and credible threat. One that made her throat dry and her heart race.

Finally he turned to face her. Trepidation iced its way to her toes.

'My decision and mine alone carries. Your timing wasn't

just wrong. It was detestable.' His voice could have frozen water in the Sahara. 'It also makes my decision incredibly easy.'

Her heart stopped. 'Wh—what decision?'

'Relieving you of your job, of course.' The smile widened. 'Congratulations. You're fired.'

CHAPTER TWO

'*WHAT?*'

'Get out.'

Sasha remained frozen, unable to heed Marco de Cervantes's command. Finally she forced out a breath.

'No. You—you can't do that. You can't fire me.' Somewhere at the back of her mind she knew this to be true—something about contracts…clauses—but her brain couldn't seem to track after the blow it had been dealt.

'I can do anything I want. I *own* the team. Which means I own you.'

'Yes, but…' She sucked in a breath and forced herself to focus. 'Yes, you own the team, but you don't *own* me. And you can't fire me. I haven't done anything wrong. Sure, the press interview was a little mistimed. But that isn't grounds to sack me.'

'Maybe those aren't the only grounds I have.'

Cold dread eased up her spine. 'What are you talking about?'

Marco regarded her for several seconds. Then his gaze slid to his brother. Reaching out, he carefully smoothed back a lock of hair from Rafael's face. The poignancy of the gesture and the momentary softening of his features made Sasha's heart ache for him, despite his anger at her. No one deserved to watch a loved one suffer. Not even Marco de Cervantes.

When his gaze locked onto her again Sasha wasn't prepared for the mercurial shift from familial concern to dark fury.

'You're right. My brother's bedside isn't the place to discuss this.' He came towards her, his long-legged stride purposeful and arrestingly graceful. His broad shoulders, the strength in his lean, muscled body demanded an audience. Sasha stared, unable to look away from the perfect body packed full of angry Spanish male.

In whose path she directly stood.

At the last second her legs unfroze long enough for her to step out of his way. 'It's okay. I'll leave.'

'Running away? Scared your past is catching up with you, Miss Fleming?'

She swallowed carefully, striving to maintain a neutral expression. Marco de Cervantes didn't know. He *couldn't*.

'I don't know what you're talking about. My past has nothing to do with my contract with your team.'

He stared into her face for so long Sasha wanted to slam on the shades dangling uselessly from her fingers.

'Extraordinary,' he finally murmured.

'What?' she croaked.

'You lie so flawlessly. Not even an eyelash betrays you. It's no wonder Rafael was completely taken with you. What I don't understand is why. He offered you what you wanted—money, prestige, a privileged lifestyle millions dream about but only few achieve. Isn't that what women like you ultimately want? The chance to live in unimaginable luxury playing mistress of a *castillo*?'

'Um, I don't know what sort of women *you've* been cavorting with, but you know nothing about me.'

Impossibly, his features grew colder. 'I know everything I need to know. So why didn't you just take it? What's your angle?' His intense gaze bored into her, as if trying to burrow beneath her skin.

It took every control-gathering technique she'd learned not to step back from him.

'I have no *angle*—'

'Enough of your lies. Get out.' He wrenched the door open, fully expecting her to comply.

Her eyes flicked to Rafael's still form. Sasha doubted she'd see him again before the team's month-long August break.

'Will you tell him I came to see him when he wakes up—please?' she asked.

Marco exhaled in disbelief. 'With any luck, by the time my brother wakes up any memory he has of you will be wiped clean from his mind.'

She gasped, the chill from his voice washing over her. 'I'm not sure exactly what Rafael told you, but you've really got this wrong.'

Marco shrugged. 'And you're still fired. Goodbye, Miss Fleming.'

'On what grounds?' she challenged, hoping this time her voice would emerge with more conviction.

'I'm sure my lawyers can find something. Inappropriate enthusiasm?'

'That's a reason you should be keeping me on—not a reason to fire me.'

'You've just proved my point. Most people know where to draw the line. It seems you don't.'

'I *do*,' she stressed, her voice rising right along with the tight knot in her chest.

'This conversation is over.' He glanced pointedly at the door.

She stepped into the corridor, reeling from the impact of his words. Her contract was airtight. She was sure of it. But she'd seen too many teams discard perfectly fit and able drivers for reasons far flimsier than the one Marco had just given her. X1 Premier Racing was notorious for its court battles between team owners and drivers.

The thought that she could lose everything she'd fought for made her mouth dry. She'd battled hard to hold onto her seat in the most successful team in the history of the sport, when every punter with a blog or a social media account had taken potshots at her talent. One particularly harsh critic had even gone as far as to debate her sexual preferences.

She'd sacrificed too much for too long. Somehow she had to convince Marco de Cervantes to keep her on.

She turned to confront him—only to find a short man wearing a suit and a fawning expression hurrying towards them. He handed Marco a small wooden box and launched into a rapid volley of French. Whatever the man—whose discreet badge announced him as Administrator—was saying, it wasn't having any effect on Marco.

Marco's response was clipped. When the administrator started in surprise and glanced towards the reception area, Sasha followed his gaze. The nurse who had let her in stood behind the counter.

The administrator launched into another obsequious torrent. Marco cut him off with an incisive slash of his hand and headed for the lifts.

Sasha hurried after him. As she passed the reception area, she glimpsed the naked distress in the nurse's eyes. Another wave of icy dread slammed into her, lending her more impetus as she rushed after Marco.

'Wait!'

He pressed the button for the lift as she screeched to a halt beside him.

Away from the low lights of the hospital room Sasha saw him—really saw him—for the first time. Up close and personal, Marco de Cervantes was stunning. If you liked your men tall, imposing and bristling with tons of masculinity. Through the gap in his grey cotton shirt she caught a glimpse of dark hair and a strong, golden chest that had her glancing away in a hurry.

Focus!

'Can we talk—please?' she injected into the silence.

He ignored her, his stern, closed face forbidding any conversation. The lift arrived and he stepped in. Sasha rushed in after him. As the doors closed she saw the nurse burst into tears.

Outraged, she rounded on him. 'My God. You got that nurse sacked, didn't you?'

Anger dissolved the last of her instinctive self-preservation and washed away the strangely compelling sensation she refused to acknowledge was attraction.

'I lodged a complaint.'

'Which, coming from you, was as good as ordering that administrator to sack her!'

Guilt attacked her insides.

'She must live with the consequences of her actions.'

'So there's no in-between? No showing mercy? Just straight to the gallows?'

Deep hazel eyes pinned her where she stood. 'You weren't on the list of approved visitors. She knew this and disregarded it. You could've been a tabloid hack. Anybody.'

His eyes narrowed and Sasha forced her expression to remain neutral.

'Or maybe she knew *exactly* who you were?'

She lowered her lids as a wave of guilty heat washed over her face.

'Of course,' he taunted softly. 'What did you offer her? Free tickets to the next race?'

Deciding silence was the best policy, she clamped her lips together.

'A personal tour of the paddock and a photo op with you once you became lead driver, perhaps?'

His scathing tone grated on her nerves.

Raising her head she met his gaze, anger at his high-handedness loosening her tongue. 'You know, just because your brother is gravely ill, it doesn't give you the right to destroy other people's lives.'

'I beg your pardon?' he bit out.

'Right now you're in pain and lashing out, wanting anyone and everyone to pay for what you're going through. It's understandable, but it's not fair. That poor woman is now jobless just because *you're* angry.'

'*That poor woman* abused her position and broke the hospital's policy for personal gain. She deserves everything she gets.'

'It wasn't for personal gain. She did it for her nephew. He's a fan. She wanted to do something nice for him.'

'My heart bleeds.'

'You do the same, and more, for thousands of race fans every year. What's so different about this?'

Dark brows clamped together, and his jaw tightened in that barely civilised way that sent another wave of apprehension through her. Again she glimpsed the dark fury riding just below his outward control.

'The difference, Miss Fleming, is that I don't compromise my integrity to do so. And I don't put those I care about in harm's way just to get what I want.'

'What about compassion?'

His brows cleared, but the volatile tinge in the air remained. 'I'm fresh out.'

'You know, you'll wake up one morning not long from now and regret your actions today.'

The lift doors glided open to reveal the underground car park. A few feet away was a gleaming black chrome-trimmed Bentley Continental. Beside it, a driver and a heavily muscled man whose presence shrieked *bodyguard* waited. The driver held the back door open, but Marco made no move towards it. Instead he glanced down at her, his expression hauntingly bleak.

'I regret a lot that's happened in the past twenty-four hours—not least watching my brother mangle himself and his car on the race track because he believed himself to be heartbroken. One more thing doesn't make a difference.'

'Your emotions are overwhelming you right now. All I'm saying is don't let them overrule your better judgement.'

A cold smile lifted one corner of his mouth. 'My *emotions*? I didn't know you practised on the side as the team's psychologist. I thought you'd ridden down with me to beg for your job back, not to practise the elevator pitch version of pop psychology. You had me as your captive audience for a full thirty seconds. Shame you chose to waste it.'

'Mock me all you want. It doesn't change the fact that you're acting like—' She bit her lip, common sense momentarily overriding her anger.

'Go on,' he encouraged softly. Tauntingly. 'Acting like what?'

She shrugged. 'Like…well, like an ass.'

His eyes narrowed until they were mere icy slits. 'Excuse me?'

'Sorry. You asked.'

Anger flared in his eyes, radiated off his body. Sasha held her breath, readying herself for the explosion about to rain on her head. Instead he gave a grim smile.

'I've been called worse.' He nodded to his bodyguard, who took a step towards them. 'Romano will escort you off the premises. Be warned—my very generous donation to this hospital is contingent on you being arrested if you set foot anywhere near my brother again. I'm sure the administrator would relish that challenge.'

Despair rose to mingle with her anger. 'You can't do this. If you don't listen to me I'll…I'll talk to the press again. I'll spill everything!'

'Ah, I'm glad to finally meet the *real* you, Miss Fleming.'

'Ten minutes. That's all I want. Let me convince you to keep me on.'

'Trust me—blackmail isn't a great place to start.'

She bit her lip. 'That was just a bluff. I won't talk to the press. But I do want to drive for you. And I'm the best mid-season replacement you'll find for Rafael.'

'You *do* place a high premium on yourself, don't you?'

Unflinching, she nodded. 'Yes, I do. And I can back it up. Just let me prove it.'

His gaze narrowed on her face, then conducted a lazy sweep over her body. Suddenly the clothes that had served as perfect camouflage against the intrusive press felt inadequate, exposing. Beneath the thin material of her T-shirt her

heart hammered, her skin tingling with an alien awareness
that made her muscles tense.

As a female driver in a predominantly male sport, she was
used to being the cynosure of male eyes. There were those
who searched for signs of failure as a driver, ready to use any
shortcomings against her. Then there were the predators who
searched for weaknesses simply because she was a woman,
and therefore deemed incapable. The most vicious lot were
those who bided their time, ready to rip her apart because she
was Jack Fleming's daughter. Those were the ones she feared
the most. And the ones she'd sworn to prove wrong.

Marco de Cervantes's gaze held an intensity that combined
all of those qualities multiplied by a thousand. And then there
was something else.

Something that made her breath grow shallow in her lungs.
Made her palms clammy and the hairs bristle on her nape.

Recalling the sheer intensity of the look he'd directed into
the camera earlier, she felt her heartbeat accelerate.

'Get in the car,' he bit out, his tone bone-chilling.

Sasha glanced into the dark, luxurious interior of the limo
and hesitated. The feelings this man engendered in her weren't
those of fear. Rather, she sensed an emotional risk—as if,
given half a chance, he would burrow under her skin, discover her worst fears and use them against her. She couldn't
let that happen.

'If you want me to hear you out you'll get in the car. Now,'
he said, his tone uncompromising.

She hesitated. 'I can't.'

'*Can't* isn't a word I enjoy hearing,' he growled, his patience clearly ebbing fast.

'My bike.' He quirked one brow at her. 'I'd *rather* not leave
it here.'

His glance towards the battered green and white scooter
leaning precariously against the car park wall held disbelief.
'You came here on *that*?'

'Yes. Why?'

'You're wearing the most revolting pair of jeans I've ever seen and a scarf that's seen better days. Add that to the oversized sunglasses and I don't need to be a genius to guess you were trying some misguided attempt to escape the paparazzi. I am right?' At her nod, he continued. 'And yet you travelled on the slowest mode of motorised transport known to man.'

She raised her chin. 'But there's the beauty—don't you see? I managed to ride straight past the paparazzi without one single camera lens focusing on me. You, on the other hand… Tell me—how did they react when you rocked up in your huge, tinted-windowed monstrosity of a car?'

His jaw tightened and he glared at her.

'Exactly. I'm not leaving my bike.'

'Security here is—'

'Inadequate, according to you. After all, *I* managed to get through, didn't I?' She threw his words back at him.

One hand gripped the door of the car. 'Get in the car or don't. I refuse to argue with you over a pile of junk.'

'It's my junk and I won't leave it.'

With a stifled curse, Marco held out his hands. 'Keys?'

'Why?'

'Romano will return the scooter to your hotel.'

Sasha's eyes widened. Romano weighed at least two hundred and fifty pounds of pure muscle. The thought of what he'd put her poor scooter through made her wince.

'And before you comment on Romano's size I'd urge you to stop and think about his *feelings*,' Marco added mockingly.

Touché, she conceded silently.

Digging into her satchel, she reluctantly handed over her keys. Marco lobbed them to his bodyguard, then raised an imperious eyebrow at her.

With a resigned sigh, Sasha slid past his imposing body and entered the limo.

The door shut on them, enclosing them in a silent cocoon that threatened to send her already taut nerves into a frenzied tailspin.

As the car glided out of the car park it occurred to her that she had no idea where Marco was taking her. She opened her mouth to ask, then immediately shut it when she saw his gaze fixed on the small box.

Despite his bleak expression, his profile was stunningly arresting. The sculpted contours of his face held enough shadow and intrigue to capture the attention of any red-blooded female with a pulse—a fact attested to by the regular parade of stunning women he was photographed with.

His strong jaw bore the beginnings of a five o'clock shadow, and an even stronger, taut neck slanted onto impossibly broad shoulders. Under the discreetly expensive cotton shirt those shoulders moved restlessly. She followed the movement, her gaze sliding down over his chest, past the flat stomach that showed no hint of flab. Her eyes rested in his lap. The bulge beneath his zipper made heat swirl in her belly.

'Have you seen enough? Or would you like me to perform a slow striptease for you?'

Her cheeks burned. Her neck burned. In fact for several seconds Sasha was sure her whole body was on fire. Mortified, she hastily plucked her sunglasses from atop her head and jammed them onto her face.

'I… You didn't say where we were going.'

'I've called a meeting with Russell and the chief engineer. I'm handing over the reins temporarily so I can concentrate on making arrangements for Rafael to be evacuated home to Spain.'

'You're moving him?'

'Not yet, but the medical team is on standby. He'll be moved the moment it's deemed safe.'

'I see.'

Sharp eyes bored into her. 'Do you? You've talked your way into a last-chance meeting and yet you're wasting time exhibiting false concern for my brother.'

She sucked in a breath. 'My concern isn't false. I'd give anything for Rafael not to be in that place.'

Sasha watched, fascinated, as his hand tightened around the box. 'In my experience *anything* tends to arrive with a very heavy price tag and a carefully calculated catch. So be very careful with your choice of words.'

Sasha licked her lips, suddenly unable to breathe at the expression in his eyes. 'I'm sure I don't know what you mean.'

The look in his eyes hardened. 'You really should try a different profession. Your acting skills are highly commendable.'

'Driving suits me just fine, thanks. Where are we going, exactly?'

Keeping his gaze on her, he relaxed back in his seat. 'My hotel.'

'Your hotel?' she repeated dully. Her senses, still reeling after she'd been caught staring at Marco de Cervantes's man package, threatened to go into freefall. The thought of being alone with him—truly alone—made anxiety skitter over her skin. 'I don't think that's a good idea.'

'You don't have a choice. You wanted this meeting.'

Desperation lent her voice strength. 'The rest of the team will be wondering where I am. Maybe I should let them know.' Tom had asked where she was going after the press conference, but she'd been deliberately evasive.

'The team will be out doing what they do after every Sunday race. Bar hopping and trying it on with the local girls.'

'I don't think they'll be doing that tonight. Not with Rafael…' She bit her lip, unable to continue as she glimpsed the flash of pain in those hazel eyes.

But he merely shrugged. 'Call them if you want. Tell them where you're going. And why.'

Not expecting her bluff to be called, Sasha floundered. The circumstances of her past made it impossible to make friends with anyone on her team. The constant whispers behind her back, the conversations that stopped when she walked into a room, made it hard to trust anyone.

Tom only cared as far as her actions impacted upon his career. The only one who had cared—really cared—had been

Rafael. A wave of pain and regret rushed through her. Until their row last night she'd foolishly let herself believe she could finally trust another human being.

Feigning nonchalance, she shrugged. 'I'll tell them later.'

Unable to stomach the mockery in Marco's eyes, she turned away.

Absently she stroked the armrest, silently apologising for calling the Bentley Continental a monstrosity. Amongst the luxury, sometimes vacuous, creations car manufacturers produced, the Bentley was one of the more ingenious styles. It had been her father's favourite non-racing car—his pride and joy until he'd been forced to sell it to defend himself.

'We're here.'

They were parked beneath the pillared portico of the Four Seasons. A liveried doorman stepped forward and opened the door on Marco's side, his bow of deference deep to the point of being obsequious.

Casting her gaze past him, Sasha felt her mouth drop open at the sheer opulence of the marbled foyer of the stunning hotel. The whole atmosphere glittered and sparkled beneath a super-sized revolving chandelier, which was throwing its adoring light on sleekly dressed patrons.

Sasha remained in her seat, super-conscious of how inappropriate her old hipster jeans and worn top were for the gold-leaf and five-star luxury spread before her. She was pretty sure she would be directed to the tradesman's entrance the moment the doorman saw her scuffed boots.

'Come out. And lose the glasses and the scarf. No one cares who you are here.'

She hesitated. 'Can't we just talk in the car?' she ventured.

He held out a commanding hand. 'No, we can't. We both know you're not shy, so stop wasting my time.'

She could argue, defend her personal reputation against the label Marco had decided to pin on her, but Sasha doubted it would make a difference. He, like the rest of the world, be-

lieved she was soiled goods because of her past and because
she was a Fleming.

What good would protesting do?

The only weapon she had to fight with was her talent behind the steering wheel.

Her father's time had been cruelly cut short, stamped out
by vicious lies that had destroyed him and robbed her of the
one person who had truly loved and believed in her.

Sasha was damned if she would let history repeat itself.
Damned if she would give up her only chance to prove everyone wrong.

Gritting her teeth, she ignored his hand and stepped out
of the car.

Marco strode across the marble foyer, the box clutched firmly
in his grip. Its contents were a vivid reminder, stamped onto
his brain.

Behind him he heard the hurried click of booted heels as
Sasha Fleming struggled to keep up with him.

He didn't slow down. In fact he sped up. He wanted this
meeting over with so he could return to the hospital.

For a single moment Marco thanked God his mother wasn't
alive. She couldn't have borne to see her darling son, the miracle child she'd thought she'd never have, lying battered and
bruised in a coma.

It was bad enough that she'd had to live through the pain
and suffering Marco had brought her ten years ago. Bad
enough that those horrendous three weeks before and after
his own crash had caused a rift he'd never quite managed to
heal, despite his mother's reassurances that all was well.

Marco knew all hadn't been well because *he* had never
been the same since that time.

Deep shame and regret raked through him at how utterly
he'd let his mother down. At how utterly he'd lost his grip on
reality back then. Foolishly and selfishly he'd thought himself in love. The practised smile of a skilful manipulator had

blinded him into throwing all caution to the wind and he'd damaged his family in the process.

His mother was gone, her death yet another heavy weight on his conscience, but Rafael was alive—and Marco intended to make sure lightning didn't strike twice. For that to happen he had to keep it together. He *would* keep it together.

'Um, the sign for the bar points the other way.'

Sasha Fleming's husky voice broke into his unwelcome thoughts.

He stopped so suddenly she bumped into him. Marco frowned at the momentary sensation of her breasts against his back and the unsuspecting heat that surged into his groin. His whole body tightened in furious rejection and he rounded on her.

'I don't conduct my business in bars. And I seriously doubt you want our conversation to be overheard by anyone else.'

Turning on his heel, he stalked to the lift. His personal porter pushed the button and waited for Marco to enter the express lift that serviced the presidential suite.

Sasha shot him a wary look and he bit back the urge to let a feral smile loose. Ever since Rafael's crash he'd been pushing back the blackness, fighting memories that had no place here within this chaos.

Really, Sasha Fleming had chosen the worst possible time to make herself his enemy. His hands tightened around the box and his gaze rested on her.

Run, he silently warned her. *While you have the chance.*

Her eyes searched every corner of the mirrored lift as if danger lurked within the gold-filigree-trimmed interior. Finally she rolled her shoulders. The subtle movement was almost the equivalent of cracking one's knuckles before a fight, and it intrigued him far more than he wanted to admit.

'We're going to your suite? Okay...'

She stepped into the lift. Behind her, Marco saw the porter's gaze drop to linger on her backside. Irritation rose to mingle with the already toxic cauldron of emotions swirling through him. With an impatient finger he stabbed at the button.

'I see the thought of it doesn't disturb you too much.' He didn't bother to conceal the slur in his comment. The urge to attack, to wound, ran rampage within him.

Silently he conceded she was right. As long as Rafael was fighting for his life he couldn't think straight. The impulse to make someone pay seethed just beneath the surface of his calm.

And Sasha Fleming had placed herself front and centre in his sights.

He expected her to flinch. To show that his words had hit a mark.

He wasn't prepared for her careless shrug. 'You're right. I don't really want our conversation to feed tomorrow's headlines. I'm pretty sure by now most of the media know you're staying here.'

'So you're not afraid to enter a strange man's suite?'

'Are you strange? I thought you were merely the engineering genius who designed the Espíritu DSII and the Cervantes Conquistador.'

'I'm immune to flattery, Miss Fleming, and any other form of coercion running through your pretty little head.'

'Shame. I was about to spout some seriously nerd-tastic info *guaranteed* to make you like me.'

'You'd be wasting your time. I have a team specially selected to deal with sycophants.'

His barb finally struck home. She inhaled sharply and lowered her gaze.

Marco caught himself examining the determined angle of her chin, the sensual line of her full lips. At the base of her neck her pulse fluttered under satin-smooth skin. Against his will, another wave of heat surged through him. He threw a mental bucket of cold water over it.

This woman belonged to his brother.

The lift opened directly onto the living room—a white and

silver design that flowed outside onto the balcony overlooking the Danube. Marco bypassed the sweeping floor-to-ceiling windows, strode to the antique desk set against the velvet wall and put the box down.

Recalling its contents, he felt anger coalesce once more within him.

He turned to find Sasha Fleming at the window, a look of total awe on her face as she gazed at the stunning views of the Buda Hills and the Chain Bridge. He took a moment to study her.

Hers wasn't a classical beauty. In fact there was more of the rangy tomboy about her than a woman who was aware of her body. Yet her face held an arresting quality. Her lips were wide and undeniably sensual, and her limbs contained an innate grace when she moved that drew the eye. Her silky black hair, pulled into a loose ponytail at the back of her head, gleamed like a jet pool in the soft lighting. His gaze travelled over her neck, past shoulders that held a hint of delicacy and down to her chest.

The memory of her breasts against his back intruded. Against him she'd felt decidedly soft, although her body was lithe, holding a whipcord strength that didn't hide her subtle femininity. When he'd held her wrist in Rafael's hospital room her skin had felt supple, smooth like silk…

Sexual awareness hummed within him, unwelcome and unacceptable. Ruthlessly he cauterised it. Even if he'd been remotely interested in a woman such as this, flawed as she was, and without a moral bone in her body, *she* was the reason his brother had crashed.

Besides, poaching had never been his style.

'So, what would it take to convince you to keep me on?' She addressed him without taking her eyes from the view.

Annoyance fizzled through him.

'You're known for having relationships with your team mates.'

Her breath caught and she turned sharply from the window. Satisfaction oozed through him at having snagged her attention.

Satisfaction turned to surprise when once again she didn't evade the question. 'One team mate. A very long time ago.'

'He also crashed under extreme circumstances and lost his drive, I believe?'

A simple careful nod. 'He retired from motor racing, yes.'

'And his seat was then given to you?'

Her eyes narrowed. 'Your extrapolation is way off base if you think it has any bearing on what has happened with Rafael.'

'Isn't it curious that you bring chaos to every team you join? Are you an unlucky charm, Miss Fleming?'

'As a former racer yourself, I'm sure you're familiar with the facts—drivers crash on a regular basis. It's a reality of the sport. In fact, wasn't a crash what ended *your* racing career?'

For the second time in a very short while the reminder of events of ten years ago cut through him like the sharpest knife. Forcing the memories away, he folded his arms. 'It's *your* circumstances that interest me, not statistics. You dumped this other guy just before a race. This seems to be your *modus operandi*.'

Her chest lifted with her affronted breath. He struggled not to let his gaze drop. 'I resent that. I thought you ran your team on merit and integrity, not rumour and hypothesis.'

'Here's your chance to dispel the rumours. How many other team mates have you slept with?'

'I had a *relationship* with one. Derek and I went out for a while. Then it ended.'

'But this…relationship grew quite turbulent, I believe? So much so that it eventually destroyed his career while yours flourished?'

She snorted. 'I wouldn't say flourished, exactly. More like sweated and blooded.'

'But you did start out being a reserve driver on his team.

And you did dump him when his seat became available to you?'

Marco watched her lips tighten, her chin angling in a way that drew his eyes to her smooth throat.

'It's obvious you've done your homework. But I didn't come here to discuss my personal life with you—which, as it happens, is really none of your business.'

'When it relates to *my* brother and *my* team it becomes my business. And your actions in the past three months have directly involved Rafael.' He reached for the box on the table. 'Do you know what's in this box?' he asked abruptly.

A wary frown touched her forehead. 'No. How would I?'

'Let me enlighten you. It contains the personal effects that were found on Rafael's person when he was pulled out of the car.' He opened the box. The inside was smeared with blood. Rafael's blood.

Blood he'd spilled because of this woman.

He lifted a gold chain with a tiny crucifix at the end of it. 'My mother gave this to him on the day of his confirmation, when he was thirteen years old. He always wears it during a race. For good luck.'

A look passed over her face. Sadness and a hint of guilt, perhaps? He dropped the chain back into the container, closed it and set it down. Reaching into his pocket, he produced another box—square, velvet.

She tensed, her eyes flaring with alarm. 'Mr de Cervantes—'

His lips twisted. 'You're not quite the talented actress I took you for, after all. Because your expression tells me everything I need to know. Rafael asked the question he'd been burning to ask, didn't he?' he demanded.

'I—'

He cut across her words, not at all surprised when the colour fled her face. 'My brother asked you to marry him. And you callously rejected him, knowing he would have to race directly afterwards. *Didn't you?*'

CHAPTER THREE

SASHA CLENCHED HER fists behind her back, desperately trying to hold it together. Even from across the room she could feel Marco's anger. It vibrated off his skin, slammed around the room like a living thing.

Her heart thudded madly in her chest. She opened her mouth but no words emerged.

'Here's your chance to speak up, Miss Fleming,' Marco incised, one long finger flipping open the box to reveal a large, stunning pink diamond set within a circle of smaller white diamonds.

She'd never been one to run from a fight, and Lord knew she'd had many fights in her life. But, watching Marco advance towards her, Sasha yearned to take a step back. Several steps, in fact…right out through the door. Unfortunately she chose that moment to look into his eyes.

The sheer force of his gaze trapped her. It held her immobile, darkly fascinating even as her panic flared higher. She'd dealt with disrespect, with disdain, even with open slurs against her.

Seething, pain-racked Spanish males like Marco de Cervantes were a different box of frogs.

'Did you refuse my brother or not?' he demanded, and his low, dangerous voice scoured her skin.

Suppressing a shiver, she said, 'You've got it wrong. Rafael didn't ask me—'

'Liar.' He snapped the box shut. 'He sent me a text last night. You said no.'

'Of course I said no. He didn't mean—'

He continued as if she hadn't spoken. 'He thought you

were just playing hard to get. He was going to try again this morning.'

Sasha knew the brothers were close, but Rafael hadn't given her any indication he was *this* close to his brother. In fact the reason she'd grown close to him, despite his irreverent antics with the team and his wildly flirtatious behaviour with every female he came into contact with, was because she'd glimpsed the loneliness Rafael desperately tried to hide. Loneliness she'd identified with.

She watched Marco's nostrils flare with ever deepening anger as he waited for her answer. She licked her lips, carefully choosing her words, because it was clear that Rafael, for his own reasons, hadn't given Marco all the facts.

'Rafael and I are just friends.'

'Do you take me for a fool, Miss Fleming? You really expect me to believe that you viewed the romantic dinners for two in London or the spontaneous trip to Paris last month as innocent gestures of a mere friend?'

Another stab of surprise went through her at the depth of Marco's knowledge. 'I went to dinner with him because Rav… his date stood him up.'

'And Paris?'

'He was appearing at some function and I was at a loose end. I tagged along for laughs.'

'For laughs? And you then proceeded to dance the night away in his arms? What about the other half a dozen times you've been snapped together by the paparazzi?' he demanded.

She frowned. 'I know you two are close, but don't you think you're taking an alarmingly unhealthy interest in your brother's private life?'

His head jerked as if she'd slapped him. His hazel eyes darkened and his shoulders stiffened as if he held some dark emotion inside. Again she wanted to step back. To flee from a fight for the first time in her life.

'It's my duty to protect my brother,' he stated, with a finality that sharpened her interest.

'Rafael's a grown man. He doesn't need protecting.'

He raised a hand and slowly unfurled his fingers from around the velvet box. 'Then what do you call this? Why did my brother, the reigning world champion, who rarely ever makes mistakes, deliberately drive into the back of a slower car?'

Her gasp scoured her throat. 'The accident wasn't deliberate.' She refused to believe Rafael would have acted so recklessly. 'Rafael wouldn't put himself or another driver in such danger.'

'I've watched my brother race since he was six years old. His skill is legendary. He would never have put himself into the slipstream of a slower car so close to a blind corner. Not if he'd been thinking straight.'

Sasha couldn't refute the allegation because she'd wondered herself why Rafael had made such a dangerous move. 'Maybe he thought he could make the move stick,' she pursued half-heartedly.

Long bronze hands curled around the box. Features tight, Marco breathed deeply. 'Or maybe he didn't care. Maybe it was already too late for him when he stepped into the cockpit?'

Horror raked through her. 'Of course it wasn't. Why would you say that?'

'He sent me a text an hour before the race to tell me he intended to have what he wanted. *At all costs.*'

Sasha's blood ran cold. 'I...no, he couldn't have said that! Besides, he didn't mean—' She bit her lip to stop the rest of her words. Although they'd rowed, she wasn't about to betray Rafael's trust. 'We're just friends.'

'You're poison.' His hand slashed through the denial she'd been about to utter. 'Whatever thrall you hold over your fellow team mates, it ends right now.'

Sliding the box containing the engagement ring into his pocket, he returned to the desk. Several papers were spread

across it. He searched through until he found what he wa
looking for.

'Your contract is a rolling one, due to end next season.'

Still reeling from the force of his words, Sasha stared a
him.

'My lawyers will hammer out the finer details of a pay-of
in the next few days. But as of right now your services are n
longer needed by Team Espíritu.'

With the force of a bucket of cold water, she was wrenche
from her numbness.

'You're firing me because I befriended your brother?'

The hysterical edge to her voice registered on the oute
fringes of her mind, but Sasha ignored it. She'd worked to
hard, fought too long for this chance to let mere hysteria stan
in her way. If she had to scream like a banshee she would d
so to make Marco de Cervantes listen to her. After years o
withstanding vicious whispers and callous undermining, sh
would not be dismissed so easily. Not when her chance to se
her father's reputation restored, the chance to prove her ow
worth, was so close.

'Do you want to stop for a moment and think how absur
that is? Do you really want to carry on down that road?' sh
demanded, raising her chin when he turned from the desk.

'What road?' he asked without looking up.

'The sexist, discriminatory road. Or are you going to fir
Rafael too when he wakes up? Just to even things up?'

His gaze hardened. 'I've been running this team for almos
a decade and no one has ever been allowed to cause this muc
disruption unchecked before.'

'What do you mean, unchecked?'

'I warned Rafael about you three months ago,' he delivere
without an ounce of remorse. 'I told him you were trouble
That he should stay away from you.'

Her anger blazed into an inferno. 'How dare you?'

He merely shrugged. 'Unfortunately, with Rafael, you only

have to suggest there's something he can't have to make him hunger desperately for it.'

'You're unbelievable—you know that? You think you can play with people's lives!'

His face darkened. 'Believe me, I'm not playing. Five million.'

Confused, she frowned. 'Five million…for what?'

'To walk away. Dollars, pounds or euros. It doesn't really matter.'

Fire crackled inside her. 'You want to pay me to give up my seat? To disappear like some sleazy secret simply because I became friends with your brother? Even to a wild nut-job like me that seems very drastic. What exactly are you afraid of, Mr de Cervantes?'

Strong, corded arms folded over his chest. His body was held so tense she feared he would snap a muscle at any second. 'Let's just say I have experience with women like you.'

'Damn, I thought I was one of a kind. Would you care to elaborate on that stunning assertion?'

One brow winged upward. 'And have you selling the story to the first tabloid hack you find? I'll pass. Five million. To resign and to stay away from the sport.'

'Go to hell.' She added a smile just for the hell of it, because she yearned for him to feel a fraction of the anger and humiliation coursing through her. The same emotions her father had felt when he'd been thrown out of the profession that had been his life.

'Is that your final answer?' he asked.

'Yes. I don't need to phone a friend and I don't need to ask any audience. My final answer—*go to hell*!'

Sasha braced herself for more of the backlash he'd been doling out solidly for the last hour. But all he did was stare at her, his gaze once again leaving her feeling exposed, as if he'd stripped back a layer of her skin.

He nodded once. Then he paced the room, seemingly lost for words. Finally he raked both hands through his hair, ruffling it until the silky strands looked unkempt in a sexy, just-got-out-of-bed look that she couldn't help but stare at.

Puzzled by his attitude, she forced her gaze away and tried to hang on to her anger. She didn't deserve this. All she'd tried to be was a friend to Rafael, a team mate who'd seemed to be battling demons of his own.

After her experience with Derek, and the devastating pain of losing the baby she hadn't known she was carrying until it was too late, she'd vowed never to mix business with pleasure. Derek's jealousy as she'd risen through the ranks of the racing world had eroded any feelings she'd had for him until there'd been nothing left.

As if sensing her withdrawal, he'd tried to hang on to her with a last-ditch proposal. When she'd turned him down he'd labelled her a bitch and started a whispering campaign against her that had undermined all her years of hard work.

Thankfully Derek had never found out the one thing he could have used against her. The one thing that could have shattered her very existence. The secret memory of her lost baby was buried deep inside, where no one could touch it or use it as a weapon against her.

Even her father hadn't known, and after living through his pain and humiliation she'd vowed never to let her personal life interfere with her work ever again.

Rafael's easy smile and wildly charming ways had got under her guard, making her reveal a few careful details about her past to him. His friendship had been a balm to the lonely existence she'd lived as Jack Fleming's daughter.

The thought that Marco had poisoned him against her filled her with sadness.

'You know, I thought it was Rafael who told *you* about my past. But it was the other way round, wasn't it?' she asked.

She waited for his answer, but his gaze was fixed on the view outside, on the picturesque towers of the Royal Castle. A stillness surrounded him that caught and held her attention.

'For as long as I can remember I've been bailing Rafael out of one scrape or another.'

The words—low, intense and unexpected—jolted aside her anger.

'He's insanely passionate about every single aspect of his life, be it food, driving or volcano-boarding down the side of some godforsaken peak in Nicaragua,' he continued. 'Unfortunately the perils of this world seem to dog him. When he was eleven, he discovered mushrooms growing in a field at our vineyard in León and decided to eat them. His stomach had to be pumped or he'd have died. Two years later, he slipped away from his boarding school to run with the bulls at Pamplona. He was gored in the arm. Save for a very substantial donation to the school, and my personal guarantee of his reformation, he would've been thrown out immediately.'

His gaze focused on her. 'I can list another dozen episodes that would raise your hair.'

'He's a risk-taker,' Sasha murmured, wondering where the conversation was headed but deciding to go with it. 'He has to be as a racing driver; surely you understand that?' she argued. 'Didn't you scale Everest on your own five years ago, after everyone in your team turned back because of a blizzard? In my book that's Class A recklessness.'

'I knew what I was doing.'

'Oh, okay. How about continuing over half the London-Dakar rally with a broken arm?'

His clear surprise made her lips twist. 'How—?'

'Told you I had nerd-tastic info on you. You own the most successful motor racing team in the history of the sport. I want to drive for you. I've done my homework.'

'Very impressive, but risk-taking on the track is expected—within reason. But even before Rafael ever got behind the wheel of a race car he was…highly strung.'

'If he's so highly strung that you have to manage him, then why do you let him race? Why own the team that places him in the very sport likely to jeopardise his well-being?'

His eyes darkened and he seemed to shut off. Watching him, Sasha was fascinated by the impenetrable mask that descended over his face.

'Because racing is in our blood. It's what we do. My father never got the chance to become a racer. I raced for him, but because I had the talent. So does Rafael. There was never any question that racing was our future. But it's also my job to take care of my brother. To save him from himself. To make him see beyond his immediate desires.'

'Have you thought that perhaps if you let him make his own mistakes instead of trying to manage his life he'll wise up eventually?'

'So far, no.'

'He's a grown man. When are you going to cut the apron strings?'

'When he's proved to me that he won't kill himself without them.'

'And are you so certain you can save him every single time?'

'I can put safety measures in place.'

She laughed at his sheer arrogance. 'You're not omnipotent. You can't control what happens in life. Even if you could, Rafael will eventually resent you for controlling his life.'

Marco's lips firmed, his eyelids descending to veil his eyes.

She gave another laugh. 'He already does, doesn't he? Did you two fight? Was that why you weren't at the track this weekend?'

He ignored her questions. 'What I do, I do for his own good. And you're not good for him. My offer still stands.'

Just like that they were back to his sleazy offer of a buy-off. Distaste filled her.

She looked around the sleekly opulent room at the highly polished surfaces, the velvet walls, the bespoke furniture and elegant, sweeping staircases that belonged more in a stately home than in a hotel. Luxurious decadence only people like Marco de Cervantes could afford. The stamp of power and authority told her she wouldn't find even the smallest chink in the de Cervantes armour.

The man was as impenetrable as his wealth was immeasurable.

In the end, all she could rely on was her firm belief in right and wrong.

'You can't fire me simply to keep me out of Rafael's way. It's unethical. I think somewhere deep down you know it too.'

'I don't need moral guidance from someone like you.'

'I disagree. I think you need a big-ass, humongous compass. Because you're making a big mistake if you think I'm going to go quietly.'

His smile didn't quite reach his eyes. 'Rafael told me you were feisty.'

What else had Rafael told him? Decidedly uncomfortable at the thought of being the subject of discussion, she shrugged. 'I haven't reached where I am today without a fight or three. I won't go quietly,' she stressed again.

Several minutes of silence stretched. Her nerves stretched along with them. Just when she thought she'd break, that she'd have to resort to plain, old-fashioned, humiliating begging, he hitched one taut-muscled thigh over the side of the desk and indicated the chair in front of it.

'Sit down. I think a discussion is in order.'

Marco watched relief wash over her face and hid a triumphant smile.

He'd never had any intention of firing Sasha Fleming. Not immediately, anyway. He'd wanted her rattled, on a knife-edge at the possibility of losing what was evidently so precious to her.

The bloodthirsty, vengeance-seeking beast inside him felt a little appeased at seeing her shaken. He also wanted to test her, to see how far she would go to fight for what she wanted. After all, the higher the value she placed on her career, the sweeter it would be to snatch it away from her. Just as he'd had everything wrenched from *him* ten years ago.

He ruthlessly brushed aside the reminder of Angelique's betrayal and focused on Sasha as she walked towards him.

Again his senses reacted to her in ways that made his jaw clench. The attraction—and, yes, he was man enough to admit to it—was unwelcome as much as it was abhorrent. Rafael was in a coma, fighting for his life. The last thing Marco wanted was to acknowledge a chemical reaction to the woman in the middle of all this chaos. To acknowledge how the flare of her hips made his palms itch to shape them. How the soft lushness of her lower lip made him want to caress his finger over it.

'Regardless of the state of the team, I have a responsibility towards the sponsors.'

His office had already received several calls, ostensibly expressing concern for his brother's welfare. In truth the sponsors were sniffing around, desperate to find out what Marco's next move would be—specifically, who he would put in Rafael's place and how it would affect their bottom line.

She nodded. 'Rafael was scheduled to appear at several sponsored engagements during the August hiatus. They'll want to know what's happening.'

Once again Marco was struck by the calm calculation in her voice. This wasn't the tone of a concerned lover or a distraught team mate. Her mind was firmly focused on Team Espíritu. In other circumstances, her single-mindedness would have been admirable. But he knew first-hand the devastation ambition like hers could wreak.

Before he could answer a knock sounded on his door. One of his two butlers materialised from wherever he'd been stationed and opened the door.

Russell Latchford, his second-in-command, and Luke Green, the team's chief engineer, entered.

Russell approached. 'I've just been to see Rafael—' He stopped when he saw Sasha. 'Sasha. I didn't know you were here.' His tone echoed the question in his eyes.

Sasha returned his gaze calmly. Nothing ruffled her. Nothing except the threatened loss of her job. The urge to see her lose that cool once again attacked Marco's senses.

'Miss Fleming's here to discuss future possibilities in light of Rafael's accident.'

As team principal, it was Russell's job to source the best drivers for the team, with Marco giving final approval. Marco saw his disgruntlement, but to his credit Russell said nothing.

'Have you brought the shortlist I asked for?' Marco asked Russell.

Sasha inhaled sharply, and he saw her hands clench in her lap as Russell handed over a piece of paper.

'I've already been discreetly approached by the top five, but every driver in the sport wants to drive for us. It'll cost you to buy out their contracts, of course. If you go for someone from the lower ranking teams it'll still cost you, but the fallout won't be as damaging as poaching someone from the top teams.'

Marco shook his head. 'Our sponsors signed up for the package—Rafael and the car. I don't want a second-class driver. I need someone equally talented and charismatic or the sponsors will throw hissy fits.'

Luke spoke up. 'There's also the problem of limited in-season testing. We can't just throw in a brand-new driver mid-season and expect him to handle the car anywhere near the way Rafael did.'

Marco glanced down at the list. 'No. Rafael is irreplaceable. I accept that the Drivers' Championship is no longer an option, but I want to win the Constructors' Championship. The team deserves it. All of these drivers would ditch their contract to drive for me, but I'd rather not deal with a messy court battle. Where do we stand on the former champion who retired last year? Have you contacted him?'

Russell shook his head. 'Even with the August break he won't be in good enough shape when the season resumes in September.'

'So my only option is to take on a driver from another team?'

'No, it isn't.' Sasha's voice was low, but intensely powerful, and husky enough to command attention.

Marco's eyes slid to her. Her stance remained relaxed, one leg crossed over the other, but in her eyes he saw ferocious purpose.

'You have something to add?'

Fierce blue eyes snapped at him as she rolled her shoulders. As last time, he couldn't help but follow the movement. Then his eyes travelled lower, to the breasts covered by her nondescript T-shirt. Again the pull of desire was strong and sharp, unlike anything he'd experienced before. Again he pushed it away and forced his gaze back to her face.

A faint flush covered her cheeks. 'You know I do. I know the car inside out. I've driven it at every Friday Practice since last season. The way I see it, I'm the only way you can win the Constructors' Championship. Plus you'd save a lot of money and the unnecessary litigation of trying to tempt away a driver mid-season from another team. In the last few practices my run-times have nearly equalled Rafael's.'

Marco silently admitted the truth of her words. He might not sit on the pit wall for every single minute of a race—the engineer and aerodynamicist in him preferred the hard facts of the telemetry reports—but he knew Sasha's race times to the last fraction.

He also knew racing was more than just the right car in the right hands. 'Yes, but you're yet to perform under the pressure of a Saturday practice, a pole position shoot-out and a race on Sunday. I'd rather have a driver with actual race experience.'

Russell fidgeted and cleared his throat. 'I agree, Marco. I think Alan might be a better option—'

'I've consistently surpassed Alan's track times,' she said of the team's second driver. 'Luke will confirm it.'

Luke's half-hearted shrug made Marco frown.

'Is there a problem?'

The other man cleared his throat. 'Not a problem, exactly, but I'm not sure how the team will react to…you know…'

'No, I don't know. If you have something to say, then say it.'

'He means how the team will react to a woman lead driver,' Sasha stated baldly.

Recalling her accusation of sexism, he felt a flash of anger swell through him. He knew the views of others when it came to employing women as drivers. The pathetically few women racers attested to the fact that it was a predominantly male sport, but he believed talent was talent, regardless of the gender that wielded it.

The thought that key members in his team didn't share his belief riled him.

He rose. 'That will be all, gentlemen.'

Russell's surprise was clear. 'Do you need some time to make the decision?'

His gaze stayed on Sasha. Her chest had risen in a sharp intake of breath. Again he had to force himself not to glance down at her breasts. The effort it took not to look displeased him immensely.

'I've requested figures from my lawyers by morning. I'll let you know my decision.'

His butler led them out.

'Mr de Cervantes—' Sasha started.

He held up a hand. 'Let me make one thing clear. I didn't refuse you a drive because of your gender. Merely because of your disruptive influence within my team.'

Her eyes widened, then she nodded. 'Okay. But I want to—'

'I need to return to my brother's bedside. You'll also find out my decision tomorrow.' He turned to leave.

'Please. I…need this.'

The raw, fervent emotion in her voice stopped him from leaving the room. Returning to her side, he stared down at her bent head. Her hands were clenched tighter. A swathe of pure black hair had slipped its knot and half covered her face. His fingers itched to catch it back, smooth it behind her ear so he could see her expression.

Most of all, he wanted her to look at him.

'Why? Why is this so important to you?' he asked.

'I…I made a promise.' Her voice was barely above a whisper.

Marco frowned. 'A promise? To whom?'

She inhaled, and before his eyes she gathered herself in. Her spine straightened, and her shoulders snapped back until her whole body became poised, almost regal. Then her eyes slowly rose to his.

The steely determination in their depths compelled his attention. His blood heated, rushing through his veins in a way that made his body clench in denial. Yet he couldn't look away.

Her gaze dropped. Marco bit back the urge to order her to look at him.

'It doesn't matter. All you need to know is if you give me a chance I'll hand you the Constructors' Championship.'

Sasha heard the low buzzing and cursed into her pillow. How the blazes had a wasp got into her room?

And since when did wasps make such a racket?

Groaning, she rolled over and tried to burrow into a better position. Sleep had been an elusive beast. She'd spent the night alternately pacing the floor and running through various arguments in her head about how she would convince Marco to keep her on the team. In the end exhaustion had won out.

Now she'd been woken by—

Her phone! With a yelp, she shoved off the covers and stumbled blindly for the satchel she'd discarded on the floor.

'Huhn?'

'Do I take it by that unladylike grunt that I've disturbed your sleep?' Marco de Cervantes's voice rumbled down the line.

'Not at all,' she lied. 'What time is it?' She furiously rubbed her eyes. She'd never been a morning person.

Taut silence, then, 'It's nine-thirty.'

'What? *Damn*.' She'd slept through her alarm. Again.

Could anyone blame her, though? Being part of Team Es-píritu meant staying in excellent accommodation, but this time management had excelled itself—the two thousand thread-count cotton sheets, handmade robes, the hot tub, lotions and potions, the finest technology and her personal maid on tap were just the beginnings of the absurd luxury that made the crew of Marco's team the envy of the circuit. But her four-poster bed and its mattress—dear Lord, the made-by-angels mattress—was the reason—

'Do you have somewhere else to be, Miss Fleming?'

'Yes. I have a plane to catch back to London at eleven.' Thankfully she didn't have a lot of things to pack, having put her restless energy to good use last night. And the airport was only ten minutes away. Still, she was cutting it fine.

'You might wish to revise that plan.'

She froze, refusing to acknowledge the thin vein of hope taking root deep within her. 'And why would I need to do that?'

'I have a proposition for you. Open your door.'

'What?'

'Open your door. I need to look into your eyes when I out-line my plan so there can be no doubt on either part.'

'You're *here*?' Her eyes darted to her door, as if she could see his impressive body outlined through the solid wood.

'I'm here. But I'll soon be a figment of your imagination if you don't open your door.'

Sasha glanced down at herself. No way was she opening the door to Marco de Cervantes wearing a vampire T-shirt that declared *'Bite Me'* in blood-red. And she didn't even want to think of the state of her hair.

'I… Can you give me two minutes?' If she could get in and out of a race suit in ninety seconds, she sure as hell could make herself presentable in a fraction of that time.

'You have five seconds. Then I move on to my next call.'

'No. Wait!' Keeping the phone glued to her ear, she rushed to the door. Pulling it open, she stuck her head out, trying her best to shield the rest of her body from full view.

And there he stood. Unlike the casual clothes of yesterday, Marco was dressed in a bespoke suit, his impressive shoulders even more imposing underneath the slate-grey jacket, blue shirt and pinstriped tie, his long legs planted in battle stance. His hair was combed neatly, unlike the unruly, sexy mess it'd been yesterday. The strong desire to see it messy again had her pulling back a fraction.

Eyes locked on hers, he lowered his phone. 'Invite me in.'

'Why? Are you a vampire?' she shot back, then swallowed a groan.

Frown lines creased his brow. '*Excuse me?* Are you high?'

Sasha silently cursed her morning brain. 'Hah—I wish. Oh, never mind. I'm…I'm not really dressed to receive guests, but I didn't want you to leave, so unless you want to extend that five-second ultimatum this will have to do.'

His frown deepened. 'Are you in the habit of answering your hotel door naked?'

Heat crawled up her neck and stung her face. 'Of course not. I'm not naked.'

'Prove it' came the soft challenge.

'Fine. See?' Belatedly she wondered at her sanity as she stepped into his view and felt the dark, intense force of Marco's gaze as it travelled over her.

When his eyes returned to hers, the breath snagged in her lungs. His hazel eyes had darkened to burnt gold with dark green flecks; the clench of his jaw was even more pronounced. He seemed to be straining against an emotion that was more than a little bit frightening.

She stepped back. He followed her in and shut the door. The luxury hotel suite that had seemed so vast, so over the top, closed in on her. She took another step back. He followed, eyes locked on her.

Her phone fell from her fingers, thankfully cushioned by

the shag-pile carpet. Mouth dry, she kept backing up. He kept following.

'I make it a point not to credit rumours, but it seems in this instance the rumours are true, Sasha Fleming.'

The way he said her name—slowly, with a hint of Latin intonation—made goosebumps rise on her flesh. Her nipples peaked and a sensation she recognised to her horror as desire raked through her abdomen, sending delicious darts of liquid heat to the apex of her thighs.

'What exactly do you think is true about me?'

'Sex is your weapon of choice,' he breathed, his eyes lingering on the telltale nubs beneath her T-shirt. 'The only trouble is you wield it so unsubtly.'

'I beg your pardon?' she squeaked as the backs of her legs touched the side of the bed. 'Did you just say—?'

'You need to learn to finesse your art.'

'What in heaven's name are you blathering about? Are you sure *you're* not the one who's high?' she flung back.

'No man likes to be bludgeoned over the head with sex. No matter how…enticing the package.'

'You're either loopy or you've got me confused with someone else. I don't bludgeon and I don't entice.'

He kept coming.

She leaned back on the bed and felt the hem of her shirt riding up her thighs. 'For goodness' sake, stop!'

He stopped, but his gaze didn't. It continued its destructive course over her, leaving no part of her untouched, until Sasha felt sure she was about to combust from the heat of it.

Desperate, she let her tongue dart out to lick her lips. 'Look…Derek—I presume that's where you got your little morsel from—said a lot of unsavoury things about me when we broke up. But I'm not who…whatever you think I am.'

'Even though I can see the evidence for myself?' he rasped in a low voice.

She scrambled over the side of the bed and grabbed the robe she'd dropped on the floor last night. With shaking fingers, and a mind scrambling to keep pace with the bizarre turn of the conversation, she pulled the lapels over her traitorous body.

Having pursued her profession in fast cars financed by billionaires with unlimited funds, Sasha knew there was a brand of women who found the whole X1 Premier Racing world a huge turn-on: women who used their sexuality to pursue racers with a single-mindedness that bordered on the obsessive.

She'd never considered for a second that she would ever be bracketed with them—especially by the wealthiest, most sought-after billionaire of them all. The idea would have been laughable if the sting of Derek's betrayal still didn't have the ability to hurt.

'Well, whatever it is you *think* you see, there's no truth to the rumour. Now, can we please get back to the reason you came here in the first place?'

Her words seemed to rouse him from whatever dark, edgy place he'd been in. He looked up from her thighs, slowly exhaled, and looked around the room, taking in the rumpled bed and the contents of her satchel strewn on the floor.

When he paced to the window and drew back the curtain she took the opportunity to tie the robe tighter around her, hoping it would dispel the electricity zinging around her body.

He turned after a minute, his face devoid of expression. 'I've decided not to recruit a new driver. Doing so mid-season is not financially viable. Besides, they all have contracts and sponsorship commitments to fulfil.'

Hope grew so powerful it weakened her legs. Sinking down onto the side of the bed, she swallowed. 'So, does that mean I have the seat for the rest of the season?'

He shoved his hands into his pockets, his gaze fixed squarely on her. 'You'll sign an agreement promising to honour every commitment the team holds you to. Half of the sponsors have agreed to let you fulfil Rafael's commitments.'

He hadn't given a definite *yes*, but Sasha's heartbeat thundered nonetheless. 'And the other half?'

'With nowhere to go, they'll come round. My people are working on them.'

Unable to stem the flood of emotion rising inside, she pried her gaze from his and stared down at her trembling hands. She struggled to breathe.

Finally. The chance to wipe the slate clean. To earn the respect that had been ruthlessly denied her and so callously wrenched from her father. Finally the Fleming name would be spoken of with esteem and not disdain. Jack Fleming would be allowed to rest in peace, his legacy nothing to be ashamed of any more.

'I…thank you,' she murmured.

'You haven't heard the conditions attached to your drive.'

She shook her head, careless of the hair flying about her face as euphoria frothed inside her. 'I agree. Whatever it is, I agree.' She wouldn't let this opportunity slip her by. She intended to grab it with both hands. To prove to anyone who'd dared to nay-say that they'd been wrong.

His eyes narrowed. 'Yesterday you promised to give *anything* not to have Rafael in hospital. Today you're agreeing to conditions you haven't even heard. Are you always this carefree with your consent? Perhaps I need to rethink making you lead driver. I shudder to think what such rashness could cost me on the race track.'

'I… Fine—name your conditions.'

He quirked a mocking brow. '*Gracias.* Aside from the other commitments, there are two that I'm particularly interested in. Team Espíritu *must* win the Constructors' Championship. We're eighty points ahead of the next championship challenger. I expect those points only to go up. Understood?'

A smile lit up her face. 'Absolutely. I intend to wipe the floor with them.'

'The second condition—'

'Wait. I have a condition of my own.'

His lips twisted. '*Déjà vu* overwhelms me. I suppose I shouldn't be surprised.'

Sasha ignored him, the need to voice a wish so long denied making her words trip from her lips with a life of their own. 'If...*when* I secure you the Constructors' Championship, I want my contract with Team Espíritu to be extended for another year.'

When his eyes narrowed further, she rushed to speak again.

'You can write it into my contract that I'll be judged based on my performance during the next three months. If we win the Constructors' you'll hire me for another year.'

'Winning a Drivers' Championship means that much to you?'

His curiously flat tone drew her gaze, but his expression remained inscrutable. Her heart hammered with the force of her deepest yearning. 'Yes, it does.'

His eyelids descended, veiling his gaze. The tension in the room increased until she could cut the atmosphere with a butter knife. But when he looked back up there was nothing but cool, impersonal regard.

'Very well. Win the Constructors' Championship and I'll extend your contract for another year.'

She couldn't believe he'd agreed so readily. 'Wow, that was easy.'

'Perhaps it's because I don't believe in talking every subject to death. My time is precious.'

'Yes, of course...'

'As I was saying, before you interrupted, my second condition is more important, Miss Fleming, so listen carefully. You'll have no personal contact with any male member of the team; you will go nowhere near my brother. Any hint of a nonprofessional relationship with another driver or anyone within the sport, for that matter, will mean instant dismissal. And I'll personally make it my mission to ensure you never drive another racing car. Do we understand each other?'

CHAPTER FOUR

'IF YOU'VE FINISHED your breakfast, I'll take you on the tour of the race track.'

Sasha looked up from her almost empty plate of scrambled eggs and ham to find Marco lounging in the doorway that connected the vast living room to the sun-drenched terrace of *Casa de León*.

She'd been here three days, and she still couldn't get her head round the sheer vastness of the de Cervantes estate. Navigating her way around the huge, rambling two-storey villa without getting lost had taken two full days.

With its white stucco walls, dark red slate roofs and large cathedral-like windows, *Casa de León* was an architect's dream. The high exposed beams, sweeping staircases and intricately designed marble floors wouldn't have been out of place in a palace. Every piece of furniture, painting and drape looked as if it cost a fortune. Even the air inside the villa smelled different, tinged with a special rarefied, luxurious quality that made her breath catch.

Outside, an endless green vista, broken only by perfectly manicured gardens, stretched as far as the eye could see... It was no wonder the countless villa staff travelled around in golf buggies.

Realising Marco was waiting for an answer, she nodded, drawing her gaze from the long, muscular legs encased in dark grey trousers. 'Sure. I'll just finish my coffee. Aren't you having anything?' She indicated the mouth-watering spread of seasonal fruit, pastries and ham slices on the table.

Disengaging himself from the doorway, he came towards her, powerfully sleek and oozing arrogant masculinity. 'I'll have a coffee, too.'

When he sat and made no move to pour it himself, she raised an eyebrow. 'Yes, boss. Three bags full, boss?'

His hazel eyes gleamed and Sasha had the distinct feeling he was amused, although not a smile cracked his lips. In fact he looked decidedly strained. Which wasn't surprising under the circumstances, she reminded herself.

Feeling the mutiny give way, she poured him a cup. 'Black?'

'*Sí*. Two sugars.'

She looked up, surprised. 'Funny, I wouldn't have pegged you for the two-sugars type.'

'And how *would* you have pegged me?'

'Black, straight up, drunk boiling hot without a wince.'

'Because my insides are made of tar and my soul is black as night?' he mocked.

She shrugged. 'Hey, you said it.' She added sugar and passed it over.

'*Gracias.*' He picked up a silver spoon and stirred his drink, the tiny utensil looking very delicate in his hand.

Sasha found herself following the movement, her gaze tracing the short dark hairs on the back of his hand. Suddenly her mouth dried, and her stomach performed that stupid flip again. Wrenching her gaze from the hypnotic motion, she picked up her cup with a decidedly unsteady hand.

'How are you settling in?' he asked.

'Do you really want to know?'

The speed with which Marco had whisked her from Budapest to Spain after she'd signed the contract had made her head spin. Of course his luxury private jet—which he'd piloted himself—had negated the tedium of long airport waits and might have had something to do with it. They'd flown to Barcelona, then transferred by helicopter to his estate in León.

He took another sip. 'I wouldn't have asked otherwise. You should know by now that I never say anything I don't mean.'

Now she felt surly. Her suite was the last word in luxury, complete with four-poster bed, half a dozen fluffy pillows and a deep-sunken marble bath to die for. Just across from where she sat, past the giant-sized terracotta potted plants and a barbecue area, an Olympic-sized swimming pool sparkled azure in the dappling morning light. She'd already sampled its soothing comfort, along with the sports gym equipped with everything she needed to keep her exercise regime on track. In reality, she wanted for nothing.

And yet…

'It's fine. I have everything I need. Thank you,' she tagged on waspishly. Then, wisely moving on before she ventured into full-blown snark, she asked, 'How is Rafael?'

Marco's gaze cooled.

Sasha sighed. 'I agreed to stay away from him. I didn't agree to stop caring about him.'

'The move from Budapest went fine. He's now in the care of the best Spanish doctors in Barcelona.'

'Since you'll probably bite my head off if I ask you to send him my best, I'll move on. How far away is the race track?'

'Three miles south.' Lifting his cup, he drained it.

'Exactly how big is this place?'

When Marco had announced he was bringing a skeleton team to Spain to help her train for her debut at the end of August, she'd mistakenly thought she would be spending most of her time in a race simulator. The half an hour it'd taken to travel from Marco's landing strip to his villa had given her an inkling of how immense his estate was.

His gaze pinned on her, he picked up an orange and skilfully peeled it. 'All around? About twenty-five square miles.'

'And you and Rafael own all of it?'

'Sí.' He popped a segment into his mouth.

Sasha carefully set her cup down, her senses tingling with warning. That soft *sí* had held a slight edge to it that made her wary. His next words confirmed her wariness.

'Just think, if only you'd said yes all this would've been yours.'

She didn't need to ask what he meant. Affecting a light tone, she toyed with the delicate handle of her expensive bone china cup. 'Gee, I don't know. The race track would've been handy, but what the hell would I do with the rest of the... What else is there, anyway?'

His gaze was deceptively lazy—deceptive because she could feel the charged animosity rising from him.

'There's a fully functioning vineyard and winery. And the stables house some of the best Andalucian thoroughbreds in Spain. There's also an exclusive by-invitation-only resort and spa on the other side of the estate.'

'Well, there you have it, then. My palate is atrociously common—not to mention that if I drink more than one glass of wine I get a raging headache. As for thoroughbreds—I couldn't tell you which end of the horse to climb if you put me next to one. So, really, you're way better off without me in your family. The spa sounds nice, though. A girl could always do with a foot rub after a hard day's work—although I have a feeling the amount of grease I tend to get under my nails would frighten your resort staff.'

A tiny tic appeared at his temple. 'Are you always this facetious, or do you practice?'

'Normally I keep it well hidden. I only show off when asked really, really nicely,' she flung back. Then she stood. 'From the unfortunate downturn of this conversation, I take it the offer of a tour is now off the table?' She tilted her chin, determined not to reveal how deep his barbs had stung.

'As much as I'm tempted to reward your petulance with time on the naughty step, that will only prove counterproductive.' Wiping his hands on a napkin, he rose to tower over her. 'You're here to train. Familiarising yourself with the race track is part of that training. I'll leave the naughty step for another time.'

Wisely deciding to leave the mention of the naughty step alone, Sasha relaxed her grip on the back of the chair. 'Thank you.'

Sasha followed him into the villa, staunchly maintaining her silence. But not talking didn't equate to not looking, and, damn it, she couldn't help but be intensely aware of the man beside her. His smell assailed her nostrils—that sharp tang of citrus coupled with the subtle undertones of musk that shifted as it flowed over his warmth.

Against the strong musculature of his torso his white polo shirt lovingly followed the superb lines of a deep chest and powerful shoulders. All that magnificence tapered down to a trim waist that knew not an ounce of fat.

Judging by his top-notch physicality, she wasn't surprised Marco had been the perfect championship-winning driver ten years ago.

'Why did you give up racing? You resigned so abruptly, and yet it's obvious you recovered fully after your crash.'

She saw his shoulders tense before he rounded on her. The icy, forbidding look in his eyes made her bite her lip.

Nice one, Sasha.

'That is not a subject up for discussion, Miss Fleming. And before you take it into your head to go prying I caution you against it. Understood?'

He barely waited for her nod before he wrenched open the front door.

Outside, two golf buggies sat side by side at the bottom of the steps. She headed towards the nearest one.

'Where are you going?' he bit out.

She stopped. 'Oh, I thought we were going by road.'

He nodded to the helipad, where a black and red chopper sat gleaming in the morning sun. 'We're touring by helicopter.'

It was a spectacularly beautiful machine—the latest in a long line of beautiful aircraft.

'Any chance you'll let me fly it?'

He flashed a mirthless grin at her. 'I don't see any pigs flying, do you?'

'Wow, this is incredible! How long have you had this race track?'

Marco glanced up from the helicopter controls, then immediately wished he hadn't. It was bad enough hearing her excitement piped directly into his headphones. The visual effects were even more disturbing.

When he'd offered her an aerial tour of the race track he hadn't taken into account how she was dressed. In most respects, her white shorts could be described as sensible—almost boyish. He'd been out with women who wore far less on a regular basis. Her light green shirt was also plain to the point of being utilitarian.

All the same, Marco found the combination of her excitement and her proximity...*aggravating*. Even more aggravating were the flashbacks he kept having of her leaning back on the bed in her hotel room, her T-shirt riding up to reveal skin so tempting it had knocked his breath clean out of his lungs...

Her naked ambition and her sheer drive to succeed were living things that charged the air around her. Marco knew only too well the high cost of blind ambition, and yet knowing the depths of Sasha Fleming's ambition and what she would do to achieve her goals didn't stop him from imagining how it would have felt to lift her T-shirt higher...just a fraction...

He was also more than a little puzzled that she'd made no attempt to gain his attention since that episode in her room. Women flaunted themselves at him at every opportunity—used every excuse in the book to garner his interest. Some even resorted to...*unconventional* means. Most of the time he was happy to direct them Rafael's way. He'd long outgrown the paddock bunny phase; had outgrown it even before Angelique, the most calculating of them all, had stepped into his orbit and turned his world upside down.

Marco sobered, seething at himself for the memories he suddenly couldn't seem to dispel so easily. Focusing on the controls, he banked the chopper and followed the straights and curves of the race track hundreds of metres below.

'I built it ten years ago,' he clipped out in answer to her question.

'After you retired?' she asked, surprised.

'No. Just before.' His harsh response had the desired effect of shutting her up, but when he glanced at her again, he noted the spark of speculation in her eyes. Before he could think about why he was doing so, he found himself elaborating. 'I thought I'd be spending more time here.' He'd woven foolish dreams about what his life would be like, how perfect everything had seemed. He'd had the perfect car; the perfect woman.

'What happened?'

The crushing pain of remembrance tightened around his chest. 'I crashed.'

She gave a sad little understanding nod that made him want to growl at her. What did she know? She was as conniving as they came.

Forcing his anger under control, he flew over the track towards the mid-point hill.

Sasha pointed to six golf buggies carrying mechanics who hopped out at various points of the track. 'What are they doing?'

'The track hasn't been used for a while. They're conducting last-minute checks on the moveable parts to make sure they're secure.'

'I can't believe this track can be reshaped to simulate other tracks around the circuit. I can't wait to have a go!'

Excitement tinged her voice and Marco couldn't help glancing over at her. Her eyes were alight with a smile that seemed to glow from within. His hands tightened around the controls.

'The track was built before simulators became truly effective. One concrete track would've served only to make a driver expert at a particular track, so I designed an interchangeable track. The other advantage is experience gained in driving on tarmac, or as close to tarmac—as you can get. Wet or dry conditions can make or break a race. This way the driver gets to practise on both with the right tyres. Electronic simulators and wind tunnels have their places, but so does this track.'

The helicopter crested another small hill and cold sweat

broke out over his skin. Several feet to the side of the track a mound of whitewashed stones had been piled high in a makeshift monument. Marco's hand tightened on the lever and deftly swerved the aircraft away from the landmark he had no wish to see up close.

'Trust me, I'm not complaining. It's a great idea. I'm just surprised other teams haven't copied the idea. Or sold their firstborn sons to use your track.'

'Offers have been made in the past.'

'And?'

He shrugged. 'I occasionally allow them to use the track I designed. But for the whole package to come together they also need the car I designed.'

A small laugh burst from her lips. The sound was so unexpectedly pleasing he momentarily lost his train of thought, and missed her reply.

'What did you say?'

'I said that's a clever strategy—considering you own the team you design for, and the only other way anyone can get their hands on a Marco de Cervantes design is by shelling out…how much does the *Cervantes Conquistador* cost? Two million?'

'Three.'

She whistled—another unexpected sound that charged through his bloodstream, making him even more on edge than he'd been a handful of seconds ago.

She leaned forward into his eyeline. He'd been wrong about the shirt being functional. Her pert breasts pressed against the cotton material, her hands on her thighs as she peered down.

Marco swallowed, the hot stirrings in his abdomen increasing to uncomfortable proportions. Ruthlessly he pushed them away.

Sasha Fleming was bad news, he reminded himself.

Rafael had got involved with her to his severe detriment. Marco had no intention of following down the same road. His only interest in her was to make sure she delivered the

Constructors' Championship. Now he knew what she really wanted—the Drivers' Championship—he had her completely at his mercy.

Control re-established, he brought the helicopter in to land, and yanked off his headphones. Sasha jumped down without his help and Marco caught the puzzled look she flashed him. Ignoring it, he strode towards Luke Green. His chief engineer had travelled ahead to supervise the initial training arrangements.

Sasha drew closer and her scent reached his nostrils. Marco's insides clenched in rejection even as he breathed her in. His awareness of her was becoming intolerable. Even her voice as she greeted Luke bit into his psyche.

'Is everything in order?' he asked.

Luke nodded. 'We're just about to offload the engine. The mechanics will check it over and make sure it hasn't been damaged during the flight.'

'It takes three hours max to assemble the car, so it should be ready for me to test this afternoon, shouldn't it?' Sasha asked, her attention so intent on the tarpaulin-covered engine Marco almost enquired if she yearned to caress it.

'No. You'll begin training tomorrow morning,' he all but growled.

Her head snapped towards him, her expression crestfallen. 'Oh, but if the car's here…'

'The mechanics have been working on getting things ready since dawn. This engine hasn't been used since last December. It'll have to go through rigorous testing before it's race-ready. That'll take most of the day—at least until sundown.'

He turned back to Luke. 'I want to see hourly engine readouts and a final telemetry report when you're done testing.'

'Sure thing, boss.'

Grabbing Sasha's arm, he steered her away from the garage. Several eyes followed them, but he didn't care. He was nothing like his brother. He had no intention of ever making a fool of himself over a woman again.

Opening the passenger door to his Conquistador, he thrust her into the bucket seat. Rounding the hood, he slid behind the wheel.

'Why do I get the feeling you're angry with me?' she directed at him.

Marco slammed his door. 'It's not a feeling.'

The breath she blew up disturbed the thick swathe of hair slanting over her forehead. 'What did I do?' she demanded.

He faced her and found her stunning eyes snapping fire at him. The blue of her gaze was so intense, so vivid, he wanted to keep staring at her for ever. The uncomfortable erotic heat he'd felt in her Budapest hotel room, when she'd strutted into view wearing that damned T-shirt that boldly announced *'Bite Me'*, rose again.

For days he'd been fighting that stupid recurring memory that strayed into his thoughts at the most inconvenient times.

Even here in León, where much more disturbing memories impinged everywhere he looked, he couldn't erase from his mind the sight of those long, coltish legs and the thought of how they would feel around his waist.

Nor could he ignore the evidence of Sasha's hard work and dedication to her career. Every night since her arrival in Spain he'd found her poring over telemetry reports or watching footage of past races, fully immersed in pursuing the only thing she cared about.

The only thing she cared about…

Grabbing the steering wheel, he forced himself to calm down.

'Marco?'

When had he given her permission to use his first name? Come to think of it, when had he started thinking of her as Sasha instead of Miss Fleming?

Dios, he was losing it.

With a wrench of his wrist the engine sprang to life, its throaty roar surprisingly soothing. Designing the Espíritu race cars had been an engineering challenge he'd relished. The *Cervantes Conquistador* had been a pure labour of love.

Momentarily he lost himself in the sounds of the engine, his mind picking up minute clicks and torsion controls. If he closed his eyes he would be able to imagine the aerodynamic flow of air over the chassis, visualise where each spark plug, each piston, nut and bolt was located.

But he didn't close his eyes. He kept his gaze fixed firmly ahead. His grip tightened around the wheel.

Her gaze stayed on him as he accelerated the green and black sports car out of the parking lot. The screech of tyres drew startled glances from the mechanics heading for the hangar. Marco didn't give a damn.

After a few minutes, when he felt sufficiently calm, he slowed down. 'It's not you.'

She didn't answer.

Shrugging, he indicated the rich forest surrounding them. 'It's this place.'

'This place? The race track or *Casa de León*?'

His jaw clenched as he tried in vain to stem the memories flooding him. 'This is where my mother died eight years ago.'

Her gasp echoed in the car. 'Oh, my God, I'm so sorry. I didn't know. You should've said something.'

He slowed down long enough to give her a hard look. 'It isn't common knowledge outside my family. I'd prefer it to remain that way.' He wasn't even sure why he'd told her. Whatever was causing him to act so out of character he needed to cauterise it.

She gave a swift nod. 'Of course. You can trust me.' Her colour rose slightly at her last words.

The irony wasn't lost on him. He only had himself to blame if she decided to spill her guts at the first opportunity. Flooring the accelerator, he sent the car surging forward as his *other* reason for wanting to escape the memories of this place rose.

Sasha remained silent until he pulled up in front of the

villa. Then, lifting a hand, she tucked a strand of hair behind her ear. 'How did it happen?' she asked softly.

Releasing his clammy grip on the steering wheel, Marco flicked a glance at the villa door. He knew he'd find no respite within. If anything, the memories were more vivid inside. He didn't need to close his eyes to see his mother laughing at Rafael's shameless cajoling, her soft hazel eyes sparkling as she wiped her hands on a kitchen towel moments before rushing out of the villa.

'For his twenty-first birthday my father bought Rafael a Lamborghini. We celebrated at a nightclub in Barcelona. Afterwards I flew down here in the helicopter with my parents. Rafael chose to drive from Barcelona—five hours straight. He arrived just after breakfast, completely wired from partying. I tried to convince him to get some sleep, but he wanted to take my parents for a spin in the car.'

The familiar icy grip of pain tightened around his chest.

'Rafael was my mother's golden boy. He could do no wrong. So of course she agreed.' Marco felt some of the pain seep out and tried to contain it. 'My father insisted later it was the sun that got in Rafael's eyes as he turned the curve, but one eyewitness confirmed he took the corner too fast. I heard the crash from the garage.' Every excruciating second had felt like a lifetime as he sped towards the scene. 'By the time the air ambulance came my mother was gone.'

'Oh, Marco, *no!*'

Sasha's voice was a soft, soothing sound. The ache inside abated, but it didn't disappear. It never would. He'd lost his mother before he'd ever had the chance to make up for what he'd put her through.

'I should've stopped him—should've insisted he get some sleep before taking the car out again.'

'You couldn't have known.'

He shook his head. 'But I should have. Except when it comes to Rafael everyone seems to develop a blind spot. Including me.'

Vaguely, Marco wondered why he was spilling his guts. To Sasha Fleming, of all people. With a forceful wrench on the door, he stepped out of the car.

She scrambled out too. 'And your father? What happened to him?'

His fist tightened around the computerised car key. 'The accident severed his spine. He lost the use of his body from the neck down. He's confined to a wheelchair and will remain like that for the rest of his life.'

Sasha looked after Marco's disappearing figure, shocked by the astonishing revelation.

Now Marco's motives became clear. His overprotective attitude towards Rafael, his reaction to the crash, suddenly made sense. Watching his mother die on the race track *he'd* built had to be right up there with enduring a living hell every time he stepped foot on it.

So why did he do it?

Marco de Cervantes was an extraordinary engineer and aerodynamicist, who excelled in building astonishingly fast race cars, but he could easily have walked away and concentrated his design efforts on the equally successful range of exclusive sport cars favoured by Arab sheikhs and Russian oligarchs.

So what drove him to have anything to do with a world that surely held heart-wrenching memories?

She slowly climbed the stairs and entered the house, her mind whirling as she went into her suite to wash off the heat and sweat of the race track.

After showering, she put on dark jeans and a striped blue shirt. Pulling her hair into a neat twist, she secured it with a band and shoved her feet into pair of flat sandals.

She met Marco as she came down the stairs. The now familiar raking gaze sent another shiver of awareness scything through her. He stopped directly in front of her, his arrest-

ing face and piercing regard rendering her speechless for
several seconds.

'Lunch won't be ready for a while, but if you want something light before then, Rosario can fix you something.'

The matronly housekeeper appeared in the sun-dappled
hallway as if by magic, wiping her hands on a white apron.

'No, thanks. I'm not hungry.'

With a glance, he dismissed the housekeeper. His gaze returned to her, slowly tracing her face. When it rested on her
mouth she struggled not to run her tongue over it, remember-
ing how his eyes had darkened the last time she'd done that.

'I have a video call with Tom Brooks, my press liaison, in
five minutes. Can I use your study?'

His eyes locked on hers. 'Why's he calling?'

'He wants to go over next month's sponsorship schedule.
I can give you a final printout, if you like.'

She deliberately kept her voice light, non-combative. Something told her Marco de Cervantes was spoiling for a fight,
and after his revelations she wasn't sure it was wise to engage him in one. Pain had a habit of eroding rational thought.

Being calmly informed by the doctor that she'd lost the
baby she hadn't even been aware she was carrying had made
her want to scream—loudly, endlessly until her throat gave
out. She'd wanted to reach inside herself and rip her body
apart for letting her down. In the end the only thing that had
helped was getting back to the familiar—to her racing car.
The pain had never left her, but the adrenaline of racing had
eased her aching soul the way nothing else had been able to.

Looking into Marco's dark eyes, she caught a glimpse of
his pain, but wisely withheld the offer of comfort on the tip
of her tongue. After all, who was *she* to offer comfort when
she hadn't quite come to terms with losing her baby herself?

Silently, she held his gaze.

For several seconds he stared back. Then he indicated his
study. 'I'll set it up for you.'

She followed him into the room and drew to a stunned halt.

he space was so irreverently, unmistakably male that her yes widened. An old-style burgundy leather studded chair nd footrest stood before the largest fireplace she'd ever seen, bove which two centuries-old swords hung. The rest of the oom was oak-panelled, with dusty books stretching from loor to ceiling. The scent of stale tobacco pipe smoke hung n the air. It wouldn't have been strange to see a shaggy-haired rofessor seated behind the massive desk that stood under he only window in the room. Compared to the contempoary, exceedingly luxurious comfort of the rest of the villa, his was a throwback to another century—save for the sleek omputer on the desk.

Marco caught the look on her face and raised an eyebrow s he activated the large flat screen computer on the immense nahogany desk.

'Did your designer fall into a time warp when he got to his room?'

'This was my father's study—his personal space. He never llowed my mother to redesign it, no matter how much she ried. He hasn't been in here since she died, and I...I feel no need to change things.'

A well of sympathy rose inside Sasha for his pain. Casting a look around, she stopped, barely suppressing a gasp. 'Is that a stag's head on the wall?' she asked, eyeing the large animal head, complete with gnarled, menacing antlers.

'A bull stag, yes.'

She turned from the gruesome spectacle. 'There's a difference?'

The semblance of a smile whispered over his lips. Sasha found she couldn't tear her gaze away. In that split second she felt a wild, unfettered yearning to see that smile widen, to see his face light up in genuine amusement.

'The bull stag is the alpha of its herd. He calls the shots. And he gets his pick of the females.'

'Ah, I see. If you're going to display such a monstrosity on your wall, only the best will do?'

He slanted her a wry glance. 'That's the general thin
ing, yes.'

'Ugh.'

He caught her shudder and his smile widened.

Warmth exploded in her chest, encompassed her who
body and made her breathless. Sasha found she didn't ca
The need to bask in the stunning warmth of his smile trump
the need for oxygen. Even when another voice intruded s
couldn't look away.

When Tom's voice came again she roused herself with d
ficulty from the drugging race of her pulse, carefully skirt
a coffee table festooned with piles of books, and approach
the desk as the screen came to life.

'Hello? Can you hear me, Sasha?' Tom's voice held its usu
touch of impatience, and his features were pinched.

Marco's smile disappeared.

Sasha mourned the loss of it and moved closer to the scree
'I'm here, Tom.'

He huffed in response, then his eyes swung over her shou
der and widened.

'Sit down,' Marco said from behind her, pushing the ma
sive chair towards her.

She sat. He reached over her shoulder and adjusted t
screen. Then he remained behind her—a heavy, domina
ing presence.

Tom cleared his throat. 'Uh, I didn't know you'd be joi
ing us, Mr de Cervantes.'

'A last-minute decision. Carry on,' Marco instructed.

'Um…okay…'

She'd never seen Tom flounder, and she bit the inside
her mouth to keep from smiling.

'Sasha, you have a Q&A on the team's website next Fr
day. I've e-mailed the questions to you. I'll need it back b
Wednesday, to proofread and get it approved by the lawyer
On Friday night you have the Children of Bravery awards
London. Tuesday is the Strut footwear shoot, followed by th

inear Watches shoot in Barcelona. On Sun— Is there a prob-
m?' he asked testily when she shook her head.

'That's not going to work. I can't take all that time off just
or sponsorship events.'

'This is the schedule I've planned. You'll have to deal with

'Seriously, I think it makes more sense to group every-
ning together and get it done in the shortest possible time—'

'*I'm* in charge of your schedule. Let *me* work out what
aakes sense.'

'Miss Fleming is right.' Marco's deep voice sounded from
ehind her shoulder. 'You have several events spaced out over
ne period of a week. That's a lot of time wasted travelling.
Do you not agree?'

'But the sponsors—'

'The sponsors need to work around her schedule, not the
ther way round. They can have Thursday to Saturday next
veek. Otherwise they'll have to wait until the end of the
nonth. Miss Fleming gets Sundays off. Your job is to man-
ge her time properly. Make it happen.'

Marco reached past Sasha and disconnected the link. Al-
hough it was a rare treat to see Tom get his comeuppance, a
arge part of her tightened with irritation.

'I'm perfectly capable of arranging my own schedule, thank
ou very much.'

'It didn't seem that way.'

'Only because you didn't give me half a chance.' She craned
ner neck to gaze up at him, feeling at a severe disadvantage.

His head went back as he glared down his arrogant nose
t her. 'I didn't like the way he spoke to you,' he declared.

Her heart lurched, then swung into a dive as a wave of
varmth oozed through her. Sasha berated herself for the fool-
sh feeling, but as much as she tried to push it away it grew
stronger.

Despite the alien feeling zinging through her, she tried for
a casual shrug. 'I don't think he likes me very much.'

A frown creased his forehead. 'Why not?'

Her bitter laugh escaped before she could curb it. Risin
she padded several steps away, breathing easier. 'Probabl
for the same reasons you don't. He doesn't think I have an
business being a racing driver. He believes I've made him
laughing stock by association.'

'Because of your gender or because of your past indiscre
tions?'

'According to you they're one and the same, aren't they'
she retorted.

The hands gripping the back of the chair tightened. 'I tol
you in Budapest your gender had nothing to do with my de
cision to fire you. Your talent as a full-time racing driver
yet to be seen. Prove yourself as the talented racing drive
you claim to be and you'll earn your seat. Until then I reserv
my judgement.'

'You reserve your judgement professionally, but you'r
judge, jury and executioner when it comes to my persona
life?'

A cold gleam had entered his eyes, but even that didn't sto
her from staring into those hypnotising depths.

'We agreed that you will have *no* personal life until you
contract ends, did we not? You wouldn't be thinking of re
neging on that agreement so soon, would you?'

Sasha just stopped herself from telling him she already ha
no personal life. That she hadn't had one since Derek's lies an
the loss of her baby had put her through the wringer. Rafae
had been her one and only friend until that had headed south

'Sasha.'

The warning in the way he said her name sent a shive
dancing down her spine. She glanced up at him and bit bac
a gasp.

When had he drawn so close? Within his eyes she coul
see the flecks of green that spiked from his irises. And th
lashes that framed them were long, silky. Beautiful. He ha

beautiful eyes. Eyes that drew her in, wove spells around her. Tugged at emotions buried deep within her...

Eyes that were steadily narrowing, demanding an answer.

She sucked in a breath, her brain turning fuzzy again when his scent—lemony, with a large dose of man—hit her nostrils. 'No, Marco. No personal life. Not even a Labradoodle to cuddle when I'm lonely.'

A frown deepened. 'A what?'

'It's a dog. A cross between a Labrador and a poodle. I used to have one when I was little. But it died.'

'Pets have no place on the racing circuit.'

She glared at him. 'I wasn't planning on bringing one to work. Anyway, it's a moot point, since my schedule isn't conducive to having one. I detest part-time pet owners.'

Her phone buzzed in her back pocket. She pulled it out and activated it. Seeing the promised e-mail from Tom, she turned to leave.

'Where are you going?' he demanded.

She faked a smile to hide the disturbing emotions roiling through her body. 'Oh, I thought the inquisition was over. Only Tom has sent the Q&A and I want to get it done so I don't take up valuable race testing time.'

Her snarky tone didn't go unmissed. His jaw clenched as he sauntered over to her. She held her breath, forcing herself not to move back.

'The inquisition is over for now. But I reserve the right to pursue it at a later date.'

'And *I* reserve the right not to participate in your little witch hunt. I read the small print and signed on the dotted line. I know exactly what's expected of me and I intend to honour our agreement. You can either let me get on with it, or you can impede me and cause us both a lot of grief. Your choice.'

She sailed out of the room, head held high. Just before the door swung shut Sasha suspected she heard a very low, very frustrated growl emitted by a very different bull stag from the one hanging on the wall.

Her smile widened as she punched the air.

Marco didn't come back for dinner. Even after Rosario told her he'd gone to his office in Barcelona Sasha caught herself looking towards the door, half expecting him to stride through it at any second.

Luke had dropped off the engine testing results, which she'd pored over half a dozen times in between listening out for the sound of the helicopter.

Catching herself doing so for the umpteenth time, she shoved away from the table, ran upstairs to her suite and changed into her gym clothes.

Letting herself out of the side entrance, she skirted the pool and jogged along the lamplit path bordering the extensive gardens. Fragrant bougainvillaea and amaranth scented the evening air. She breathed in deeply and increased her pace until she spotted the floodlights of the race track in the distance. Excitement fizzed through her veins.

A few hours from now she'd start her journey to clear her father's name. To prove to the world that the Fleming name was not dirt, as so many people claimed.

Fresh waves of sadness and anger buffeted her as she thought of her father. How his brilliant career had crumbled to dust in just a few short weeks, his hard work and sterling dedication to his team wiped away by vicious lies.

The pain of watching him spiral into depression had been excruciating. In the end even his pride in her hadn't been enough...

Whirling away from her thoughts, and literally from the path, she jogged the rest of the way to the sports facility half a mile away and spent the next hour punishing herself through a strenuous routine that would have made Charlie, her physio, proud.

Leaving the gym, Sasha wandered aimlessly, deliberately

emptying her mind of sad memories. It wasn't until she nearly stumbled into a wall that she realised she stood in front of a single-storey building. Shrouded in darkness, it sat about half a mile away from the house, at the far end of the driveway that led past the villa.

About to enter, she jumped as the trill of her phone rang through the silent night.

Hurriedly, she fished it out, but it went silent before she could answer it. Frowning, she returned it to her pocket, then rubbed her hands down her arms when the cooling breeze whispered over her skin.

Casting another glance at the dark building, she retraced her steps back to the villa. Her footsteps echoed on the marble floors.

'Where the hell have you been?'

Marco's voice was amplified in the semi-darkness, drawing her to a startled halt. He stood half hidden behind one of the numerous pillars in the vast hallway.

'I went to the gym, then went for a walk.'

His huge frame loomed larger as he came towards her. 'The next time you decide to leave the house for a long stretch have the courtesy to inform the staff of your whereabouts. That way I won't have people combing the grounds for you.'

There was an odd inflection in his voice that made the hairs on her neck stand up.

'Has something happened?' She stepped towards him, her heart taking a dizzying dive when he didn't answer immediately. 'Marco?'

'*Sì*, something's happened,' he delivered in an odd, flat tone.

He stepped into the light and Sasha bit back a gasp at the gaunt, tormented look on his face.

'Rafael… It's Rafael.'

CHAPTER FIVE

FEAR PIERCED THROUGH her heart but she refused to believe the worst. 'Is he…?' She swallowed and rephrased. 'How bad is it?'

Marco shoved his phone into his pocket and stalked down the hall towards the large formal sitting room. Set between two curved cast-iron balconies that overlooked the living room from the first-floor hallway, a beautifully carved, centuries-old drinks cabinet stood. Marco picked up a crystal decanter and raised an eyebrow. When she shook her head, he poured a healthy splash of cognac into a glass and threw it back in one quick swallow.

A fire had been lit in the two giant fireplaces in the room. Marco stood before one and raked a hand through his hair, throwing the dark locks into disarray. 'He's suffered another brain haemorrhage. They had to perform a minor operation to release the pressure. The doctors…' He shook his head, tightly suppressed emotion making his movements jerky. 'They can't do any more.'

'But the operation worked, didn't it?' She didn't know where the instinct to keep talking came from. All she knew was that Marco had come looking for her.

He sucked in a deep, shuddering breath. 'The bleeding has stopped, yes. And he's been put into an induced coma until the swelling goes down.'

She moved closer, her heart aching at the pain he tried to hide. 'That's good. It'll give him time to heal.'

His eyes grew bleaker. He looked around, as if searching for a distraction. 'I should be there,' he bit out. 'But the doctors think I'm in their way.' He huffed. 'One even accused me of unreasonable behaviour, simply because I asked for a third opinion.'

The muttered imprecation that followed made Sasha bite her lip, feeling sorry for the unknown hapless doctor who'd dared clash with Marco.

She sucked in a breath as his gaze sharpened on her.

'Nothing to say?'

'He's your brother. You love him and want the best for him. That's why you've hired the best doctors to care for him. Maybe you need to leave them alone to do their jobs?' He looked set to bite her head off. 'And if he's in intensive care they probably need to keep his environment as sterile as possible. Surely you don't want anything to jeopardise his recovery?'

His scowl deepened and he looked away. 'I see you not only wear a psychologist's hat, you also dabble in diplomacy and being the voice of reason.'

Although Sasha did not enjoy his cynicism, she felt relieved that his voice was no longer racked with raw anguish. 'Yeah, that's me. Miss All-Things-To-All-People,' she joked.

Eyes that had moments ago held pain and anguish froze into solid, implacable ice. '*Sí*. Unfortunately that aspect of your nature hasn't worked out well for my brother, has it? Rafael needed you to be *one* thing to him. And you failed. *Miserably.*'

'I tried to talk some sense into him…'

Rafael hadn't taken it well when she'd pointed out the absurdity of his out-of-the-blue proposal. He'd stormed out of her hotel in Budapest the night before the race, and she'd never got the chance to talk to him before his accident.

Marco turned from the mantel and faced her. 'Don't tell me… You were *conveniently* unsuccessful?' he mocked.

'Because he didn't mean it.'

He pounced. 'Why would any man propose to a woman if he didn't mean it?'

When she didn't answer immediately, his scowl deepened. In the end, she said, 'Because of…other things he'd said.'

'What *other* things?' came the harsh rejoinder.

'*Private* things.' She wasn't about to deliver a blow-by-blow account. It wasn't her style. 'I thought he was reacting to his last break-up.'

He dismissed it with a wave of his hand. 'Rafael and Nadia broke up two months ago. Are you suggesting this was a re-bound?' Marco asked derisively. 'My brother's bounce-back rate is normally two *weeks*.'

Sasha frowned. 'Rafael's changed, Marco. To you he may have seemed like his normal wild, irreverent self. But—'

'Are you saying I don't know my own brother?' he demanded.

Slowly, Sasha shook her head. 'I'm just saying he may not have told you everything that was going on with him.'

Her breath caught at the derisive gleam that entered Marco's eyes.

'His text told me everything I needed to know. By refusing him, you gave him no choice but to come after you.'

'Of course I didn't!'

'Liar!'

'That's the second time you've called me a liar, Marco. For your own sake I hope there isn't a third. Or I'll take great pleasure in slapping your face. Contract or no bloody contract. Whatever Rafael led you to believe, I *didn't* set out to ensnare him, or encourage him to fall for me—which I don't think he did, by the way. And I certainly didn't get him riled up enough to cause his accident. Whatever demons Rafael's been battling, they finally caught up with him. I'm tired of defending myself. I was just being his friend. Nothing else.'

Heart hammering, she took a seat on one of the extremely delicate-looking twin cream and gold striped sofas and pulled in a deep breath to steady the turbulent emotions coursing through her. Emotions she'd thought buckled down tight, but which Marco had seemed to spark to life so very easily.

'I find it hard to believe your actions have taken you down the same path twice in your life.'

'An unfortunate coincidence, but that's all it is. I have to live with it. However, I refuse to let you or anyone else label me some sort of *femme fatale*. All I want is to do my job.'

He sat down opposite her. When his gaze drifted down her body, she struggled to fight the pinpricks of awareness he ignited along the way.

'You're a fighter. I admire that in you. There's also something about you...'

His pure Latin shrug held a wealth of expression that made her silently shake her head in awe.

'An unknown quality I find difficult to pinpoint. You're hardly a *femme fatale*, as you say. The uncaring way you dress, your brashness, all point to a lack of femininity—'

Pure feminine affront sparked a flame inside her. 'Thanks very much.'

'And normally I wouldn't even class you as Rafael's type. Yet on the night before his accident he was fiercely adamant that *you* were the one. Don't get me wrong, he's said that a few times in the past, but this time I knew something wasn't quite right.'

Despite his accusation, sympathy welled inside her. 'Did you two fight? Was that why you didn't come to Friday's practice?'

His nod held regret. 'I lost it when he asked for the ring.'

'You had it?'

He pinched the bridge of his nose and exhaled sharply. 'Yes. It belonged to our mother. She didn't leave it specifically to either of us; she just wanted the first one of us to get married to give it to his bride.' He shook his head once. 'I always knew it would go to Rafael since I never intend—' He stopped and drew in a breath. 'Rafael has claimed to be in love with many girls, but this was the first time he'd asked for the ring.'

'And you were angry because it was me?'

His jaw clenched. 'You could have waited until the race was over,' he accused, his voice rough with emotion.

'Marco—'

'He'd have had the August hiatus to get over you; he would've mended his broken heart in the usual way—ensconced on a yacht in St Tropez or chasing after some Hollywood starlet in LA. Either way, he would've arrived back on the circuit, smiled at you, and called you *pequeña* because he'd forgotten your name. Instead he's in a hospital bed, fighting for his life!'

'But I couldn't lie,' she shot back. 'He didn't want me—not really. And I'm not on the market for a relationship. Certainly not after—' She pulled herself up short, but it was too late.

He stood and pulled her up, caught her shoulders in a firm grip. 'After what?'

'Not after my poor track record.'

'You mean what happened with your previous lover?'

She nodded reluctantly. 'Derek proposed just before I broke up with him. I'd known for some time that it wasn't working, but I convinced myself things would work out. When I declined his proposal a week later he accused me of leading him on. He said I was only refusing him because I wanted to sell myself to the highest bidder.'

Derek had repeated that assertion to every newspaper and team boss who would listen, and Sasha's career had almost ended because of it. She pushed the painful memories away.

'Rafael knew there was no way I'd get involved with him romantically.'

Marco's grip tightened, his gaze scouring her face as if he wanted to dig out the truth. Sasha forced herself to remain still, even though the touch of his hands on her branded her—so hot she wanted to scream with the incredibly forceful sensation of it.

'Do you know the last thing I said to him?' he rasped.

Her heart aching for him, she shook her head.

'I told him to stop messing around and grow up. That he was dishonouring our mother's memory by treating life like his own personal playground.' His eyelids veiled his gaze for several seconds and his jaw clenched, his emotions riding very near the surface. 'If anything happens to him—'

'It won't.'

Without thought, she placed her hand on his arm. Hard muscles flexed beneath her fingers. His eyes returned to her face, then dropped to her mouth. Sharp sensation shot through her belly, making her breath catch.

Sasha felt an electric current of awareness zing up her arm—a deeper manifestation of the intense awareness she felt whenever he was near. *Comfort*, she assured herself. *I'm offering him comfort. That's all.* This need to keep touching him was just a silly passing reaction.

'He'll wake up and he'll get better. You'll see.'

Face taut and eyes bleak, he slowly dropped his hands. 'I have to go,' he said.

She stepped back, her hands clenching into fists behind her back to conceal their trembling. 'You're returning to the hospital?'

He shook his head. 'I'm going to Madrid.'

Her belly clenched with the acute sense of loss. 'For how long?' she asked lightly.

'For however long it takes to reassure my father that his precious son isn't dying.'

The state-of-the-art crash helmet was no match for the baking North Spanish sun. Sasha sat in the cockpit of the Espíritu DSI, the car that had won Rafael the championship the year before. Eyes shut, she retraced the outline of the Belgian race track, anticipation straining through her.

Sweat trickled down her neck, despite the chute pumping cold air into the car. When she'd mentally completed a full circuit she opened her eyes.

They burned from lack of sleep, and she blinked several times to clear them. She'd been up since before dawn, the start of her restless night having oddly coincided with the moment Marco's helicopter had lifted off the helipad. For hours she'd lain tangled up in satin sheets, unable to dismiss the look on Marcus's anguished face from her mind. Or the heat of his touch on her body.

Firming her lips, she forcibly cleared her mind.

She wrapped fireproof gloved hands around the wheel and pictured the Double S bends at Eau Rouge, and the exact breaking point at La Source. Keeping her breathing steady, she finally achieved the mental calm she needed to block out the background noise of the mechanics and the garage. She emptied every thought from her mind, the turmoil of the past few days reduced to a small blot. She welcomed the relief of not having to dwell on anything except the promise of the fast track in front of her.

Her eyes remained steady on the mechanic's *STOP/GO* sign, her foot a whisper off the accelerator.

When the sign went up, she launched out of the garage onto the track. Adrenalin coursed through her veins as the powerful car vibrated beneath her. Braking into the first corner, she felt G-forces wrench her head to the left and smiled. This battle with the laws of physics lent an extra thrill as she flew along the track, the sense of freedom making her oblivious to the stress on her body as lap after lap whizzed by.

'You're being too hard on your tyres, Sasha.'

Luke's voice piped into her earphones and she immediately adjusted the balance of the car, her grip loosening a touch to help manoeuvre the curves better.

'That's better. In race conditions you'll need them to go for at least fifteen laps. You can't afford to wear them out in just eight. It's early days yet, but things look good.'

Sasha blinked at the grudging respect in Luke's voice.

'How does the car feel?'

'Er…great. It feels great.'

'Good. Come in and we'll take a look at the lap times together.'

She drove back into the garage and parked. Keeping her

focus on Luke as he approached her, she got out and set her helmet aside.

He showed her the printout. 'We can't compare it with the performance of the DSII, but from these figures things are looking very good for Spa in three weeks' time.'

Reading through the data, Sasha felt a buzz of excitement. 'The DSII is great at slow corners, so I should be able to go even faster.'

Luke grinned. 'When you have the world's best aerodynamicist as your boss, you have a starting advantage. We'll have a battle on the straight sections, but if you keep up this performance we should cope well enough to keep ourselves ahead.'

Again she caught the changed note in his voice.

Although she'd tried not to dwell on it, throughout the day, and over the following days during testing, Sasha slowly felt the changing attitude of her small team. They spoke to her with less condescension; some even bothered to engage her in conversation before and after her practice sessions.

And the first time Luke asked her opinion on how to avoid the under steering problem that had cropped up, Sasha forced herself to blink back the stupid tears that threatened.

Marco heard the car drive away as he came down the stairs. He curbed the strong urge to yank the door open and forced himself to wait. When he reached the bottom step he sat down and rested his elbows on his knees, his BlackBerry dangling from his fingers.

Light footsteps sounded seconds before the front door opened.

Sasha stood silhouetted against the lights flooding the outer courtyard, the outline of her body in tight dark trousers and top making sparks of desire shoot through his belly.

Clenching his teeth against the intensity of it, he forced himself to remain seated, knowing she hadn't yet spotted him in the darkened hallway. Her light wrap slipped as she turned to shut the door, and he caught a glimpse of one smooth shoulder and arm. Her dark silky hair was tied in a careless knot on top of her head, giving her neck a long, smooth, elegant line that he couldn't help but follow.

He found himself tracing the lines of her body, wondering how he'd ever thought her boyish. She was tall, her figure lithe, but there were curves he hadn't noticed before—right down to the shapely denim-clad legs.

Shutting the door, she tugged off her boots and kicked them into a corner.

She turned and stumbled to a halt, her breath squeaking out in alarm. 'Marco! Damn it, you *really* need to stop skulking in dark hallways. You nearly scared me to death!'

'I wasn't skulking.' He heard the irritation in his voice and forced himself to calm down. 'Where have you been? I called you several times.'

She pulled the wrap tighter around her shoulders, her chin tilting up in silent challenge. 'I went for a drink with the team. They're all flying out tomorrow morning and I wanted to say goodbye. I know that wasn't part of the deal—me socialising with the team—but they kept asking and it would have been surly to refuse.'

Annoyance rattled through him. The last thing he wanted to discuss was his team, or the deal he'd made with Sasha Fleming. *Dios*, he wasn't even sure why he'd come back here. He should be by his brother's bedside—even if the doctors intended to keep him in his induced coma until the swelling on his brain reduced.

'And you were having such a great time you decided not to answer your phone?'

'I think it's died.'

'You *think*?'

'You're annoyed with me. Why?'

Sasha asked the question in that direct way he'd come to expect from her. No one in his vast global organisation would dare to speak to him that way. And yet…he found he liked it.

Rising, he walked towards her. A few steps away, the scent

of her perfume hit his nostrils. Marco found himself craving more of it, wanting to draw even closer. 'Why bother with a phone if you can't ensure it works?'

'Because no one calls me.'

Her words stopped him in his tracks. For a man who commanded his multi-billion-euro empire using his BlackBerry, Marco found her remark astonishing in the extreme. 'No one calls you?'

'My phone never rings. I think *you* were the last person to call me. I get the occasional text from Tom, or Charlie, my physio, but other than that…zilch.'

Marco's puzzlement grew. 'You don't have any friends?'

'Obviously none who care enough to call. And, before you go feeling sorry for me, I'm fine with it.'

'You're fine with being lonely?'

'With being *alone*. There's a difference. So, is there another reason you're annoyed with me?'

She raised her chin in that defiant way that drew his gaze to her throat.

He shoved his phone into his pocket. 'I'm not annoyed. I'm tired. And hungry. Rosario had gone to bed when I arrived.'

'Oh, well, that's good. Not the tired and hungry part. The not annoyed part.' She bit her lip, her eyes wide on his as he moved even closer. 'And about Rosario…I hope you don't mind, but I told her not to wait up for me.'

Marco shook his head. 'So where did you go for this drink?' He strove to keep his voice casual.

'A bodega just off Plaza Mayor in Salamanca.'

He nodded, itching to brush back the stray hair that had fallen against her temple. 'And did you enjoy your evening out?'

Her shrug drew his eyes to her bare shoulder. 'León is beautiful. And I was glad to get out of the villa.'

Her response struck a strangely discordant chord within him. 'You don't like it here?'

'I don't mind the proximity to the track, but I was tired of knocking about in this place all by myself.'

Marco stiffened. 'Do you want to move to the hotel with the rest of the team?'

She thought about it. Then, 'No. The crew and I seem to be gelling, but I don't want to become overly familiar with them.'

Marco found himself breathing again. 'Wise decision. Sometimes maintaining distance is the only way to get ahead.'

'*You* obviously don't practise that dogma. You're always surrounded by an adoring crowd.'

'X1 Premier Racing is a multi-million-spectator sport. I can't exist in a vacuum.'

'Okay. Um…do you think we can turn the lights on in here? Only we seem to be making a habit of having conversations in the dark.'

'Sometimes comfort can be found in darkness.'

Facing up to reality's harsh light after his own crash ten years ago had made him wish he'd stayed unconscious. Angelique's smug expression as she'd dropped her bombshell had certainly made him wish for the oblivion of darkness.

Sasha gave a light, musical laugh. The sound sent tingles of pleasure down his spine even as heat pooled in his groin. His eyes fell to her lips and Marco experienced the supreme urge to kiss her. Or to keep enjoying the sound of her laughter.

'What's so funny?' he asked as she reached over his shoulder and flipped on the light switch.

'I was thinking either you're very hungry or you're very tired, because you've gone all cryptic on me.'

He *was* hungry. And not just for food. A hunger—clawing and extremely ravenous—had taken hold inside him.

Pushing aside the need to examine it, he followed her as she headed towards the kitchen. The sight of her bare feet on the cool stones made his blood thrum faster as he studied her walk, the curve of her full, rounded bottom.

'I could do with a snack myself. Do you want me to fix you something?'

Walking on the balls of her feet made the sway of her hips different, sexier. He tried to stop himself staring. He failed.

'You cook?' he asked past the strain in his throat.

'Yep. Living on my own meant I had to learn, starve or live on takeaways. Starving was a bore, and Charlie would've had conniptions if he'd seen me within a mile of a takeaway joint. So I took an intensive cookery course two years ago.'

She folded her wrap and placed it on the counter, along with a small handbag. Only then did he see that her top was held up by the thinnest of straps.

Opening the fridge, she began to pull out ingredients. 'Roast beef sandwich okay? Or if you want something hot I can make pasta carbonara?' she asked over her shoulder.

Marco pulled up a seat at the counter, unable to take his eyes off her. 'I'm fine with the sandwich.'

Her nod dislodged more silky hair from the knot on her head. 'Okay.' Long, luxurious tresses slipped down to caress her neck.

She moved around the kitchen, her movements quick, efficient. In less than five minutes she'd set a loaded plate and a bottle of mineral water before him. He took a bite, chewed.

'This is really good.'

Her look of pleasure sent another bolt of heat through him.

He waited until she sat opposite him before taking another bite. 'So, how long have you lived on your own?'

'Since…' She hesitated. 'Since my father died four years ago.'

She looked away, but not before he caught shadows of pain within the blue depths.

'And your mother? Is she not around?'

She shook her head and picked up her sandwich. 'She died when I was ten. After that it was just Dad and me.'

The sharp pain of losing his own mother surfaced. Ruthlessly, he pushed it away.

'The team are wondering how Rafael is,' Sasha said, drawing him away from his disturbing thoughts.

'Just the team?'

She shrugged. 'We're all concerned.'

'Yes, I know. His condition hasn't changed. I've updated Russell. He'll pass it on to the team.'

He didn't want to talk about his brother. Because speaking of Rafael would only remind him of why this woman who made the best sandwich he'd ever tasted was sitting in front of him.

'How is your father holding up?'

He didn't want to talk about his father either.

Recalling his father's desolation, Marco shoved away his plate. 'He watched his son crash on live TV. How do you think he's doing?'

A flash of concern darkened her blue eyes. 'Does he…does he know about me?' she asked in a small voice.

'Does he know the cause of his son's crash is the same person taking his seat?' He laughed. 'Not yet.'

He wasn't sure why he'd kept that information from his father. It certainly had nothing to do with wondering if his brother's version of events was completely accurate, despite Rafael's voice ringing in his head… *She's the one, Marco.*

Sasha's gaze sought his, the look into them almost imploring. 'I didn't cause him to crash, Marco.'

Frustrated anger seared his chest. 'Didn't you?'

She shook her head and the knot finally gave up its fight. Dark, silky tresses cascaded over her naked shoulders and everything inside Marco tightened. It was the first time he'd seen it down, and despite the fury rolling through him the sudden urge to sink his fingers into the glossy mass, feel its decadent luxury, surged like fire through his veins.

'Then what did? Something must have happened to make him imagine that idiotic move would stick.'

Her lips pursed. The look in her eyes was reluctant. Then she sighed. 'I saw him just before the race. He was arguing with Raven.'

Marco frowned. 'Raven Blass? His physio?'

She nodded. 'I tried to approach him but he walked away. I thought I'd leave him to cool off and talk to him again after the race.'

Marco's muttered expletive made her brows rise, but he was past caring. He strode into the alcove that held his extensive wine collection. 'I need a drink. White or red?'

'I shouldn't. I had a beer earlier.' She tucked a silky strand behind one ear.

Watching the movement, he found several incredibly unwise ideas crowding his brain. Reaching out, he grabbed the nearest bottle. 'I don't like drinking alone. Have one with me.'

Her smile caused the gut-clenching knot to tighten further. 'Is the great Marco de Cervantes admitting a flaw?'

'He's admitting that his brother drives him *loco*.' He grabbed two crystal goblets.

'Fine. I was going to add another twenty minutes to my workout regime to balance out the incredible *tapas* I had earlier. I'll make it an even half-hour.'

Marco's gaze glided over her. 'You're hardly in bad shape.'

Another sweet, feminine laugh tumbled from her lips, sparking off a frenzied yearning.

'Charlie would disagree with you. Apparently my body mass index is *way* below acceptable levels.'

Marco uncorked the wine, thinking perhaps Charlie needed his eyes examined. 'How long is your daily regime?'

'Technically three hours, but Charlie keeps me at it until I'm either screaming in agony or about to pass out. He normally stops once I'm thoroughly dripping in sweat.'

His whole body froze, arrested by the image of a sweat-soaked Sasha, with sunshine glinting off her toned body.

Dios, this was getting ridiculous. He should not be feeling like this—especially not towards the woman who was the every epitome of Angelique: ruthlessly ambitious, uncaring of anything that got in her way. Sasha had nearly destroyed his brother the way Angelique had destroyed Marco's desire ever to forge a lasting relationship.

And yet in Barcelona he'd found himself thinking of Sasha…admitting to himself that his sudden preoccupation with her had nothing to do with work. And everything to do with the woman herself. The attraction he'd felt in Budapest was still present…and escalating.

Which was totally unacceptable.

He took a deep breath and wrenched control back into his body. While his brother was lying in a coma, the only thing he needed to focus on was winning the Constructors' Championship. And teaching Sasha Fleming a lesson.

He poured bold red Château Neuf into one glass and set it in front of her. 'I've seen the testing reports. You'll need to find another three-tenths of a second around Eau Rouge to give yourself a decent chance or you'll leave yourself open to overtaking. Belgium is a tough circuit.'

She took a sip and his gaze slid to the feline-like curve of her neck. Clenching fingers that itched to touch, he sat down opposite her.

'The DSII will handle the corners better.'

His eyes flicked over her face, noting her calm. 'You don't seem nervous.'

Another laugh. A further tightening in his groin.

Madre di Dios. It had been a while since he'd indulged in good, old-fashioned, no-holds-barred sex. Sexual frustration had a habit of making the unsavoury tempting, but this…this yearning was insane.

Mentally, he scanned through his electronic black book and came up with several names. Just as fast he discarded every one of them, weariness at having to disentangle himself from expectation dampening his urge to revisit old ground.

Frustration built, adding another strand of displeasure to his already seething emotions.

'Believe me, I get just as nervous as the next racer. But I don't mind.'

'Because winning is everything, no matter the cost?' he bit out.

Her eyes darkened. 'No. Because nerves serve a good purpose. They remind you you're human; they sharpen your focus. I'd be terrified if I wasn't nervous. But eighteen years of experience also helps. I've been doing this since I was seven years old. Having a supportive father who blatantly disregarded the fact that I wasn't a boy helped with my confidence too.'

'Not a lot of parents agree with their children racing. You were lucky.'

She smiled. 'More like pushy. I threw a tantrum every time he threatened to leave me with my nanny. I won eventually. Although I get the feeling he was testing me to see how much I wanted it.'

'And you passed with flying colours.' He raised his glass to her. 'Bravo.'

Unsettlingly perceptive blue eyes rested on him. 'Oops, do I detect a certain cynicism there, Marco?'

He clenched his teeth as his control slipped another notch. 'Has anyone told you it's not nice to always go for the jugular?'

Her eyes widened. 'Was that what I was doing? I thought we were having a get-to-know-each-other conversation. At least until you went a little weird on me.'

'*Perdón*. Weird wasn't what I was aiming for.' He took a large gulp of his wine.

'First an admission of a flaw. Now an apology. Wow—must be my lucky night. Are you feeling okay? Maybe it would help to talk about whatever it is that spooked you?'

Perhaps it was the mellowing effect of the wine. Perhaps it was the fact that he hadn't had an engaging conversation like this in a while. Marco was surprised when he found himself laughing.

'I have no memory of ever being spooked. But, just for curiosity's sake, which hat will you be wearing for this little heart-to-heart? Diplomat or psychologist?'

Her gaze met his squarely. 'How about friend?' she asked. His laughter dried up.

She wanted to be his friend.

Marco couldn't remember the last time anyone had offered to be his friend. Betrayal had a habit of stripping the scales from one's eyes. He'd learnt that lesson well and thoroughly.

He swallowed another gulp of wine. 'I respectfully decline. Thanks all the same.'

A small smile curved her lip. 'Ouch. At least you didn't laugh in my face.'

'That would have been cruel.'

One smooth brow rose. 'And you don't do cruel? You've come very close in the past.'

'You were a threat to my brother.'

'*Were?* You mean you're not under that impression any more?'

Realising the slip, he started to set her straight, then paused. *You can't control what happens in life...Rafael will resent you for controlling his life...* 'I'm willing to suspend my judgement until Rafael is able to set the picture straight himself.'

Her smile faded. 'You don't trust me at all, do you?'

He steeled himself against his fleeting tinge of regret at the hurt in her voice.

'Trust is earned. It comes with time. Or so I'm told.'

So far no one had withstood the test long enough for Marco to verify that belief. Sasha Fleming had already failed that test. She was only sitting across from him because of what he could give her.

She hid her calculating nature well, but he knew it was there, hiding beneath the fiercely determined light in her eyes.

'Well, then, here's to earning trust. And becoming friends.'

Marco didn't respond to her toast because part of him regretted the fact that friendship between them would never be possible.

CHAPTER SIX

'THIS WAY, SASHA!'

'Over here!'

'Smile!'

The Children of Bravery awards took place every August at one of the plushest hotels in Mayfair. Last year Sasha had arrived in a cab with Tom, who had then gone on to ignore her for the rest of the night.

Tonight flashbulbs went off in her face the moment Marco helped her out of the back of his stunning silver Rolls-Royce onto the red carpet.

Blinking several times to help her eyes adjust, she found Tom had materialised beside her. Before he could speak, Marco stepped in front of him.

'Miss Fleming won't be needing you tonight. Enjoy your evening.'

The dismissal was softly spoken, wrapped in steel. With a hasty nod, a slightly pale Tom dissolved back into the crowd.

'That wasn't very nice,' she murmured, although secretly she was pleased. Her nerves, already wound tight at the thought of the evening ahead, didn't need further negative stimulus in the form of Tom. 'But thank you.'

'De nada,' he murmured in that smooth deep voice of his, and her nerves stretched a little tighter.

When he took her arm the feeling intensified, then morphed into a different kind of warmth as another sensation altogether enveloped her—one of feeling protected, cherished...

She applied mental brakes as her brain threatened to go into meltdown. Forcing herself away from thoughts she had no business thinking, she drew in a shaky breath and tried to project a calm, poised demeanour.

'For once I agree with the paparazzi. *Smile.* Your face looks frozen,' Marco drawled, completely at ease with being the subject of intense scrutiny.

He seemed perfectly okay with hundreds of adoring female fans screaming his name from behind the barriers, while she could only think about the ceremony ahead and the memories it would resurrect.

Pushing back her pain, she forced her lips apart. 'That's probably because it is. Besides, you're one to talk. I don't see you smiling.'

One tuxedo-clad shoulder lifted in a shrug. 'I'm not the star on show.' He peered closer at her. 'What's wrong with you? You didn't say a word on the way over here and now you look pale.'

'That's because I don't *like* being on show. I hate dressing up, and make-up makes my face feel weird.'

'You look fine.' His gaze swept over her. 'More than fine. The stylist chose well.'

'She didn't choose this dress. I chose it myself. If I'd gone with her choice I'd be half naked with a slit up to my cro—' She cleared her throat. 'Why did you send me a stylist anyway?'

When she'd opened the door to Marco's Kensington penthouse apartment to find a stylist with a rack of designer gear in tow, Sasha had been seriously miffed.

'I didn't want to risk you turning up here in baggy jeans and a hippy top.'

'I'd never have—!' She caught the gleam of amusement in his eyes and relaxed.

Another photographer screamed her name and she tensed.

'Relax. *You* chose well.' His gaze slid over her once more. 'You look beautiful.'

Stunned, she mumbled, 'Thank you.'

She smoothed a nervous hand over her dress, thankful her new contract had come with a lucrative remuneration package that meant she'd been able to afford the black silk and lace floor-length Zang Toi gown she wore.

The silver studs in the off-the-shoulder form-fitting design flashed as the cameras went off. But even the stylish dress, with its reams of material that trailed on the red carpet, couldn't stem the butterflies ripping her stomach to shreds as the media screamed out for even more poses. Nor could it eliminate the wrenching reason why, on a night like this, she couldn't summon a smile.

'Stop fidgeting,' he commanded.

'That's easy for you to say. Anyway, why are you here? I don't need a keeper.' Nor did she need the stupid melting sensation in her stomach every time his hand tightened around her arm.

'I beg to differ. This event is hosting many sport personalities, including other drivers from the circuit. Your track record—pardon the pun—doesn't stand you in good stead. The one thing you *do* need is a keeper.'

'And you're it? Don't you have better things to do?'

When he'd pointed out after they'd landed this morning that it was more time-efficient for her to stay with him in London, than to come to the ceremony from her cottage in Kent, she hadn't bargained on the fact that he'd appoint himself her personal escort for the evening.

His rugged good looks lit up in sharp relief, courtesy of another photographer's flash, but he hardly noticed how avidly the media craved his attention. Nor cared.

'The team has suffered with Rafael's absence. It'll be good for the sponsors to see me here.'

The warmth she'd experienced moments ago disappeared. She felt his sharp gaze as she eased her arm from his grasp.

'How long do we have to stay out here?' The limelight was definitely a place she wasn't comfortable in. However irrational, she always feared her deepest secret would be exposed.

'Until a problem with the seating is sorted out.'

She swivelled towards him. 'What problem with the seating?'

Relief poured through her as he steered her away from the cameras and down the red carpet into the huge marble-floored foyer of the five-star hotel.

The crowd seemed to pause, both men and women alike staring avidly as they entered.

Oblivious to the reaction, Marco snagged two glasses of champagne and handed one to her. 'Some wires got crossed along the line.'

Sasha should have been used to it by now, but a hard lump formed in her throat nonetheless. 'You mean I was down-graded to nobody-class because my surname is Fleming and not de Cervantes?'

He gave her a puzzled look. 'Why should your name matter?'

'Come on. I may have missed school the day rocket science was taught, but I know how this works.' Even when the words weren't said, Sasha knew she was being judged by her father's dishonour.

'Your surname has nothing to do with it,' Marco answered, nodding greetings to several people who tried to catch his eye. 'When the awards committee learned I would be attending, they naturally assumed that I would be bringing a plus one.'

A sensation she intensely disliked wormed its way into her heart. 'Oh, so I was bumped to make room for your date. Not because…?'

He raised a brow. 'Because?'

Shaking her head, Sasha took a hasty sip of her bubbly. 'So why didn't you? Bring a date, I mean?' When his brow rose in mocking query, she hurried on. 'I know it's certainly not for the lack of willing companions. I mean, a man like you…' She stumbled to a halt.

'A man like me? You mean The Ass?' he asked mockingly.

Heat climbed into her cheeks but she refused to be cowed. 'No, I didn't mean that. The other you—the impossibly rich, successful one, who's a bit decent to look at….' Cursing her runaway tongue, she clamped her mouth shut.

'*Gracias*…I think.'

'You know what I mean. Women scale skylights, risk life and limb to be with you, for goodness' sake.'

'Skylight-scaling is a bit too OTT for me. I prefer my women to use the front door. *With* my invitation.' His gaze connected with hers.

Heat blazed through her, lighting fires that had no business being lit. His broad shoulders loomed before her as he bent his head. As if to… As if to… Her gaze dropped to his lips. She swallowed.

Chilled champagne went down the wrong way.

She coughed, cleared her throat and tried desperately to find something to say to dispel the suddenly charged atmosphere. His eyelids descended, but not before she caught a flash of anguish. Stunned, she stared at him, but when he looked back up his expression was clear.

'To answer your question, this is a special event to honour children. It's not an event to bring a date who'll spend all evening checking out other women's jewellery or celebrity-spotting.'

'How incredibly shallow! Oh, I don't mean you date shallow women—I mean… Hell, I've put my foot in it, haven't I?'

The smile she'd glimpsed once before threatened to break the surface of his rigid demeanour. 'Your diplomatic hat is slipping, Sasha. I think we should go in before you insult me some more and completely shatter my ego.'

'I don't think that's possible,' she murmured under her breath. 'Seriously, though, you should smile more. You look almost human when you do.'

The return of his low, deep laugh sang deliciously along her skin, then wormed its way into her heart. When his hand arrived in the small of her back to steer her into the ballroom a whole heap of pleasure stole through her, almost convincing her the butterflies had been vanquished.

The feeling was pathetically short-lived. The pictures of children hanging from the ceiling of the chandeliered ballroom punched a hole through the euphoric warmth she'd dared to bask in. Her breath caught as pain ripped through her. If her baby had lived she would have been four by now.

'Are you sure you're okay?' Marco demanded in a low undertone.

'Yes, I'm fine.'

Unwilling to risk his incisive gaze, she hurried to their table and greeted an ex-footballer who'd recently been knighted for his work with children.

Breathing through her pain, it took a moment for her to realise she was the subject of daggered looks and whispered sniggers from the other two occupants of the table.

Feeling her insides congeal with familiar anger, she summoned a smile and pasted it on her face as the ex-footballer's trophy wife leaned forward, exposing enough cleavage to sink a battleship.

'Hi, I'm Lisa. This is my sister, Sophia,' she said.

Marco nodded in greeting and introduced Sasha.

Sophia flashed Marco a man-gobbling smile, barely sparing Sasha a glance.

A different form of sickness assailed Sasha as she watched the women melt under Marco's dazzling charisma. Eager eyes took in his commanding physique, the hard beauty of his face, the sensual mouth and the air of authority and power that cloaked him.

He murmured something that made Sophia giggle with delight. When her gaze met Sasha's, it held a touch of triumph that made Sasha want to reach out and pull out her fake hair extensions. Instead she kept her smile and turned towards the older man.

If fake boobs and faker lashes were his thing, Marco was welcome to them.

Marco clenched his fist on his thigh and forced himself to calm down. He'd never been so thoroughly and utterly ignored by a date in his life.

So Sasha wasn't technically his date. So what? She'd arrived with him. She would leave with him. Would it hurt her to try and make conversation with *him* instead of engaging in an in-depth discussion of the current Premier League?

Slowly unclenching his fist, he picked up his wine glass.

Sasha laughed. The whole table seemed to pause to drink it in—even the two women who had so rudely ignored her so far.

By the time the tables were cleared of their dinner plates he'd had enough.

'Sasha.'

She smiled an excuse at the older man before turning to him.

'Yes?'

At the sight of her wide, genuine smile—the same one she'd worn when she'd offered her friendship at *Casa de León*—something in his chest contracted. He forced himself to remember the reason Sasha Fleming was here beside him. Why she was in his life at all.

Rafael. The baby brother he'd always taken care of.

But he isn't a child any more…

Marco suppressed the unsettling voice. 'The ceremony's about to start. You're presenting the second award.'

Her eyes widened a fraction, then anxiety darkened their depths.

'Yes, of course. I…I have my speech ready. I'd better read it over one more time, just in case…' Her hands shook as she plucked a tiny piece of paper from her bag.

Without thinking, he covered her hand with his. 'Take a deep breath. You'll be fine.'

Eyes locked onto his, she slowly nodded. 'I… Thanks.'

The MC took to the stage and announced the first award-giver. Sasha smiled and clapped but, watching her closely, Marco caught a glimpse of the pain in her eyes. Forcing himself to concentrate on the speech, he listened to the story of a four-year-old who'd saved her mother's life by ringing for an ambulance and giving clear, accurate directions after her mother had fallen down a ravine.

The ice-cold tightening his chest since he'd stepped from the car increased as he watched the little girl bound onto the stage in a bright blue outfit, her face wreathed in smiles. Forcing himself not to go there, not to dwell in the past, he turned to gauge Sasha's reaction.

She was frozen, her whole body held taut.

Frowning, he leaned towards her. 'This is ridiculous. Tell me what's wrong. *Now.*'

She jumped, her eyes wide, darkly haunted with unshed tears. Her smile flashed, only this time it lacked warmth or substance.

'I told you, I'm fine. Or I would if I'd remembered to bring a tissue.'

Wordlessly, he reached into his tuxedo jacket and handed her his handkerchief, a million questions firing in his mind.

Accepting it, she dabbed at her eyes. 'If I look a horror, don't tell me until I come back from the stage, okay?' she implored.

It was on the tip of his tongue to trip out the usual platitudes he gave to his dates. Instead he nodded. 'Agreed.'

Marco watched her gather herself together. A subtle roll of her shoulders and a look of determination settled over her features. By the time she rose to present the award her smile was fixed in place.

Watching the lights play over her dark hair, illuminate her beautiful features and the generous curve of her breasts, Marco felt the familiar tightening in his groin and bit back a growl of frustration.

'As most of you know, Rafael de Cervantes was supposed to present this award to Toby this evening. Instead he's skiving off somewhere in sunny Spain.'

Laughter echoed through the room.

'No, seriously, just as Toby said a prayer before rushing into his burning home to save his little sister and brother, so we should all take a moment to say a prayer for Rafael's speedy recovery. Toby fought for his family to live. Not once did he give up. Even when the rescuers told him there was no hope for his little brother he ignored them and rescued him. Why? Because he'd promised his mother he'd take care of his siblings. And he never once wavered from that promise. There are lessons for all of us in Toby's story. And that's never to give up. No matter how small or big your dreams, no matter how tough or impossible the way forward seems, never give up. I'm delighted to present this award to Toby Latham, for his outstanding bravery against all odds.'

Sasha's voice broke on the last words. Although she tried to hide it, Marco caught the strain in her face and the pain behind her smile even as thunderous applause broke out in the ballroom.

Automatically Marco followed suit, but inside ice clenched his heart, squeezing until he couldn't breathe. It was always like this when he allowed himself to remember what Angelique had taken from him. What his weakness had cost him. He'd failed to take care of his own.

Never again, he vowed silently.

Sasha stepped down from the stage and made her way back to her seat. Despite the rushing surge of memories, he couldn't take his eyes off her. In fact he wanted to jump up, grab her hand and lead her away from the ballroom.

She reached the table and smiled at him. 'Thank God I didn't fall on my face.'

Sliding gracefully into the seat, she tucked her hair behind one ear. In that moment Marco, struggling to breathe and damning himself to hell, knew he craved her.

Impossibly. Desperately.

Sasha caught the expression on Marco's face and her heart stopped.

'What's the matter? Oh, my God, if you tell me I have food caught in my teeth I'll kill you!' she vowed feverishly.

Desperately blinking back the threatening tears, she trie
to stem the painful memories that looking into Toby Latham
face had brought. She couldn't afford to let Marco see he
pain. The pain she'd let eat her alive, consume her for year:
but had never been able to put to rest.

She heard sniggers from across the table but ignored then
her attention held hostage by the savagely intense look i
Marco's eyes.

'Your teeth are fine,' he replied in a deep, rough voice.

'Then what? Was my speech that bad?' Caught in the trau
matising resurgence of painful memories, she'd discarded he
carefully prepared notes and winged it.

'No. Your speech was…*perfecto*.'

Her heart lurched at his small pause. Before she could ques
tion him about it the MC introduced the next guest. With n
choice but to maintain a respectful silence, she folded he
shaking hands in her lap.

Frantically, she tried to recall her speech word for word
Marco was obviously reacting to something she'd said. Ha
she been wrong to mention Rafael? Had her joke been to
crass? A wave of shame engulfed her at the thought.

She waited until the next award had been presented, the
leaned over. 'I'm sorry,' she whispered into his ear.

His head swivelled towards her. His jaw brushed her cheek
sending a thousand tiny electric currents racing through he

'What for?' he asked.

'I shouldn't have made that crack about Rafael skiving off
It was tasteless—'

'And exactly what Rafael himself would've done had th
situation been reversed. Everyone's been skirting around th
subject, either pretending it's not happening or treating it wit
kid gloves. You gave people the freedom to acknowledge wha
had happened and set them at ease. I'm no longer the object o
pitying glances and whispered speculation. It is I who shoul
be thanking you.'

'Really?'

'*Sí*,' he affirmed, his gaze dropping to her mouth.

'Then why did you look so…*off*?'

His eyes darkened. 'Your words were powerful. I was touched. I'm not made of stone, Sasha, contrary to what you might think.'

The reproach in his voice shamed her.

'Oh, I'm sorry. It's just… I thought…'

'Forget it.'

He gave a tight smile, turned away and addressed Sophia, who flashed even more of her cleavage in triumph.

As soon as the last award was given, Sophia turned to Marco. 'We're going clubbing.' She named an exclusive club frequented by young royals. 'We'd love you to join us, Marco,' she gushed.

Sasha gritted her teeth but stayed silent. If Marco wanted to party with the Fake Sisters it was his choice. All the same, Sasha held her breath as she waited for his answer, hating herself as she did so.

'Clubbing isn't my scene, but thanks for the offer.'

'Oh, we don't have to go clubbing. Maybe we can do something…*else*?'

Sasha stood and walked away before she could hear Marco's response.

She'd almost reached the ballroom doors when she felt his presence beside her. The wave of relief that flooded her body threatened to weaken her knees. Sternly, she reminded herself that Marco's presence had nothing to do with her personally. He was here for the team's sake.

'Are you sure you'd rather not be out with the Fa… Sophia? She seemed very eager to show you a good time. Seriously, I can take a taxi back.'

His limo pulled up. He handed her inside, then slid in beside her. 'I prefer to end my evening silicone-free, *gracias*.'

She laughed. 'Picky, picky! Most men wouldn't mind.'

Perfect teeth gleamed in the semi-darkness of the limo.

'I am not most men. No doubt you'll add *that* to my list of flaws?'

His eyes dropped to her chest, abruptly cutting off her laughter.

'You had better not be examining me for silicone. I'll have you know these babies are natural.'

'Trust me, I can tell the difference,' he said, in a low, intense voice.

She swallowed hard. The thought that she was suddenly treading unsafe waters descended on her. Frantically, she cast her mind around for a safe subject.

'So you don't like clubbing?'

'It's not how I choose to spend an evening, no.'

'Let me guess—you're the starchy opera type?'

'Wrong again.'

She snapped her fingers. 'I know—you like to stay indoors and watch game shows.'

Low laughter greeted her announcement. Deep inside, a tiny part of Sasha performed a freakishly disturbing happy dance.

Encouraged, she pressed on. 'Telemetry reports and aerodynamic calculations?'

'Now you're getting warm.'

'Ha! I knew you were a closet nerd!'

He cast her a wry glance. 'I prefer to call it passion.'

She shrugged. 'A passionate nerd who surrounds himself with a crowd but keeps his distance.'

He stiffened. 'You're psychoanalysing me again.'

'You make it easy.'

'And *you* make baseless assumptions.'

'Good try, but you can't freeze me out with that tone. You're single-minded to the point of obsession. I wiki-ed you. You have more money than you could ever spend in ten lifetimes and yet you don't let anyone close. You have the odd liaison, but nothing that lasts more than a few weeks. According to your girlfriends, you never stay over. And there's a time limit on every relationship.'

'You shouldn't believe everything you read—especially in the tabloid press.'

'Tell me which part is false,' she challenged.

His gaze hardened. 'I'll tell you which part is right—every relationship ends. For ever is a concept made up to sell romance novels.'

'Didn't you have a long liaison once, when you were still racing? What was her name…? Angela? Ange—?'

'Angelique,' he bit out, his face frozen as if hewn from rock. 'And she wasn't a liaison. We were engaged.'

'She must be the reason, then.'

Cold eyes slammed into her. 'The reason?'

'For the way you are?'

'Did Derek Mahoney turn you into the intrusive woman you are today?' he fired back, his tone rougher than sandpaper. 'Because I'd like to find him and throttle the life out of him.'

Sasha knew she should let it go. But somehow she couldn't.

'Yes. No.' She sighed and looked out of the window at Kensington's nightlife. 'Damn, I wish I smoked.'

An astounded breath whistled from his lips. 'Why would you wish that?'

'Because trying to have a conversation with you is exhausting enough to drive anyone to drink. But since I have to be up at the crack of dawn tomorrow, and I've reached my one-glass drink limit, smoking would be the other choice—if I smoked.' Abandoning the view, she turned back to him. 'Where was I?'

A mirthless smile lifted one corner of his mouth. 'You were dissecting my life and finding it severely deficient.'

'Mockery? Is that your default setting?'

He lowered his gaze to her lips and her insides clenched so hard she feared she'd break in half. The limo turned a sharp corner. She grabbed the armrest to steady herself. Too late she realised the action had thrust her breasts out. Marco's gaze dropped lower. Heat pooled in her belly. Her breasts ached, feeling fuller than they'd ever felt.

He leaned closer. Her heart thundered.

'No, Sasha,' he said hoarsely. '*This* is my default setting.'

Strong hands cupped her cheeks, held her steady. Heat-filled eyes stared into hers, their shocking intensity igniting a fire deep inside her.

Sasha held her breath, almost afraid to move in case…in case…

He fastened his mouth to hers, tumbling her into a none-too-gentle kiss that sent the blood racing through her veins. He tasted of heat and wine, of tensile strength and fiery Latin willpower. Of red-blooded passion and intoxicating pleasure. And he went straight to her head.

Sasha felt a groan rise in her throat and abruptly shut it off. She wasn't *that* easy. Although right now, with Marco's mouth wreaking insane havoc on her blood pressure, *easy* was deliciously tempting.

His tongue caressed hers and the groan slipped through, echoing in the dim cavern of the moving car. One hand slipped to her nape, angling her head. Although he didn't need to. She was willingly tilting her head, all the better to deepen the pressure and pleasure of his kiss. Her mouth opened, boldly inviting him in.

His moan made her triumphant and weak at the same time. Then she lost all thought but of the bliss of the kiss.

Lost all sense of time.

Until she heard the thud of a door.

Their lips parted with a loud, sucking noise that arrowed straight to the furnace-hot apex of her thighs.

Marco stared down at her, his breath shaking out of his chest. '*Dios,*' he muttered after several tense, disbelieving seconds.

You can say that again. Thankfully, the words didn't materialise on her lips. Her eyes fell to his mouth, still wet from their kiss, and the heat between her legs increased a thousandfold.

Get a grip, Sasha. She reined herself in and pulled away as reality sank in. She'd kissed Marco de Cervantes—fallen into him like a drowning swimmer fell on a life raft.

'We're here,' he rasped, setting her free abruptly to spear a hand through his hair.

'Y-yes,' she mumbled, cringing when her voice emerged low and desire-soaked.

With one last look at her, he thrust his door open and helped her out.

They entered the exclusive apartment complex in silence, travelled up to the penthouse suite in silence. Sasha made sure she placed herself as far from him as possible.

After shutting the apartment door he turned to her. Sasha held her breath, guilt rising to mix with the desire that still churned so frantically through her.

'I have an early start—'

'Sasha—'

Marco gestured for her to go first.

Sasha cleared her throat, keeping her gaze on his chest so he wouldn't see the conflicting emotions in her eyes. 'I have an early start tomorrow. So…um…goodnight.'

After a long, heavy pause, he nodded. 'I think that's a good idea. *Buenos noches.*'

All the way down the plushly carpeted hallway she felt his gaze on her. Even after she shut the door behind her his presence lingered.

Dropping her clutch bag, she traced her fingers over her lips. They still tingled, along with every inch of her body. Resting her head against the door, she sucked in a desperate breath.

One hand drifted over her midriff to her pelvis, where desire gripped her in an unbearable vice of need. A need she had every intention of denying, no matter how strong.

Wanting Marco de Cervantes was a mistake. Even if there

was the remotest possibility of a relationship between them it would be over in a matter of weeks. And she knew without a shadow of a doubt that it would also spell the end of her career.

And her experience with Derek had taught that no man—no matter how intensely charismatic, no matter how great a kisser—was worth the price of her dreams.

CHAPTER SEVEN

'COFFEE...I SMELL coffee,' she mumbled into the pillow, the murky fog of her brain teasing her with the seductive aroma of caffeine. 'Please, God, let there be coffee when I open my eyes.'

Carefully she cracked one eye open. Marco stood at the foot of her bed, in a dark green T-shirt and jeans, a steaming mug in his hand.

'If I demand to know what you're doing in my bedroom so early, will you withhold that coffee from me?'

There was no smile this morning, just an even, cool stare, but awareness drummed beneath the surface of her skin nonetheless.

'It's not early. It's eight o'clock.'

With a groan, she levered herself up, braced her back against the headboard. 'Eight o'clock is the crack of dawn, Marco.' She held out her hand for the cup. He didn't move. 'Please,' she croaked.

With an uncharacteristically jerky movement he rounded the bed and handed it to her. Sasha tried not to let her eyes linger on the taut inch of golden-tanned skin that was revealed when he stretched. Her brain couldn't handle anything so overwhelming. Not just yet.

She took her first sip, groaned with pleasure and sagged against the pillow.

'You're not a morning person, are you?'

'Oops, my secret is out. I think whoever decreed that anything was important enough to start before ten o'clock in the morning should be hung, drawn and quartered.' She cradled the warm mug in her hand. 'Okay, I guess now I'm awake enough to ask what you're doing in my room.'

'I knocked. Several times.'

She grimaced. 'I sleep like the dead sometimes.' She took another grateful sip and just stopped herself from moaning again. Moans were bad. 'How did you know to bring me coffee?'

'I know everything about you,' he answered.

Her heart lurched, but she managed to keep her face straight. Marco didn't know about her baby. And she meant to keep it that way.

'I forgot. You have mad voodoo skills.'

His eyes strayed up from where he'd been examining the vampire on her T-shirt. 'No voodoo. Just mad skills. As to why I'm here—I have a meeting in the city in forty-five minutes—'

'On a Saturday?' She caught his wry glance. 'Oh, never mind.'

'I wanted to discuss last night before I left.'

Her breath stalled in her chest. 'Yes. Last night. We kissed.'

A sharp hiss issued from his lips. Then, '*Sí*, we did.'

She bravely met his gaze, even as her heart hammered. 'Before you condemn me for it, you need to know I don't make a habit of that sort of thing.'

His very Latin shrug drew her eyes to the bold, strong outline of his shoulders. 'And yet it happened.'

'We could blame the wine? Oh, wait, you barely touched your glass all evening.'

'How would you know? You were neck-deep in discussing the Premier League.'

She sighed. 'What can I say? I love my footie. Which club do you support?'

'Barcelona.'

She grimaced. 'Of course. You seem the Barcelona type.'

He shook his head. 'I don't even want to know what that means.'

Silence encased them. She took a few more sips of her coffee, instinctively sensing she'd need the caffeine boost to withstand what was coming.

Marco raised his head and looked at her. The tormented gleam in his eyes stopped her breath. 'What happened last night will not happen again.'

Despite telling herself the very same thing over and over last night, she felt a sharp dart of disappointment and hurt lance through her. She feigned a casual tone. 'I agree.'

'You belong to my brother,' he carried on, as if she hadn't spoken.

'I belong to no one. I'm my own person.'

His gaze speared hers. 'It can't happen again.'

Again the uncomfortable dart of pain. 'And I agreed with you. Are you trying to convince me or yourself?'

He shook his head. 'You know, I've never met anyone so forthright.'

'I believe in being upfront. I'm nobody's yes-woman. You need to know that right now. I kiss whomever I want. But kissing you was a mistake. One that I hope will not jeopardise my contract.'

His gaze hardened. 'You value being a racing driver more than personal relationships?'

'I haven't had a successful run with relationships but I'm a brilliant driver. I think it's wise to stick to doing what I do best. And I'd prefer not to lose my job because you feel guilty over a simple kiss. I also understand if you have some reservations because of your brother. Really, it's no big deal. There's no need to beat yourself up over it.'

Running out of oxygen, she clamped her mouth shut.

This was yet another reason why she hated mornings. At this time of day the natural barrier between her brain and her mouth was severely weakened.

Throw in the fruitless soul-searching she'd done into the wee hours, and the resultant sleep-deprivation, and who knew what would come out of her mouth next?

He shoved a forceful hand through his hair. '*Dios*, this has nothing to do with your contract. If you were mine to take

I'd have no reservations. None. The things I would do to you. *With* you.'

He named a few.

Her mouth dropped open.

Lust singed the air, its fumes thick and heavy. Her fingers clenched around her mug. Silently, desperately, she willed it away. But her body wasn't prepared to heed her. Underneath her T-shirt her nipples reacted to his words, tightening into painful, needy buds.

'Wow! That's…um…super, *super*-naughty.'

Hazel eyes snapped pure fire at her. 'And that's just for starters,' he rasped.

Her breath strangled in her chest.

In another life, at another time…

No! Even in a parallel universe having anything to do with Marco would be bad news.

'I hear a *but* somewhere in there. Either you still think I'm poison or it's something else. Tell me. I can take it.'

He gave a jerky nod of his head in a move she was becoming familiar with. 'Last night, at the awards, you spoke of Rafael like a friend.'

'Because that's what he is. Just a friend.'

His jaw clenched. 'You're asking me to take your word over my brother's?'

'Not really. I'm saying give us both the benefit of the doubt. See where it takes you.'

He shook his head. 'As long as Rafael sees you as his there can be nothing between us.'

Despite the steaming coffee in her hand, she felt a chill spread through her. 'The message has been received, loud and clear. Was there something else?'

For a full minute he didn't answer. Then, 'I don't want you to think that the kiss has bought you any special privileges.'

'You mean like expecting you to bring me coffee every morning?' she replied sarcastically, a surprisingly acute pain scouring its acidic path through her belly.

'My expectations from you as a driver haven't changed. In fact nothing has changed. Understood?'

Setting down her mug on the bedside table, she hugged her knees. 'All this angst over a simple kiss, Marco?' The need to reduce the kiss to an inconsequential blip burned through her, despite her body's insistence on reliving it.

He prowled to the window and turned to face her. 'Women have a habit of reading more into a situation than there actually is.' His raised hand killed her response. 'While taking pains to state the contrary. But I want to be very clear—I don't *do* relationships.'

Her breath fractured in her lungs. 'I'm not looking for one,' she forced out.

His whole body stiffened. 'Then it stands to reason that there shouldn't be a problem.'

She hugged her knees tighter. 'Again I sense a *but*.'

'*But*…for some reason you're all I think about.'

The statement was delivered with joyless candour. Yet her heart leapt like a puppet whose string had been jerked. And when his eyes met hers and she saw the heat in them something inside her melted.

He strode back towards the bed, shoving clenched fists into his pockets. She stared up at him, her pulse racing. 'And you're annoyed about that?'

His gaze raked her face slowly. Then slid to her neck, her breasts, and back up again. Molten heat burned in his eyes. 'Livid. Frustrated. Puzzled. Intensely aroused.'

Of their own volition her eyes dropped below his belt-line. Confronted with the evidence, she felt a deep longing melt between her legs. She swallowed as heat poured through her whole being.

Looking away, she muttered, 'Don't do that.'

A strained sound escaped his throat. 'I was just about to demand the same of you.'

'I'm not doing anything. You, on the other hand—you're…' She sucked in a desperate breath.

'I'm what?' he demanded, his voice low, ferocious.

'You're all brooding and…and fierce…and angry…and… aroused. You're cursing your desire for me and yet your eyes are promising all sorts of rampant steaminess.' Her eyes darted back to the bulge in his trousers and a lump clogged her throat. 'I…I think you should leave.'

'You don't sound very sure about that.'

'*I am.* I don't want you. And even if I did you're off-limits to me, remember? So you can't…can't present me with…*this*!'

A pulse jerked in his jaw. 'I never said the situation wasn't without complications.'

'Well, the solution is easy. You hired me to do a job so let me get on with it. We don't have to see each other until the season ends and we win the Constructors' Championship. We'll stand on the top podium and douse ourselves in champagne. Then we'll go our separate ways until next season starts.'

'And you will have fulfilled this promise you made?'

Surprise zapped through her. He remembered. 'Partly, yes,' she replied, before thinking better of it.

His gaze turned speculative. 'To whom did you make the promise?'

She dragged her eyes from his, the sudden need to spill everything shocking her with its intensity. But she couldn't. Marco didn't trust her. And she wasn't prepared to trust him with the sacred memory of her father.

She shook her head. 'It's none of your business. Are you going to leave me alone to get on with it?'

His mouth firmed into a hard line. 'The team has too much riding on this for me to take my eye off the ball at this juncture. So do our sponsors. Once you have proved yourself—'

'Yes, I've heard it all before.' She couldn't stop the bitterness from spilling out. 'Prove myself. Don't bewitch anyone on the team. *Especially* not the boss. Message received and understood. Perhaps you could take your frustrations elsewhere, then, and spare me the thwarted lust backlash?'

He stiffened with anger. '*Dios.* Has no one ever told you

that the difference between attractive feistiness and maddening shrew is one bitchy comment too many?'

'No one has dared,' she threw back.

'Well, take it from me. You need to stop throwing blind punches and learn to pick your fights.' He strode towards the door. 'Romano will drive you to your appointment and bring you back here.'

'That's not necessary. I've hired a scooter.'

He whirled to face her. 'No. Romano will drive you.' His tone brooked no argument.

'Seriously, Marco, you need to dial back the caveman stuff—'

'And *you* need to take greater responsibility for your welfare. If you come off your scooter and break an arm or a leg the rest of the season is finished. I thought you wanted the drive? Or do you think you're invincible on those little piles of junk you like to travel on?'

She bit back a heated retort. Marco was right. All her hard work and sacrifice would amount to nothing if she couldn't ensure she turned up to her races with her bones intact.

'Fine. I'll use the car.'

Pushing back the covers, she slid her feet over the edge and stood. The air thickened once more as Marco tensed.

Sasha refused to look into his face. His brooding, tempting heat would weaken her sorely tested resolve.

'I need to get ready for the shoot.'

He made a sound she couldn't decipher. She squeezed her thighs together and fingered the hem of her T-shirt.

'Your breakfast will be delivered in half an hour.' He moved towards the door. 'Oh, and Sasha...?'

Unable to stop herself, she looked. Framed in the doorway, his stature was impressively male and utterly arresting. 'Yes?' she rasped.

'Unless you want things to slide out of control, don't wear that T-shirt in my presence again. You may not be mine, but

I'm not a saint. The next time I see you in it I may feel obliged to take advantage of its instruction.'

His words hit her with the force of a tsunami. By the time he shut the door, a hundred different images of Marco using his teeth on her had short-circuited her brain.

The photo shoot was horrendously tedious. Several hours of sitting around getting her hair and make-up done, followed by a frenzied half-hour of striking impossible poses, then back to repeating the whole process again.

Sasha returned to the hotel very near exhaustion, but she had gained a healthy respect for models. She also now understood why men like Marco dated them. The sample pictures the photographer had let her keep showed an end result that surprised her.

After pressing the button for the lift, she fished the pictures out of her satchel, shocked all over again by how different she looked—how a few strokes of a make-up brush could transform plain to almost…*sexy*. Or was it something else? All day she'd been unable to dismiss last night's kiss from her mind. Her face burned when she reached the picture of her licking her tingling lips. She'd been recalling Marco's moan of pleasure as he'd deepened their kiss.

So really it was Marco's fault…

Opening the door to the suite, she stopped in her tracks as strains of jazz music wafted in from the living room. Following the sound, she entered the large, opulent room to find Marco lounging on the sofa, an electronic tablet in his hand and a glass of red wine on a table beside him.

'I thought you were going to be late?' The words rushed out before she could stop them. Her suddenly racing pulse made her dizzy for a few seconds.

His gaze zeroed in on her. 'I wrapped things up early.'

'And you couldn't find anyone in your little black book to spend the evening with?'

The thought that he hadn't gone out and vented his sexual frustration on some entirely willing female sent a bolt of elation through her, which she tried—unsuccessfully—to smash down.

She couldn't read the hooded look in his eyes as he set aside the gadget.

'It's only seven-thirty. The night is still young,' he replied.

Something crumpled into a small, tight knot inside her, and the sharp pang she'd felt that morning returned. 'That's just typical. You're going to call some poor woman out of the blue and expect her to be ready to drop everything to go out with you, aren't you?' she mocked.

One corner of his mouth quirked. 'Luckily, the women I know are kind enough to *want* to drop everything for me.'

She snorted. 'Come off it. We both know kindness has nothing to do with it.'

As she'd seen first-hand at the awards ceremony, women would crawl over hot coals to be with Marco. And many more would do so regardless of his financial status or influence. With a body and face like his, he could be penniless and still attract women with a snap of his fingers. As for that lethal, rarely seen smile, and the way he kissed—

Her thoughts screeched to a halt as he stood and came towards her.

'Maybe not,' he conceded, with not a hint of arrogance in sight. 'How was the shoot?'

The question wrenched her from her avid scrutiny of his body. 'Aside from the free shoes, it was a pain in the ass,' she replied.

'Of course,' he agreed gravely. Then without warning he reached out and plucked the pictures from her fingers. 'Maybe you'll even get around to wearing them instead of going barefoot or wearing those hideous boots—'

He stopped speaking as he stared at the pictures. Awareness crawled across her skin as he slowly thumbed through them, lingering over the one where she was draped over the bonnet of the not-yet-released prototype of his latest car, the

Cervantes Triunfo. Eventually he returned to *that* one. And looked as if he'd stopped breathing.

'Marco…'

She stretched out her hand to retrieve the pictures. He ignored her, his attention fixed on the picture, his skin drawn tight over the chiselled bones of his face.

'Marco, I don't want to keep you. I have plans of my own.'

His head snapped up. 'What plans?' he demanded, his tone rough and tight.

Sasha couldn't think how to answer. Her whole mind was paralysed by the way his eyes blazed. Shaking her head, she tried to turn away. He grabbed her arm in a firm hold.

No! Too hot. Too irresistible. Too much.

'Let me go,' she murmured, her voice scraped raw with desire.

'What plans?' he gritted out.

'Are you sure you want to know? You may not approve.'

His hand tightened on her arm, his eyes darkening into storm clouds that threatened thunder and lightning. 'Then think carefully before you speak.'

She sighed. 'Fine. You've busted me. I was going to beg your chef to make me that T-bone steak and salad he made for us yesterday, followed by chocolate caramel delight for dessert—I'll think about the calories later. Afterwards I intend to have a sweltering foursome with Joel, LuAnn and Logan.'

The hand that had started to relax suddenly tightened, harder than before.

'Excuse me?' Marco bit out, his voice a thin blade of ice slicing across her skin.

Reaching into the handbag slung over her shoulder, she pulled out the boxed set of her favourite TV vampire show.

He released her and reached for it. After scrutinising it, he threw it down onto the sofa along with the pictures.

'Take a piece of advice for free, *pequeña*. It's a mistake to keep goading me. The consequences will be greater than you ever bargained for.' His voice was soft. Deadly soft.

Sasha felt a shiver go through her. Most people mistakenly assumed partaking in one of the most dangerous sports in the world meant X1 Premier Racing drivers were fearless. Sasha wasn't fearless. She had a healthy amount of fear and respect for her profession. She knew when to accelerate, when to pull back the throttle, when to pull over and abandon her car.

Right now the look on Marco's face warned her she was skidding close to danger. She heeded the warning. Lashing out because of the maelstrom of emotions roiling inside her would most likely result in far worse consequences than she'd endured with Derek.

'Understood. Let me go.'

Surprise at her easy capitulation lit his eyes. Abruptly he released her.

'I need a shower. I guess you'll be gone when I come out. Enjoy your evening.'

Shamelessly, she fled.

Marco watched her go, frustration and bewilderment fighting a messy battle inside him.

He prided himself on knowing and understanding women. After Angelique, his determination never to be caught out again had decreed it. Women liked to think they were complicated creatures, but when it came down to it their needs were basic, no matter how much they tried to hide it. Hell, some—like Angelique—even spelled it out.

I want fame, Marco. I want excitement! I can't be with a man who's a has-been.

The memory slid in, reminding him why he now ensured the women he associated with knew there was no rosy future in store for them and had no surprises waiting to trap him.

A reality devoid of surprises suited him just fine.

His eyes followed Sasha's tall, slim figure down the hallway.

She surprised him, he admitted reluctantly. She also infuriated him. She made his blood boil in a way that was so basic, so...*sexual*—even without the benefit of those pictures...

Dios! With a growl, he whirled towards the window. When he'd gone to her room to set things straight this morning the last thing he'd expected was for her to reassure him that it had been no big deal.

Despite being totally into the kiss—as much as he'd been—she'd walked away from him last night. A situation he'd never encountered before.

Was it because she didn't really want him? Or was she merely waiting for his brother to wake up so she could resume where they'd left off?

Acid burned through his stomach at the thought. But even the corrosive effect couldn't wash away the underlying sexual need that seared him.

He'd rushed through his meeting with every intention of calling one of the many willing female acquaintances on his BlackBerry. But once he'd returned, his need to go out again had waned. He withdrew from examining why too closely.

He turned back from the window and his eyes fell on the pictures on the sofa. To the one of her draped all over his car...

Blindly he stumbled towards his jacket and dug around for his phone. Two minutes later reservations were made. By the time his Rolls collected him from the foyer, Sasha Fleming had been consigned to the furthest corner of his mind.

Marco stood outside the door ninety minutes later, caught himself listening for sounds from inside, and grimaced in disbelief. He'd spent the last hour or so wining and dining a woman whose name he couldn't now remember.

He'd stared at his date's in-your-face scarlet lips and thought of another set of lips. Plump, freshly licked lips, captured in perfect celluloid. Lips that had responded to his kiss in a way that had sent the most potent pulse of excitement through him.

Forbidden lips.

In the end he'd thrown down his napkin and extracted

several large notes. 'You'll have to forgive me. I'm terrible company tonight. I shouldn't have disturbed your evening.'

The practised pout had reappeared. 'You know I'll forgive you anything, Marco.'

Candy? Candice? had leaned forward in another carefully calculated pose, designed to showcase her body to its best advantage.

'Listen, I have an idea. I know how much you like your coffee. When I was filming in Brazil last month I absolutely fell in love with the coffee and brought some back with me. Why don't we skip dessert and go back to my place and I'll give you a taste?'

Barely containing rising distaste, he'd shaken his head. 'Sorry, I'll take a rain check.'

He'd led her out amid soft protests and further throaty promises of the delights of her cafetière. But coffee, or sex with Candy/Candice had been the last thing on his mind.

His sudden hunger for chocolate caramel had become over-powering.

'Take my car. I'll walk,' he'd said.

And now here he stood, skulking outside his own apartment like a hormonal teenager on his first date.

He entered and approached the living room.

She was curled up on the sofa, a bowl of popcorn in her lap. Her head snapped towards him. As if she'd been listening out for him too. The thought pleased him more than it should have.

The striking blue of her eyes paralysed him.

'You're still awake.' *Excelente, Marco. First prize for stating the obvious.*

She blinked. 'It's only nine-fifteen.' Her eyes followed him as he shrugged off his jacket and dropped it on the sofa. When her gaze lingered on his chest he felt the blood surge stronger than before.

He watched her fingers dance through the bowl of popcorn, the movement curiously erotic. His heart hammered harder. 'You didn't have the chocolate caramel after all?'

'Charlie's disapproving face haunted me. Popcorn is healthier.' She looked away. 'So, how was your date?' she asked, her voice husky.

He wrenched his gaze from her fingers. 'You really want to know?'

Her sensual lips firmed and she shook her head.

The need to gauge her true feelings drew him closer. 'Jealous?'

She inhaled sharply. 'I thought we weren't doing this?'

His eyes fell to her lips. 'Maybe I've changed my mind.'

'Well, change it back. Nothing has changed since this morning. I can't handle your...baggage. And I don't want a relationship. Of any sort.'

Marco opened his mouth to tell her he didn't want anything from her either. But he knew he was lying. His very presence in this room belied that.

Forbidden or not, he wanted her with a compulsive need that unnerved and baffled him. But the fact that he wanted her didn't mean he would have her. He was known for his legendary control. He sat down next to her, caught her scent, and simply willed himself not to react.

Forcing his body to relax, he nodded towards the television. 'You have a thing for vampires?'

'Doesn't everyone?' she replied breathlessly.

He wanted to look at her. But he denied himself the urge and kept his gaze fixed ahead. 'What's the story about?'

She hesitated, fidgeted and sat forward. From the corner of his eye he saw her lick her lips. Fiery heat sang through his veins.

'Oh, you know—it's the usual run-of-the-mill storyline. Two brothers in love with the same girl.'

Something tightened in his chest and his stomach muscles clenched. 'I see.'

'You don't have to watch it.' She shifted backwards, out of his periphery.

'Why not? I'm intrigued.' The two male protagonists faced off on the screen, fangs bared. 'What are they doing now?'

Again she hesitated. 'They're about to fight to the death for her.'

His muscles pulled tighter. Blood surged through his veins and he forcibly relaxed the clenched fist on his thigh.

'Which one are you rooting for?' he asked, the skin on his nape curiously tight as he waited for her answer.

It occurred to him how absurd the conversation was. How absurd it was to be so wound up by a TV show. But every second he waited for her answer felt like an eternity.

'Neither.'

Illogically, his insides hollowed. 'You don't care if either one of them dies?' The words grated his throat.

'That's not what I said. I said neither because I know they won't kill each other. They might tear chunks out of each other, but ultimately they love each other too much to let a woman come between them. No matter how difficult, or how heart-wrenching it is to watch, I know they'll work it out. That's why I love the show. Popcorn?'

The bowl appeared in front of him.

He declined and nodded at the screen as a female character walked on. 'Is she the one?'

Sasha laughed. 'Yep. LuAnn—*femme fatale extraordinaire*. With those huge brown eyes and that body she can have any man she wants. On *and* off the screen.'

'She may look innocent onscreen but off-screen is another matter.'

It was her gasp that did it. That and her scent, mingled with the strangely enticing aroma of popcorn.

Control failed and his eyes met Sasha's stunning blue. Marco wondered if she knew how enthralling they were. How captivating. How very easily she could give LuAnn a run for her money.

'You've met her?'

'Briefly. At one of Rafael's parties.'

Her eyes returned to the screen. 'As much as I'm dying to know the details of your no-doubt salacious meeting, I don't really want the illusion spoiled. Do you mind?'

Again Marco was struck by Sasha's contrast to the other women he'd dated. They would have been bowled over by his mention of a celebrity, dying to know every single detail. Her refreshingly indifferent attitude made him relax a little more.

When he found himself munching on popcorn another bolt of surprise shot through him.

When was the last time he'd relaxed completely like this? Shared an enjoyable evening with a woman that hadn't ended in sex if he'd wanted it to?

He glanced at Sasha. Her eyes were glued to the screen, her lower lip caught between her teeth. Heat ratcheted through him. Correction—an evening that wasn't going to end in sex because sex was forbidden?

He reached for another mouthful of popcorn and his hand brushed hers. Her breath caught but she didn't look away from the screen. When he reluctantly forced his gaze away from her, he saw LuAnn caught in a heated clinch with Joel.

As a thirty-five-year-old man, who knew that sex onscreen was simulated, he shouldn't have found the scene erotic. Especially not with those damned fangs thrown in.

Nevertheless, when Sasha's breath caught for a second time he turned to her, his heart pounding so loudly in his ears he couldn't hear anything else.

'You should be watching the screen, not me.'

Her husky murmur thrummed along his nerve-endings and made a beeline for his groin.

'I was never much of a spectator. I prefer to be a participant.'

Dios! He was hard—so hard it was a toss-up as to whether the feeling was pain or pleasure. The logical thing to do was to get up, walk away.

Yet he couldn't move. Couldn't look away from this woman his body ached for but his mind knew he couldn't have.

Her eyes found his. 'Marco…'

Again it was a husky entreaty.

His fingers brushed her cheek. 'Why can't I get you out of my head? I took a beautiful woman to dinner but I can barely remember what she looked like now. I ate but hardly tasted the food. All I could think about was you.'

'Do you want me to apologise?'

'Would you mean it?'

Her pink tongue darted out, licked, darted back in. He groaned in pain.

'Probably not. But I may have an explanation for you.'

A few feet away the TV belted out the closing sequence of the show. Neither of them paid any attention. His forefinger traced her soft skin to the corner of her mouth, the need to taste her again a raging fever flaming through his veins. 'I'm listening.'

She shrugged. 'Maybe you share a trait with your brother after all. Deny you something and you want it more?'

Marco didn't need to think about it to answer. 'No. The difference between Rafael and me is that he wouldn't have hesitated to take—consequences be damned. He sees something he wants and he takes it.'

'Whereas you agonise about it endlessly, then deny yourself anyway? It's almost as if you're testing yourself—putting yourself through some sort of punishment.'

Her eyes darkened when he froze. She moved her head and her lips came closer to his finger. Marco couldn't speak, needing every single ounce of self-control to keep his shock from showing. He *deserved* to put himself through punishment for what he'd done. He'd lost the most precious thing in life—a child—because he'd taken his eye off the ball.

'Maybe you should learn to bend a little…take what is being offered? What is being offered freely.'

An arrow of pain shot through the haze of desire engulfing him. He gave a single shake of his head and inhaled. 'I

stopped believing in *free* a long time ago, Sasha. There are
always consequences. The piper always expects payment.'

'I don't believe that. Laughter is free. Love is free. It's hate
that eats you up inside. Bitterness that twists feelings if you
let them. And, no, I'm not waxing philosophical. I've experienced it.'

'Really?' he mocked, dropping his hand. When his senses
screeched in protest he merely willed the feeling away. 'To
whom did you make your promise?' he asked, the need to
know as forceful as the need raging through his veins.

Wariness darkened her eyes. Then her shoulders rolled.
'My father.'

'What did you promise him?'

'That I'd win the Drivers' Championship for him.'

'Out of some misguided sense of duty, no doubt?' he de-
rided.

Anger blazed through her eyes. 'Not duty. *Love.* And it's
about as misguided as your bullheaded need to coddle Rafael.'

'There's a difference between responsibility and your illu-
sionary love,' he rebutted, irate at this turn of the conversation.

'I suffer no illusions. My father loved me as unconditionally as I loved him.'

Tensing, he sat back in the seat. 'Then you were lucky.
Not everyone is imbued with unconditional love for his or her
child. Some even use their unborn children as bartering tools.'

Her breath caught. 'Did you…? Are you saying that from
experience?'

A cold drench of reality washed over him at how close he'd
come to revealing everything.

Surging to his feet, he stared into her face. 'I was merely
making a point. As much as I want you, Sasha, I'll never take
you. The consequences would be too great.'

CHAPTER EIGHT

THE CONSEQUENCES WOULD be too great.

Sasha tried to block out the words as she adjusted the traction control on her steering wheel. The tremor in her fingers increased and she clenched her fists tighter around the wheel.

Shears, Marina Bay, Raffles Boulevard. Watch out for Turn Ten speed bump—Padang, pit lane exit, look after the tyres...

Her heart hammered, excitement and adrenaline shooting through her as she went through the rigorous ritual of visualising every corner of the race. At her third attempt, fear rose to mingle with her emotions.

She'd secured pole position for the first time in her racing career, but despite the team's euphoria afterwards she'd sensed a subtle waning of their excitement as speculation as to whether she could do the job trickled in. Sasha had seen it in their faces, heard it in Luke's voice this morning when he'd grilled her over race strategy for the millionth time. Even Tom had weighed in.

Consequences...responsibility...last chance...

Sweat trickled down her neck and she hastily sipped at her water tube. She couldn't afford dehydration. Couldn't afford to lose focus. In fact she couldn't afford to do anything less than win.

Beyond the bright lights of the circuit that turned night into day at the Singapore Grand Prix thousands of fans would be watching.

As would Marco.

He hadn't spoken to her since that night on his sofa in London, but he'd attended every race since the season had resumed and Sasha knew he was somewhere above her, in the exclusive VIP suite of the team's motor home, hosting the Prime Minister, royalty and a never-ending stream of celebrities.

Some time during the sleepless night, when she'd been looking down at the race track from her hotel room, she'd wondered whether he'd even bother to grace the pit with his presence if she made it onto that final elusive step on the podium. Or whether he would be too preoccupied with entertaining his latest flame—the blonde daughter of an Italian textile magnate who never seemed far from his side nowadays.

She tried desperately to block him from her mind. Taking pole position today—a dream she'd held for longer than she could remember—should be making her ecstatic. She was one step further towards removing the dark stain of her father's shame from people's minds. To finally removing herself from Derek's malingering shadow.

Yet all she could think about was Marco and their conversation in London.

She clenched her teeth in frustration and breathed in deeply.

Luke's voice piped through her helmet, disrupting her thoughts.

'Adjust your clutch—'

She flicked the switch before he'd finished speaking. The sheer force of her will to win was a force field around her. Finally she found the zen she desperately craved.

Focusing, she followed the red lights as they lit up one by one. Adrenaline rushed faster, followed a second later by the drag of the powerful car as she pointed it towards the first corner.

She made it by the skin of her teeth, narrowly missing the front wing of the number two driver. Her stomach churned through lap after gruelling lap, even after she'd established a healthy distance between her and the car behind.

What seemed like an eternity later, after a frenzied race, including an unscheduled pitstop that had raised the hairs on her arms, she heard the frenzied shouts of her race engineer in her ear.

'You won! Sasha, you won the Singapore Grand Prix!'

Tears prickled her eyes even as her fist pumped through the air. Her father's face floated through her mind and a sense of peace settled momentarily over her. It was broken a second later by the sound of the crowd's deafening roar.

Exiting the car, Sasha squinted through the bright flashes of the paparazzi, desperate to see familiar hazel eyes through the sea of faces screaming her name.

No Marco.

A stab of disappointment hollowed out her stomach. With a sense of detachment, she accepted the congratulations of her fellow drivers and blinked back tears through the British national anthem.

Dad would be proud, she reminded herself fiercely. *He* was all that mattered. Plastering a smile on her face, she accepted her trophy from the Prime Minister.

This was what she wanted. What she'd fought for. The team—*her* team—were cheering wildly. Yet Sasha felt numb inside.

Fighting the alarming emptiness, she picked up the obligatory champagne magnum, letting the spray loose over her fellow podium winners. Brusquely she told herself to live in the moment, to enjoy the dream-come-true experience of winning her first race.

Camera flashes blinded her as she stepped off the podium. When it cleared Tom stood in front of her, a huge grin on his face.

'I *knew* you could do it! Prepare yourself, Sasha. Your world's about to rock!'

The obligatory press conference for the top three winning drivers took half an hour. When she emerged, Tom grabbed her arm and steered her towards the bank of reporters waiting behind the barriers.

'Tom, I don't really want—'

'You've just won your first race. *"I don't really want"* shouldn't feature in your vocabulary. The world's your oyster.'

But I don't want the world, she screamed silently. *I want Marco. I want not to feel alone on a night like this.*

Feeling the stupid tears build again, Sasha rapidly blinked them back as a microphone was thrust in her face.

'How does it feel to be the first woman to win the Singapore Grand Prix?'

From deep inside she summoned a smile. 'Just as brilliant as the first man felt when he won, I expect.'

Beside her she heard Tom's sharp intake of breath.

Behave, Sasha.

'Are you still involved with Rafael de Cervantes?' asked an odious reporter she recognised from a Brazilian sports channel.

'Rafael and I were never involved. We're just friends.'

'So now he's in a coma there's nothing to stop you from switching *friendships* to his brother, no?'

Tom stepped forward. 'Listen, mate—'

Sasha stopped him. 'No. It's fine.' She faced the reporter. 'Marco de Cervantes is a world-class engineer and a visionary in his field. His incredible race car design is the reason we won the race today. It would be an honour for me to call him my friend.' She tagged on another smile and watched the reporter's face droop with disappointment.

Tom nodded at a British female reporter. 'Next question.'

'As the winner of the race, you'll be the guest of honour at the rock concert. What will you be wearing?'

Mild shock went through her at the question, followed swiftly by a deepening sense of hollowness. The X1 Premier Rock Concert had become a fixture on every A-List celebrity's calendar. No doubt Marco would be there with his latest girlfriend.

'It doesn't matter what I'll be wearing because I'm not going to the concert.'

Sasha dashed into the foyer of her six-star hotel, grateful when the two burly doormen blocked the chasing paparazzi.

She heaved in a sigh of relief when she shut her suite door behind her.

The ever-widening chasm of emptiness she couldn't shake threatened to overwhelm her. Quickly she stripped off her clothes and showered.

The knock came as she was towelling herself dry. For a second she considered not answering it.

A sense of *déjà vu* hit her as she opened the door to another perfectly coiffed stylist, carting another rack of clothes.

'I think you've got the wrong suite.'

The diminutive Asian woman in a pink suit simply bowed, smiled and let herself in. Her assistant sailed in behind her, clutching a large and stunningly beautiful bouquet of purple lilies and cream roses.

'For you.' She thrust the flowers and a long oblong box into Sasha's hand.

Stifling a need to scream, Sasha calmly shut the door and opened the box. On a red velvet cushion lay the most exquisite diamond necklace she'd ever seen. With shaking fingers, she plucked the card from the tiny peg.

Pick a dress, then they'll leave. Romano is waiting downstairs.

Sasha stared at Marco's bold scrawl in disbelief. When she looked up, the women smiled and started pulling clothes off the hangers.

'No—wait!'

'No wait. Twenty minutes.'

'But…where am I going?' she asked.

The stylist shrugged, picked up a green-sequinned dress barely larger than a handkerchief, and advanced towards her. Sasha stepped back as the tiny woman waved her hand in front of her.

'Off.'

With a sense of damning inevitability…and more than a

little thrill of excitement…she let herself be pulled forward. 'Okay, but definitely not the green.'

The stylist nodded, trilled out an order in Mandarin, and advanced again with another dress.

Twenty minutes later Sasha stepped from the cool, air-conditioned car onto another red carpet. This time, without Marco, she was even more self-conscious than before. On a warm, sultry Singapore night, the cream silk dress she'd chosen felt more exposing than it had in the safety of her hotel room. At first glance she'd refused to wear the bohemian mini-dress because…well, because it had no back. But then the stylist had fastened the draping material across her lower back and Sasha had felt…*sexy*—like a woman for the first time in her life.

Her hair was fastened with gold lamé rope, her nails polished and glittering. The look was completed with four-inch gold stilettos she'd never dreamt she'd be able to walk in, but she found it surprisingly easy.

Romano appeared at her side, his presence a reminder that somewhere beyond the wild flashes of the paparazzi's cameras Marco was waiting for her.

All the way from her hotel she'd felt the emptiness receding, but had been too scared to acknowledge that Marco had anything to do with it. Now she couldn't stop a smile from forming on her face as the loud boom of fireworks signalled the start of the rock concert.

The VIP lounge teemed with rock stars and pop princesses. She tried to make small talk as she surreptitiously searched the crowd for Marco. Someone thrust a glass of champagne in her hand.

Half an hour later, when a Columbian platinum-selling songstress with snake hips asked who her designer was, Sasha started to answer, then stopped as an ice-cold thought struck her. Was Marco even here? Had she foolishly misinterpreted his note and dressed up only to be stood up?

The depths of her hurt stunned her into silence.

She barely felt any remorse as the pop star flounced off
in a huff. Blindly she turned for the exit, humiliation scouring through her.

'Sasha? You're heading for the stage, right?' Tom grabbed
her arm and stopped her.

'The…the stage?'

'Your favourite band is about to perform. Marco had me
fly them out here just for you.'

'He *what*?' A different kind of *stun* stopped her heart.

'Come on—you don't want them to start without you.'

A thousand questions raced through her brain, but she
didn't have time to voice a single one before she was propelled
onto the stage and into the arms of the band's lead singer.

Torn between awe at sharing the stage with her favourite
band, and happiness that she hadn't misinterpreted Marco's
note after all, Sasha knew the next ten minutes were the most
surreal of her life. Even seeing herself super-sized on half
a dozen giant screens didn't freak her out as much as she'd
imagined.

She exited the stage to the crowd's deafening roar. Tom
beamed as he helped her down the stairs.

'Have you seen Marco?' Sasha attributed her breathless-
ness to her onstage excitement—not her yearning to see Marco
de Cervantes.

Tom's smile slipped and his gaze dropped. 'Um, he was
around a moment ago…'

She told herself not to read anything into Tom's answer.
'Where is he?'

'Sasha…' He sighed and pointed towards the roped-off
area manned by three burly bodyguards.

At first she didn't see him, her sight still fuzzy from the
bright stage lights.

When she finally focused, when she finally saw what her
mind refused to compute, Sasha was convinced her heart had
been ripped from her chest.

Each step she took out of the concert grounds felt like a

walk towards the opening mouth of a yawning chasm. But Sasha forced herself to keep going, to smile, to acknowledge the accolades and respect she finally had from her team.

Even though inside she was numb and frozen.

The knock came less than ten minutes later.

Marco leaned against the lintel. The buttons of his shirt were *still* undone; his hair was unkempt. As if hands—*female hands*—had run through it several times. He stood there, arrogantly imposing, larger than life.

She hated him more than she could coherently express. And yet the sight of him kicked her heart into her throat.

'What do you want?' she blurted past the pain in her throat.

His gaze, intense and unnerving, left her face to take in the bikini she'd changed into. 'Why did you leave the concert?'

'Why aren't you back there, being pawed by your Italian sexpot?'

'You left because you saw me with Flavia?'

'You know what they say—two's company, three's a flash mob. Now, if you'll excuse me…' She grabbed her kaftan from the bed and the box containing the diamond necklace. 'Here—take this back. I don't want it.'

'It's yours. Every member of the team receives a gift for the team's win. This is yours.'

Her mouth dropped open. 'You're kidding me?'

'I'm not. Where are you going?'

She stared at the box, not sure how to refuse the gift now. 'For a swim—not that it's any of your business.'

'A swim? At this hour?'

'Singapore is the longest race on the calendar. It's even longer when you're leading and trying to defend your position. If I don't warm up and do my stretching exercises my muscles will seize up. That's what I'd planned to do before… Whatever—will you please get out of my way?'

His gaze dropped to her legs. A hoarse sound rumbled

from his throat. A look entered his eyes—one that made her excited and afraid at the same time.

'Marco, I said—'

'I heard you.' Still, he didn't move away. Instead, he extracted his phone and issued a terse command in Spanish, his gaze on her the whole time.

Sasha dropped the box on the bed and took a deep calming breath, willing her skin to stop tingling, her heartbeat to slow down. Her senses were too revved up, ready to unleash the full power of her conflicted feelings for this man.

'Let's go.' He finally moved out of the doorway.

'I'm not going anywhere with you until you tell me what you're doing here,' she responded.

He speared a hand through his hair, mussing up the luxurious strands even more. 'Does it matter why I'm here, Sasha? Are you happy to see me?' he demanded in a low, charged tone.

She hated the fire that raced through her veins, stinging her body to painful life in a way even her first race win hadn't been able to achieve.

'Less than half an hour ago you had another woman all over you. Last time I checked, my name wasn't Sloppy Seconds Sasha.'

He swore under his breath. 'You know, you're the most difficult, infuriating woman I know.'

Despite the raspy vehemence in his tone, she smiled. 'Thank you.'

He took her arm and led her to the lift. 'It wasn't a compliment.'

'I know. But I'll take it as one.' She tried not to breathe too deeply of his scent as he stepped in beside her.

The lift whisked them upwards. From the corner of her eye she saw him turn his phone off and shove it into his pocket.

The doors opened onto a space that was so beautiful Sasha couldn't speak for several seconds. In the soft breeze potted palm trees swayed. Strategically placed lights gave the space an exotic but intimate feel that just begged to be enjoyed. Several feet away an endless, boomerang shaped infinity pool poised over the tip of the hotel's tower glimmered blue and silver.

Then she noticed what was missing. 'It's empty.' There wasn't a single soul on the sixtieth-floor skydeck.

'*Sì.*'

The way he responded had her turning to face him.

'You had something to do with it?'

A simple nod.

'Why?'

His shook his head in disbelief. 'That's the hundredth question you've asked since I knocked on your door. I didn't want your swim to be interrupted.'

She kicked away her slippers, her temperature rising another notch when his gaze dropped to her bare feet. 'This pool is three times the size of an Olympic pool. It's hardly cramped.'

His gaze turned molten. 'I wanted privacy.' He released the last button on his shirt and it fell open to reveal a golden washboard torso.

Heat piled on. Beneath the Lycra bikini, her nipples tightened, and her stomach muscles quivered with a need so strong she could barely breathe. 'I see. Will you snarl at me if I ask why?'

'Yes,' he snarled.

Striding to her, he drew the hem of her kaftan over her head and tossed it over his shoulder. Then he took her hair tie, raked his fingers through the strands and secured her hair on top of her head.

Fresh waves of desire threatened to drown her. 'Marco…'

'How many laps do you need to be less tense?'

'Tw—twenty.' She couldn't drag her eyes from the beauty of his face, from the sensual, inviting curve of his mouth.

'Twenty laps it is, then.' He shrugged off his shirt, then released his belt.

Her eyes widened. 'What are you doing?'

'What does it look like?'

'Um…'

Without warning he leaned forward and sniffed the skin between her neck and shoulder. 'You're covered in *eau de* Sleazy Rock Star. I smell of cloying Italian perfume. What say we wash the scent of other people off our skin, and then we'll talk, *si*?'

'Marco…'

He swore under his breath. 'Go, Sasha. I need to cool off, or *Dios* help me, I won't be responsible for my actions.'

She went, with the heaviness of his hot gaze scorching her skin.

Pausing at one end of the pool, she stretched her arms over her head. At his sharp intake of breath, she let a sensual smile curve her lips.

The water was a welcome but temporary relief from the sensations arcing between them. He dived in after her a second later, quickly caught up with her and matched her stroke for stroke. When she swam faster, to escape the frenzied need clawing inside, he kept up with her.

His presence made every stroke of water against her skin feel like a caress. At the last lap he increased his pace and heaved himself out of the water. She clung to the side, her lungs heaving, and watched the play of water on his magnificent body as he returned to the poolside.

'Out,' he commanded tersely, his hand holding out a towel like a bull-baiting matador.

She rose out of the pool, careful not to look at the wet clinginess of his boxers. He folded the towel around her, his movements brisk as he rubbed the moisture off her. Then he swung her into his arms and carried her to the enclosed cabana a few feet away.

Two silk-covered loungers stood side by side, separated by a table laid out with several platters of food, from local delicacies to caviar on blinis. In a sterling silver tub a linen-draped bottle of vintage champagne chilled on ice.

Marco set her down on the lounger and picked up the bottle.

Sasha forced her gaze from the play of muscles and looked at the table. 'There's enough here to feed an army.' Reaching for a small plate, she dished out grilled prawns and fragrant rice.

'You don't like caviar?'

She grimaced. 'It smells funny and tastes disgusting. I don't know why people eat the stuff.' She took a mouthful of her food and felt the explosion of textures on her tongue. Thankfully she managed to swallow without choking. 'Now, *this* is heavenly.' She took another mouthful and groaned.

Marco took his seat across from her and held out one glass of champagne, his gaze never leaving hers. What she glimpsed in the heated depths made her heart quicken.

'Marco—'

'Eat. We'll talk when you're done.'

How can I eat? she wanted to ask. Especially when his eyes followed her every move. But words refused to form on her lips. It was as if he'd cast some sort of spell on her. Maybe he was a vampire after all, she thought hysterically.

The thought should have lightened her mood, made it easier for her to cope, but all it did was cause a fevered shudder to race down her spine.

Clawing in a desperate breath, she set the plate aside. 'Let's talk now. You invited me to the concert, then ignored me to make out with your girlfriend. What else is there to talk about?'

'Flavia's not my girlfriend, and I wasn't making out with her. She was congratulating me on the team's win, just like a lot of people have done tonight.'

'She was *all* over you. And you didn't seem to mind.'

'I was…preoccupied.'

She snorted. 'Evidently.'

'*Para el amor de Dios!* I was waiting in the VIP room for

you! The Prime Minister turned up when I was about to come and meet you. I tried to get away as quickly as possible, only to find you were more interested in plastering yourself all over your favourite rock star. It was very evident you didn't have a bra on, but tell me—were you even wearing panties under that dress?'

A harsh flush of anger tinged his cheekbones. This was the angriest she'd ever seen Marco. The reason why stopped her breath.

'You were jealous?'

His jaw clenched. 'Do you mean was that what I expected when I had the band flown over for you? No. Did I want to break every bone in his pathetically thin body? *Sì*. For starters.'

The air thickened around them.

A thousand different questions rushed into her mind. One emerged.

'I'm not stupid, Marco, I know where this is going. But what about the consequences? The ones that made you avoid me for the past three weeks?'

He abandoned his glass and rested his hands on his knees, his eyes never leaving hers. 'Seeing you in another man's arms has simplified my decision. For the sake of my sanity, and to avoid murder charges, no more staying away,' he rasped.

'Right. Well, I'm happy for you and your sanity. But what about what *I* want?'

His eyes dropped to her lips. 'If you know where this is going then you know how badly I want to kiss you. Come here.'

Her mouth, the subject of his very intense scrutiny, tingled so badly she had to curb the urge to bite it. 'I meant what I said in London. I don't want a relationship.'

A hard look passed through his eyes. 'I don't want a relationship either.'

'What about *your* clause?'

'I'm not a racing driver and I don't work for the team so I'm exempt. Come here, Sasha.'

'No. Aren't you twisting the rules?'

'No. I can quote them verbatim for you later. Right now I want you to come over here and kiss me.'

Her breath shortened. 'What if I don't want to?'

His gaze darkened. 'Then I'll return to the concert, find your reedy rock star and decorate the VIP lounge with him.'

A roar went up a few miles away. The throb of the rock concert echoed superbly the blood surging through her veins as Marco continued to watch her.

'I hope you won't expect me to bail you out of jail.'

He shrugged. 'I live in hope for a lot of things, *querida*. At this moment I'm hoping you'll stop arguing and crawl into my lap. Would it help if I said that not a day went by these past three weeks when you didn't feature in my thoughts?' He lifted a winged brow.

'Maybe that helps. A little…'

Without warning he reached across the table and scooped her up. Settling her in his lap, he freed her hair and sighed in pleasure as the heavy tresses spilled into his hands. Then he lowered her until her back rested on the upraised lounger.

Despite her bikini's relative modesty, Sasha had never felt more exposed in her life. Especially when Marco took his time to trail his fierce gaze over her, missing nothing as he scoured her body, and followed more slowly with one long, lazy finger.

'You're doing it again.' Her voice was smoky with lust, her flesh alight wherever he touched.

'What?' he murmured, his eyes resting at the apex of her thighs.

Beneath her bottom the hard ridge of his erection pressed into her flesh, its heat making her skin tighten in feverish anticipation.

'The thing with your eyes. And your hands. And your body.'

'If you want me to stop you'll have to kiss me.'

'Maybe I don't want you to stop. Maybe this is what I'll allow before I decide this is a very bad idea.'

His finger paused on her belly. 'You think this is a bad idea?'

A thread of uncertainty wheedled through her desire. 'My last involvement left a lot of bruises.'

He tensed. 'Derek physically hurt you?'

'No, but he influenced a lot of people against me. You included.'

He shook his head. 'I make up my own mind. If you truly don't want this, say the word and I'll stop.'

The thought of denying herself made her heart lurch painfully.

Her body moved closer of its own volition. He hissed out a breath, the skin around his mouth tightening as he visibly reined in control. 'If you intend to stop that's not a great idea, *querida*.'

Sasha had had enough. Marco had spent far too much of his life controlling everything. For once she yearned to see him lose his cool, to crack the shell of tightly reined-in emotion. She wriggled again.

His gaze connected with hers. The dark hunger in its depths made her breath catch. Giving in to the urge, she slipped her hand over his nape and urged his head down.

He took control of her lips in a kiss so driven, so desperate, she cried out against his mouth. He fisted one hand in her hair to hold her still, his other hand sliding over her bottom to drag her closer.

Sasha went willingly, her body a fluid vessel of rampant desire that craved only him. Every single doubt that crowded in her brain drowned under ever-increasing waves of sensation.

She might be risking everything to experience a few hours of pleasure, but Sasha could no more push Marco away than she could voluntarily stop breathing. She would deal with regret in the morning.

Losing herself in the kiss, she boldly thrust her tongue

against his. His body jerked, making a tiny fizz of pleasure steal through her.

When his fingers squeezed her buttock, she moaned.

He pulled back. 'You like that?' he rasped, his gaze heavy and hooded.

She nodded and licked her lips, already missing the feel of his mouth against hers.

'Tell me what else you'd like, *mi tentación.*' He released the tie of her bikini top and trailed his mouth over her skin.

'You…not to be so overdressed…' she gasped out.

Another roar from the concert ripped through the night air. Momentarily she remembered where they were.

'On the other hand, maybe that's not so bad—'

'We won't be disturbed.'

The finality of the statement, along with the graze of his teeth over one Lycra-clothed nipple, melted the last of her reservations. Giving her feelings free rein, she slid her hand over his shoulders, touching the smooth skin of his nape before exploring his damp, luxurious hair.

Her urgency fed his. With renewed vigour he kissed her again, pulling off the wet cloth and tossing it aside. Reversing their positions, he eased her onto the lounger, then tugged off her bikini bottoms.

In the soft, ambient light of the enclosed cabana his skin gleamed golden, the dark silky hairs on his chest making her fingers tingle to touch.

'I want to touch you all over.' The heated words had slipped out before she could stop them.

His face contorted in a pained grimace. Tugging off his boxers, he stretched out next to her. Leaning down, he ran his tongue over her mouth. 'I believe I mentioned the near insanity that has plagued me these past weeks? Touching me all over is not a good idea right now.'

Her breath rasped through her chest. Breathing had become increasingly difficult. 'Oh. Then I guess it's not a good time to mention I also intend biting a few strategic places?'

A heartfelt groan preceded a few heated Spanish words muttered against her lips. 'Do me a favour, *mi tentadora*. Keep your thoughts to yourself for the time being. You have my word. I'll let you vocalise your every want later.'

Swooping down, he captured one exposed nipple in his mouth, his fierce determination to shut her up working wonders. Words deserted her as sensation took over. Liquid heat pooled at the apex of her thighs, the flesh of her sex swelling and pulsating with the strength of her need. By the time he transferred his attention to her other nipple Sasha was incoherent with desire.

Marco traced his lips lower, ruthlessly turning her inside out with pleasure, but when she felt his mouth dip below her navel she froze.

Sensing her withdrawal, he raised his head. 'You don't want this?'

'I *do*.' So much so the force of her need shocked her. 'I do... But you don't have to if...' Her words fizzled out at the searing heat in his eyes.

'I've spent endless nights imagining the taste of you, Sasha.' He parted her legs wider, licked the sensitive skin inside her thigh, his eyes growing darker at her breathless groan. 'But I've always preferred reality to dreams.'

He put his mouth on her, slowly worked his tongue over the millions of nerve-endings saturated with pleasure receptors. Sasha screamed, and came in a rush of pleasure so intense her whole body quivered with it.

Before the last of her orgasm had faded away Marco was surging over her. His kiss was less frantic but no less demanding. And, just like the engine of a finely tuned car, her body responded to his demands, anticipation firing her blood like nothing had ever done in her life.

Tension screamed through Marco's body as he raised himself from the intoxicating kiss. The sound of Sasha's orgasm echoed in his head like a siren's call, promising him pleasure beyond measure. He couldn't remember ever being so fired up about sex—so impatient he'd nearly forgotten protection.

Luckily sanity prevailed just in time.

Sasha moved restlessly beneath him, her sultry gaze steady on his as he parted her thighs.

Every single night of the past three weeks he'd woken with an ache in his groin and a sinking sensation that he was fighting a losing battle. He'd congratulated himself on staying away, but he'd known deep down it was a hollow victory.

Truth was he'd never wanted a woman as much as he wanted Sasha. He'd stopped trying to decipher what made her so irresistible. She just *was*. He'd also made discreet enquiries and verified that she'd spoken the truth—she hadn't been involved with Rafael.

So just this once he was going to take. Sasha Fleming had worked her way under his skin like no other woman had and now this was the inevitable conclusion. Her underneath him, her thighs parted, her sultry gaze steady on his. Just as he'd dreamed...

With a groan he sank into her.

'Thank God!' she cried. 'For a second there I thought you were about to change your mind.'

As if to stop him taking that route, her muscles clamped tight around him.

Another groan tore from his throat. 'I thought I told you to shut up?' He pulled back and surged into her once more, pleasure such as he'd never known rocking through him.

'I am... I will... Just please don't stop.' Raking her nails down his back, she clamped her hands around his waist.

As if he could even if he wanted to. He was past the point of no return, his need so great he was almost afraid to acknowledge its overwhelming scope. Instead he lost himself in her pleasure, in the hitched sounds and feminine demands of her body as she welcomed him into her sweet warmth.

'*Dios*, you feel incredible,' he rasped as sensation piled upon sensation.

Inevitably the bough broke. Ecstasy rode through him, blinding him to everything else but the glorious satisfaction of unleashed passion.

With her cry of bliss he followed off the peak, the muscles in his body tightening with the force of his orgasm as he emptied himself into her.

He collapsed on top of her, her soft, sweat-slicked body a cushion to his hardness. He remained there until their breathing calmed then, rolling onto the lounger, he tucked her against his side.

As the last of the haze faded away he felt the first inevitable twinge of regret. He'd succumbed to temptation. Now the piper would expect payment. And for the first time in his life Marco was afraid at just how much he was willing to pay.

CHAPTER NINE

'WHAT—?' SASHA jerked awake.

The solid body curved around hers and the arm imprisoning her kept her from falling off the lounger. Opening her eyes, she encountered Marco's accusing gaze.

'You fell asleep.'

The wide expanse of muscled chest scrambled her brain for a few seconds, before a few synapses fired a thought. She'd had sex with Marco. Wild, unbelievable, pleasure-filled sex. After which—

'You fell *asleep*,' he incised a second time, affront stamped all over his face.

'Uh…I'm sorry…'

'I get the feeling you don't mean that.'

'And I get the feeling I'm not following this conversation at all.' Before she could stop it a wide yawn broke through.

His glare darkened.

'Did I not please you?' He seemed genuinely puzzled, and a little unsure. One hand curved under her nape to tilt her face up to his.

Thoughts of their lovemaking melted her insides. 'Of course you did,' she said, struggling to keep from blushing at recalling her cries of pleasure. Lifting her hands, she framed his face. 'I've never felt more pleasure than I did with you.'

'It was so good you fell asleep straight after?'

'Take it as a compliment. You wore me out.'

His lids veiled his eyes. 'This is a first, I admit.'

'Wearing a woman out?' she asked, stunned.

'Of course not. The falling asleep part.'

Laughter bubbled up from deep within her, delight filling her. Leaning up, she pressed her lips against his in a light kiss.

Marco took over and turned it into a long, deep kiss.

By the time he was done with her she struggled to breathe. And he…he was fully engorged, his erection a forceful presence against her belly. Emboldened by the thought that she could arouse him again so quickly, she caressed her fingers down his side, eliciting a shuddered groan from him that released a wanton smile from her.

'Like I said, I'm sorry. How can I make it up to you?' She slid her hand between them and gripped him tight. His lips parted on another groan. She caressed up and down, marvelling at the tensile strength of him.

His mouth trailed over her face to the juncture between her neck and shoulder. Erotic heat washed through her.

When her grip tightened, his breath shuddered out. '*Sí, mi querida*, that's the right way to make it up to me.'

His hips bucked against her hold, heat and strength pulsing through her fingers. Liquid heat gathered between her thighs. She was unbelievably turned on by the pleasure she gave him.

At yet another caress he suddenly reared up and flipped her over. 'You're getting carried away.'

She slid her thighs either side of him and lowered herself until her wet heat touched him. The feel of his strong hands sliding down her back to capture her bottom made her shiver with delight.

'Then me being on top wasn't the best idea, was it?'

His predatory gaze swept over her, lingering on her breasts, making them peak even more painfully.

'It's time you learned that I can control you from whichever position I'm in,' he breathed.

He surged into her, filling her so completely stars exploded behind her closed lids. He captured her nape, forced her down and took her mouth in a scorching kiss. His tongue seeking the deep cavern of her mouth, he took her over completely, escalating the desire firing through her until Sasha was aflame with a pleasure so intense it frightened the small part of her brain that could still function.

Sasha hung on as he clamped one hand in the small of her back to hold her still. His pace was frantic, frightful in its demand and exquisite in its delivery of pleasure. She whimpered when he freed her mouth, only to blindly seek his for herself before she could draw another breath. Sensation spiralled out of control as bliss gathered with stunning speed.

'Open your eyes. Let me see your eyes when you come for me.'

She obeyed. Then wished she hadn't when the heat in his eyes threatened to send her already flaming world out of control.

'Marco…'

'*Sì*, I feel it too.'

She believed him. The sheen of sweat coating his skin, the unsteady hand that caressed down her face before recapturing her nape, the harsh pants that escaped his lungs all attested to the fact that he was caught in this incredible maelstrom too.

Pleasure scythed through her heart, arrowed down into her pelvis, forcing her to cry out one last time as her orgasm exploded through her.

Beneath her, still controlling their pleasure, Marco thrust into her release, groaning at the sensation of her caressing convulsions, then found his own satisfaction.

Their harsh breaths mingled, hearts thundering as the breeze cooled their sweat-damp skin. Far away, another burst of fireworks lit up the sky.

Inside the cabana, the intensity of their shared pleasure sparked a threat of fear through her.

To mask her feelings, she hid her face in his shoulder. 'I'd love to compose a sonnet to you right now. But I have no words.'

A short rumble of laughter echoed through his heated chest. 'Sonnets are overrated. Your screams of pleasure were reward enough.'

Sasha sighed, put her head on his chest and tried to breathe. The alarm that had taken root in that small part of her brain grew. Something had happened between their first and second lovemaking.

Then she'd felt safe enough to fall asleep in Marco's arms.

Now... Now she felt exposed. Her emotions felt raw, naked. Unbidden, tears prickled her eyes. She scrambled to hide her composure but Marco sensed her feelings.

Pushing her head gently off his shoulder, he stared into her face. 'You're crying. Why?'

How could she explain something she had no understanding of?

When she tried to shrug he shook his head. 'Tell me.'

'I'm just feeling a little overwhelmed. That's all.'

After a second he nodded and brushed a hand down her cheek. '*Sí*. This is your first victory. That feeling can never be equalled.'

For several heartbeats Sasha didn't follow his meaning. When she realised he was talking about the race, and not the roiling aftermath of their lovemaking, her heart lurched.

Panic escalating, she grasped the lifeline. 'I wish my father had been there.'

Marco nodded. 'He would've been proud of you.'

Surprise widened her eyes. 'You knew my father?'

'Of course. He was the greatest driver never to win a championship. I've seen every single race of his. Clearly you inherited his talent.'

The unexpected compliment made her feel even more tearful. She tried to move away but he caught her back easily, lowered his head and kissed his way along her arm. When she shivered, he shook out a cashmere throw and pulled it over them, one muscular leg imprisoning both of hers.

She was grateful for the cover—not least because the familiar feeling of humiliation had returned. 'You know what happened to him, then?'

'He bet on another car to win and deliberately crashed his car.' The cold conviction in his voice sent an icy shiver down her spine, bleeding away the warmth she'd felt in his arms.

This time she moved away forcefully. Standing, she grabbed her kaftan and slid it over her head, even though it did little to cover her nakedness.

'The allegations were false!'

Marco folded his arms behind his head. 'Not according to the court that found him guilty.'

'He never managed to disprove the claims. But *I* believed him. He would *never* have done that. He loved racing too much to crash deliberately for money.'

'I was on the board that reviewed the footage, Sasha. The evidence was hard to refute.'

Shock and anger twisted in her gut. '*You* were one of those who decided he was guilty?'

He lowered his feet to the floor. 'He didn't do much to defend himself. It took him weeks to even acknowledge the charges.'

'And that makes him automatically guilty? He was devastated! Yes, he should have responded to the allegations earlier, but the accusations broke his heart.'

Her voice choked as memories rushed to the fore. Her father broken, disgraced by the sport he'd devoted his life to. It had taken Sasha weeks to convince her father to fight to clear his name. And in those precious weeks his reputation in the eyes of the public had been sullied beyond repair. By the time Jack Fleming had taken the stand his integrity had been in tatters.

'So he gave up? And let you carry the weight of his guilt?'

'Of course not!'

'Why did you promise him the championship?'

Sasha floundered, pain and loss ripping through her. 'He started drinking heavily after the trial. The only time he stopped was when I had a shot at the Formula Two Championship. When I crashed and had to stay a while in hospital he started drinking again.'

'You were in hospital? And the father you claim loved you *unconditionally* wasn't there for you?'

Hazel eyes now devoid of passion taunted her.

Tears prickled her eyes but she refused to let them fall. In her darkest, most painful moments after losing her baby she'd asked herself the same question.

Blinking fiercely, she raised her chin. 'Whatever point you're trying to make, Marco, make it without being a total bastard.'

He sighed and ran a hand over his chin.

She stayed at the other end of the cabana, her arms curved around her middle.

'Did you hire another lawyer to appeal?'

'Of course we did. He... Dad died before the second trial.'

His gaze softened a touch. 'How did he die?'

'He drove his car off a bridge near our cottage.' Pain coated her words. 'Everyone thinks he did it because he was guilty. He was just...devastated.'

'And you feel guilty for this?'

She plucked at the hem of her kaftan. 'If I hadn't got involved with Derek I'd have won a championship earlier. Maybe that would've saved my father...'

Marco's hand slashed through her words. 'Your life is your own. You can't live it for someone else. Not even your father.'

'Who's got their psychoanalysing hat on now?'

His brow lifted. 'You can dish it out but you can't take it?'

Sasha tried to stem the wave of guilt that rose within her. After his trial she'd suggested her father not come to her races, because she'd watched him slide deeper into depression after attending every one.

'Whatever he was, he wasn't a cheat. And I intend to honour his memory.'

Marco rose from the lounger, completely oblivious to his sheer masculine beauty and the effect it had on her tangled emotions. Sasha wanted to burrow into him, to return to the warm cocoon of his arms. But she forced herself to stay where she was.

'Come here.'

She shook her head. 'No. I don't like you very much right now.'

His smile made a mockery of her words as he strolled towards her. 'That's not true. You can't keep your eyes off me. Just like I can't take mine off you.'

'Marco…'

He cupped her jaw and lifted her face to his. Her heart stuttered, then thundered. 'You made your promise out of guilt—'

'No, I want to win the Championship.'

'Sometimes the best deal is to walk away.'

'I don't intend to. So don't stand in my way.'

He brought his mouth within a whisper of hers. Sasha swayed towards him, her willpower depleting rapidly.

'Determination is a quality I admire, *querida*. But remember I won't tolerate anything that stands in the way of *my* desires.'

Tugging her firmly into his arms, he proceeded to make her forget everything but him. Including the fact that he'd never believed her father's innocence.

Marco attended the next two races, flying back each time from Spain, where Rafael was still in a coma. When she won in Japan he took the whole team to celebrate, after which he took Sasha to his penthouse for a private celebration of their own.

After a tricky, hair-raising start, Korea secured her yet another victory. But one look at Marco's taut expression when she emerged from the press conference told her there would be no team celebrations this time.

'Marco?'

'We're leaving. Now.'

He whisked her away from the Yeongam Circuit in his helicopter, his possessive fingers tense around hers all through the flight to a stunning beach house on the outskirts of Seoul City, where he proceeded to strip off her race suit and her underclothes.

'You know that by dragging me away like that in front

of the team you've blown this thing between us wide open, don't you?' she asked, in the aftermath of another pulse-melting session in his bed.

His lovemaking had been especially intense, with an edge that had bordered on the frenzied. And, as much as she'd loved it, he'd left her struggling for breath, in danger of being swept away by the force of his passion.

He brushed a damp curl from her cheek and studied her face. 'Does it bother you?'

She gave the matter brief thought. 'There was speculation even before we were together. Paddock gossip can make the tabloid press look like amateurs.'

He pulled back slightly, his earlier tension returning. 'That doesn't answer my question.'

'They knew I was a good driver before I started sleeping with you. They just didn't want to acknowledge it because of who I am. I only care about what they think of me as a driver. What they think of me personally doesn't matter. It never has.'

'You're a fighter,' he said, his expression reflective.

'I've had to fight for what I've achieved.' She cast him a droll look. 'As you well know.'

When he didn't smile back, a cloud appeared on the horizon of her happy haze. 'It bothers you that I don't care what other people think about me?'

'Single-mindedness has its place.'

'I smell a *but* in there somewhere.'

His gaze because suspiciously neutral. 'Following a single dream is risky. When it's taken from you you'll have nothing.'

'*When?* Not *if*? Are you trying to tell me something?'

'Nothing lasts for ever.'

'You must be jet-lagged again, because you've gone all cryptic on me. I'm three races away from securing the Constructors' Championship for you. Unless I don't finish another single race, and our nearest rival wins every one, it's pretty much a done deal.'

He got out of bed and pulled on his boxer shorts. For a man

who embraced nudity the way Marco did, the definitive action sent a shiver of unease down her spine.

'Done deals have a way of coming undone.'

Her anxiety escalated. 'Enough with the paradoxes. What's going on, Marco?'

Marco strode to the champagne chilling in a monogrammed silver bucket, filled up a glass and brought it back to her. Returning to the cabinet, he poured a whisky for himself and downed it in one go.

He slammed the glass down and spun towards her. '*Madre di Dios*, you nearly crashed today!'

Her fingers tightened around the delicate stem of her glass as the full force of his smouldering temper hit her. Her car had stalled at the start of the race, leaving her struggling to retain pole position. Her rivals hadn't hesitated in trying to take advantage of the situation. She'd touched tyres with a couple of cars and nearly lost a front wing.

'I found myself in a slightly hairy situation. I dealt with it.' She glanced at him. 'Were you worried?'

'That my lover would end up in a mangled heap of metal just like my brother did mere weeks ago? What do you think?' he ground out.

She trembled at the harshness in his tone even while a secret part of her thrilled that he'd been worried about her. 'I know what I'm doing, Marco. I've been doing it almost all my life.'

He speared a hand into her hair, tilting her face up to his. 'Rafael knew what he was doing too. Look where he ended up. You can't do it for ever. You do realise that, don't you?'

The question threw her, for Sasha had been deliberately avoiding any thoughts of the future. Even the end of the racing season didn't bear thinking about. If by some sheer stroke of bad luck she lost the Constructors' Championship then she was out of a job.

If she won her professional future would be secured for another year. But what about her personal future?

The reality was that she'd fallen into Marco's bed expecting little more than a one-night stand. But with each day that passed she was being consumed by the magic she experienced there. With no thought to the future…

'Yes,' she finally whispered. 'I realise nothing lasts for ever.'

'Bueno,' he breathed, as if her answer had satisfied him.

He shucked his boxers in one smooth move. 'Are you going to drink that? Only, after watching you nearly crash, I feel an urgent need to re-affirm life with you again. Repeatedly.'

She passed him the glass and opened her arms.

It wasn't until their breaths were gasping out in the aftermath of soul-shattering orgasms that she tensed in disbelief.

'Marco!'

'What?' He raised his head, a swathe of hair falling seductively over one eye.

'We didn't… We forgot…' Frantically she calculated dates.

He let loose a single epithet. *'Dios.* Please tell me you're on the Pill?' he rasped.

His voice was a choked sound that chilled her.

Reassured with the dates, she nodded, then noticed his pallor. 'Hey, it's okay. Even if the Pill doesn't work it's the wrong time of the month.'

'Are you sure?' he demanded.

Frowning, Sasha laid a hand on his cheek, which had grown cold and clammy. 'I'm sure. Relax.'

Marco eased away from Sasha, steeling himself against her throaty protest as he left the bed. Pulling on a robe, he went into his study. His laptop was set up on his desk, his folders neatly arranged by his assistant. He bypassed it, threw himself into the leather sofa and scrubbed a hand down his face.

He hadn't meant to lose it with Sasha like that earlier.

But seeing her come within a whisker of crashing had set him on a knife-edge of fear and rage he hadn't been able to completely dismiss. Now his loss of control had made him forget his one cardinal rule—contraception. *Always*.

He hadn't slipped once in ten years. Until tonight. Thank goodness Sasha was as against accidentally conceiving a child as he was...

Grimly reining in the control that seemed to be slipping from him, he strode to his desk and picked up the top folder. A sliver of guilt rose inside him but he quashed it.

Enough. He'd done what needed to be done. He refused to feel guilty for protecting what was important to him. Nothing mattered except keeping his family safe.

He picked up the phone and called his brother's doctors. Once he'd been updated on Rafael's condition, he placed another call.

Fifteen minutes later he slammed down the lid of his laptop and pushed away from the desk, at peace with his decision.

Feeling a sense of rightness, he returned to the bedroom and slid into bed, his need for Sasha overcoming the wish to let her rest. With a soft murmur she wound her supple body around his. The sense of rightness increased, making his head spin.

'I missed you. Where have you been?'

Another wave of guilt hit him—harder than before. Inhaling the seductive scent of her, he pushed away the disturbing feeling. 'I needed to take care of something.' Bending his head, he placed his lips against the smooth skin of her neck. His body stirred, transmitting its persistent message.

'Um. And have you?' she murmured.

'Sí.' His voice emerged gruffer than he wished. 'It's all taken care of.'

CHAPTER TEN

SASHA WATCHED MARCO turn the page of his newspaper, a frown creasing his brow before it smoothed out again. Watching him had become something of a not-so-secret pleasure in the last few weeks. On cue, she experienced the slow drag of desire in her belly as her gaze drifted over the sensual curve of his lips, the unshaven rasp of his jaw and the strong column of his throat to the muscled bare torso which she'd caressed to her heart's content last night and this morning.

As if sensing her gaze, his eyes met hers over the top of the paper. One brow lifted. 'You want to go back to bed?'

He laughed at her less-than-convincing shake of the head. The remnants of breakfast lay scattered on the table, long forgotten as they basked in the South Korean sun.

'I didn't know you could read Korean,' she said, eager for something to distil the suffocating heat of the desire that was never far from the surface.

Marco smiled and folded away the paper. 'It's Japanese. I never quite mastered Korean.'

'Wow. You're freely admitting *another* flaw? Shocking!'

He shrugged. 'It was down to a choice of which was the most useful.'

She wrinkled her nose. '*Useful?* Do you ever do anything just for pleasure?'

His droll look made her colour rise higher.

'Besides sex,' she mumbled.

'Sex with you is all the pleasure I crave, *mi corazón.*'

'You have other interests, surely? Everyone does.'

His throaty laugh made her pulse pound harder. 'What did you have in mind?'

'Some culture. An exhibition. Something other than…'

Flustered, she waved her hand towards the severely rumpled bed beyond the sliding doors leading into the master suite, trying not to think of all the *other* places—the highly polished teak floor, the wooden bench in his outdoor bathroom, the hammock overlooking the stunning beach—where Marco had pleasured her during the long night.

Leaning over, he slid a hand around her nape and pulled her in for a hot kiss. 'I'd much rather spend the day with you in my bed. But if you insist—'

'I insist.'

Because Sasha had woken up this morning with a fearful knowledge deep in her heart. She was in danger of developing feelings for Marco de Cervantes. Feelings that she dared not name. Feelings that threatened to overwhelm her the more time she spent locked in his embrace.

At least away from this place, real life would impede long enough to knock some sense into her. To remind her that she couldn't afford to lose her head over a man like Marco—a man whom she knew deep down grappled with his guilt for being attracted to her. After all, hadn't it taken him three weeks to decide he could be with her?

He was also a man who believed her father to be guilty of fraud, a small voice added.

A sharp pang pierced through the concrete she'd packed around her pain. She hadn't been able to raise the subject with Marco since that night in Singapore. Somehow knowing he'd painted her father with the same brush of guilt as everyone else hurt so much more. Which made her a fool. Why should he believe any differently? Just because they were sleeping together it didn't mean the taint of her name had disappeared.

'You have fifteen minutes to get ready.'

She roused herself to find Marco ending a call. 'Ready for what?'

He tossed his phone on the table and brushed his knuckle along her jaw. Sparks of pleasure lit along her skin.

'You want culture, *mi encantadora*. Korea awaits.'

'Oh, my God,' Sasha whispered as her bare feet touched the wet flagstones that led to the ancient lake temple, unable to tear her gaze away from the magnificent vista before her.

'I'm finding that I don't like you using that expression unless it relates directly to me, *pequeña*,' Marco complained, releasing her hand as she leapt onto the next flagstone.

'Are you jealous?' she asked on a laugh.

He raised a mocking brow. 'Of your insane adoration of old temples and ancient monuments?' He rolled up his trouser cuffs and stepped on to the flagstones, bringing his warmth and addictive body up close and personal. 'Not a chance. But I suggest you alter your phraseology, because every time you say *Oh, my God* in that sexy tone I want to flatten you against the nearest surface and have my way with you.'

He grinned at her gasp and his head started to descend.

'No.' She pulled away reluctantly.

He frowned. *'Qué diablos?'*

'Shh, we're in a holy place,' she whispered. 'No kissing. And no swearing.'

She giggled at his muted growl and skipped over the rest of the flagstones until she stood in front of the temple.

'Wow.'

'*Wow* I can live with.'

'You'll have to. I have no other words.'

From where they stood the small temple seemed to float on the water, its curved eaves reminiscent of a bird in flight. In the light of the dying sun huge pink water lilies glowed red, their rubescent petals unfurled to catch the last of the sun's rays.

'It's all so beautiful. So stunning.' With reverent steps Sasha approached the temple doors. 'Can we go in?'

He nodded. 'It's not normally open to visitors. But on this occasion…'

Unbidden, a lump rose to her throat. 'Thank you.'

'*De nada.* Go—explore to your heart's content.'

With legs that felt shaky, and a heart that hammered far too hard to be healthy, Sasha paused to wipe her feet, then entered the temple.

Like every single place Marco had taken her to since he'd summoned his car after breakfast, the temple was breathtakingly exquisite. The *shoji* scrolls lining the walls looked paper-thin and fragile, causing her to hold her breath in case she damaged the place in any way. Examining one, she wished she had a translator to explain the three lines of symbols to her.

'"Peace through wisdom. Wisdom through perspicacity,"' Marco murmured from behind her. 'This temple was originally Japanese. It changed owners a few times before the Shaolin monks took over in the fourth century.'

'It puts everything into perspective, doesn't it?'

'Does it?'

'You said nothing lasts for ever. This temple proves some things do.'

For a long moment he didn't answer. His hooded gaze held hers, but in the gathering dusk she couldn't read the expression in his eyes.

'Come, it is time to leave. Romano will think you've kidnapped me.'

'What? Little ol' me?'

He laughed—a sound she was finding she liked very much. 'Romano knows you have a black belt in Jujitsu.'

'I'd still think twice before I tried to drop-kick a man of his size. So you're safe with me.'

'*Gracias.*' He threaded his fingers through hers, then signalled to Romano to bring the car round.

She waited until they were in the car before leaning over to press her lips to his. 'Thank you for showing me Seoul.'

His hand tightened around her waist and pulled her closer. 'The tour isn't over yet. I have one last treat for you.'

Pleasure unfurled through her. 'Really?'

'The night is just beginning. I know a little place where, if you're really nice to the staff, they'll name a dish after you. Will you allow me to show it to you?' He picked up her hand and kissed the back of it.

Watching the dark head bent over her hand, Sasha experienced that irrational fear again. Only this time it was ten times worse. Her heart hammered and her pulse raced through her veins as the reason for her feelings whispered softly through her mind.

No. She *wasn't* falling for Marco de Cervantes. Because that would be stupid.

And reckless.

Marco didn't do relationships. And she'd barely survived being burned once.

His lips caressed the sensitive skin of her wrist.

At her helpless sigh, he smiled. 'On second thoughts, a Michelin-star-chef-prepared meal on the beach sounds very appealing.'

Resisting temptation was nearly impossible. But Sasha forced herself to speak. 'It's not fair to dangle the opportunity to have a dish named after me and then withdraw it. Now it's on my lust-have list.'

He reached out and cupped her breast. 'I have only one thing on *my* lust-have list.'

'You're insatiable,' she breathed, unable to stop her moan when his thumb passed over her nipple.

Bending his head, he brought his lips close to hers. 'Only for you do I have this need,' he muttered thickly. 'And, *por favor*, I won't have it denied.' He drew closer until their breaths mingled.

'What about dinner…the dish…?' she whispered.

'You'll have it,' he vowed. 'Just…later.'

With a muted groan, he closed the gap, sealing them in a hot cocoon of fevered need so intense it stopped her breath.

The cocoon held them intimately all the way through their torrid lovemaking in Marco's bed and in the shower afterwards, where he explored every inch of her body as if seeing it for the first time.

His phone rang as they dressed for dinner. At first she thought it was a business call. Then she noticed his ashen pallor.

Their cocoon had been shattered.

'Who was that?' she asked, even though part of her knew the answer.

'It was the hospital. Rafael's suffered another bleed.'

'What the hell are you doing under there? Freebasing engine oil?'

Sasha froze at the voice she hadn't heard in six long sleepless nights and forced herself to breathe. 'Hand me the wrench.'

'Didn't the staff tell you no one's allowed in here?' The harsh censure in his voice grated on her already severely frayed nerves.

'They probably *tried*.'

'You didn't listen, of course?'

'I don't speak Spanish, remember? Are you going to hand me the wrench or not?'

His designer-shod feet moved, then a wrench appeared underneath the body of the 1954 Fiat 8V Berlinetta.

'Not that one. The retractable.'

The right wrench reappeared. 'Thanks.'

She hooked the wrench on to the bolt and pulled. Nothing happened.

'Come out from under there.'

'No.'

'Sasha…' His voice held more than a hint of warning.

Her mouth compressed. She didn't want to see his face,

didn't want to breathe his scent. In fact she wanted to deny herself everything to do with Marco. To deny that every single atom of her being yearned to wheel herself from under the car and throw herself into his arms.

She gripped the wrench and yanked harder, reminding herself of how almost a week ago he'd ordered Romano to bring her to *Casa de León* and walked away.

As if Seoul had never happened.

'We need to talk.'

Her heart clenched. 'So talk.'

An expensively cut suit jacket landed a few feet from her head, followed a millisecond later by Marco's large, tightly packed frame.

'What are you doing?' she squeaked, holding herself rigid as his shoulder brushed hers.

He ignored her, taking his time to study the axle she'd been working on. 'Hand me the wrench and move over.'

'Why? Because you think you're bigger and stronger than me?'

'I *am* bigger and stronger than you.'

'Sexist pig.'

'Simple truth.'

'I see you still live in the Dark Ages.'

'Only when it comes to protecting what's mine.'

Realising he wasn't going to go away, she shrugged. 'Fine. Knock yourself out.'

His gaze sharpened. 'No arguments, *querida*? That's how it works between us usually, isn't it? I say something, then you argue my words to death until I kiss you to shut you up?'

'I don't crave arguments—or your kisses, if that's what you're implying. In fact I'd love nothing better than for you to leave me alone,' she suggested. 'You've managed it quite successfully for almost a week.'

Silently he held out his hand. She slapped the wrench into his palm. With a few firm twists he loosened the bolt on the axle.

'Show-off,' she quipped. 'What do you want?'

'I thought you'd want an update on Rafael.' His gaze stayed intense on hers.

'I thought he was off-limits?'

'If I still believed you and he were involved I wouldn't have taken you to my bed.'

'Okay. So how is he?'

'He's doing better. The doctors managed to stop the bleed. They expect him to wake up any day now.'

Licking her lips carefully, she nodded. 'That's great news.'

'*Sì.*'

The intensity in his eyes sent a bolt of apprehension through her. Without warning, his gaze dropped to her lips. Belatedly Sasha realised she was licking them. She stopped. But the quickening was already happening. The cramped space underneath the car became smaller. The air grew thinner.

'You didn't have to come back here to tell me that. A simple phone call would've sufficed. I'll pack my things and leave this afternoon.'

He stiffened. 'Why would you do that?'

'Rafael will need you when he comes home. I can't be here.'

'Of course you can. I want you here.'

Despite the thin hope threading its way through her, she forced herself to speak. 'That wasn't the impression I got from your six-day silence.'

He sucked in a weary breath and for the first time she noticed the lines of strain around his eyes.

'I didn't expect to be away this long. I'm sorry.'

When her mouth dropped open in surprise at the ready apology he grimaced.

'I know. I must be losing my touch.' He glanced around, his strained look intensifying. 'How did you get in here? The door is combination locked.'

'Rosario let me in. She recognises stir-craziness when she sees it. So—twenty-five vintage cars locked away in a garage? Discuss.'

He inhaled sharply, then flung the wrench away. 'I refuse

to have this conversation underneath a car, with grease dripping on me.'

'You should've thought of that before you crawled down here.'

'*Dios*, I've missed your insufferable attitude.' He paused. 'This is your chance to tell me you've missed me too.'

The stark need to do just that frightened her. 'Are you sure you don't want me to leave? I can go home for a few days before the team leaves for Abu Dhabi next week. Maybe it's for the best.'

'And maybe you need to shut up. Just for one damn moment,' he snarled, then grabbed her arm and turned her into his body.

The heat of his mouth devoured hers. Fiery sensation was instantaneous. Sasha held nothing back. Her fingers gripped his nape, luxuriating in the smooth skin before spearing upward to spread through his hair. His deep groan echoed hers. Willingly, she let her mouth fall open, let his tongue invade to slide deliciously against hers.

His hand snaked around her waist and veered downwards, bringing her flush against his heated body. Need flooded her. To be this close again with him, to feel him, to be with him, made her body, her heart sing.

She wanted to be close. Closer. Physically and emotionally. Because… Because…

Infinitely glad he'd shed his jacket, she explored the large expanse of his shoulders.

When the demands of oxygen forced them apart his gaze stayed on her. One hand cupped her bottom. Against her belly she felt the ripe force of his erection.

'You do realise we're making out under a car, don't you?' she asked huskily.

'It's the only thing stopping me from pulling you on top of me and burying myself inside you. Tell me you missed me.'

'I missed you.'

'*Bueno.*' He fastened his mouth to hers once more.

By the time he freed her and pulled them from underneat the car her brain had become a useless expanse seeking onl the pleasure he could provide. When he undressed her, le her to the back door of a 1938 Rolls-Royce, she was a willin slave, ready to do his every bidding.

Snagging an arm around her waist, he speared a han through her hair and tilted her face to his. 'You have no ide how long I've wanted to do this.'

'What?' she breathed.

His mouth swooped, locked on the juncture where he shoulder met her neck, where her pulse thundered franticall

Her blood surged to meet his mouth. When his teeth graze her skin she cried out. The eroticism of it was so intens that liquid heat pooled between her legs, where she throbbe plumping up for the studied and potent possession only h could deliver.

He took his time, tasted her, his mouth playing over the del icate, intensely aroused skin. Just when she thought it couldn' get any more pleasurable his tongue joined in. Ecstasy lashe at her insides, creating a path of fire from her neck to he breasts, to her most sensitive part and down to her toes. No where was safe from the utter bliss rushing through her.

Finally, satisfied, he lifted his head. He took a step for ward, then another, until the edge of the car seat touched he calves. With his gentle push she fell back onto the wide seat

He followed immediately, his warmth surrounding her. I his arms she felt delicate, cared for, as if she mattered. As i she was precious. Which was silly. For Marco this was jus sex. But for her...

She shut her mind off the painful train of thought. ' thought you wanted me on top?'

His teeth gleamed in a slow, feral smile. 'In good time *mi tentación*. We have a long way to go. Now, don't move.'

He cupped her breasts, toying with the nipples, torturin her for so long she wriggled with pleasure.

'I said don't move,' he gritted through clenched teeth, the harsh stamp of desire tautening his face.

'You expect me to just lie here like a ten-dollar hooker?'

Despite the intense desire threatening to swallow them whole, laughter rumbled through his chest. 'Never having been graced with the attentions of a ten-dollar hooker, I can't answer that. But if you don't stop tormenting me with your body I won't be responsible for my actions.'

'Oh, *now* you're just threatening me with a good time.'

'*Dios*, woman. Your mouth…'

'You want to kiss it?' It was more of a plea than a question. Her head rose off the seat in search of his.

He pulled away. 'It's a weapon of man's destruction.'

She groaned. 'You can always kiss me to shut me up. I can't promise I won't blow you away, though.'

He mumbled something low and pithy under this breath. And then he kissed her.

A long while later, stretched out alongside Marco's warm length on the back seat of the car, she finally acknowledged her feelings.

She was happy. It was a happiness doomed to disaster and a short lifespan, but no matter how delusional she wanted it to last a little while longer.

Glancing down, she noticed Marco's wallet had dropped onto the floor of the car. Spying a picture peeking out, she picked up the wallet and peered closer.

The long, unruly hair was unfamiliar, as was the small go-kart in the background. But the determination and fierce pride in those hazel eyes looked familiar.

'This picture of you is adorable. Now I know what your children will look like.' She tried not to let the pain of that thought show on her face. 'I bet they'll be racers just like you and Rafael.'

Marco stiffened, his eyes growing cold and bleak. 'There won't be any children.'

The granite-like certainty in his voice chilled her soul.
'Why do you say that?'

For a long, endless moment he didn't answer. Then he took the wallet from her. Reaching for his trousers, he opened the car door, stepped out and pulled them on.

'Come with me.'

Despite already missing his arms around her, she sat up. 'Where are we going?'

The look in his eyes grew bleaker. 'Not far. Put your clothes on. I don't want to get distracted.'

She was all for distracting him if it meant he wouldn't look so cold and forbidding. But she did as he said.

Marco led her to the far side of the garage. Keying in a security code, he threw open the door and stepped inside, pulling her behind him.

With a flick of a switch, light bathed the room. Sasha looked around and gasped at the contents of many glass cabinets.

'These are all yours?' she whispered. Walking forward she opened the first cabinet and lifted the first trophy.

'*Sí.*' Marco's voice was husky with emotion. 'I started racing when I was five.'

There were more trophies than she could count, filling four huge cabinets. 'I know.'

He walked to the farthest cabinet and picked up the lone trophy standing in a case by itself. 'This was my last trophy.'

'You never told me why you gave up racing,' she murmured.

When he tensed even more, she went to him and grasped his balled fists.

'Tell me what happened.'

His eyes bored into hers, as if judging her to see if he could trust her with his pain. After an eternity his hand loosened enough to grasp hers.

'I got my first contract to race when I was eighteen. By twenty-one I'd won two championships and acquired a degree in engineering. I was on the list of every team, and I had the choice of picking which team to drive for. A week after I signed for my dream team I met Angelique Santoro. I was twenty-four, and foolishly believed in love at first sight. And even by then I'd had my fill of paddock bunnies. She was… different. Smart, sexy, exciting—far older than her twenty-five years. All I wanted to do was race and be with her. She convinced me to sack my manager and take her on instead. Six months later we were engaged and she was pregnant.'

A shiver of dread raced over Sasha. Deep inside her chest a ball of pain, buried but not forgotten, tightened.

There won't be any children.

'You didn't want the baby?' she whispered in horror.

He laughed. A harsh, tortured sound that twisted her heart. 'I wanted it more than I'd ever wanted anything in my life.'

Sasha frowned. 'But…what happened?'

'I rearranged my whole life around that promise of a family. I designed the *Casa de León* track so I could train there, instead of going away to train at other tracks. My parents moved here. My mother was ecstatic at becoming a grandparent.'

The note of pain through his voice rocked her.

'Angelique wasn't satisfied?'

'She wholeheartedly agreed with everything. Until I crashed.'

Her hand tightened around his. 'I don't understand. Your crash was serious, yes, but nothing you couldn't come back from.'

'I was in a coma for nine days. The team hired someone else to replace me when the doctors told my parents and Angelique it was unlikely I'd race again.'

'They must have been devastated for you.'

'My parents were.'

Sadness touched her soul. 'I'm sorry. I can't imagine what you must have gone through.'

He slid a finger under her chin and lifted her face to his, an echo of pain in his eyes. 'Nor would I want you to. But this…' he pulled her closer, his gaze softening a touch '…this helps.'

With a smile, she lifted her mouth to his. 'I'm glad.'

Their kiss was gentle, a soothing balm on his turbulent revelations.

When they parted, she glanced again at the trophies. 'Is that why you don't let anyone in here? Because it reminds you that your racing career is over?'

'When I accepted that part of my life was over I locked them away.' He pulled her away from the cabinet.

'Wait. You said your parents were devastated? What about Angelique?'

He stiffened again, his gaze turning hooded as he thrust his hands into his pockets. 'When it turned out I was destined for a job designing cars instead of racing them, she lost interest,' he said simply, but his oblique tone told a different story.

'That's not all, is it?'

Pain washed over his face before he could mask it. 'Before I crashed Angelique was almost three months pregnant. When I woke from my coma she was no longer pregnant.'

Sasha's horrified gasp echoed through the room. 'She had an abortion?'

His eyes turned almost black with pain. '*Sí*. Two months later she married my ex-team boss.'

A wave of horror washed over her. 'Are you even sure she was pregnant in the first place?' Considering how heartless the woman had been, Sasha wouldn't be surprised if she'd faked the pregnancy.

Marco's movements were uncharacteristically jerky as he reached for his wallet. Beneath the photo, a small grey square slid out. In the light of the trophy room Sasha saw the outline of a tiny body in a pre-natal scan.

Tears gathered in her eyes and fell before she could stop them. With shaking hands she took the picture from him, the memory of her own loss striking into her heart so sharply she couldn't breathe.

'I was there the day this was taken. The thing was, all along I suspected Angelique was capable of that. She was extremely ruthless—driven to the point of obsession. But since she channelled all that into being my manager I chose to see it as something else.'

'Love?' she suggested huskily.

His jaw tightened. 'I blinded myself to her true colours. My mother tried to warn me, but I wouldn't listen to her. I almost cut her out of my life because of Angelique.' He sucked in a harsh breath. 'I lost my child…she lost her grandchild… because I chose to bury my head in the sand. She was devastated, and I don't think she really got over the damage I did to our family.'

Brushing a hand across her cheek, she asked, 'Why do you keep this?'

Marco took the scan and placed it back in his wallet. 'I failed to protect my daughter. This reminds me never to fail my family again.'

CHAPTER ELEVEN

MARCO LEFT AGAIN the next day and didn't return for another two. When he returned Sasha met him in the hallway. His dragged her into his study and proceeded to kiss her with brutal need.

His confession in the garage had afforded her a glimpse into the man he was today. She now truly understood why he was so ferociously protective of Rafael. And why she couldn't afford for him to find out the true depth of her feelings.

Taking a deep breath, she forced herself to vocalise what she'd been too afraid to say over the phone the night before.

'Marco, I think I should leave. You can stay in Barcelona and not keep flying back here to see me. I can use the race track back home to train.'

His face clouded in a harsh frown. 'What the hell are you talking about?' Roughly he pulled her into his arms and kissed her again. 'You're not going anywhere.'

She tried to pull back but he held her easily. 'But—'

His smile was strained through tiredness. 'Rafael woke briefly last night. Only for a few minutes. But he appeared lucid, and he recognised me.' The relief in his voice was palpable.

Sasha smiled. 'I'm glad. But I think that's even more of a reason for you to stay in Barcelona. What if he wakes again when you're not there?'

Setting her free, he stabbed a hand through his hair. 'He's been moved to a private suite and I've set up video conferencing so I have a live feed into his room. Nothing will happen to him without my knowledge. I've also hired extra round-the-clock staff for when he comes home—including that nurse who was fired from the hospital in Budapest. So, you see, I'm not a total ass.'

'I know you're not. But you're splitting yourself in two when it's really Rafael who needs you most now.'

'Maybe I want to put my needs ahead of Rafael's for once in my life.' He threw his hands up in the air. 'What exactly do you want from me, Sasha?'

She was unprepared for the question. But she had one of her own burning at the back of her mind.

'What do *you* want from *me*? What is the real reason you want me to stay here? Am I here just so you can have sex on tap or is this something more…?' She faltered to a halt, too afraid to voice the words traipsing through her mind.

His eyes narrowed. 'I hardly think this is the time to be having a *where is this relationship going?* conversation.'

'Is there ever a right time? Besides, you don't *do* relationships, remember?'

He shrugged off his jacket and flung it onto a nearby chair. 'I want you here with me. Isn't that enough?' he rasped.

Another question she wasn't prepared for. Not because she didn't know the answer. It was because she knew the answer was *no*. Wanting was no longer enough. She was in love with Marco: with the boy whose heart had been shredded by a heartless woman and the formidable man who'd loved his unborn child so completely he'd closed his heart to any emotion.

She loved him. And it scared the hell out of her. The urge to retreat stabbed through her. Marco's obvious reluctance to discuss their relationship frightened her. But looking at him, his face haggard, his hands clenched on the desk in front of him, she knew she couldn't leave. Not just yet. Not when he was so worried about Rafael.

'I'll stay,' she said.

Naked relief reflected in his eyes. *'Gracias.'* He pulled her into his arms. 'Don't mention leaving again. Even the mere thought makes me want to hurl something.'

She hated herself for the thrill of pleasure that surged

through her. 'It was for your own good—even if you don't
want to see it.' And not just for Marco's sake. She had to find
the strength to walk away. Because the longer she stayed, the
more she risked losing everything.

'If you want suggestions on what's good for me, I have several ideas—' He stopped and cursed when his phone started
ringing.

'Before you start hurling things, I'll remove myself to the
garage. Your '65 Chevelle Impala's chrome finish needs pol-
ishing.'

'It also has extra wide front seats, if I recall.'

Desire weakened her. 'Marco…'

'Fine. But before you go—'

He plastered his lips against hers and proceeded to show
her just how foolish her decision to leave had been.

By the time Sasha stumbled from the study she knew her
heart was in serious trouble.

Marco threw himself into his seat two days later and barely
stopped himself from punching a hole in the wall behind him.

Even though she'd changed her mind about leaving, Marco
had sensed a withdrawal in Sasha he couldn't shake. It was
almost as if Rafael's impending emergence from his coma
had put a strain between them.

But why? If there was nothing between them Sasha should
be happy that Rafael was recovering. Unless…? The thought
that Sasha had feelings for Rafael after all sent a wave of anger
and jealousy through him.

No. He dismissed the thought.

She'd listened to him bare his soul, held him in her arms
as he'd relived Angelique's betrayal. Sasha had shed tears for
him; he refused to believe the raw pain he'd seen in her eyes
wasn't real.

But he couldn't deny something was wrong.

Only when they made love, when he held her afterwards,
did he feel he had the real Sasha back. Even now, mere hours

before she was due to leave for London, she'd locked herself away in his garage, hell-bent on restoring his vintage cars to even more pristine condition than they'd originally been in. While he sat here, grappling with confusion and a hunger so relentless he was surprised he didn't spontaneously combust from want.

No. It was more than want. This craving for Sasha, whether she was within arm's reach or he was in Barcelona, went beyond anything he'd ever known. The few times he'd contemplated whether it would be better if she wasn't at the villa at all he'd felt a wrench so deep it had shaken him.

Angelique had never made him feel like this, even though at the time he'd thought he would never yearn for another woman the way he'd yearned for her.

What he felt for Sasha was different...deeper...purer...

Marco stiffened, the breath trapped in his chest as he tried to get to grips with his feelings. But the more he tried to unravel the unfamiliar feeling, the more chaotic and frantic it grew.

He glanced out of his study window towards his garage. The feeling that she was slipping through his fingers wouldn't fade. But he couldn't deal with it now. There were too many loose ends left to tie up.

As if on cue, his phone rang. With a muttered curse, he picked it up.

All the way to his suite Sasha forced herself to breathe. Despite the cold lump of stone in her stomach, she needed to do this. She couldn't continue to string things along any longer.

She entered the suite and heard the shower running. Without pausing, she crossed the room and slid open the door.

Water streamed off Marco's naked, powerful body. The need that slammed through her threatened to weaken her resolve. It took several seconds before she could speak.

'Marco, I...I've decided...I'm not coming back here after the next race.'

He whirled about, looked stricken for a moment, then his jaw clenched. 'I thought we had this conversation already.'

Even now, with the wrenching pain of losing him coursing through her, she couldn't resist the intense pull of desire that watching the water cascade over his body brought.

She steeled herself against it. 'I tried to talk. You laid down the law.'

He snapped a towel off the heated rack and stepped from the shower. 'You timed it perfectly, didn't you?'

'Excuse me?'

'Your exit strategy. At first I didn't want to believe it, but now it makes perfect sense.'

She frowned. 'Perfect sense… What are you talking about?'

'You can drop the pretence. I had a call twenty minutes ago. From Raven Blass.'

Her eyes widened in surprise. 'Raven? Why—?'

'She's in Barcelona. She wants to see Rafael. I gave the hospital permission to let her see him, but funnily enough she was more worried about how *you* would feel about her visit.'

'Marco—'

'Apparently you're very *territorial* about Rafael. She said something about warning Rafael to stay away from her the day he crashed?'

'That wasn't how it was—'

He tied the towel around his trim waist. 'What was the plan? Use me as a stopgap until Rafael was on his feet, then go back to him?'

'Of course not!'

'You started withdrawing from me the moment I told you Rafael was about to wake up. Well, I'm glad to have been of service. But if you have any designs on my brother, kill them now. He won't like soiled goods.'

She flinched and bit back her gasp. For a moment he appeared to regret his words, then his expression hardened again.

'Wow. Okay, I guess your mind's made up.'

'I mean it, Sasha. Come anywhere near Rafael and I'll crush you like a bug.'

Pain congealed into a crushing weight in her chest. 'I suspected this, and I see I was right. Rafael will always come first with you—no matter how much you protest about putting yourself first. I just hope you don't have to give up something you really want one day.'

He frowned. 'There's nothing I want more than my family safe.'

'Well, that says it all, doesn't it?'

Whirling, she hurried from the room, cursing the stupid tears that welled up in her eyes.

In her room, she grabbed her suitcase and stuffed her belongings into it. She was snapping it shut when her door flew open.

'What are you doing?'

'Leaving. *Obviously.*'

'Your flight is not for another four hours.'

She picked her case off the bed. 'Oh? And what? You want one last shag for old times' sake?'

His eyes darkened in a familiar way even as his jaw clenched.

A stunned laugh escaped her. 'Let me get this straight. You want more sex with me even though I'm "soiled goods" you wouldn't let your own brother touch?'

Dull colour swam into his cheeks. 'Don't put it like that.'

'You know when I said you weren't an ass? I was stupendously wrong! You're the biggest ass in the universe.' She stalked towards the door.

'Sasha—'

'And to think I fooled myself into thinking I was in love with you. You don't deserve love. And you certainly don't deserve mine!'

Had she looked back as she sped through the door, pleased

with herself for not breaking down in front of him, she would have seen his stunned face, his ashen pallor.

Sasha flew home to Kent after the Indian Grand Prix, one step closer to cementing the Constructors' Championship.

Returning home for the first time in months felt bittersweet. Glancing round the familiar surroundings of the home she'd grown up in, she wanted to burst into tears. Pictures of her father graced the mantel. A wooden cabinet in the dining room held their trophies. They weren't as numerous as Marco's, but she was proud of every single one of them. Unlike Marco, who'd chosen to hide his away the way he'd chosen to close off his heart…

But had he? He'd shown her that he would fight to the death to protect his family. Didn't that prove it was *her* who wasn't worth fighting for? The thought hurt more than she could bear.

With an angry hand she dashed away the tears. She refused to dwell on him. Her only goal now was finishing the season. She couldn't summon the appropriate enthusiasm for next year.

Wearily, she trudged to the kitchen and put on the kettle. Mrs Miller, her next door neighbour, had texted to let her know the fridge was fully stocked.

Sasha opened the fridge, caught a whiff of cheese and felt her stomach lurch violently. She barely made it to the bathroom seconds before emptying the contents of her stomach. Rinsing her mouth, she decided to forgo the tea in favour of sleep. Dragging herself to the shower, she washed off the grime of her transatlantic flight and fell into bed.

The stomach bug she suspected she'd caught in India, along with half of the team, didn't go away immediately, but by the time she arrived in Brazil three and a half weeks later she was in full health.

And three points away from securing the championship.

São Paolo was vibrant and exhilarating. The pit was abuzz with the excitement of the season's final race, and Team Espíritu even more so with a potential championship win only a few short hours away.

Sasha had taken the coward's way and hidden in her hotel room until the last minute, in case she bumped into Marco. In Abu Dhabi she'd declined his invitation to an after-race party on his sprawling yacht. It seemed he was back to entertaining dignitaries and A-list celebrities with barely a blink in her direction.

Whereas she…she just wanted the season to be over.

The joy had gone out of racing.

With a sharp pang she realised Marco had been right—her guilt about her father had blinded her to the fact that she didn't need to prove to anyone that she was good enough. Nor did she need to defend Jack Fleming's integrity. With her deeper integration and final acceptance into the team she'd discovered that most people remembered Jack Fleming as the great driver he'd been. Her guilt lingered, but she would deal with that later.

First she had to get through the press interviews before and after the race.

She spotted Tom heading her way as she was pulling on her jumpsuit. She winced at the sensitivity of her breasts as the Velcro tightened over them.

She paused, then suddenly was scrambling madly for dates, calculating frantically and coming up short every time. Panic seized her.

'Are you all right? You've gone pale. Here—have some water.'

Tom poured water into a plastic cup and handed it to her. His attitude had undergone a drastic change since she'd become involved with Marco. Snarkily, Sasha wondered whether he'd go back to being insufferable once he found out she and Marco were no longer together.

'It's the heat,' she replied, setting the cup aside. 'I'm fine,' she stressed when he continued to peer at her in concern.

'Okay. Your last interview is with local TV.' He rolled his eyes. 'It's that smarmy one who interviewed you in Singapore. I'd cut him out of the schedule, but since we're on his home turf we don't have any choice. Don't worry. If he looks as if he's straying into forbidden territory I'll stop him.'

He went on to list the other interviewers, but Sasha was only half listening. She'd finally worked out her period dates and breathed a sigh of relief. She'd had her last albeit brief period just before she'd left León. And her cycle was erratic at the best of times.

Reassured, she followed Tom around to the paddock and spoke to the journalists.

The race itself was uneventful. With her eight-second lead unchallenged after the first six laps she cruised to victory, securing the fastest lap ever set on the Interlagos circuit. She managed to keep a smile plastered on her face all through the celebrations and the myriad interviews that followed, sighing with relief as she entered the team's hospitality suite for her last interview.

Despite having done dozens of interviews, she still suffered an attack of nerves whenever a camera was trained on her. And, unlike nerves during a race, interview nerves never worked to her advantage.

'Don't worry, Miss Fleming. It will be all right.'

The note of insincerity in the interviewer's thick accent should have been her first warning.

The first few questions were okay. Then, 'How does it feel to be dating the team boss? Has it earned you any advantages?'

From the corner of her eye she saw Tom surge from his seat. Her 'no comment' made him relax a little.

'After winning the Constructors' Championship, surely your seat for next year is secured?'

'No comment.'

He shrugged. 'How about your ex, Derek Mahoney? Have you heard he's making a comeback to racing?'

Sasha tensed. 'No, I haven't heard.'

'He gave us an interview this morning. And he mentioned something quite interesting.'

Icy dread crept up her spine. 'Whatever it is, I'm sure it has nothing to do with me.'

'On the contrary, it has everything to do with you.'

Her interviewer rubbed his chin in a way that was probably supposed to make him appear smart. It only confirmed the slimeball he really was.

'You see, Mr Mahoney claims you were pregnant with his child when you broke up, and that you deliberately crashed to lose the baby because you didn't want a child to hamper your career. What's your response to that?'

The room swayed around her. Vaguely she heard Tom shouting at the cameraman to stop filming. Inside she was frozen solid, too afraid to move. The buzz in the room grew louder. Someone grasped her arm and frogmarched her into another room. The sole occupant, a waitress cleaning a table, looked from her to the TV and quickly made herself scarce.

'Sasha... I... God, this is a mess,' Tom stuttered. 'Will you be all right? I need to secure that footage...'

'Please, go. I...I'll be fine,' she managed through frozen lips.

He hurriedly retreated and she was alone.

Dropping her head between her thighs, she tried to breathe evenly, desperately willing herself not to pass out. The TV hummed in the background but she didn't have the strength to walk over to turn it off.

Oh, God, how had Derek found out? Not that it mattered now. Her secret was out. Out there for the whole world to pore over...

Tears welled in her eyes. Derek was all about causing maximum damage. But she'd never dreamed he'd sink this low.

The door flew open and Marco walked in.

Her gaze collided with his, and every single thing she'd told herself over the last three weeks flew out of the door.

He'd lost weight. The gap at the collar of his light blue shirt showed more of his collarbones and his jacket hung looser. But he was just as arresting, just as breathlessly beautiful, and her heart leapt with shameless joy at the sight of him.

'I need to talk to you,' he said tautly, his gaze roving intensely over her before capturing hers again.

She licked her dry lips. 'I…I need to tell you…' How could she tell him? She'd never vocalised her pain, never told another human being.

'What is it?' He came over and took her hands. 'Whatever it is, tell me. I can handle it.'

That gave her a modicum of strength. 'You promise?'

'*Sí*. I have a few things I need to tell you too, *mi corazón*. The things I said in León…' He paused and shook his head, a look of regret in his eyes. 'You were right. I'm an ass.'

'I didn't…' *I didn't mean it*, she started to confess, but her eyes had strayed to the TV. There, like a vivid recurring nightmare, her interview was being replayed.

Seeing her distraction, Marco followed her gaze.

Just in time to hear the interviewer's damning question.

Marco dropped her hands faster than hot coals and surged to his feet. '*No!* It's a lie. Isn't it, Sasha? *Isn't it?*' he shouted when she couldn't speak.

'I…'

He paled, his cheekbones standing out against his stark face as he stepped back from her.

'Marco, please—it wasn't like that.' She finally found her voice. But it was too late.

He'd taken several more steps backwards, as if he couldn't stand to breathe the same air as her.

'Did you race knowing you were pregnant?' he insisted, his voice harsh.

'Not the day Derek's talking about—'

'But you *did* race knowing you were pregnant?'

'I suspected I was—'

'Dios mio!'

'I'd already lost the baby when I crashed. That was *why* I crashed! Racing was all I knew. After the doctor told me I'd lost the baby I didn't know what else to do.'

'So you got straight back in your car? You didn't even take time to mourn the loss of your child?' he condemned in chilling tones.

Somehow she found the strength to stand and face him. 'The doctor said it wasn't my fault. The pregnancy wasn't viable to begin with. But I still cried myself to sleep every night for years afterwards. If you're asking if I carry a picture of a scan to punish myself with, or as an excuse to push people away, then no, I don't. She lives in my heart—'

"She?" His voice was a tortured rasp, his fists clenching and unclenching and his throat working as he paled even more.

Tears spilled from her eyes and she nodded. 'Mine was a girl too. She lives in my heart and that's where I choose to remember her. You say you don't live in the past, but that's exactly what you're doing. You're judging *me* by what happened to you ten years ago.'

He inhaled sharply. 'And you've proved to me just how far you'll go. I told you about Angelique, about my child, and you said nothing. Because a small thing like a lost pregnancy is less important to you than your next race, isn't it?'

She swayed as pain clamped her chest in a crushing vice. 'You know why I wanted to race!'

'I was a fool to believe you were trying to preserve the memory of your father. You were really just seeking to further your own agenda.'

Pain arrowed through her. 'Don't pretend you don't think he was guilty.'

'I said he was *found* guilty. I didn't say I agreed with the verdict.'

'But—'

He slashed a hand through her words. 'I had my lawyers investigate the case. Some of the testimony didn't add up. If your father had spent less time feeling sorry for himself and more time getting his lawyers to concentrate on his case he'd have realised that. That's one of the things I came here to tell you.'

Tears stung the backs of her eyes, her throat clogging with unspoken words. 'Marco, please—can't we talk about this?'

He gave a single, finite shake of his head. 'I'm not interested in anything you have to say. I'm only grateful I never made you pregnant. I don't think I could survive another child of mine being so viciously denied life for the sake of ruthless ambition.'

Her insides froze as his words cut across her skin.

With one last condemning look he headed towards the door. Panic seized her. 'Marco!'

He stilled but didn't turn around, one hand on the doorknob. 'What else did you come to say to me?'

The cold malice in his eyes when he turned around made her heart clench.

'I sold the team six weeks ago. In Korea. The paperwork was finalised today. As of one hour ago your contract is null and void.'

CHAPTER TWELVE

SHE WAS PREGNANT with Marco's child. Sasha had been certain of it almost as soon as Marco had walked out on her in São Paolo. Taking the pregnancy test once she'd returned home had only established what she'd known in her heart.

There was no doubt in her mind that she would tell him he was about to become a father. The only problem was when.

He'd made his feelings clear. Her own emotions were too raw for her to face another showdown with Marco. She doubted he would believe whatever she had to tell him anyway.

Gentle fingers stroked over her belly. The doctor had confirmed today that she was almost three months pregnant. Her fingers stilled. Angelique had terminated Marco's child at three months. Sadness welled inside her as she recalled Marco's face when he'd shown her his scan.

Making up her mind before she lost the courage, she dug out her phone. Her fingers shook as she pressed the numbers.

'*Si?*' came the deep voice.

'Marco, it's me.'

Taut silence.

'I know you don't want to speak to me…but there's something I need to tell you.'

'I'm no longer in the motor racing business, so you're wasting your time.' The line went dead.

Sasha stared at the phone, anger and pain churning through her. '*Ass.*'

She threw the phone down, vowing to make Marco beg before she let him anywhere near his child.

Two days later Sasha was standing at her fridge stacking groceries when she heard the agonisingly familiar sound of helicopter rotorblades. The aircraft flew directly over her small cottage before landing in a field half a mile away.

Even though she forced herself to finish her task, every sense was attuned to the knock that came less than five minutes later.

Heart hammering, she opened her door to find Marco standing there, tall, dark and windswept.

'You know you'll have my neighbours dining out on your spectacular entrance for years, don't you? What the hell are you doing here anyway? I recall you wanting nothing to do with me.'

Hazel eyes locked on hers, the look in them almost imploring. 'Invite me in, Sasha.'

'I don't invite heartless bloodsuckers into my home. You can stay right where you are. Better yet, jump back into your vampire-mobile and leave.'

'I'm not leaving until you hear what I have to say. I don't care what your neighbours think, but I get the feeling *you* do. There's a blue-haired one staring at us right now.' Brazen, he waved at Mrs Miller, who shamelessly waved back and kept right on staring at them.

Firming her lips, Sasha stepped back and waved him in. 'You think you're very clever, don't you?'

Expecting a quick comeback, she turned from shutting the door to find him staring at her, a tormented grimace on his face.

'No, I don't think I'm clever at all. In fact, right now, I'm the stupidest person I know.'

Her mouth dropped open.

His grimace deepened. 'Yes, I know. Shocker.'

'Marco…' She stopped and finally did what she'd been dying to do since he knocked on her door. She let her eyes devour him. Let her heart delight in the sheer magnificent sight of him. He went straight to her head. Made her sway where she stood.

He stared right back at her, a plethora of emotions she was

too afraid to name passing over his face. He opened his mouth a couple of times but, seemingly losing his nerve to speak, cast his gaze around her small living room, over the pictures and racing knick-knacks she and her father had accumulated over the years.

Finally he dug into his jacket pocket. 'This is for you.'

Sasha took the papers. 'What are these?'

'Signed affidavits from two former drivers who swear your father wasn't involved in the fraud. He was the fall guy.'

Hands shaking, she read through the documents. 'How…? Why…?' Tears clogged her throat, making the words difficult to utter. Finally she could clear her father's name.

'The how doesn't matter. The why is because you deserve to know.'

She didn't realise she was crying until the first teardrop landed on her hand. Sucking in a sustaining breath, she swiped at her cheeks. 'I…I really don't know what to say. After what happened…' She glanced down at the papers again and swallowed. 'Thank you, Marco,' she said huskily.

'De nada,' he replied hoarsely.

'You didn't have to deliver it in person, though.'

His watchful look intensified. 'I didn't. But I needed the excuse to see you.'

'Why?' she whispered, too afraid to hope.

He swallowed. 'Rafael woke up—really woke up yesterday.'

Her heart lurched. 'Is he okay?'

Marco nodded. 'I went to see him this morning. He told me what happened in Budapest.'

Sasha sighed. 'I know it was stupid, but I lost it when I found out what Rafael was doing.'

'You mean deliberately using your friendship to make Raven jealous?'

She nodded. 'I think she was smitten with Rafael when she first joined the team. That changed when she found out he'd dated most of the women in the paddock. She refused to have anything to do with him after that.'

Marco pursed his lips. 'And he, of course, found it a challenge when she kept refusing him. Why didn't you tell me?' he demanded.

'You told me the significance of your mother's ring. I didn't think you needed to know Rafael was intending to use it to…'

'Get lucky?' He grimaced, then sobered. 'He's over that now, I think. He's seems different—more…mature. I think the accident was a wake-up call for him.'

His eyes locked on her, their expression so bleak it broke her heart.

'For me too. You were right.'

'I was?'

He moved towards her suddenly. '*Sí*. I was living in the past. I knew it even before you left León. I knew it when I came to see you in São Paolo. Hearing Rafael tell me what I already knew—how great you are, how much of a friend you'd been to him…' He stopped and swallowed. 'Did I mention I'm the stupidest person I know right now?'

'Um, you may have.'

'What I said in São Paolo was unforgivable…' His anxious gaze snared hers. 'I was in shock, but I never should've said what I did. I'm sorry you lost your baby. I think you would've made a brilliant mother.'

'You do?'

'*Sí*. I saw how the Children of Bravery Awards affected you. You held it together despite your pain. Watching you on stage with the kids made me wish my child had had a mother like you. At least then she would've had a chance.'

Tears filled her eyes. 'Oh, Marco…' She could barely speak past the lump in her throat.

Another grimace slashed his face. 'I've made you cry again.' He sat next to her and gently brushed away her tears. 'This wasn't what I intended by coming here.'

'Why did you come here, Marco?'

He sucked in a huge breath. 'To tell you I love you. And to beg your forgiveness.'

'*You love me?*'

He gave a jerky nod. 'It ripped me apart to learn I'd had your love and lost it because I'd been so stupid. When you called two days ago—'

'When you hung up on me?'

'I panicked. The hospital had just called about Rafael. I thought you knew and were calling to ask to see him.' He frowned. 'Why *did* you call?'

'I had something to tell you. When you hung up on me I wrote a letter instead.'

'A letter?'

'Well, it was more like a list.'

She'd done it to stop herself from crying—something she couldn't seem to stop doing lately.

Reaching into her pocket, she pulled it out and held it towards him. 'Here.'

He stared at the paper but didn't take it, his face ashen. 'Is forgiveness anywhere on that list, by any chance?'

Her gaze sharpened on him. 'Forgiveness?'

'Yes. Forgiveness of judgemental bastards who don't know the special gift of love and beauty and goodness when it's handed to them.'

'Er…' She glanced down at the list, her thundering heartbeat echoing loudly in her ears. 'No. But then I've only had two days to work on it.'

Dropping down on his haunches, he cupped her face in his hands. 'Then consider this a special request, *por favor*. I know I have a lot of grovelling to do for judging you harshly from the beginning.'

'You were hurting. And you were right. I *was* acting out of guilt.'

'No. You were doing whatever it took for you to move on—whereas I let one stumbling block shatter me. I resented you for that.'

'The blows you were dealt were enough to knock anyone sideways.'

'But I let it colour my judgement. I told myself I had recovered, that I didn't care, but I did. Do you know that until you came to León I hadn't entered that garage in over ten years? You opened my eyes to what a barren life I'd led until then.'

'Look at the letter, Marco.'

He inhaled sharply and stood. 'No. If you're going to condemn me I'd rather hear it from you.'

'You might want to sit down.'

He stuffed his fingers into his coat pockets, but not before she caught the trembling of his hands.

'Just tell me.'

'Fine. But if you faint from shock don't expect me to help you. You're too big—'

When he made an incoherent sound racked with pain, she unfolded the paper.

Anxiety coursed through her. He'd said he loved her, but what if Marco truly didn't want another child? What if the loss of his unborn child had been too great a pain for him ever to move on from?

'Sasha, *por favor.*'

'That's the second time you've said please in the last five minutes,' she whispered.

When his eyes grew dark, she read aloud. *"'Marco, you were an ass for hanging up on me but I think you should know—'"* She looked up from the sheet. *"'You're going to become a father.'"*

For a full minute he didn't move. Didn't breathe, didn't blink. Then he stumbled into the chair. His hands visibly shook when he reached out and cupped her cheek. 'Sasha. Please tell me this isn't a dream,' he rasped.

'This isn't a dream. I'm pregnant with your child.'

A look of complete reverence settled over his face before his eyes dropped to her still-flat stomach.

'Are you okay? Is everything all right?' he demanded.

'You mean with the baby?'

'With both of you.'

'Yes. I saw the doctor. Everything is fine. Does that mean you want the baby?'

'*Mi corazón*, you've given me a second chance I never would've been brave enough to take on my own. I may have burned my bridges with you, but, yes, I want this baby.' His eyes dropped to her stomach, and lingered. '*Por favor*, can I touch?'

Sweet surprise rocked through her. 'You want to touch my belly?'

'If you'll allow me?'

'You know the baby isn't any larger than your thumb right now, don't you?'

'*Sí*, but my heart wants what it wants. Please?'

Renewed tears clogged her throat as she nodded and unbuttoned her jeans.

Warm fingers caressed her belly. Watching his face, she felt the breath snag in her chest at the sheer joy exhibited there. Then his eyes locked on hers and his fingers slid under her sweater, heating her bare flesh.

Her heart kicked, the fierce love she felt for this man and for her baby making her throat clog with tears. Reluctantly she withdrew from his seductive warmth. 'Marco, I haven't finished reading the letter.'

A look of uncertainty entered his eyes. 'I know what a hard bargain you can drive. Is there any room for negotiation?'

'You need to hear what's in it first.'

He gave a reluctant nod, his joy fading a little.

'"*If it's a boy I would like to name him after my father. One of his names, at least.*"'

A quick nod met her request. 'It will be so.'

'"*I want our child to be born in Spain. Preferably in León.*"'

He swallowed hard. 'Agreed.'

She looked up from the paper. '"*I'd like to stay there after the baby's born. With you.*"'

His eyes widened and he stopped breathing. 'You want to stay in León? With me?'

Her heart in her throat, she nodded. 'Our child deserves two parents who don't live in separate countries.'

Disappointment fleeted over his face. 'You're right.'

'Our child also deserves parents who love each other.'

Pain darkened his eyes. 'I intend to do everything in my power to earn your love again, Sasha.'

She shrugged, her heart in her throat. 'You'll need to focus your energies on other things, Marco. Because I love you.'

He sucked in a breath. 'You...love me...?'

'Yes,' she reiterated simply. 'I knew in León, even though I'd convinced myself it wouldn't work.'

'I didn't exactly make it easy. I felt my life unravelling and I got desperate.'

Shock rocked through her. 'Was that why you sold the team?'

He grimaced. 'Rafael's accident and your near-collision in Korea convinced me it was time to get out of racing. But I managed to bulldoze my way through that too. I also may have left a tiny detail out regarding your firing.'

'Oh?'

'The sale contract included a stipulation that you were to have first refusal of the lead driver's seat. If you wanted it.'

Lifting loving hands, she cradled his face. 'Didn't you read Tom's press release last week?'

'What press release?'

'I've retired from motor racing.'

He frowned. 'What about your promise to your father?'

'He would've been proud that I helped you win the Constructors' Championship. But what he really wanted was for me to be happy.'

'And are you?'

'Tell me you love me again and I'll let you know.'

'I am deeply, insanely in love with you, Sasha Fleming, and I can't wait to make you mine.'

She flung the letter away and slid her arms around his neck. 'Then, yes, I'm ecstatically happy.'

EPILOGUE

'HAPPY BIRTHDAY, *MI PRECIOSA.*'

Sasha turned from where she'd been watching another stunning León sunset and tucked the blanket around their two-month-old baby.

'*Shh.* You'll wake him.'

Marco joined her at the crib. With a look of complete adoration on his face, he brushed a finger down his son's soft cheek. 'Jack Alessandro de Cervantes can sleep through a hurricane—just like his mother.' He pressed a kiss on his son's forehead, then held out his hand to her. 'Come with me.'

'Marco, you're not giving me another present? You've already given me six—oh, never mind.' By now she knew better than to dissuade her husband when he was on a mission. Today his mission was to shower her with endless gifts.

'*Sí,* now you're learning.'

As Marco led her to their bedroom she glanced down at the large square diamond ring he'd slid next to her seven-month-old wedding ring this morning. Not a week went by without Marco giving her a gift of some sort. Last week he'd presented her with the most darling chocolate Labradoodle puppy, and then grumbled when she'd immediately fallen in love with the dog.

'I hope it's not another diamond. There's only so much bling a girl can wear before she's asking for a mugging.'

'It's not a diamond. This present is much more…personal.' He shut the door behind them, settled his hands on her hips and pulled her closer, his hazel eyes growing dramatically darker. 'The kind of *personal* that happens when you wear this T-shirt.'

'Why do you think I'm wearing it?'

He gave a low, sexy laugh. '*Dios,* you're merciless.'

'Only when it comes to you. Turning you on gives me a huge buzz.'

Stretching up, she wrapped her arms around his neck, luxuriating in their long kiss until she reluctantly pulled away.

At his protest, she shook her head. 'I have something to show you before we get too carried away.'

Reaching towards her bedside table, she handed him a single piece of heavily embossed paper.

He read through the document before glancing up at her. 'It's finalised?'

Happiness burst through her chest. 'Yes. The mayor's office sent over confirmation this afternoon. I'm officially patron of the De Cervantes Children's Charity. My programme to help disadvantaged kids who're interested in racing is a go!'

His devastating smile held pride even as he sighed. 'Between that and you being spokeswoman for women motor racers, I see my cunning plan to keep you busy in my bed having babies fast disappearing.'

Her smack on his arm was rewarded with a kiss on her willing mouth.

He sobered. 'Are you sure you don't want to go back to racing? You know you'd have my support in that too.'

Sasha blinked eyes prickling with tears and pressed her mouth against his. 'Thank you, but that part of my life is over. The chance to work with children is another dream come true. As for making more babies with you—it's my number one priority. Right up there with loving you for ever.'

His eyes darkened. 'I love you too, *mi corazón*.'

'Enough to take advantage of the instruction on my T-shirt?' she asked saucily.

With a growl, he tumbled her back onto the bed and proceeded to demonstrate just how good he was at taking instruction.

* * * * *